MARK OF DAMNATION

SCHULZE WAS STANDING over the second corpse. 'There's some marks on this one, sir. Come and see.' The body lay about twenty feet away, sprawled and twisted, face-down. A pattern of intersecting lines had been cut deep into the flesh of its back: a rectangle with horns that branched out over the man's shoulder-blades. The wound was puffy and dribbles of blood had run from it over the skin. Hoche recognised the crossed bars and flinched. Sweat pricked against his skin.

'It's a weird thing,' Schulze said, and knelt to touch the body.

'Don't!' Hoche shouted. Schulze's outstretched arm froze.

'What is it, sir?'

'It's the mark of the being some call Khorne, the Blood God. These men weren't killed by wolves and didn't die in a fight – they were sacrificed.'

A WARHAMMER NOVEL

MARK OF DAMNATION

JAMES WALLIS

For Marc and Maggie of course.
Thanks to Psion5 and the staff
of Caffé Nero in Clapham Common

A BLACK LIBRARY PUBLICATION

BL Publishing,
An imprint of Games Workshop Ltd.,
Willow Road, Lenton,
Nottingham, NG7 2WS, UK

First US edition, March 2003

10 9 8 7 6 5 4 3 2 1

Distributed by Simon & Schuster
1230 Avenue of the Americas,
New York, NY 10020

Cover illustration by Clint Langley

ISBN 0-7434-4350-0

Set in ITC Giovanni

Printed and bound in Great Britain by
Cox & Wyman Ltd, Cardiff Rd, Reading, Berkshire RG1 8EX, UK

See the Black Library on the Internet at
www.blacklibrary.com

Find out more about Games Workshop
and the world of Warhammer at
www.games-workshop.com

THIS IS A DARK age, a bloody age, an age of daemons and of sorcery. It is an age of battle and death, and of the world's ending. Amidst all of the fire, flame and fury it is a time, too, of mighty heroes, of bold deeds and great courage.

AT THE HEART of the Old World sprawls the Empire, the largest and most powerful of the human realms. Known for its engineers, sorcerers, traders and soldiers, it is a land of great mountains, mighty rivers, dark forests and vast cities. And from his throne in Altdorf reigns the Emperor Karl-Franz, sacred descendant of the founder of these lands, Sigmar, and wielder of his magical warhammer.

BUT THESE ARE far from civilised times. Across the length and breadth of the Old World, from the knightly palaces of Bretonnia to ice-bound Kislev in the far north, come rumblings of war. In the towering World's Edge Mountains, the orc tribes are gathering for another assault. Bandits and renegades harry the wild southern lands of the Border Princes. There are rumours of rat-things, the skaven, emerging from the sewers and swamps across the land. And from the northern wildernesses there is the ever-present threat of Chaos, of daemons and beastmen corrupted by the foul powers of the Dark Gods. As the time of battle draws ever near, the Empire needs heroes like never before.

Chapter One
PATIENCE

THE QUEEN OF wands fell on the king of swords, and the prince of coins on the queen of wands. Ten of cups on the prince, followed by a sequence of low-numbered sword cards. There was nothing there that he could use, and only a handful of cards still face-down. The pattern was blocked, the reds and the blacks balanced, a stalemate in the making.

It was hard to read the cards. Outside, beyond the open door of the tent, the night was hot and still and the rest of the sleeping army camp was bathed in the pale silver-green light of the full moon, but only a little filtered through to reach the spread of cards on the floor near the back, where Karl Hoche was sat cross-legged, a glass of Kislevite kvas to his side, contemplating and listening to the silence. Nobody glancing into the tent could see he was awake, passing the night by playing cards, and waiting.

Behind him Rudolf Schulze, his orderly, grunted in his sleep and twitched a leg. Hoche waited until he had settled again, then flipped a card from the deck he held in one hand. He frowned. It was the Wise Fool, the wild card that could work for any of the four suits. But that would be in a

7

normal game, with opponents you could see. This game was played by different rules, and the Fool didn't fit them. It shouldn't have been in the deck, should have been removed from play before the game started. He put it down beside his glass, drew another card, and froze. He could hear horses.

He sat absolutely still, listening. Five, maybe six horses moving through the camp, led by people on foot. If they were wearing tack then it was muffled: no bridles clinked, no saddle-leather squeaked. The soft footfalls walked down the path between the tents and he heard the animals' breath as they were led past the open flaps of his tent. It was past midnight, the third watch, and these people were taking trouble not to be heard.

The figures moved on and Hoche let out his breath silently. He had been right. Since the army had set up its summer camp here, every night that one of the two moons had been full he had heard horses and people moving in the late hours. This was the third time, but the first since he had vowed to discover the reason. Now the time had come.

He put down the deck of cards, took a sip of kvas and moved towards Schulze's bed, then paused for a second and flipped over the card that had been under the Fool. He grimaced. It was the two of hearts, an insignificant card, only useful at the start of the game. He could see no fortune or omen in it.

Hoche leaned over Schulze's sleeping form and put his hand gently over the man's moustached face. 'Shh, Schulze,' he whispered. 'They're about. Time to move.'

Schulze's eyes were instantly open and alert, and he nodded his understanding. Hoche smiled for a moment. Schulze always claimed that he'd been a farm-labourer before he joined the Empire's armies three years ago, but Hoche knew he had the knowledge and instincts of an expert hunter. It was one of the reasons he'd chosen the man to be his orderly.

Hoche picked up his sword from next to the field of cards, then crept to the tent door and peered out. To the west, directly under the full moon, lay the camp's stables. He could see shapes moving there, and hear low murmurs of conversation. Behind him Schulze moved, and there was a *tink* as he knocked over the glass of kvas. Hoche held up a hand. 'Stay,' he said. 'The last thing we need is for them to know someone's following.'

He watched as the figures paused for a moment, then they moved off toward the centre of the camp. He counted six, but it was impossible to tell who they were or which regiment they belonged to. Long minutes passed. Clouds moved across the sky, west to east. Hoche watched them go, then he gestured to Schulze. Together, the two men stepped out into the moonlight and walked towards the stables, Schulze at Hoche's right hand and a half-pace behind.

The stables were at the corner of the camp, a fenced-in area with long tents on either side for cover and for the grooms' quarters. Hoche walked to the entrance of the first of them, where the group had stood a handful of minutes earlier. Inside, a figure lay on its back on a straw mattress, snoring gently. Hoche observed it.

'You're not asleep,' he said.

The figure sat up slowly. 'No, sir, but I'm giving it my best try,' it replied. 'Not helped by you.'

'Nor by the men who brought their horses here a few minutes ago,' Hoche said. 'Who were they?'

The groom came to the mouth of the tent. Hoche recognised him but didn't know his name: a man in his thirties with a Talabheim accent, a Tilean nose and the scars of smallpox across his face. His tunic was stained with soup and there was straw in his hair. The groom looked him up and down, registering Hoche's white Reikland uniform with the ornate red tassels that marked him as a lieutenant. He said nothing.

'You can tell me now,' said Hoche, 'or you can tell the duke's men in the morning.'

The man looked from Hoche to the shorter figure of Schulze beside him. 'No offence meant, masters,' he said, 'but my mind is slow at night. They were officers of the Knights Panther, back from some hunting by moonlight. A good time for deer, it is, a night like this.'

Hoche stared at him, not sure if the man believed his own story or not. 'Show us the horses,' he said.

'Sir?'

'I want to see their horses.'

The groom frowned. 'With respect sir,' he said, 'you Reiklanders are infantrymen. What are you wanting with the Knights Panthers' horses? They'll not be pleased when they hear.'

Hoche bent towards him, using his advantage in height to stare down at the man, his face inches from the groom's. 'When an officer gives you an order, you obey, immediately and without thinking. You do not take word of it to anyone else. You are a disgrace to your uniform, which is also a disgrace. Smarten up, or you'll be on a charge the moment the sun rises. Have you got that?'

'Yes, sir. Sorry, sir.' The groom dropped his head, unwilling to meet Hoche's eyes, and silently led the two men into the stable. A single lantern lit the area, casting long shadows across the stalls, piles of straw and racks of equipment. Close to the entrance, six fine warhorses were tethered, each with a grey blanket across its back. Hoche walked over to the first.

'Hunting, you say?' he asked.

'Aye.'

Hoche ran a hand across the flank of one of the huge beasts. Its coat was warm but not damp. 'These horses haven't been ridden hard. There's no heat or sweat to them,' he said.

'I rubbed them down, sir.'

'All six, in the last few minutes? Don't cover for your officers. They could be up to anything, and you know as well as I do that whatever they were doing tonight, it wasn't chasing deer.' Hoche nodded to Schulze. Together they left the stable-tent, walking towards the camp gate.

'Think he'll go to the Knights Panther?' asked Schulze.

'Of course,' Hoche said. 'The question is how quickly. If he's privy to their plans then he'll inform them immediately that people have been asking questions, but the Knights Panther are too elite, too well-bred, too...'

'Snobbish?'

'Exactly. Too snobbish to involve lower ranks in their secrets. Whatever those might be. I think he'll wait until morning.' Hoche paused and leaned against the side of a supply-cart that bracketed one end of a row of tents. 'Schulze, do you feel like a walk?'

'Where, sir?'

'To learn what six Knights Panther do outside the camp, long past midnight, every full moon.'

Schulze yawned. 'In truth I'd prefer my sleep, sir, but if it's an order–'

'It's not. This isn't official business, but there's a mystery here and I'd welcome your help in solving it. I trust your skills, your sword and your discretion. Will you come?'

Schulze looked up and grinned. Hoche smiled back.

'Good man. I knew I could depend on you. Good evening, gentlemen, a fine quiet night.' They had reached the gate and the sentries acknowledged Hoche's greeting with a nod as he and Schulze left the camp. Hoche walked down the hard earth track that led away from the gate, stopped and looked back at the camp's fortifications: its dry ditch, low earth ramparts and palisade of sharpened stakes hiding the rows of tents, carts and fires within. Beside him, Schulze moved to the side of the track, leaned against a lone tree and dabbed the sweat off his brow with a handkerchief. The air was still and hot, filled with the heavy dry-grass scent of late summer nights.

'See anything?' Hoche asked.

'What am I supposed to see, sir?'

Hoche grimaced. 'I'm not some master-sleuth like Zavant Konniger prancing through some penny-dreadful tale of deduction, Schulze. You're the expert. It rained this afternoon and those horses should have left fresh tracks. Can you find them in this light?'

Schulze looked at him, and Hoche knew he was considering what he saw: the young officer, fresh-faced and newly promoted, who had dragged him out of bed because he'd heard horses. But he knew Schulze was also seeing the man who had led his company of Reiklander pikemen at the Battle of Wissendorf last summer, the only company that had stood against the Bretonnian charge, the action that had turned the tide of the fight but had left the young officer close to death, his scalp ripped open by a Bretonnian lance.

Hoche hoped Schulze trusted him as he hoped all his men trusted him: implicitly, no matter how seemingly foolish or foolhardy the job. Then Schulze smiled, and Hoche knew his hopes were justified.

'I spotted them as we left the gate, sir,' Schulze said. 'The tracks head straight out down the road. They come back in along the bank of the stream over there.' He pointed.

'We'll follow those ones, the return track,' Hoche said. 'They may have taken a detour away from the camp to shake off followers.'

Schulze looked at him askance. 'On foot, sir? They could have ridden for miles.'

'That,' said Hoche, 'is what we have to find out.'

THE TRACKS OF the horses followed the stream, and the stream followed the undulations of the heathland as it rose slowly towards the foothills of the Grey Mountains, their shapes visible on the horizon as dark masses against the star-filled sky. Schulze led the way, sure-footed through the half-seen scrub grass and heather. Small creatures scurried out of their path. From time to time they heard the screech of a hunting owl, and once sensed the shadowed form of a larger predator as it silently padded into sight ahead of them, sprang across the stream and loped away into the night. It did not bother them, and they did not bother it.

'Wolf?' asked Hoche. Schulze shook his head.

'Mountain cat,' he said, 'but away from home. Maybe something's driven it from its territory, fire or a lack of food. Could be the orc army moving north.'

'I don't believe the orc army exists,' Hoche said.

'You don't?'

'No. There are warbands and we've tangled with some of them, but the greenskins are still regrouping from the pounding they got from the dwarfs last winter. They lost two or three leaders, and it'll take a while for the new ones to get their forces together. I think the reports of early raidings were exaggerated and we're wasting our time scouring the hills for an army that isn't there.'

'Hope you're right, sir. I could do with being home in time for the harvest.'

'I wouldn't mind some leave myself,' said Hoche. His thoughts went to Grünburg where he had grown up, his family – his father in his black Sigmarite robes, leading the great services at the temple, his grey-haired mother boiling apples – and Marie, always Marie, the dark-haired angel from the house across the stream. Sloe-eyed Marie who had smiled at him for twenty years, kissed him in secret for five, and would marry him within the next. 'Home,' he said wistfully.

Schulze looked back at him, moonlight leaving half his face in shadow. 'So you're bored, sir? Is that why we're tramping across moorland tonight?'

Hoche chuckled and shook his head. 'I'm not bored, but I think some of our fellow soldiers may be. I want to see what they've found to fill their time.'

'Deer hunting?'

'Not likely. You, Schulze, I know you'd have a fine time stalking and poaching deer out here on foot with a crossbow. But only a lunatic would gallop a horse across ground like this by night. And even I can read these tracks and tell these horses weren't chasing anything.'

There was a silence. Schulze broke it. 'Truth be told, sir, I used to use a longbow. Takes a touch more skill, but the range and penetration are better.'

Hoche laughed.

They walked another half-mile. The outlines of clouds moved silently across the sky. To the north, the half-crescent shape of Mannslieb, the second moon, was sinking below the horizon, but Morrslieb still poured its sickly light over the landscape. The stream curved away to the right, towards the woodlands that covered the nearer hills. Schulze stopped and studied the ground, then pointed left. Hoche stared up the side of the shallow valley to where his orderly was pointing. A copse of trees stood against the sky.

'What is that place?' he asked

'An old ruin,' Schulze said. 'The locals avoid it.'

As they drew close to it, Hoche could see that the copse was a wall of trees surrounding an open, overgrown area within. He'd seen similar things elsewhere: this was a fortified manor house or farm, abandoned for a couple of centuries and fallen into dilapidation, its protective boundary of elms and poplars now reaching high to the heavens. In this lonely place, so close to the Grey Mountains, he could guess what had happened: overrun by greenskins, its inhabitants butchered, its shell used as a camp until the beasts' own filth drove them from it and its walls were reclaimed by Taal, god of the wild places. If not greenskins then mutants or beastmen. The races changed but their methods were depressingly predictable.

He could see the outlines of the buildings now, between the trees. One wall still stood but the rest were rubble, over-grown with brambles and young trees, ash and sycamore. He could make out the plan of the building; its stone floor had probably survived. Against the one remaining wall was a large rectangular block, probably the remains of a stone oven. Shapes moved around it, low and grey, sinuous in the moonlight. One raised its head towards them and bared gleaming, growling teeth.

'Now those,' said Schulze in a low voice, 'are wolves.'

'What do we do?' Hoche asked.

'Back off but don't look away. Meet their eyes, stare back like you're a predator too. If there's only the three of them we'll be safe. Scavengers, wolves are. They'll only attack live prey if they have the weight of numbers.'

'What are they scavenging?' Hoche said. His answer was a growl from behind them and he whirled, drawing his sword. Two more were there.

'Oh, Sigmar,' Schulze said.

'Stand back to back,' Hoche said urgently. 'If they–' and the first wolf sprang at him. He slashed at it, cutting the air in front of its jaws, and it paced away, out of range, watching him with dark eyes. Behind him he heard a snarl, a slash, and Schulze's oath. The next one was on him, biting at his arm as another leaped, and he was parrying, cutting, dodg-ing, swinging for his life. No amount of sword practice or warring against the Bretonnians had prepared him for this. This wasn't a battle, it was a brute animal struggle.

A wolf came in from his left, snapping at his leg. He side-stepped and swept his sword at it, but the blade struck at an angle and glanced off. Hoche swore. It was the wrong weapon for this fight; a thrusting weapon, designed to pierce armour, its flat blade shaped for parrying, not cutting through thick fur and skin. At his rear he could tell Schulze was having a worse time of it: the man's blows were frenzied, panicked, lacking in structure or strategy. Then two wolves closed in on him and he was lost in his own fight, ducking right as one lunged at him, slashing at its sleek form and swinging through to block the other's run, smashing the edge of his blade into its face.

The two backed away and the pack followed. Hoche hoped for an instant that they had had enough of this prey that fought back. Instead they waited, circling, their eyes hard and greedy. Hoche watched them. One was limping badly, one had dark streaks of blood in its fur from a long cut along its back and a third was wounded across the face, blinded in one eye. But they were still five against two men.

Hoche studied the shapes of the predators, trying to identify the pack leader. There: larger than the rest, and darker too; perhaps only three summers old. A young leader, its movements confident, assured. The great wolf raised its head and stared back at him down its sharp muzzle. Hoche met its gaze, unblinking.

'How are you faring, Schulze?' he asked.

'Not well, sir.' Schulze's voice was shaky. 'What are we going to do?'

'If we defend, we die,' Hoche said and launched himself across the open space, his sword point low. The pack scattered but the dark leader stood firm, legs wide, its teeth bared in a snarl to receive his attack. Hoche swung the blade in a low arc and the wolf jerked its head up, leaping high at him to avoid the blade. Hoche had anticipated the leap, turned his arm and his swing became a straight thrust backed with all the weight of his charge. The sword met the wolf's leap, pierced its throat and ran deep into its body. The animal fell, wrenching the sword hilt from Hoche's grip as thick blood gushed from the open wound. The wolf convulsed. It tried to rise, tried to snarl, bared its teeth and died.

Hoche whirled, his arms raised to defend himself against another wolf's teeth, but the pack had scattered into the night. He bent to the dead leader and pulled his sword from its body. It had been an excellent thrust, fifteen inches deep: the steel had slipped in above its ribcage and must have hit heart and lungs on its way. Hoche nodded, satisfied with his work, and picked a handful of grass to clean the blade.

'That seems to have dealt with that, eh, Schulze?' he said.

Schulze didn't reply, and as Hoche turned he saw why. The soldier was clutching his left arm, his tunic sleeve ripped to tatters and soaked with blood. Claws had raked across his face, tearing open one cheek. Schulze looked at him in speechless pain, and sank to his knees.

'By Shallya,' Hoche muttered, pulling off his own tunic and shirt, tearing the linen into strips for bandages. Schulze's arm was a mess, the flesh torn where sharp fangs had ripped across the muscles. The cuts on his face were not as bad as they had first appeared, but they would leave scars. Schulze winced as Hoche swabbed the wound on his arm with a cloth soaked in kvas from his flask.

Hoche grinned. 'You'll live, old soldier. Come on, I need to know what those wolves were here to scavenge.'

The moat of the farmhouse was dry and overgrown with brambles, but there was an earth bridge across it. Schulze walked slowly up to it and studied the ground. 'They tethered their horses to the trees over there,' he said. 'Quite a few men, and one – no, two of them barefoot. The wolves must have come later.'

Hoche stared across the rubble at the end of the bridge to the dirt-deep stone floor of the old house, and knew why. Two shapes lay in broad moonlight where they had been tugged and torn by the scavenging wolves. Limbs lolled, spines contorted, heads twisted. There were dark holes in their naked bodies. Once, quite recently, they had been human.

Hoche stepped down from the rubble towards them. After a moment he realised that Schulze was staying back, wary of entering this place. Hoche didn't blame him. There was something about the ruin, a sense of taint, of pollution. It raised the hairs on the back of his neck.

'Schulze, they're only bodies,' he said. 'You've seen plenty – you've created enough among the Bretonnians.' The older man scrambled, still clutching his bandaged arm, to stand at Hoche's side as the young officer put the toe of his boot to the first body's shoulder and pushed. It rolled over and lay flat on its back, staring sightlessly up at the stars that banded the heavens. The wolves had torn much of its flesh away, but

the face was still whole and young. Hoche crouched down
beside the body.

'I know this one,' Schulze said. 'He's one of the
Bögenhafen boys that deserted last week.'

Hoche didn't look up. 'Deserted?'

'Always the same on a long campaign, men drifting away
all the time. But these two – no word to their friends, and
most of their equipment left behind.'

'I don't think they deserted,' said Hoche, 'though we were
meant to believe so. This one's flesh is still loose; no stink,
no maggots, no putrefaction. He's been dead no more than
a few hours. Why desert to hide out for a week in a wood
three miles from the camp you've left? It makes no sense.' He
stared at the corpse's face. The soldier couldn't have been
more than seventeen: his skin was clear, his torso hairless. A
pit in his chest gaped wide, the ends of ribs showing.
Whatever end the boy had met, it had been violent and not
caused by wolves. But there wasn't enough blood around to
explain an ungentle death like this.

Hoche reached out towards him and closed his cold eyes.
He hoped it would make the boy's face look more at peace,
but it didn't; it made him look like a blind man in hell.

Schulze was standing over the second corpse. 'There's
some marks on this one, sir. Come and see.' The body lay
about twenty feet away, sprawled and twisted, face-down. A
pattern of intersecting lines had been cut deep into the flesh
of its back: a rectangle with horns that branched out over
the man's shoulder-blades. The wound was puffy and dribbles of blood had run from it over the skin. Hoche
recognised the crossed bars and flinched. Sweat pricked
against his skin.

'It's a weird thing,' Schulze said, and knelt to touch the
body.

'Don't!' Hoche shouted. Schulze's outstretched arm froze.
'What is it, sir?'

'It's the mark of the being some call Khorne, the Blood
God. These men weren't killed by wolves and didn't die in a
fight – they were sacrificed. This place is unclean.' Hoche
could feel a slight tremor in his voice and a rising tension in
his mind, and fought it down. Orcs and wolves were one

thing, but worshippers of the Dark Gods were in another, much more powerful league.

He had seen marks like these before, years ago, when his father had been called to cleanse a secret temple discovered in an abandoned warehouse by the town watch. He wished his father was here now; for his knowledge as a priest of Sigmar, and for the sense of support and moral certainty that only a father can give. He felt afraid in a way he had never known before, not of the two corpses before him but of what they meant.

'The Knights Panther...?' said Schulze, giving a name to the fear.

'I don't know,' Hoche said. 'I don't know. Sigmar! This is very bad.'

'What do we do?'

'Let's cover them up.' Hoche glanced around. A dark red cloth had been spread over the stone block he had noticed earlier. It had been used as an altar, he realised. 'Get that cloth, bring it here.' He studied the marks. There could be no doubt: it was Khorne's symbol, carved deep with a dagger. Here too, there seemed to be less blood than there should be.

Schulze cried out, and Hoche whirled. His orderly was standing by the altar, one hand extended and shaking. 'The cloth, sir, it's–' and Hoche suddenly knew what had happened to the men's blood. He didn't want to see it or even think about it, but he knew he must.

The cloth was soaked in blood. It dripped from the edges, congealing in strings that hung down to the ground and pooled there, crusting. It stank of death. Through the thickening, tar-like contours of the awful liquid, Hoche could make out the seams and patches of embroidery on the fabric below, forming a pattern he knew well. It was the crest of the Emperor, the banner of the Empire, the army's battle-standard. Drenched in the blood of the Empire's soldiers.

At the centre of the cloth lay two objects, bulbous and fleshy, strange and glistening. Hoche knew with a sickening revulsion what they were. The crushed ribcages, the holes in the men's chests – these were their hearts.

Two hearts.

There was a long silence filled with Hoche's horrified thoughts. It was broken by Schulze staggering to a bush and being noisily sick. Hoche shook himself, and tried to regain the cool composure, the self-assurance with which he had started the evening.

'Right,' he said. 'One of us needs to get back to the camp and rouse the duke. The other needs to wait here under cover in case whoever did this comes back. We don't know for sure it was the Knights Panther, and even if it was, we don't know which of them are involved. Schulze, you're wounded, and besides the duke is more likely to listen to me. Find yourself some cover and don't move from it.'

Schulze spat a string of bile onto the ground and coughed. 'What if the wolves come back?' he asked.

'It's not likely but if they do then climb a tree.'

'With this arm?'

Hoche looked at him. 'I give you an order, it's up to you to obey it. If I don't return in four hours, make your own way back to the camp.' Schulze grunted something about sleep and Hoche put a hand on his shoulder. 'Look, if we can unearth a nest of Chaos worshippers, there's a good chance of promotion for both of us. That's worth a night's sleep.' He laughed. The sound had a high, shrill edge, and he wished he hadn't.

Hoche turned and began the long jog back towards the camp. Faint light lifted in the eastern sky and the landscape began to take on the day's colours, grey fading into greens and browns. A new dawn was coming.

Chapter Two
CHALLENGE

As HE RAN, thoughts pounded through Hoche's brain. Two men had been sacrificed to Khorne. Could one of the oldest and most elite regiments in the Emperor's armies be involved in such a thing? Only six knights had ridden out, but the idea that even six of the Knights Panther might be worshippers of Khorne was shocking enough.

Khorne. The Blood God, the basest and most brute of the four foul lords of Chaos. Hoche knew little about the possessor of the Brass Throne, although when he was younger his father had tried to teach him something of Chaos, separating out some truth from the folklore, superstition and fear.

Most cultists and followers of the Dark Gods gathered in secret to practise their foul rites, but Khorne was another matter. The Blood God demanded sacrifice and slaughter from his adherents, and much of it. The civilized lands of the Empire made it impossible to hide such bloody worship, and so it was certain – no, Hoche thought, it was assumed – that there were no cults of Khorne in the Empire's cities. The beastmen of the great forests were generally worshippers of the Blood God, and many of the fearsome warriors from the far north across the Sea of Claws or the frozen lands of Kislev were Khorne's forces. But of the four Chaos Gods, most scholars assumed that Khorne was the one who affected the Empire least. So why had two men been sacrificed to the Blood God this night?

And he had heard horsemen riding out of the camp at full moon at least twice before. Had other men disappeared and been put down as deserters, to meet unholy deaths at the hands of cultists? If not missing soldiers, then perhaps people had been taken from nearby farms and villages?

There would have to be a full-scale investigation. And someone, Hoche thought, would have to be appointed to lead it. Commanding a company of Reikland pike-soldiers was all well, but he wanted a new challenge: one that would exercise his brain as well as his voice and sword-arm.

The sun was above the horizon by the time he reached the camp gates and the army was beginning to wake up. Two Reiklanders from the Sixth Pikemen, the sister-company to Hoche's command, stood guard.

'Halt!' one of them shouted.

'For Sigmar's sake,' said Hoche, 'when you challenge someone, butt one end of your pike in the earth and point the other at their throat. You're supposed to be stopping an attacker, not waving like a flag-signaller. Get it right next time.' He walked in.

INSIDE THE CAMP, tent flaps were pulled back and men half-in, half-out of uniform were stretching, yawning, shaving, fetching water, walking to the latrines, polishing armour, talking to their friends. There was a smell of cooking oatmeal. It seemed like a completely normal morning, but Hoche felt separated from it by the things he had seen and the new knowledge he held.

The officers' quarters were at the far end of the camp, the ground sloping up gently to reach them. The tents here were larger, newer and better spaced. Servants, orderlies and uniformed batmen were doing the menial tasks while the officers lay in bed a few minutes longer, or broke their fast in their tents. Hoche walked through them, towards Duke Heller's tent.

'Hoi! Watch yourself, soldier!' someone shouted and Hoche, jerked from his thoughts, looked up to see a horse bearing down on him. On its back was an officer in Knights Panther colours, gesticulating, his proud face angry. Hoche froze. The rider pulled on his mount's reins, and stared down at him with arrogant disdain.

Hoche stepped out of the way, staring back. Had he been recognised? Was this one of the men? What would he do if he was challenged?

After a long moment the knight turned his head away and horse and rider moved past and away between the rows of tents. Hoche watched them for a second, then strode on to the open area at the top of the row and the great high tent at its centre, from where Duke Heller, the hero of the Carroberg campaign, military legend thrice decorated by the Emperor himself, commanded the army below.

THE GUARDS AT the tent mouth were in full armour, their breastplates and halberds shining. They stared ahead implacably as Hoche walked between them and into the cool canvas space beyond. Sunlight filtered through the pale fabric overhead, throwing soft light on the furniture, the hangings on the walls, the maps and papers on the table, and the patterned rug underfoot. A man sat at the table in the centre of the space, his back to Hoche, reading a roll of parchment. A messenger in the colours of the Imperial Service stood beside him, at attention. A curtain sectioned off the rear of the tent, a fold in its centre marking the way through. A servant moved between the tent poles, refilling the oil-lamps that hung from them.

Hoche halted and saluted smartly, clicking his heels together. The reader didn't look round. Hoche coughed. Still no reaction. He waited a second, then strode to the far side of the table and saluted again before looking down at the man seated opposite him. The man looked up, an expression of irritation on his face. It wasn't the duke. Hoche recognised him as the general's aide-de-camp, but couldn't remember his name.

'Lieutenant Karl Hoche, Fifth Reiklanders. I need to speak with Duke Heller on a matter of great urgency,' he said.

'Lieutenant,' the man said, drawing out the syllables of the word. 'The general is dealing with Imperial business. I will pass him your message.' He smiled.

Bohr, that was his name. Johannes Bohr, Hoche recalled. He knew his reputation for cool efficiency, but something of this importance had to go to the duke before all other men.

'If he's dealing with Imperial business, why aren't you at his side?' Hoche asked, and didn't wait for an answer. 'Listen, I understand the niceties of protocol, but this matter is too serious and too urgent. I have to see the duke.'

'He is indisposed.'

'Then dispose him.' Hoche stared at Bohr. He guessed the man was only a year or two older than himself but his black hair was already streaked with lines of silver. A scar ran down one cheek to lose itself in the thick hair of a neatly trimmed beard. Bohr raised his head and stared back at Hoche. His eyes were vulpine and piercing blue. He did not blink.

'Are you sure he will want to hear your news?' he asked.

'It is news no commander wants to hear,' said Hoche. 'That is what makes it important.'

Bohr stroked his beard for a second, impassive, then stood and rolled up the parchment. 'We will have a reply in three hours,' he said to the messenger, who saluted and left the tent. The aide-de-camp went to the fold in the curtain and held it open to speak through it: 'Lieutenant Karl Hoche of the Reiklanders, sir. I apologise, but he has news he says is urgent.'

A voice came from the other side, muffled by the thick fabric. Hoche recognised it as the duke's but couldn't make out the words. Bohr could, however: 'He will not tell me, sir,' he said. Another muffled sentence. 'He's most insistent.' He turned to Hoche. 'The general will see you now.'

Hoche followed Bohr through the gap in the curtain, into the duke's private quarters. There was a four-poster bed here, rich hangings on the walls and a smell of incense. The duke was being helped into the ornate folds of his uniform by a liveried servant. A table to one side carried the remains of a roast chicken, still steaming, and an open bottle of wine. The duke's appetite for life was as well known as his hunger for glory.

The great commander turned as they entered. His face was cragged and lined, like channels carved in rock by the passage of time. Hoche was surprised to see how thin and lank his hair was, in contrast to his great bush of a moustache.

Hoche saluted. He was conscious that Bohr, at his side, did not.

'At ease, Lieutenant Hoche,' the duke said. 'I know you. You fought with me at Wissendorf.'

'It was my honour to command the fifth company there, sir, as I do here.'

The duke smiled. 'Yes. Hope you do as well this time out. Now what's so urgent that it interrupts my dressing?'

Hoche glanced at Bohr. The duke caught the movement. 'Johannes is my personal secretary and aide-de-camp. I have no secrets from him. Speak freely.'

Hoche took a deep breath. 'Sir, two soldiers were murdered last night by worshippers of Chaos.' He felt as if someone in the room had twisted a cord; the other men tensed with a twitch, as if a puppeteer had jerked their strings. He had been right: it was news that nobody wanted to hear.

The duke said slowly, 'Murdered?'

'Sacrificed, sir. Their bodies lie in a small wood some three miles distant. One of my men is standing watch over them.' He thought briefly of Schulze, wounded and on duty. There was a silence. Hoche felt the atmosphere of the room change, grow heavy, its pressure bearing down on him. He said: 'I have evidence that the murderers are knights in this army.'

Nobody spoke. The duke pressed his thumb against the spot between his eyes, rubbing it. Then he gestured to Bohr and the servant, and they left without a word. The duke sat in the leather-backed chair on the far side of the table and pointed at another that stood against the tent wall. Hoche pulled it into the centre of the room to sit before his commander.

'You were right to come to me at once,' the duke said. 'Start at the beginning and don't leave anything out.'

* * *

TEN MINUTES LATER the duke drained his second goblet of wine and pushed his chair back from the table. 'By Sigmar, I hope you're wrong.' he said. 'Knights Panther! This could upset a lot of things all the way to Altdorf.'

'How do we proceed?' asked Hoche. 'There'll have to be a full investigation.'

The duke looked thoughtful. 'First thing, get the priest out to the old farmhouse, see what he can tell us. Probably worth taking the battle-wizard too; you never know.'

'What about the Knights Panther?'

'We do nothing. Only six of them are implicated, and we have no idea who. We can't arrest all of them. They're an elite regiment, personal favourites of the Emperor. Their generals have powerful connections. For the moment, till we know more, we can't let them know that they're suspected. And it's possible that they're not involved at all; the riders may have been hunting, stopped at the farm, and their tracks became muddled with those of the real cultists.'

He's already trying to cover for them, thought Hoche. He doesn't want to believe that one of the Empire's great regiments could be involved in such a thing. 'The guards on the gate may be able to identify the riders,' he said out loud. 'The groom at the stable too, he knew for sure who they were.'

The duke stood. 'Then we should find these people and question them,' he said. 'Obviously we have to treat this with utter discretion. Only those who have to know about it should be told. We'll need someone to lead the investigation here until we can summon some witch hunters, and I – what on earth...?'

A faint vibration trembled from the ground beneath their feet. From outside the tent there was the sound of thundering hoof-beats, of many heavy horses galloping through the camp. It sounded like a stampede, or a cavalry charge. Shouts and cries followed them, the clash of steel, and then the crack of a flintlock pistol being discharged.

Hoche turned, focusing, following the source of the sound. The horses were heading away – from the stables, he guessed, racing down the hill and towards the main gate.

Beside him, the duke had stood and was pulling on a velvet jerkin. 'I have a notion this may be connected to your discovery,' he said. 'Come with me.'

Hoche followed as the older man pulled the curtain aside and stepped into the outer chamber of the tent. Bohr was seated there, still reading the same parchment. 'Bohr, go to the captain of the Templars. Tell him to put the Knights Panther under close arrest, on my authority, and bring Sir Valentin to me at once. Then find the high priest and bring him here.'

'This hour, sir?' said Bohr.

'At once. Though I fear we are already too late.'

THE CAMP WAS in uproar. Fires blazed as burning tents, dry from the summer's heat, threw flames at the sky. Further down the camp, rows of tents lay flattened, their guy-ropes severed. Men lay slashed, bleeding, their limbs broken or severed, their fellow soldiers bandaging their wounds and pouring brandy into their mouths. Beyond the gate and down the road, thirty horsemen galloped away into the distance, the banner of the Knights Panther waving proudly above them. Sunlight glinted off their bright armour. Nobody was giving chase. There had been no time to react.

There was a sense of shock and silence.

'One thing you have to say for the Panthers,' said the duke, 'they're highly effective soldiers. No other regiment could have done so much damage in so little time.'

'We should be following them,' Hoche said.

The duke snorted. 'They set light to the stables. I'll wager they cut the other horses' throats too, as well as that groom. Destroy evidence, prevent pursuit and spill blood for their god. Damnably effective soldiers.'

Hoche nodded, unsure how to answer.

They walked through the camp, surveying the damage. At the stables, where the canvas walls still blazed and the air was filled with the smell of fresh-roasted horseflesh, the groom he had spoken to the night before lay in a water-trough half-filled with his own blood, his neck opened to the bone, his teeth bared in a red grimace.

They spoke with the wounded, hearing how the Knights had charged through the camp, slashing wildly from their saddles at anything in their way. The Reiklanders on the gate were dead, cut down as the Knights galloped out. Hoche wondered if they had tried to use their pikes properly, or if they had even had a chance to turn the unwieldy twelve-foot weapons as they realised that this time the threat came from inside, not outside the camp.

He cursed himself for not being more attentive, more suspicious. Had he been followed back from the ruined farm? Had someone been watching the gate, ready to tip off the Knights that they had been discovered? Or had someone been listening outside the general's tent, by chance or on purpose? Still, if he was leading the coming investigation there would be plenty of time to track down witnesses, trace everyone's movements, put together a picture of exactly what had happened.

Outside the burning remains of the Knights Panther quarters, the captain of the Templars and his men were holding the remaining Knights, their wrists in chains. Sir Valentin, their leader, was not among them. Hoche counted them: nineteen. He'd guessed at thirty riders. That left eleven still around the camp, or dead in the burning ruins of the order's tents.

The Knights seemed subdued, oddly quiet. There was none of the protesting and arguing that Hoche had expected. It was as if they accepted their guilt: their comrades' traitorous actions had brought shame on them all, their regiment and everything it stood for. Half their number had proved to be worse than enemies.

A blond man with his head bowed was led out, his wrists chained. It was the young knight he had seen that morning, who had almost ridden him down. What a change there was in his face; from arrogant pride to a humbled prisoner. Then he looked up, directly at Hoche, and his expression twisted for a moment before blanking, expression neutral, eyes straight ahead.

I've changed too, Hoche thought, and he knows why. Everything's changed. It's too late to try to pull away; I must see this through, wherever it leads.

Beside him, Bohr said something to the duke in a low voice, and pointed off into the distance. The duke turned to look. 'Is that the wood you talked about?' he said, nodding in the direction of Bohr's finger. Across the valley, a column of grey smoke was rising lazily into the still morning sky. There was a flicker of fire among the trees. Hoche stared at it, feeling a rising horror. Deliberately, he forced the muscles of his face to relax, to show nothing, like the blond knight.

'The Knights must be destroying the evidence there too,' Hoche said. 'The sacrifices and everything that could connect them.' With cold certainty he knew that they would have killed Schulze too. His orderly and friend was dead, and it was his order that had condemned him.

They had killed all the witnesses now – except one, he thought, and wondered when they would come for him.

IT WAS NOON. Seven men were gathered in Duke Heller's quarters, seated around the large table. The duke was at its head with Johannes Bohr at his right hand, taking notes. To left and right were his chief officers and advisors. Hoche stood at the end of the table and felt thirsty. Outside, the day was hot and dry. The Knights Panthers's quarters had burnt to the ground, and men doused the hot ashes with water, seeing what had survived the flames and trying to identify the dead. On the horizon, the wood still burned.

'There's no solid evidence,' said Lord Hanft, leader of the Knights Templar. His loose jowls, shaggy facial hair and dogmatic way of thinking reminded Hoche of a wolfhound. 'Anything that was in the Panthers' quarters was either taken with them or destroyed in the fire, as was their place of worship. Anyone who saw them last night has been killed. Obviously we can work out a list of those who fled. But beyond that, and Lieutenant Hoche's testimony, we have no proof that these men were involved in things of... er...'

'Chaos,' said Duke Heller. 'One of the most prestigious regiments in the Empire's forces, making sacrifices to a Chaos cult. I didn't want to believe it when I heard the evidence, but their flight has proved their guilt. And Sir Valentin gone as well. It beggars the soul.'

Father Reikhart, the regimental priest of Sigmar, raised a hand. 'I have a suggestion,' he said. 'Nobody outside this room knows about the evidence we've heard, not even the other Knights Panther. There are stories flying around the camp but, as Lord Hanft says, no proof.

'Now: think of the impact on the morale of the army – not just this camp but all the Empire's forces – if word spreads that certian members of an elite regiment with a noble and holy history can fall victim to the temptations of the force it has sworn to oppose. It would be devastating. It would signal that even our strongest can be destroyed from within. Our defenders would lose hope; our foes gain succour.'

Hoche felt his skin flushing red, unexpected sweat pricking at his brow. 'What are you saying?' he demanded, a rising note of anger in his voice. The priest turned to look at him.

'I am saying that we should do nothing,' he said. 'A plausible cover-story, a request for reinforcements, doubling the sentries in case they should come back, but nothing more.'

'But–' Hoche struggled to find words to express his anger. He could not believe he was hearing such things from a priest of Sigmar. 'It's Chaos! You can't tell us to ignore it!'

'He's not asking us to ignore it, lieutenant,' the duke said. 'He's asking us to not mention it to those who need not know. Reports will be sent to the relevant authorities in Altdorf. There will be an investigation, but it will be a quiet one. We will remain vigilant. Part of the power of Chaos is its ability to instil fear. If we tell everyone, then we have given it a victory, and we cannot do that.

'You understand? Good. Any further questions? No? Then I suggest that we tell the men that the Panthers' cook accidentally added a poisonous mushroom to last night's stew, creating madness and blood-frenzy in those who ate it. They are beyond our help now. The remaining Panthers either did not eat the stew or are immune to the mushroom's effects, and can therefore be freed. Thank you for your time, gentlemen.' He stood, and the others began to stand too.

'Wait,' said Hoche. 'There are things I'd like to know.'

'There are things we would all like to know,' the duke said, looking at him. 'That's why there will be an investigation. If you have any questions then ask my aide-de-camp, who is leading it.' Across the table Bohr smiled like a fox, with too many teeth to be friendly. It was an expression of superiority, and what felt to Hoche like hostility too.

He and Bohr were the last to leave the meeting-table, and they entered the outer chamber of the duke's tent together.

'What were your questions?' Bohr asked.

'The duke answered one of them.' Hoche paused and looked away. He didn't trust this smooth man, but right now there were few people he did trust.

'The duke is a shrewd judge of men's thoughts,' Bohr said.

Yes, Hoche thought, that's why he didn't notice half of his elite cavalry were making sacrifices to the Blood God. His estimation of the duke dropped a little, of Bohr even further. 'So you lead the investigation?'

'Yes.' Bohr said, as if expecting another question. Then: 'Oh. Were you hoping for the post? A promotion?'

Hoche said nothing, but his expression betrayed him. Bohr gave a polite laugh. 'Karl – I may call you Karl? – I apologise. You are a soldier of rare ability, but your ways are too blunt. An enquiry of this kind needs people who are diplomats as well as soldiers, familiar with military and Imperial protocol, who can ask questions so sharp that the answerer doesn't realise how far under his skin they are, and who can persuade someone to give up a secret or break an oath without thinking about it. With all respect, you don't yet have those skills.' There was a tone in his voice that some people would have called smug, and Hoche was one of them.

Bohr looked down at his table and began to sort through a pile of sealed papers. 'Besides,' he said, 'you have your own role to play.'

'I won't be part of a cover-up,' Hoche said.

Bohr smiled the fox-smile again. 'Quite the opposite, Karl. We want you to help the investigation. You're to take the news to Altdorf.'

Hoche was taken by surprise. It was all he could do to say, 'What?'

'Word of what happened needs to reach the authorities as soon as possible. You saw it, they'll want to hear it from your lips. I'll give you letters of introduction to the Knights Panther, the High Priest of the witch hunters at the Cathedral of Sigmar, and the head of the Untersuchung. I suggest you visit them in that order.'

Hoche shook his head. 'What is the Untersuchung? I've never heard of them.'

Bohr looked him in the eye, and the look was cold and long. 'Count yourself lucky. The Untersuchung are conspiracy-hunters. They investigate cults and networks of subversive, illegal, treasonous and blasphemous activity, mostly in the army and the Imperial court, but their cloak is spread wide. They specialise in dealing with Chaos and magic. They're part of the Reiksguard but they keep a low profile.'

'Isn't that the witch hunters' job?'

'The Untersuchung is more structured than the witch hunters. Much more structured.' Bohr sat in his chair at the table, took out his quill knife, selected a goose feather from a pot, and began sharpening it to a point. 'If a witch hunter sees a hornet, he kills it. The Untersuchung follow it back to its nest and burn them all. Their investigations can take years. Decades sometimes.'

'You sound like you know them well.'

'I've...' Bohr paused. 'I've had dealings with them.'

Hoche sat in silence, digesting what he had heard. Altdorf. The Untersuchung. Perhaps a chance to go home, to see Marie and his family. It had been a long, hard summer. A week of rest would be welcome. Something else itched at his mind. The only sound in the room was the scraping of Bohr's knife.

'I'll go,' he said.

'Good,' said Bohr without looking up. 'As this is an order from the duke, you'd be court-martialled if you didn't. Go via the barracks in Nuln, get them to send us more horses.'

'You'll look after my men?' Hoche said.

'Of course.'

'You'll recover Schulze's body from the woods and see that he gets a proper burial.'

'Assuming he's dead.'

'It's a fair assumption.'

There was a pause.

'What I don't understand,' Hoche said, 'is why half the Knights Panther fled, if only six of them were involved in the sacrifice last night.'

Bohr dipped the quill in ink, and bent over a sheet of parchment to write. 'Either there were more cultists in the regiment, or some decided it would be better to be with their valiant comrades than part of a shamed regiment.'

'That's not what I meant. If thirty of the Panthers were Khorne worshippers, why did only six of them ride out last night?'

Bohr looked up from his writing. 'That's one reason why there will be an investigation.'

Hoche looked down at him. 'Who tipped off the Panthers this morning?' he demanded.

'I intend to find out. Karl, the most useful place for you is in Altdorf. Come back in an hour, I will have the letters ready for you, and you can ride with the Imperial messenger. When you return we have great things planned for you. An important role. But until then, we both have much to do.'

Hoche stood and headed for the door. As he reached it, he looked back. Bohr was still crouched over his writing, the tip of the quill moving slowly as it described each ornate black letter.

'No cover-up,' Hoche said.

'On the honour of my name,' said Bohr without looking up. Hoche turned and headed out into the bright world beyond the tent, leaving him in the cool darkness.

HIS TENT FELT empty of a familiar presence. The spilled kvas glass still lay on the floor, blurring the ink on some of the playing cards. Normally Schulze would have cleared it up, but the chances Schulze were still alive were nil. Hoche felt the death of any of his men, but Schulze had been a particular friend. He would light a candle for him in the soldiers' chapel in Altdorf, he decided. He sighed and began to pack the kit he would need for the trip, and the formal uniform he would wear in Altdorf.

Someone knocked on the tent-pole closest to the door and coughed. Hoche recognised the sound. 'Come in, Sergeant Braun,' he said.

A stocky man walked in and saluted, then used the same hand to wipe the floppy hair from his brow. 'We heard the news, sir. Is it true that you're bound for Altdorf?'

'It's true, but I'm not staying there long. I have some reports I need to make. I'll be back before the campaign breaks for the year. This isn't a promotion.'

'That's good,' said Braun. 'Good it is. We were feared you'd become a stuffed shirt with ideas above us.'

Hoche laughed. 'Braun, I'm not done leading you and the men to famous victories yet.' He thought a second, holding a jerkin. 'I want you to keep your eyes open while I'm gone. Anything suspicious, anything that feels not right, make a note of it and tell me when I'm back.'

'Sir.'

'And in the meantime, if you get some temporary officer and he's not good enough for the Reiklanders, then you give him hell.'

Braun saluted smartly. 'That we'll do, sir. That we'll do.'

IT WAS NOT until Hoche, astride one of the horses that had escaped the Knights Panthers' carnage and with the Imperial messenger riding beside him, had put fifteen long, dry miles between himself and the camp that it occured to him that sending him far away, riding with only one companion through an area reputedly heavy with orcs would be the best way to begin a cover-up of the whole filthy business.

He weighed the thought, trying various possibilities, remembering things that Bohr had said to him earlier in the day. Then he smiled wryly, placed the idea out of his mind and put the spurs to his horse, urging it on. Altdorf lay ahead, and great prospects.

Chapter Three
GREAT PROSPECTS

THE SUN WAS setting and the guards were preparing to shut the great city gates as Hoche rode into Altdorf from the south. The journey had taken him over a fortnight, and on the last day the weather had turned, soaking his woollen cloak and slowing his pace to a trot. His muscles ached, and after eight nights sleeping in rough inns with bug-ridden beds or wrapped in a blanket beside the road he was looking forward to a decent meal and a night's rest.

Even with the sun partly hidden by grey clouds, Altdorf was magnificent. The tower of the Cathedral of Sigmar was visible from miles out, and as he had drawn closer Hoche had been able to see the roof of the Imperial Palace over the city's foreboding stone walls. Inside, the streets were crowded with people moving fast, not looking at each other in that big-city way as they tried to get home before night fell. He hadn't been in the capital for years, and he didn't like it any better this time. He felt trapped, the overhang of the tall buildings on either side blocking out the light and closing in on him.

Hoche rode across the Old Bridge and the river towards the Königplatz and the Black Goat Inn. The Reiklanders did not have a barracks in Altdorf, but the regiment's officers had an agreement with the inn that gave them room and board on account. By the time he reached the square the daily market had been packed away, the barrows and carts had been pushed to the side of the road, and the Königplatz was empty apart from the cluster of tall statues of dead emperors at its centre. The entrance to the inn's courtyard was open.

'Seen any action lately, sir?' the stable-boy asked conversationally as Hoche handed him the reins of his horse and dismounted.

'Not the kind you mean,' Hoche said. He stretched his arms and bent at the knees, exercising muscles stiff from the long ride, then began unstrapping his saddle-bags. The boy patted the horse's nose.

'What's your business in Altdorf, sir?' he asked.

'Upsetting people,' said Hoche. 'What's the time?'

The boy stared at him oddly, then looked at the sky. 'Eight bells soon enough,' he said.

'Good. That's very good.' There would be enough time for him to get to the Knights Panther barracks before they sat down to their evening meal, and Hoche felt it was important that they were told tonight, before the others. It was the honour of their regiment that was at stake, and besides, Bohr had told him to see them first. He dug in the saddlebags for the letters he had been given, pocketed them and dropped the bags at the boy's feet with a couple of groats. 'See to the horse, then take these inside. Lieutenant Hoche of the Reiklanders. I need a room for the night and a bloody good meal. I'll be back in an hour.'

He headed out into the darkening streets.

THE ROOM WAS panelled with ornately carved oak, gold leaf highlighting the names of battles dating back a thousand years, and above it all the splendid crest of the Knights Panther, the great beast's head snarling, white-fanged and lash-tongued, under a gold crown. Below, across the table, the three officers who faced Hoche were no less splendid: their faces lined by age and faded scars, unmarred by fat, loose skin or the signs of high living. Any of them would be glad of the chance to lead a battle-charge tomorrow. But they couldn't. These men were the acting senior officers, crippled in battle, who stayed behind in Altdorf when the regiment and its generals went campaigning, left in charge of supplies, logistics, numbers and servants, dreaming of valour and glory.

In front of them a leg of roast mutton lay uneaten, growing cold as Hoche had told his story. The three goblets of wine were empty, and the decanter was empty too. The three men sat still and silent in their chairs, digesting.

'Circumstantial.' Colonel Jäger said, and pushed his heavy chair back. 'Circumstantial, but utterly damning.'

'Thirty men,' said Major Arnau, scratching absent-mindedly at his jewelled eye-patch. 'Thirty of our finest, and Sir Valentin among them. What can have possessed them?'

'Evidently the foul spirit of Khorne possessed them. What matters now is how we protect the regiment from this.' Colonel Raschke looked down at the piece of paper where he'd been jotting notes with a lead pencil as Hoche had described his experiences. He reached for the decanter, found it empty, and pulled the bell to summon a servant. The officers' discussion paused as more wine was brought. Hoche felt it was as if he was not present. Even when one of them looked at him, it was as if he was a witness in a trial, or a letter containing bad news. A thing, not a person.

'There will have to be an investigation,' Colonel Jäger said. 'All loose ends must be found and tied up. The reputation of the Knights Panther is at stake and the taint of Chaos must not be allowed to stain it.' He touched the shirt over his heart in the quick outline of the hammer of Sigmar. 'I trust you understand me, gentlemen?'

'The regiment must be protected,' said Major Arnau.

'Quite so,' Colonel Raschke said. He swallowed wine from his goblet and turned to Hoche. 'No doubt you will be reporting this incident to other parties in Altdorf. Or have you already done so?'

'I came to you directly I reached the city,' Hoche said. His throat was dry; he had had nothing to drink since arriving in Altdorf, nobody here had offered him water or wine, and telling his story and answering the men's questions had

taken over an hour. 'At dawn tomorrow I see the witch
hunters and the Untersuchung,' he added.

'The Untersuchung. Hmm,' Raschke said. 'It would be better if they were not involved in this. But you have orders
from Duke Heller.' He glanced at his colleagues, then at the
piece of paper in front of him. 'Thank you for your news.
Stay a while, have something to eat. We will arrange for an
escort to return you to your inn.' He picked up the paper,
wadded it and dropped it to the floor. 'The streets of Altdorf
are not safe for the unguarded,' he said.

THE STEW WAS excellent. Hoche tasted both beef and venison
in it, their flavours not masked but accentuated by the spiced
gravy. The goblet of wine seemed to clear his head after the
day's long journey and he felt like a new man, revitalised,
with new purpose. He sat back, alone in the chamber, and
thought over the day.

There was a knock on the door and two men entered. One
was blond, young, crop-headed, moustached and slick, the
other older and grey-haired with hands like a pound of
sausages and a face that the sun had beaten against for too
many years. Both wore dark cloaks, and Hoche could tell
from the way the cloth hung at their hips that each man carried a sword.

'Your escort, sire,' said the older of the two. Their faces did
not have the aristocratic cast that Hoche expected of Knights
Panther but then, he reflected, they were probably servants
or guards. Cavalry officers could hardly be expected to escort
a man through the city's dark streets, no matter how important the information he carried.

The two men led him through the Knights Panthers' headquarters, and out into the night. The warm night air was a
shock after the cool stone atmosphere of the rooms inside.
Hoche did not recognise the street they were on, but the
gothic bulk of the Imperial Palace loomed against the darkened sky to the west, so the Old Bridge must lie to the north.

'This way,' said Grey-hair, nodding towards the east.

Hoche stopped. 'Isn't it this direction?' he said.

Grey-hair shook his head. 'It's past ten bells. The ferrymen
have gone home and the Old Bridge and West Bridge are

closed for the night. We'll have to cross the river at the docks.' He set off, not looking back to see if Hoche was following. Blond took a burning, smoking torch from a bracket beside the door and waited to follow the young officer.

Hoche steadied himself for a moment, feeling a little unstable, then walked after the man's cloaked back. He was tired, and perhaps his hosts' wine had been stronger than he had thought. Grey-hair walked on in front of him while Blond brought up the rear. Good defensive formation, he thought. The Knights Panther had planned well.

The city was quiet, the day's heat deadening the night air. Hoche and his silent protectors walked down unfamiliar streets towards the Reik. He could smell it over Altdorf's familiar summer stink. They were moving into the docks district, past shuttered shops, tall warehouses, broad tenement buildings and the occasional tavern with low light and muted conversation drifting from its doorway. Only a few people were on the streets, most of them walking swiftly, not looking at other night-travellers. They hadn't passed a single watch patrol.

The first bridge was stone, wide enough for two carts to pass, the Reik below it oily in the faint light. Hoche took the chance to pause and lean on the stone parapet, feeling unsteady on his feet. He stared west, to where the river joined with the Talabec a few hundred yards downstream, the waters of the two merging to form a greater whole that flowed out to the great port of Marienburg hundreds of miles downstream, and the Sea of Claws. If Altdorf was the heart of the Empire, as men said, then the Reik was its spine. It might stink of garbage and human waste, but in the moonlight it was glorious.

Beyond lay the docks, a shambles of warehouses and cheap houses, new dwellings crammed into every available space, and piled on top of each other. Hoche knew its reputation as a place of lowlifes and reprobates; and though he should have felt safe with his two guards, for some reason he shivered. The road narrowed, the cramped buildings almost meeting overhead, pathways and alleys twisting and intersecting with others like veins in a great sleeping creature. Hoche felt like a parasite, an alien, out of place. He shouldn't be here. He thought about the army camp and about his men, now training under a new officer, and then for a moment he thought of home and Marie, smiling. How surprised she would be to see him, how proud of his lieutenant's tassels. 'Why didn't you send word you were coming back?' she would say, and he...

Grey-hair turned right off the street, away from the smell of the river, into a narrow lane dark with shadow.

'Is this the way?' asked Hoche.

'Short-cut to the second bridge,' Blond said from behind him. Hoche paused, looked up and down the street, failed to get his bearings, shrugged and followed.

Grey-hair was waiting, of course, his sword drawn.

A flood of realisation poured into Hoche's mind and he turned to run, his hand groping for his own weapon. It was all a trap. His movements felt slow, as if he was swimming in the muggy air. Behind him the blond man had cut off his retreat. His sword was drawn too, but he had dropped the torch and the alley was deep in shadow.

Hoche threw his eyes around the alley in desperation. The ground was rough cobbles with piles of garbage. The walls were flat plaster, featureless and dirty, with no handholds or pipes, much less a window or door. There was no way out.

He backed towards the nearest wall, protecting his back, trying to watch both men as they edged closer. With his left hand he unfastened the laces that held his money-pouch to his belt. 'Don't hurt me,' he said, holding it out to the older man in front of him. 'Here, I have money. Take it all.'

'We'll take it,' said Grey-hair, 'and your life too.' Hoche hurled the open pouch at his face in a spray of gold and silver coins. Grey-hair threw up his hands to protect himself, and Hoche thrust high at him with his sword.

He was aiming for the man's throat but his aim was off and the blade pierced the right shoulder instead. It wasn't deep but it was enough; Grey-hair dropped his weapon with a yowl. An instant later Hoche shoulder-rammed him, knocking him down and out of the way. Hoche heard him fall and shout, then the sound of Blond's footsteps giving chase. He didn't pause to look back: he ran.

The alley twisted left and right, then ended in a wider street. Hoche went left, his boots ringing against the cobblestones. The sound of pursuit wasn't far behind him, but as far as he could tell there was only one man on his heels.

The sudden energy of the fight had cleared his mind but not his legs; he knew he was slower than his chaser. Normally he would have run until he reached the city wall or a guard patrol, but he knew they would catch him first. He didn't try to work out why he'd been attacked. Time for that if he survived.

He dived down another alley, turned right at the end, knowing that Blond was a few feet behind him, and there beyond a low wall was the river – not the Reik but the Talabec, the other branch, glistening, its dark banks broken with wharves and moored barges. The road ran beside it in either direction but the darkness of the water beyond seemed an implacable barrier. Stop, it said. You can run no further.

Hoche gazed at it in despair, then in a desperate movement flung himself around, his body low, feet braced to steady himself, sword outstretched. Blond came hurtling out of the alley and saw the blade too late. He tried to throw himself sideways but his momentum was too strong and Hoche was too quick. The weight of Blond's rush carried him onto the sword and down to its hilt as the steel slid into him below the ribs. Then his body slammed into Hoche and the impact carried them both backwards, face to face. Blond's sword hit the ground with a clatter.

Hoche's buttocks whacked into the edge of the wall, and he felt himself begin to topple backwards, with the weight of the other man on top of him. With his left hand he tried to grasp the brickwork to steady himself. The wall was too smooth. Blond, dying, was pushing him over the edge into the river. He tried to release his right hand but it was trapped between them. For a frozen moment they hung there, balanced between land and water, life and death. Hoche stared up into Blond's eyes, an inch from his. He could feel the heat of the dying man's body pressed hard against him.

'Who are you?' he said. 'Who sent you?'

Blond's face twisted to almost a smile. He opened his mouth as if to speak and blood surged out, gushing over

Hoche's face, filling his eyes and mouth, matting his hair, soaking his uniform. He pushed back blindly and felt the man slump off him and fall to the ground. There was no other sound. Hoche leaned forward off the wall, wiped the blood from his face, and opened his eyes in time to see Grey-hair emerge from the alley at a run, sword in his left hand.

The man stopped. 'Sigmar's balls!' he said.

Hoche bent, picked up Blond's sword, and took a duelling stance. Grey-hair disappeared back into the alley, the sound of his footfalls fading into the distance.

Maybe he's gone to fetch the watch, Hoche thought. That would be ironic: he had no way to prove his innocence or the other's guilt. No way of finding out who the man was, either. He leaned back against the wall, feeling the cool air from the river brush over his face. Then something lurched inside him, and he turned and bent over the edge, emptying his stomach into the river below in a rush of vomit.

He dropped Blond's sword and tugged his own out of the corpse, wincing as it scraped against a bone. Then he untied the dead man's cloak, pulled it from under his body and put it on. It was soaked with blood, but the stains wouldn't show against the dark fabric as much as they did on his light uniform. His face must be caked in the drying blood of his would-be assassin.

He looked both ways along the street. Nobody in sight. Hoche wiped his sword on the edge of the cloak, sheathed it, and stood for a moment, working out where he was. From the position of the bridges downstream he reckoned it should be a fifteen-minute walk to the Black Goat; time enough to think through what had just happened.

BY THE TIME he reached the Königplatz he had three possibilities. Either the Knights Panther had tried to have him killed, to remove the last witness to the regiment's dishonour. But that was ludicrous. Much more likely, he thought as he cleaned the blood from his face in a horse trough, was that the Knights' porter had hired two street-toughs as linkmen to escort him, not knowing they were robbers. Or two of the Knights' staff had resolved to rob and kill him – that wasn't likely, but was less improbable than a regiment's officers conspiring to have a messenger killed. This was a civilised time; nobody killed messengers any more.

Whichever was right, it wasn't the welcome to Altdorf that he had expected. He shivered, and hoped Frau Kolner had kept some food hot for him.

He stepped into the inn. Nobody was around but an oil-lamp still burned in the cubby-hole where Frau Kolner's idiot brother usually sat next to the stairs, waiting for bags to carry. There was no sign of a bell or rapper to bring attention, and no smell of food either. Then he heard heavy boots on the floor upstairs, and voices.

Some instinct, he couldn't say what, made him duck into the shadows under the staircase. Several pairs of footsteps rattled down above his head, and he caught snatches of conversation:

'...for your help... tragedy... death.'

'...important... be returned... regiment.'

'A sad... collect his horse...'

'I'm sorry to hear of it.' That was Frau Kolner's voice, from the foot of the stairs. 'That the city streets are so unsafe, it's a worry. My sympathies to the young man's family.'

So someone staying at the inn had died. Hoche peered out from his hiding place, wondering how to emerge without looking a fool. Frau Kolner had her back to him as she talked to three soldiers. They wore tunics with the Knights Panther crest, and one carried saddlebags over his arm. They were Hoche's saddlebags.

Hoche ducked back into the shadows and pressed himself against the wall, out of sight, until the figures had left. There was no mistaking them: those were his bags. Images and parts of ideas pounded through his brain: all that had happened today. He focused, concentrating on the conversation. They had told Frau Kolner someone was dead. Who?

Then in the distance he heard the great bell of the Cathedral of Sigmar strike once, and he thought: time. In the time it took me to walk from the docks to the Black Goat, Grey-hair could not have returned to the Knights Panther to tell them I was still alive, and then the soldiers walk to the inn. They must have left just after I did. They don't know I'm still alive. They were talking about *me*. They think I'm dead in an alley.

He thought: the Knights Panther tried to have me killed.

He thought: they drugged my food, to slow my reactions. That's why I was sick.

He thought: I have to get word to the witch hunters and the Untersuchung. Tonight. That is what the knights aim to prevent, so that is what I must do. They assume I'm dead now; but will Grey-hair have taken them the news that I'm not?

He thought: I will find out.

HOCHE STOPPED BEFORE the end of the road, in the darkness. The vastness of the Cathedral of Sigmar lay behind him, its buttresses and spires rearing into the night sky. Ahead and smaller, though clearly built by the same hands, the headquarters of the Order of Witch Hunters brooded, cloaked by shadows. At its doorway, four uniformed men leaned in too-casual idleness. They looked bored, and armed. They were waiting for someone.

Hoche knew who. He turned and slunk away into the night.

THE HEADQUARTERS OF the Reiksguard was a newer building, brick-built foursquare around a series of courtyards. Bohr had told Hoche about its layout. Its main doors, fifteen feet high, were closed but the man-sized wooden door cut into the right-hand one was open. Four men stood outside, lit by the breeze-tossed flames of a torch in a wall-holder. Two were in the uniform and helmets of the Reiksguard, and the others wore dark tunics of a familiar noble cut. There were other doors into the imposing compound, but they were closed and bolted. He wondered what the Knights Panther had told the Reiksguard sentries about him. A spy? An assassin? An escaped prisoner? Anything to make him sound like a threat.

He walked away slowly, studying the surrounding streets. No buildings close enough to cross from roof to roof. No watch-patrols or beggars he could use to distract the sentries or draw them away. No way to climb over the wall. The god who had smiled on him earlier this evening, blessing him with two overconfident thugs, seemed to have deserted him now.

Hoche remembered something his father had said to him many times, but most recently on the day Hoche had left to join the army before Wissendorf. The old priest had put his hand on his son's forehead, making the mark of the hammer. 'In times of trouble, ask yourself what Sigmar would do,' he said. 'He was a soldier too.'

Sigmar, the warrior-king who had united the Empire two millennia ago: what would he have done? Major Sprang would have said that Sigmar would charge into every fight, giving no quarter, but Major Sprang had died at Wissendorf trying just that, and little good it had done his wife and babies. Sigmar would not have fought here, but he would have not shied away from the challenge. Sigmar faced every problem like he faced every foe: head-on.

Hoche walked to the end of the street and peered around the corner. The four guards were still there. He took several deep breaths, willed his shaking nerves into stillness and forced his fear to the back of his mind. Then he fastened his cloak tightly around him and stepped out into the main road, walking briskly towards the gate, his boots loud against the cobbles.

The guards turned towards him and he raised a hand in friendly greeting. 'A fine dry night, gentlemen,' he said in his best Altdorf accent. 'Tell me, is your stable-gate guarded at night?' He pointed back round the corner.

'No,' said one of the Reiksguard. 'Why?'

Hoche shrugged. 'Someone's left a rope hanging over it.'

There was a second's pause until one of the knights exclaimed, 'He's climbed in! You, with me,' and tapped a Reiksguard. The two ran westwards. *I only have moments,* Hoche thought. He pulled out his flask of kvas, took a swig and offered it to the knight standing by the open door.

The man held up a hand. 'No thanks, I–'

Hoche thrust the flask at him, splashing the strong spirit into his face. He staggered back, his hands on his eyes. Hoche was through the door before the remaining guard had moved, forcing it shut with his entire weight. A body crashed into it from the other side. Hoche pushed back, slamming it closed again.

He ran a hand down the outer edge of the door until his fingers hit the cold iron of the bolt and rammed it home. Then he was running across the courtyard on the other side, leaving the noise of swearing and hammering behind him, mouthing thanks to Sigmar under his breath.

There was the passageway that led towards the stable-block. Hoche followed the directions Bohr had given him, what felt like a lifetime ago. The passage emerged into a second court-yard full of the smell of hay and manure. The only light came from the moon, but there was enough for him to count the doors in the north wall. There, the third one. He reached it, pushed and it swung open. He closed it behind him.

Inside, down a pitch-black corridor and up a flight of stairs, was a second door. Hoche pushed it, but it was solid oak reinforced with iron nails and didn't budge. He knocked, banging his fist against the wood. The timber resounded with deep, funereal thuds that reverberated into silence.

Hoche listened for movement on the other side. Nothing. He realised he had no idea if there would be anyone to let him in. Perhaps these were day-offices and the Unter-suchung's members slept elsewhere. Perhaps it was all a fake, nothing behind the door except a hayloft, tack-room or armoury. Perhaps Bohr and Duke Heller were in on the cover-up, trying to arrange his death. Perhaps the Untersuchung would hand him straight to the Knights Panther. Perhaps Sigmar's sense of humour was as hard as his legendary warhammer.

Outside, he could hear alarms being raised.

Hoche knocked again, harder this time. Still no response. The wood seemed to absorb the energy of his blows, sapping his strength. Why had he assumed there would be someone here? It was past midnight. He hadn't thought his strategy through, he had failed, and he deserved it. He leaned against the door, feeling the pattern of square nail-heads through his stolen cloak, and let himself slide to the floor, overcome by the exhaustion and stress of the day. He felt drained, empty, helpless.

There were sounds from the stableyard outside: shouts, running feet, banging on doors. It didn't matter. Everything would be over soon. He just wanted to lie here and sleep. He didn't care what happened. He was out of his depth.

Behind him a muffled voice said, 'The sun is in the seventh house.'

Hoche said, 'What?' Below, he heard the outside door opening. 'Bring a torch!' someone said.

'The sun is in the seventh house,' the voice repeated testily.

'I don't know the password. But I have a letter for the Untersuchung,' Hoche said, scrambling to his feet.

'Oh, for Sigmar's sake,' said the voice. 'Move away: the door opens outwards.' It swung towards him. On the other side he could see a long room filled with desks, lit by a single candle. A man was silhouetted against it. 'Get in here,' he said.

Hoche did. The man closed the door and slid two bolts across it. 'Sit,' he said, and Hoche did. Heavy thuds came from outside, and a muffled voice shouting. Hoche watched the man, who looked back at him, his face an expressionless mask. Hoche guessed he was in his early forties, with salt-and-pepper hair, white at the temples. The unforgiving candlelight didn't hide the deep lines on his skin and around his eyes, or the scars. It was a face that didn't smile much.

The man counted off ten seconds on his fingers, then slid open a small panel on the door. 'The sun is in the seventh house,' he said. Hoche couldn't hear the response from outside, but from the tone it was a demand.

'I know who you are. No password, no entry,' said Salt-and-pepper, not taking his eyes from Hoche.

Another demand from outside.

'Absolutely not.'

An angry command.

'You have no jurisdiction here, and you know it. Go and bang on someone else's door.' The man slid the panel closed, listened for a moment to the guards' oath and retreating footsteps, then turned to Hoche.

'So you're the man who has the Knights Panther in a muck sweat,' he said.

'I'm afraid I am,' said Hoche.

'Captain Gottfried Braubach of the Untersuchung,' the man said. He was holding out his hand. Hoche moved to shake it, but the officer stepped back, making the candle-flame flicker. Light scattered across the room, revealing the small flintlock pistol he held. It must have been there since he opened the door. It was trained on Hoche.

'You said you had an important letter,' he said.

'Yes,' said Hoche.

'But you are more important than it is.'

'Possibly.'

'Start at the beginning,' Braubach said.

Hoche started.

THE CANDLE HAD burnt down two inches, long streaks of wax down its side. An empty wineskin lay beside two empty wine-cups, the crust of a loaf of bread and the remains of some cheese, scattered across stacks of papers. Hoche's bloodstained clothes were piled beside his chair and he sat back in his shirt and hose, laces undone, his body relaxed for the first time that day. Across the desk, Braubach leaned forward, resting his chin on his fists, looking intently at the young officer. The pistol had been put away. Behind them, the long room stretched into silent shadow and darkness.

Mostly Hoche had done the talking. Occasionally Braubach had stopped him, asking precise, focused questions. He had demanded to know the exact position of the hearts on the altar, and had made Hoche draw the bodies of the sacrificed men, to show their wounds and the symbols carved into their backs. He had asked Hoche to speculate on the direction and depth of the knife-cuts. Then they had moved through the events after he returned to the camp, his journey to Altdorf, and the evening's happenings.

Hoche reached for his cup and drained its last dregs. There was silence.

'What do you think?' he asked.

'You told them far too much,' Braubach said.

'The Knights Panther?'

'Yes. They're mad if they think they can brush this scandal away, but making you disappear would buy them time to make plans, limit the potential damage. If you'd told them less they might have thought you were less of a threat.'

'I'm a threat?'

'Very much,' said Braubach. He lifted his cup but it was empty. 'Hold a moment.' He rose to his feet and moved to another desk, opening a drawer. 'Messner usually has some of that Estalian stuff in his... here we go.' Brandishing a dark glass bottle, he returned to his seat and poured a dark, pungent liquid into their cups. 'Where was I? Yes, you're a threat. They couldn't let you bring your news to the witch hunters or us. Word would have been all over the city by noon. And what is a regiment like the Knights Panther if not its history and reputation? Your news strikes at their heart. Of course they want you dead.' He paused. 'Stupid of them,' he said. 'Predictable, but stupid.'

Hoche sipped the Estalian spirit. It was strong but smooth, making rivers of fire down his tired throat. 'What happens now?' he asked.

'The Panthers will do everything they can to stop the word getting out. We'll investigate, but we'll do it subtly. The witch hunters – that depends. If you'd reached them first there'd have been an almighty fuss, but if I was a betting man – I'm not – I'd lay odds one of the generals you met has already seen their Lord Protector, Lord Gamow, and asked him to tread softly.'

'I meant for me,' said Hoche. 'What should I do?'

Braubach lifted his head and gazed across the desk. 'You?' he said. 'You're a dead man.'

'What!'

'Seriously. You've made powerful enemies, and not just among Chaos cultists. Whoever it was who told you to visit the Knights Panther first, they signed your death warrant. Who was it? Duke Heller?'

'It was a man called Bohr,' Hoche said. 'He gave me a letter for you.'

'Ah yes,' said Braubach, 'the letter.'

'Actually it's addressed to the Untersuchung's commanding officer,' said Hoche, 'but under the circumstances...'

Braubach smiled. 'Flexibility is an important lesson. You're learning.'

* * *

BRAUBACH PUT DOWN the letter. He looked puzzled.

'The mystery deepens,' he said. 'It's a letter of introduction. Completely normal. "This is to introduce Lieutenant Karl Hoche of the Fifth Reiklanders, distinguished in battle and high in honour, who has information *et cetera et cetera.*" Boilerplate stuff. But you told me a man called Bohr wrote this?'

'Yes. Johannes Bohr, the general's aide.'

'Wrong. He's called Gunter Schmölling, and he works for us.' Braubach turned the piece of paper and pointed at the name printed neatly under the duke's seal. It was in Bohr's writing, but it didn't say Johannes Bohr.

'Gunter is one of our deep-cover agents. A man of rare ability, following his own discretion on a long-term mission. Actually,' Braubach paused and coughed, 'I thought he was in Marienburg. An excellent fellow, witty, diplomatic and charming.'

Hoche thought of Bohr, with his sleek features, vulpine smile, hard blue eyes and supercilious manner. It did not sound like the same man. He remembered what Braubach had said about saying too much, and said nothing. He was learning.

'So,' Braubach took a sip of the spirit in his cup, then stood and walked to one of the bookshelves that lined the room, 'you can assume he knew about the Chaos worshippers you discovered. Your observant nature and clean-hearted desire to bring evil to justice has probably laid waste to years of investigation. This signature tells me all that, but wouldn't have given the Knights Panther anything. A cunning man, Gunter.' He ran his finger across the spines of the leather tomes.

'I see.' Hoche swallowed hard, his throat dry. Earlier he had felt over his head; now he felt he was sinking, dragged down by the weight of things he barely understood. The room fell silent. Braubach sipped at his cup.

'Why are you trusting me with this information?' Hoche asked. 'Why give me the name of one of your agents?'

'Because you're a dead man,' said Braubach cheerily. Hoche flinched as he did.

'Please stop saying that.'

'I can stop saying it, but it won't stop being true.' Braubach selected a book and pulled it off the shelf, carrying it back to the desk in both hands. He opened it and began leafing through the hand written pages. 'What do you think will happen to you when you leave here? Now the Panthers know they can't cover things up, you're the person who brought shame on their regiment. You'll get it in the neck. My bet is they'll sink your corpse in the Reik. Or feed your body to the regiment's hunting dogs.' He stopped and focused on the page in front of him, his brow furrowed.

'I refuse to accept this fate,' Hoche said. 'They can't kill me. This is the Empire. I'm a soldier of the Emperor. There are laws.'

Braubach looked up and shrugged. 'Maybe they won't kill you, but they can guarantee your life as a soldier ends. Not that you were going to rise much higher – senior officers are sons of nobles, not sons of priests from Grünburg – but they can finish your career simply by making it known you're out of favour in Altdorf. Which you are now.'

'Won't you protect me?' asked Hoche.

'Why should we?' Braubach asked. 'You have no ties to our division, you've already given us all your information, and you appear to have wrecked one of our long-term investigations. What's more, protecting you would put us in a difficult position.'

'Put *you* in a difficult position?' Hoche echoed. He felt sick.

'Yes.'

'I don't understand.'

Braubach sighed, or possibly yawned, and flipped more pages. 'You're a soldier, you think of the army as a united force. Well and good. That's the way it should be in the field, even if sometimes it goes differently.'

Hoche nodded. 'The battle of Bechafen, General Roland switching allegiance after the Kislevite charge.'

'I was thinking more of thirty Knights Panther turning out to be Khorne worshippers,' Braubach said. 'But that's by the bye. On the battlefield, things are simple. Here in Altdorf, it's different. You can't get promoted by proving your worth in battle so you do it by undermining your superiors or back-stabbing your fellow officers. Regiments spend their time trying to do each other down, recruiting their rivals' most promising officers or breaking their legs in tavern brawls, spreading slander, gossip and lies. It's a political pit-fight. Everyone's competing for status, prestige, resources. Power.

'Yes, we could give you sanctuary. That would make us a political target; it would give the Knights Panther and every other regiment and Imperial agency a reason to demand our budget be slashed, our responsibilities reallocated, our work stopped. So no, we won't protect you. Why should we?'

Hoche raised his head from thoughts that had led nowhere. He was exhausted, physically and mentally. 'What can I do?' he asked.

'Well,' Braubach pursed his lips, leaned back in his chair and stared at the ceiling, where shadows from the candle-light swayed and twisted. 'As I see it, you have two choices. You can resign your commission in the army, return to Grünburg, start a job that will keep you away from soldiers for the next five or six years...'

'Or?'

'Or you find allies or a new patron. Someone with influence, someone in Altdorf. Duke Heller is too far away to do you any good.'

Hoche could tell that this conversation was leading somewhere, but he was too tired to go there himself. He let Braubach show him the way. 'What are you saying?'

Braubach leaned forward abruptly. 'The only way you can save yourself is to join the Untersuchung, Karl. The Knights Panther won't dare come near you if you're one of us. Face it, your career as a soldier is over. This is not the army, not as you think of it, but it's a prestigious role in a prestigious team, and it's still a chance to serve the Emperor. You're the sort of intelligent officer we need.' He paused. 'Plus it'll save your life.'

Hoche sat still. The suggestion was a shock and yet it was as if the whole discussion had been leading up to it. What Braubach said made sense: although he enjoyed army life, he knew that without noble rank, he would never rise much further – even before this cursed business. Besides, the

Untersuchung was part of the Reiksguard, the Emperor's personal guards, much higher in status than a Reikland foot-regiment. He guessed the wages would be better too. And Altdorf was much closer to Grünburg. Perhaps he could persuade Marie to move here once they were married. It would be a new direction for his life but, he felt in his gut, a better one. A clear path cut through his tired mind.

'Yes, I'll join you,' he said.

'You don't need time to think?' Braubach said.

'No.'

'You're a man of swift decisions and firm action. Once you've signed all the paperwork and a transfer request from your old regiment, we'll teach you how unwise that can be. But welcome aboard.' He gestured to a table in the corner of the room. 'There's a mattress and a couple of blankets under there. Get some sleep. You'll need it.'

Chapter Four
LEARNING

HOCHE WAS DROWNING. Black water enclosed him, pushing down on him as he sank, his lungs straining for air, his tied arms struggling against their bonds. Far above lay the surface, life, and freedom but a dreadful weight dragged him down. The heavy fabric of his clothes restrained him so he could not swim free. In another second the air would burst from his mouth, he would inhale the dark, cold water and die. Who had done this to him? Who had brought him to this end? Had he come all this way to die?

HE WOKE SUDDENLY. The panic of the dream stayed vivid for a second or two, then faded. The long office of the Untersuchung was brighter in the sunlight that streamed from the slit windows in the east wall. By daylight the room looked smaller and shabbier. Every desk was taken by people reading, making notes, comparing documents, talking to their neighbours. They did not wear uniforms, and Hoche was startled to see women and nonhumans among them. Nobody paid him any attention.

He clambered to his feet, brushing dust and creases from his clothes. A few desks away Braubach was talking to a rotund man, probably in his mid-twenties but already balding and with several double chins. The discussion was animated. Hoche walked over. Braubach looked round.

'Awake and refreshed, I hope?' he said. 'Well, roll up your mattress and stow it. I know you Reiklanders are country boys but you don't have to prove you were brought up in a hovel.'

Hoche smiled. 'Right away. Where can I get some breakfast?'

Braubach scowled. 'Lieutenant Hoche. You are about to join the Untersuchung, which means I will be your superior officer. We may not be as formal as the army and we do many things differently, but you will address me as "sir". If we lose order, we become our enemy. Remember that.'

Hoche saluted. 'Sir.'

'Good,' said Braubach. 'Breakfast must wait. We have urgent business.' He led the way down the long room, towards a closed door at its far end. It opened into a small hallway with a bare wooden staircase leading upwards. There were no paintings or tapestries to cover the bare white plaster walls of the stairwell and the windows were small. Braubach went first and Hoche followed, feeling underdressed in his shirt and britches. At the top a corridor headed back along the length of the building, plain doors on either side. Braubach strode down it, pointing them out in turn.

'Meeting room, cypher room – your training will cover that – closed case files, administration and requisitions, the armoury for – ah, let's call them specialist weapons. Down there is the major-general's office, but you'll have to get past his private secretary. That–' he nodded to a set of narrow steps heading skywards, 'goes onto the roof; there's a loft of messenger-pigeons for communicating with agents in the field and the other Imperial agencies in the city.'

'Can't you send a regular messenger?'

Braubach turned, and his expression was displeased. 'Messengers can be bribed or captured. If you bring down a pigeon in flight, you may be able to decode its message but it's nigh-impossible to tell where it came from or where it was going. I'm dismayed, Karl. Use your head before you ask another question like that. Untersuchung agents should be able to work these things out themselves. Here we are.' He knocked on a door and pushed it open without waiting for a reply.

Inside, five people sat in an arc around a circular table. Braubach closed the door and made the introductions. 'Gentlemen, this is Lieutenant Karl Hoche, of whom you will have undoubtedly recently heard. Lieutenant, these are your new colleagues. Major-General Zerstückein, our commander-in-chief—'

A uniformed man, whose aristocratic beard and flamboyant moustache sat at odds with the pasty, corpulent flesh of his face, nodded to Hoche.

'Ernst Slavski, our administrator and historian—'

A gaunt man, his head shaved and shining, squinting through eyes with dark rims of shadow.

'Jakob Bäcker, our expert on Khorne—'

The jelly-fat man looked barely older than a student. His hair was long and unkempt, and he was using a quill-knife to clean dirt from his fingernails. He didn't make eye-contact.

'Bruno Veldt, recently returned from duties in the north—'

Middle-aged and dressed like a merchant, he seemed the most relaxed man in the room.

'And Hunni von Sisenuf, our resident wizard, who will know if you lie to us.'

'So don't,' she said, and smiled. Her voice had a western accent. Curls of red hair outlined her freckled face, brown eyes and a large mouth that would have been attractive if it hadn't revealed a graveyard of crooked teeth every time she smiled. Mid-thirties, Hoche guessed, a woman accustomed to working in a man's world, and trying too hard to put me at my ease.

Braubach sat down. Karl was reminded of the meeting in Duke Heller's tent. He stood to attention. The major-general coughed.

'Don't stand on ceremony. Make us all feel uncomfortable if you stay up like that. There's a chair. Sit.' Karl sat. Braubach turned to him.

'Karl, tell us again what happened,' he said.

The room was quiet. Hoche looked at the faces surveying him from the other side of the table. It was going to be a long, hungry morning.

Tilted Windmill, Altdorf
Noon, 28th day of Vorgeheim

'SO,' SAID BRAUBACH, 'according to Jakob your Panthers' rituals fit the same pattern as a cult from a small town north of Salzenmund thirty years ago, and most of them were mercenaries and local traders in the sausage business. Where in Sigmar's name did the Knights Panther get their information?'

'Parallel development?' asked Hoche. 'A coincidence? The same daemon messengers from Khorne?'

Braubach shook his head. 'You've got a lot to learn, Karl. Firstly, nothing in this job is ever a coincidence. There's always a link. Secondly, if Khorne sends you a daemonic messenger it won't teach you, it'll rip your head off and eat it. Thirdly, if you're going to say "daemon" and "Khorne" in public, then for Sigmar's sake keep your voice down.'

They were sitting in one of the booths of the Tilted Windmill tavern, two streets away from the barracks, with the bread, meats and cheese of a late breakfast spread over their table. It was quiet and empty before the midday crowd, and the atmosphere was warm and heavy. Hoche pulled at his beer and wiped his mouth. Relaxing and eating felt good after the morning's discussions, introductions, letters and paperwork.

'Tell me about the Untersuchung,' he said.

'Sir,' said Braubach.

'Tell me about the Untersuchung, sir.'

'Better.' Braubach speared a chunk of ham on his knife. 'History-wise, there's not much to tell. We were set up sixty years ago to find and eliminate Chaos worship and the rogue use of magic in the army. A decade later there was a scandal in the Reiksguard – you can read about it in the records – and we got responsibility for the Imperial court as well. That's our official role. Unofficially, we track down and monitor cults across the Empire. Not just the Ruinous Powers.

Renegade wizards, heretics, political conspiracies, mutants, the works. We keep a low profile. Our job is easier if people don't know we exist.'

Hoche chewed a piece of soft cheese. 'Isn't that the witch hunters' job?'

'Yes,' said Braubach, 'but they're incompetent. Too fanatical and no organisation. So we do the long-term investigating, and when a situation comes to a head we call them in to arrest everyone and do the trials and the burnings. It works well. But they resent us for it all the same.'

'What's the Untersuchung's strength? How many soldiers?' Hoche asked. He felt absurdly uninformed about the regiment he had just joined, and self-conscious about asking the question. From the moment Braubach had opened the door of the Untersuchung to him he had felt like he was a new recruit again.

Braubach seemed not to notice. 'We're not soldiers. Even though we're part of the Reiksguard, technically we're civilians. Right now there are about forty agents in Altdorf, another fifty in the field – we have another barracks in Talabheim – and the rest, about the same number again, are on long-term assignments or deep-cover agents, living normal lives but feeding us information.'

Hoche added them up and felt his mouth go dry. What Braubach was describing did not sound like the 'prestigious role in a prestigious team' he had described the previous night. He thought he was going to be a soldier in a division of the Reiksguard. This wasn't what he had expected at all. He felt misled and trapped, but tried to keep his expression calm and his questions neutral. A moment from the drowning dream flashed in his mind's eye.

'That's not many,' he said.

'Our numbers are down. It's been a bad year. An operation went wrong in Carroberg and we lost twelve agents.' Braubach reached across for another lump of cheese.

'Lost them?'

'Seven dead, three hopeless cripples, two disappeared without trace. Bad business.'

'What happened?'

Braubach chewed bread and scratched his unshaved chin. 'Karl, we have this thing we call "need-to-know". If you don't need the information then you don't get it, and you don't need to know about the Carroberg mess yet. You'll hear enough things to worry about in the next few weeks, never fear.'

'Next few weeks?' Hoche sensed another setback. He'd assumed that after a couple of days of orientation he'd be on active duty, working.

Braubach nodded. 'You've got a lot to learn. More than you can imagine. You'll be trained for the next month or two. Then you'll–' He stopped and looked up. Hoche followed his eyes. A priest of Sigmar was walking across the room towards them – no, not a priest, a priestess. The loose black robe gave away nothing about the body beneath it, but the head above was utter woman: long black hair framing a face that was full and feminine, with dark eyes and ample, symmetrical lips. A southern face with a touch of Tilean or Estalian blood in the skin, thought Hoche. She was coming towards them.

Spurred by manners, he stood up. Braubach followed him. 'Good morning, sister,' he said. 'Can we help you?'

She stopped and faced Braubach. 'Are you Karl Hoche?' she asked. There was something in the way she said it that made Hoche uneasy. It was, he thought, as if she already knew that wasn't who she was looking for, and this was an act. How had she known to come straight to their table?

'I'm Hoche,' he said. 'How can I help you?'

'I am Sister Karin Schiffer, assistant to Lord Gamow, Lord Protector of the Order of Witch Hunters,' she said. 'Come with me; my lord wishes to see you urgently.'

Hoche opened his mouth to reply but Braubach beat him to it. 'This is an Untersuchung matter,' he said smoothly, smiling, 'concerning as it does a Chaos cult within the Imperial army, as you know from the letter delivered to your high priest two hours ago.'

The priestess did not appear flustered. 'We need to question this man,' she said. 'If you will not–'

'Furthermore, Lieutenant Hoche is a serving officer of the Untersuchung,' continued Braubach, 'having transferred

from his regiment this morning. If you wish to request a
meeting with him then you must go through the proper
channels. Until then you have no jurisdiction here and you
are interrupting our meal, which breaches both protocol and
etiquette. You're welcome to join us if you promise not to
talk shop. I can recommend the hard cheeses.'

'Damn your cheeses! Think of the safety of the Empire!'
she barked, and Hoche was surprised at the force and anger
in her voice. He looked across at Braubach. His superior's
face was calm, but Hoche could tell he was enjoying himself.

'While you're busy thinking of that,' he said, 'I suggest you
also think about section 17 of the Imperial Regulations,
which lays down the conditions for the interrogation of
members of other Imperial agencies. The third page is particularly apposite. If I may summarise, it says that unless
you're going to join us for a drink, you might as well go
home. Two more dark beers here.' That was to the pot-boy,
who carried over a jug to fill up the men's tankards, bumping its spout against the pewter cups. The dull clinks were
resonant in the silence. Braubach reached for his beer, held
it up to Sister Karin in salute, and drank deeply. Her dark
eyes stared at him.

'You'll hear from me,' she said, turned on the balls of her
feet and walked away, out of the tavern. Hoche watched
Braubach. Braubach was watching the priestess's departing
rear until the door closed behind it.

'Sigmar!' said Hoche. 'What was that about?'

'Business as usual,' Braubach said. 'Like I said, everyone
resents us. The witch hunters don't like us because we're
doing their job better than they do, plus we got our hands
on you before they could. The Reiksguard feel they should
be responsible for guarding the Emperor–'

'But the Untersuchung is part of the Reiksguard?'

'Only technically. All we get from them is a corner of their
barracks. The temple of Sigmar believes only priests should
deal with policing heresy and magic. The Colleges of Magic
don't like non-magicians meddling in their business; and
the Knights Panther – well, let's say there's some history
there too. And then there's all the smaller agencies like the
Palisades, who make trouble just to get themselves noticed.'

He broke off a chunk of black bread, wrapped it round a fatty lump of mutton and masticated thoughtfully.

Hoche paused, then shook his head. 'Just now, that wasn't it. There was something else, something more personal between you and her. What was it?'

'More history,' said Braubach. He swallowed, reached for his tankard and drained it, long and slow. 'Drink up. There's a lot to do.'

Untersuchung Barracks, Altdorf
Morning, 30th day of Vorgeheim

JAKOB BÄCKER WAS rounded and oily and young. He spoke like a man twice his age and licked his lips every time he said the word 'blood'. As he was the Untersuchung's expert on Khorne, he licked his lips a lot. Hoche sat on the other side of Bäcker's desk, a pile of dusty books separating him from the agent-scholar. Around them the office bustled and chatted, fetched books, scratched words on parchment.

'Khorne cults are unusual,' Bäcker said, 'but not unknown. They tend to spring up among the naturally violent – beastmen or exiled mutants, for example – or those who feel their lives have little value. They're base cults, unlearned, and they either fizzle out or explode in a characteristic burst of self-annihilatory violence.

'What's interesting about your case–' he leaned forward, 'is two points. Firstly the rarity of such cults in the upper echelons of society, implying that this is a sect of unusually strong faith, devoted to Khorne *qua* Khorne, not to a quest for personal power, revenge, anti-societal tendencies, self-loathing, the more usual things. Also, the upper classes almost always go for the more intellectual and decadent Chaos gods, Tzeentch or Slaanesh.

'The second is the ritual. Khorne cults either devise their own, since they arise spontaneously, or they despise such things as strongly as they despise magic. They abhor learning, so there's rarely any teaching or writing to pass their knowledge on to the next generation of worshippers. Finding signs of a pre-existing ritual, particularly one with ancient roots, is unusual.'

'Ancient roots?' Hoche asked. Sitting so close to Bäcker made him feel uncomfortable.

'Oh yes. Comparatively ancient. I've found a reference to the ritual cuts and use of blood' – Bäcker licked his lips – 'that you described.' He opened the thick cover of a tray-sized book in front of him, revealing pages hand-written on vellum and illustrated with scratchy diagrams and drawings. It smelled of wax and soot. 'It dates back at least two hundred years, to the last Incursion of Chaos. So either there is a hitherto unknown teaching-line of Khorne worshippers within the Empire, or the renegade Panthers had been doing some scholarship amidst forbidden texts like this.'

'Which do you – no, wait,' said Hoche. His hand hovered over the large book; he didn't want to touch it. 'What do you mean, a forbidden text?'

'This? No, no, you misunderstand. This is our copy of the *Ermittlungsergebnis of Ute Nicol*, a two-hundred year-old diary of one man's inculcation into a Khorne cult. Possession of an actual copy is a capital offence. But this is a synopsis, a précis, and quite legal.'

Something in the man's voice boasted of more. 'But you have seen an actual copy,' Hoche said.

'Two, actually,' Bäcker sounded pleased with himself, like a schoolboy answering a teacher's question. 'In the closed library of the Cathedral of Sigmar. We have reading rights.' He saw Hoche's horrified expression and laughed. 'I was forgetting that your father was a priest. It must be a shock for you, hearing these things.'

Hoche was stunned. Here was a man who boasted of having read books of Chaos doctrine. Even the thought of such things repulsed him.

'They are abominations that should be burnt,' he said flatly. 'They are things of Chaos, tainted by it. They carry its message and its infection.'

'They're books,' Bäcker said, 'and they contain words. We study them and use their information to fight back against Chaos. Like an enemy's plan, it's much less dangerous if you have a copy.'

Hoche sat silently. He had been brought up to abhor Chaos. Now he was working with people who joked about it and treated it as something that could be studied and learned without danger. Something clenched in his gut, telling him they were wrong, that they were in deadly peril if they continued. Something was very bad here. He could feel sweat forming on his temples and the palms of his hands.

Calm down, he thought. Think of Braubach. Braubach is a rational, intelligent, sardonic man. He wouldn't be here if these people were dangerous. This is only for a few weeks. After that I can leave for active service again, away from here. I can bear it for that long.

'There are no forbidden texts here, are there?' he asked.

'Of course not,' said Bäcker. 'Bringing heretical tomes into an army barracks? We'd all be burnt on the spot.' Hoche nodded, but he had seen the man's eyes flick for a nervous instant towards a shelf across the room.

Street of Tailors, Altdorf
Afternoon, 3rd day of Nachgeheim

'EVEN THOUGH WE'RE not training you as a deep-cover agent, there will be times when you're going to have to operate undercover or in disguise,' said Braubach. 'We'll give you advice about changing your face and hair, your accent, your walk, all of that. We'll teach you about creating bolt-holes, emergency equipment caches and safe drop-points for information and things you need to hide in a hurry, how to mark them, and how to find ones that other Untersuchung agents have left. But none of that is as important as your mask.'

'You mean my disguise?' Hoche asked.

'Not your disguise, the set of your mind. You still think like a soldier. First we have to get you thinking like an agent, and then we have to teach you how to think like someone else entirely. When you're undercover, disguised, you must become the person you're dressed as. Knowing who they are, how they think, how they'll react to surprises or attack isn't enough. Don't pretend to be them, become them.'

'Like an actor, you mean?' Hoche asked. Braubach scowled.

'Nothing like an actor. Actors' disguises are physical. I'm asking you to put on a mental disguise, a mask over your own thoughts. Keep your own thoughts in the background, be alert, monitor and watch what's going on – but in the front of your mind, think as this new person.'

'I don't understand,' Hoche said.

'You will. You've heard of the Tilean spy caught because someone swore at him in his own language, and he swore back without thinking? You must learn to play a new role so deeply that it becomes your life. It's the only way to survive in the long term, to convince people that you're who they believe you are, capable of doing what they believe you can.'

'You've done this?' asked Hoche.

'All the time,' Braubach said. 'All the time.'

Untersuchung Barracks, Altdorf
Night, 6th day of Nachgeheim

IT WAS LATE, and dark. Candles still burned on two desks at the other end of the long room, casting shadows of hunched readers against the far walls. Outside the bells struck nine, the holy hour. The late service would be starting in the temples.

Hoche put down the papers he was reading, stood and walked casually to a bookshelf across the room from Bäcker's empty desk, where volumes of ancient Middenheim civic records sat on sturdy shelves, presenting their faded spines to the room. He pulled one down and paged through its dusty history of long-forgotten transactions and taxations. The second and third were the same. On a hunch he bent and peered into the narrow space left between the books on the shelf. There was nothing behind them except white plaster.

Hoche replaced the third volume of records with a thump. Something didn't sound quite right. He pulled the book out, then pushed it back against the wall, listening to the sound. Then he rapped with his knuckles on the shelf. It sounded hollow. So did the ones above and below it. Fetching his candle, he held it close to the edge of the shelf. He could just see a hairline crack hidden in the grain of the wood.

Carefully he removed all the volumes from the shelf, putting them on the floor, then put his thumbs against the edge of the shelf and pushed up. The top half lifted like a box lid, revealing a shallow cavity. Inside were four slim books with aged leather bindings. He didn't try to read their titles. Their concealment was enough to show they were nothing good.

'"We'd all be burnt on the spot",' he thought, and felt himself shiver.

Old Bridge, Altdorf
Noon, 8th day of Nachgeheim

HOCHE LEANED ON the parapet of the river-bridge and gazed upstream along the sunlit waters of the Reik. His thoughts were far from Altdorf and the stuffy room where he had spent the morning being schooled by Hunni von Sisenuf in recognising the signs of wizardry.

In his mind's eye he could see Grünburg, a hundred and fifty miles upstream. Mentally he walked its narrow streets, seeing the familiar signs of the businesses, the stall-holders in the Marktstrasse, the temple where his father officiated. He missed his father's wisdom and advice. The last few days had been bewildering, so much learning and training packed into every hour. He needed perspective, distance, to set it all in place in his mind. A week in Grünburg would refresh his spirits, but until he could get there this mental journey was the only one he could make.

He stared down into the rolling waters. He had dreamed of drowning twice more, but somehow the Reik comforted him. Upstream, a great river-barge was in mid-river, sailing down from the Talabec docks, its mast half-stepped to pass under the city's bridges. Should he sail or ride to Grünburg? Riding would be faster.

Someone grabbed the back of his cloak, pushing him against the parapet. 'Gebhard Mannheim,' a voice said, 'we arrest you for deserting from the Emperor's armies.'

'I'm not–' Hoche said. Someone else put a sword against his throat, and he shut up. Hands grabbed his wrists, pulling them to the small of his back. All Hoche could see of his assailants was the hand holding the sword against his neck. It was a large hand, muscled, used to carrying a heavy weapon. It had a ring on its third finger with the profile of a panther's head.

This wasn't a case of mistaken identity.

Hoche threw himself sideways and back, into the space where the sword-holder had to be. His shoulder made solid contact with something, sending a numbing jar down his arm but knocking the other man off balance. Someone grabbed for his cloak but Hoche, his arms already behind him, let them pull it off him. He leaped onto the wide parapet and sprinted down it towards the middle of the bridge. The barge was closer now, making good speed with the current, heading for the centre arch.

He glanced back. A few yards behind him three men, all in anonymous dark leather jerkins, were pushing through the people on the bridge. He turned and drew his sword. The three stopped, their own weapons out. The crowd moved away from them, alarmed.

'Back off!' he shouted.

'You've caused us much trouble,' said one, the tallest. His voice had an aristocratic edge. The three spread out, approaching him from all sides, blocking his escape.

'I was only the messenger,' Hoche said, glancing at the river. It was a long way down and the water was dark and foul. He took four steps to the left. The three followed, not taking their eyes from him. There was no way past them, and one against three was a fool's fight.

'We're at an impasse,' he said. 'Can't we make a deal?'

'There are no deals where honour is concerned,' said the tall one. 'You have stained our reputation and we will pursue you till that stain is erased.'

'Yes?' said Hoche. 'Pursue me, then.' He dropped his sword and leaped out into the sky above the river. The half-stepped mast of the great river-barge was ahead and below him, its rigging stretched out like a cage of cords. He fell towards it, grabbing out at a master-rope with both hands. His grip slipped off it, twisting him off balance, and he was plunging out of control.

He crashed into the sail with a great sound of ripping canvas, tearing it open, falling through the tear. His body hit the deck hard, and lay still. The sail fell to cover him like a shroud.

* * *

Tilted Windmill, Altdorf
Evening, 8th day of Nachgeheim

'UNBELIEVABLE,' SAID HUNNI von Sisenuf.

'In broad daylight, on a major thoroughfare,' said Bruno Veldt. 'Extraordinary.'

'That wasn't what I meant,' Hunni said.

The back room of the Tilted Windmill was warm with the late-evening air. Sounds from the main room filtered through the closed and curtained door. The three sat around the end of the long table closest to the door. Hoche's right leg was stretched out across a chair, his sprained ankle heavily bandaged. Under his shirt, more bandages encased his broken ribs. After the surgeon had left, his colleagues had invited him out for an evening's drinking, and although his better judgement had told him he needed rest, he felt the need to be around people this night. Partly, he admitted to himself, he was lonely. Partly, he also admitted, he was scared.

'I was lucky,' he said.

'Lucky you didn't end up in the Reik,' said Bruno, and guffawed. Nobody else did. The room fell silent; one of those strange silences that drift over conversations. A ghost passing through the room, Hoche remembered his mother saying, a reminder to everyone present that they will die.

'How are you finding the Untersuchung, Karl?' Hunni asked. 'Is it what you expected?'

Hoche laughed. It hurt his ribs, and made him cough, and that hurt his ribs more. 'What did I expect?' he said. 'I expected to deliver a letter and go back to my regiment.'

Hunni and Bruno exchanged a look. He went back to his tankard; she turned back to Hoche. 'Well, how are you finding us?' she asked.

Hoche stared, his gaze unfocused. It was a fatuous question, but this was his first real chance to spend informal time with his colleagues, and he knew Hunni was only trying to be friendly. Like many intellectuals he had known, there wasn't much depth to her social skills. 'It's Braubach,' he said. 'I can't get a handle on Braubach.'

'Gottfried?' Hunni said. 'Yes. He's a... He can be a difficult man. He's not been the same since...' Her voice trailed off.

Hoche said nothing. Hunni eyed Bruno.

'A year ago?' she said.

'A little more,' said Bruno. 'Sommerzeit last year.'

Hunni turned back. 'Braubach spent the last nine years pursuing a cult of hidden learning across the Empire,' she said. 'Last summer he located their headquarters and leader here in Altdorf, under our noses. There was a big raid. It didn't go well.'

'It went astonishingly badly,' Bruno said. 'All the cultists escaped and the building burnt down, destroying everything in it. Then the next morning Braubach's assistant, a lieutenant called Andreas Reisefertig, disappeared.'

'Disappeared?' Hoche asked.

Hunni sipped her beer. 'He took a horse from the stables and left the city before dawn. There were rumours that he'd tipped off the cultists, that he'd been a cultist himself or a mole on the inside. Nothing was proved, no blame was placed, but the whole thing crushed Braubach. He'd trained Reisefertig, you see? Nine years of his life, and he'd achieved nothing except creating a turncoat. That's why he's so cynical about the world. It's a protection, his armour against everything else.'

'Instructing you is the first thing that's interested him since,' Bruno said. Hunni glanced across the table.

'Not quite,' she said. 'There was that girl.'

Bruno looked blank for a second. 'Oh yes,' he said, reaching for his tankard.

'A girl?' asked Hoche.

'A recruit, training to be a deep-cover agent,' Hunni said. 'She and Gottfried began to get close. Then they had to finish because she was assigned.'

'Who was she? Where was she assigned?' Hoche asked. Evidence of Braubach's humanity interested him. He sat up, his broken ribs grated, and he grunted with pain. Hunni examined him.

'That's need-to-know, Karl,' she said. 'Everything about deep-cover agents is. You should know that.' She looked at him, her dark eyes filled with suspicion. Even among colleagues over a friendly drink, Hoche realised, there were things that were not asked. He took a long swallow of beer to drown his questions about forbidden books and whether there had ever been any cultists in the Untersuchung. Those would wait.

Cathedral Square, Altdorf
Afternoon, 14th day of Nachgeheim

RAIN DRIZZLED ON Hoche and Braubach as they entered the great square of the Cathedral of Sigmar. Traffic was light, people driven off the streets by the first of the cold autumn rains, though a few hawkers and barrow-boys still stood by their stalls. Braubach looked up at the great building.

'What do you think of Sigmar?' he asked.

'Sigmar?' It was an odd question. 'He is our god and my patron, in whose temple I was blessed at my birth. He was the foundation of the Empire and he is its salvation, our hope in times of need. He fights for us against the evils of the world. He–'

'Beyond the doctrine,' Braubach said. 'Have you ever seen the hand of Sigmar or felt his guidance? What has Sigmar ever done for you?'

Hoche was confused. Was this a test? 'As I have said. Sigmar is my patron, my strength and guide.'

'You're fortunate,' Braubach said. 'You've never had to question your faith.' He stood, looking up at the great steeple as it thrust up into the grey sky. Rain ran down his face.

'I'll warn you,' he said, 'times will come and you'll be confronted with things that rip away all the nice words you've ever learned about the gods. That's when you'll find if Sigmar really is your strength. We can't train or test you for that, and yet it's something that all Untersuchung agents have to meet. But remember this, when it comes: Sigmar's not a strong god, and he's not a wise god. Some would say that he isn't even a sane god. But in the stretch, he and your sword are the only true allies you have.'

Hoche said nothing, because he could think of nothing to say.

'Enough of that. Let's get to work.' Braubach wiped the rain from his face and walked on around the square, stopping outside a house on the unfashionable side. Its shutters were closed, its plaster discoloured and peeling, its front door shut. He pointed to it.

'At ten bells yesterday, a man came out of there wearing a crimson cloak and a flat hat in the Tilean style,' he said. 'He was carrying a book under his cloak. You have four hours to bring me that book. Think you can do it?'

'Yes,' Hoche said, 'if he's still in the city. Where will you be?'

Braubach took a step back. 'Work it out,' he said. 'This is a training exercise, not a game of "Where's Waldermeier?".' He walked away towards the cathedral, stopping to talk at the stall of a damp orange-seller. Hoche then stood and considered. Should he ask the street-traders first? No, the man might have left a footprint by the door: it would be useful to know what shoes he was wearing. He put all thoughts of whether his teacher was a heretic to the back of his mind, knelt and studied the wet ground.

Tilted Windmill, Altdorf
Evening, 16th day of Nachgeheim

BRAUBACH RAPPED HIS knuckles on the red leather cover of the book in front of him, and looked over at Hoche. 'Well done. Very impressive,' he said. 'Your instincts for tracking and searching are well honed. However, you need to work on a couple of things.'

Hoche grinned back at him, a foam moustache from his pint of dark ale crescenting his upper lip. 'Like what?'

'Observing when people are lying to you,' said Braubach. He wasn't smiling. 'This is the wrong book. The right one was next to it on the shelf. But you took the Tilean at his word, and accepted the first one he offered.'

'I had a sword to his throat!' Hoche protested.

'But he could tell you weren't prepared to use it, and you didn't realise,' said Braubach. 'For that mistake, you forfeit your beer.' He pulled the tankard across the table and drained half of it in a long swallow, wiping his mouth with the back of his hand. 'Tomorrow we start you on face-reading. Also interrogation techniques: how to ask questions so they get the right answer, and how to avoid giving answers to people you don't want to know your business. That includes resisting torture.'

'What? Is that necessary?' Hoche asked.

'Almost certainly not.' Braubach finished the beer. 'But it'll keep us out of the rain.'

Oldenhaller warehouse, Altdorf docks
Night, 32nd day of Nachgeheim

THE WAREHOUSE DOOR creaked open and the light of a lantern shone through the crack, illuminating the stillness and emptiness. Two cloaked and cowled figures crept in from the night.

'Nobody here,' said one.

'He said two bells,' said the other.

Hoche snapped open the hood of his own lantern, filling the centre of the room with a circle of light. 'I bring greetings from Ernst's mother,' he said.

The two men moved into the circle, their steps confident. 'I hear she is much changed,' said the first, completing the pass-phrase. His Middenheim accent was strong.

'Welcome to Altdorf, my brothers in Tzeentch,' Hoche said. He placed his lantern on the floor, shrinking the illumination around them, and walked forward to embrace the first man, throwing his arms around him.

The warehouse was bathed in sudden light. 'Nobody move!' Bruno yelled, jumping down from a stack of crates, his short-sword drawn.

Hoche clenched his arms tight around the man he was holding and pushed himself forward, hard. They fell together to the floor, Hoche fighting to hold the larger man down, immobilising him.

'In the name of the Emperor,' Bruno shouted, 'we arrest you for the worship of daemons, consorting with forces of Chaos, conspiracy to–'

The larger cultist struggled against Hoche's weight. Hoche held him. In the corner of his eye, he saw the shorter man gesture, arms outstretched, his lips moving with arcane syllables.

'Spellcaster!' he yelled. There were cracks from across the room and two crossbow bolts buried themselves in the man, one in his breast, one in his neck. He looked shocked, and dropped, beginning the messy business of dying.

Hoche turned back to the man under him. An acre of hard forehead struck the bridge of his nose. Suns raced across his eyes. At the same moment he felt something rear up from inside the man's cloak, twisting between their bodies. It flashed across his vision, cord-like and whip-thin, and wrapped itself fast and tight around his neck. He tried to cry out, but it throttled his shouts. He couldn't breathe.

The cultist head-butted him again. This time his head was held by the thing round his neck and couldn't jerk back. Bone cracked in his nose and blood spurted across his face. Whatever was wrapped round his neck squeezed harder. It felt as though his bones would break and his head burst. In his chest, a long way below, his lungs burned like a blacksmith's furnace.

Dimly, from nearby, he heard Bruno say, 'You can get up, lieutenant. He's covered.'

Hoche tried to say something but had no breath to form words. He tried to roll off the man he imprisoned, but was held firm. He tried to slap the floor, to signal he needed help, but his hands were like soft cloth. His head was full of darkness. Something close made the sound bones make when they splinter.

He was falling into a hot dark place. Somewhere on the other side of the world, Bruno said, 'Sigmar!' A month of seconds later he said, 'Get a knife!' and then, 'Now!' and 'Now!' again. There were people around him, hundreds of miles away, pulling at him, rolling him over. He couldn't think any more. He was dead.

Something struck him hard on the chest, forcing the air from his lungs. He gasped, drew breath, felt traces of life returning to his mind. He blinked and saw only blurs, but they began to clear. Bruno was kneeling over him.

'Lie still. The healer is coming,' he said.

Hoche lay on his back, hurting. His lungs ached. His head felt as if it had been ripped from his body. All his senses told him he should obey Bruno and not move, but he had to know. With his hands, he pushed himself over onto his side. It hurt.

There was a length of rope on the floor beside him, cut into pieces and bloody. His eyes followed it back to the body of the cultist where it lay on the floor a few feet away. The man's clothes had been sliced away, his bare skin exposed, and the rope snaked across him and into a strange extrusion of flesh below his ribs, weirdly veined and sinuous like the umbilical cord of a newborn babe. Not a rope, then. And not a man – a mutant, his body strangely reshaped by the powers of Chaos. Hoche had never seen one before.

Four or five more rope-like tentacles snaked out from the same lump of flesh. Two reached upwards across the corpse, to wrap tightly around the dead cultist's own neck. Hoche could tell from the way his head was hanging that his neck was broken. That must have been the bone-crack. The man had killed himself rather than be taken alive, and had tried to do the same to him.

'Sweet Sigmar, what a foul-up,' Bruno said from behind him. 'The message from Middenheim said the large one was the sorcerer.'

'Maybe they both were,' said someone else.

'We can't ask them, can we? They're dead!' Bruno was losing his temper. 'The whole point was to take them alive so we could interrogate them. The whole operation's a scratch. The old man will not be happy.' He kicked something on the floor, hard. 'And the lieutenant's first job at the hard end almost gets him killed. What a nightmare.'

HOCHE'S NIGHT-EYES opened and he found himself in thick undergrowth. There were men around him. Beyond the circle of brush a river flowed deep and dark through the night. Across the whispering waters was a wooded island, its trees silhouettes against the moonless sky. There was no sign of movement from within them but Hoche knew that his true comrades were there, waiting. They hear everything, he thought, and they do not sleep.

The men around him were moving out, wading silently through the river, taking up positions for an ambush or a night assault, their weapons drawn and ready. He was part of this force, he realised, but he did not know why.

Then he was shouting a warning across the river in a strange voice he did not recognise. The attackers, not ready, reacted with shock and alarm. Movement came from the island, the sound of armour, the first battle-cries. Good, he thought. Sneak attacks were not the way true warriors fought. There would be blood tonight, and he rejoiced in the thought of it.

In his narrow bed, in his cold attic room above the barracks, he woke suddenly. He was damp with sweat and shaking, every muscle tense, and could not remember why.

Untersuchung barracks basement, Altdorf
Noon, 1st day of Erntezeit

'MUTATIONS,' SAID BRAUBACH. 'The outward and visible sign of an inner contagion by the powers of Chaos. Which does not mean that every mutant is a worshipper of the dark gods. Mutations can arise spontaneously in the bodies of virtuous men. Nevertheless, it's usually a sign that something is rotten within.'

Hoche held the lantern higher so its light glinted off the regiment of glass jars arranged over the shelves that lined the room. He didn't step through the doorway. 'These are all mutants?'

'Or bits of mutants,' Braubach said. 'They have one other thing in common too: they're all dead. Nothing to be scared of.'

Hoche reluctantly stepped in. Wax-skinned things gazed blindly at him with milk-white eyes from jars of yellow fluid. There was a dog with eight segmented eyes, an arm that became a crab-like pincer below the elbow, a man's head with fangs for teeth and tentacles growing from the eye-sockets, a baby with—. He turned away. Braubach watched him.

'If you think these are horrible, wait till you see live ones,' he said. 'The tentacle that nearly strangled you, that's almost mundane. I've seen men with transparent skin, hair that blazes like fire, hollow people...' He collected himself. 'The more excessive the change, the greater the chance it's a gift from the bearer's god. But even the smallest mutation will grow and spread, taking over the victim's body and mind until he either goes mad, flees into the forests to join the beastmen, or is discovered and burnt.'

'Poor sods,' Hoche said. 'Is there nothing that can be done for them? No cure? No blessing or spell to remove the taint?'

Braubach looked at him with a fixed gaze. 'I've already told you,' he said. 'We burn them. Or pickle them.' He rubbed his hands. 'The morning's lesson is over. Lunch?'

Tilted Windmill, Altdorf
Night, 7th day of Erntezeit

THEY WERE BACK in the back room of the Tilted Windmill: Hoche, Hunni and Bruno, and this time Anna who had been recruited from the Knights of the Blazing Sun after she'd disguised herself as a man and spent two years as a squire, and Anders, a black-bearded dwarf who was the Untersuchung's expert on his race's rune-magic and the cult of humans who had twisted it to their own ends. As usual they were on the dark beer.

'Vile,' said Anders. 'Not fit to wash a pig. Typical human brew, not fermented a month.'

Hoche turned away; it was an old argument and he was bored of it. On the other side of the table, Hunni was looking at him. He'd caught her doing that a lot recently.

'How are your ribs?' she asked.

'They're mended,' he said. 'They're fine. My neck too.'

There was a pause.

'You're quiet this evening,' she said, her gaze not shifting from his face. 'A groat for your thoughts?'

'I'm fine.'

'Don't lie to me,' she said. 'I know when you're lying. Tell me what's wrong.'

Hoche was silent for a while more, looking at the trails of froth on the head of his beer. Then he said, 'It's not what I expected, you know? Not at all.'

'How so?' she asked.

'What Braubach described to me the night I joined sounded like something glorious, an elite military unit, rooting out Chaos and putting it to the torch. That's what I thought I was joining. You know the old Reman saying – something something *custodies custodeamus*–'

'"We are the guards of the guards of hell"' Hunni quoted. 'But Karl, that's what we are.'

'No you're not. You're not guarding anything. There's no honour or glory in what the Untersuchung does. You skulk around with your noses buried in books, dressing up as Chaos worshippers to infiltrate their cults, and doing it so well that you sometimes convince yourselves. Nobody's scared of you, because nobody knows you exist.'

Hoche paused as he realised how drunk he was. He rubbed his neck. Was it wise to have this discussion now? Perhaps not wise, but important. He needed to talk to someone, to explain how he felt. This was the first chance he'd had since he'd arrived. And these were things he couldn't say if Braubach was around.

'This isn't what I wanted,' he said. 'The Untersuchung saved my skin, don't think I'm not grateful. But this isn't what I want to do, it's not what I'm good at, and it worries me. Last week Braubach told me that Sigmar is mad – that's heresy. I know that there are banned books hidden in the barracks – that's madness. And the collection of pickled mutants in the basement… We could all be burnt.'

He took a swallow of beer and a moment to think. 'If I fight Chaos, I want it to be on the battlefield, staring it in the face,' he said. 'I don't want to skulk and hide and lie and learn heresies, and become my enemy to fight my enemy, to spend nine years being a scholar to chase down other scholars, and then find they've outwitted me. I don't want to become…'

'Braubach,' said Hunni. 'You don't want to become Braubach. Because you don't want to fail.'

Hoche stared at her. 'Yes,' he said finally.

Hunni leaned forward, her dark eyes close and deep enough to drown him. 'Karl, what the Untersuchung does is vital to the Empire. You know that. If we didn't exist then neither the witch hunters nor the Reiksguard could take our place. I know you're uncomfortable here. It takes a while to get used to our way of doing things. But whether you realise it or not, many people think you're right for the Untersuchung.'

'What? Who?'

Hunni's brow furrowed. 'Don't tell me you've never thought this through,' she said.

'Thought what through?'

'Why you had to join the Untersuchung.' Hoche said nothing. Hunni slapped the table. 'Oh, for... Karl, why did Gunter Schmölling send you to the Knights Panther first?'

'They're the highest-ranked, and it was their soldiers...' Hunni scowled and Hoche realised that was not what she wanted him to understand. A small part of his mind was telling him that she was a very attractive woman. He told it to shut up. This was more important.

'What do you mean?' he said

'Work it out, Karl.'

Hoche stared at her for a long time. 'My soul,' he said. 'You mean... Schmölling knew the Knights Panther would try to stop me telling the witch hunters and you. He knew they'd try to kill me, to silence me for the honour of their regiments. And he still told me to go to them first.'

'Yes.'

'So...' In his mind the chart was revealed, the network of connections and points, the links of cause-and-effect, and he felt sick. 'So that I'd need a sanctuary. I'd be so desperate that I'd accept any offer if it meant my survival. Braubach saw the letter, understood Schmölling's intent, and made me that offer. And I took it. Like a puppet.'

Hunni sat back and raised her glass to him. 'Welcome to the Untersuchung, Lieutenant Hoche.' Her voice carried no irony, only a trace of sadness.

Hoche sat in stunned silence. The candle-flame guttered and drips of wax spilled onto the table. At the other end of the room, the others were discussing snotball. They could have been miles away.

He stared at Hunni. 'How did Schmölling know the Panthers' killers would fail?'

'He didn't. But if you couldn't defend yourself, you aren't the kind of person the Untersuchung needs.'

'But why?' he asked. 'Why me? Why at all?'

'Because Schmölling noticed you, Karl. He saw you work, and he realised that the Untersuchung could make better use of you than the army. But he knew that if he asked you directly, you'd refuse because you saw yourself as a soldier. So he forced your hand.' Hunni tossed her head and her hair fell in bright curls around her shoulders. 'I can't believe you hadn't worked it out,' she said. 'It's one of the standard ways the Untersuchung recruits.'

'This has happened before?'

Hunni drained her beer, stood, and cast him a look of utter despairing contempt. 'My dear, sweet Karl,' she said. 'How do you think they got me?'

Karl looked up, speechless.

'And you know why?' she said. 'Because they needed me. They need you too. You're a special person with unique skills. It's been a lot of work to bring you to this point, here, today. You should be flattered. Very flattered.' She picked her long, soft wool robe from the back of the chair and spread it over her shoulders. 'The hour is late, and I hear you have a way of dealing with ruffians. Walk a girl back to her room?'

He wanted to, but shook his head. 'I need another drink.'

Top floor, Untersuchung barracks, Altdorf
Evening, 12th day of Erntezeit

'SIX WEEKS, LIEUTENANT Hoche. We are very pleased. You've done well.' Major-General Zerstückein looked up from the papers on his desk. His expression was hidden by his moustache and beard, but his eyes were tired and drawn. 'How do you feel about it all?'

Hoche stood to attention on the carpet in front of the desk, facing the general. At the edge of his vision, outside the pool of candlelight that surrounded the two of them, he could see Braubach sitting motionless in a carved wooden chair, watching him. Was this a test? An appraisal? A rejection?

'It's not what I had been led to expect, sir,' he said.

'So we gather.' The major-general tapped the paper in front of him. 'Don't look surprised, man. If you're going to talk about these things in a tavern, you have to expect someone will be listening. But expectations aside, do you feel you've settled? Do you have a place in the Untersuchung?'

Hoche was silent. He felt Braubach's eyes on him.

'Let me put it another way,' said Zerstückein. 'I have a letter here, commending you in the highest terms for the assistance you have rendered us, and transferring you back to

your old regiment. If you wish, I will sign it and you're free
to go.' He leaned forward, his shadow large on the wall
behind him. 'You're a good man, Hoche. Everyone says so.
But the Untersuchung is a calling more than a job. Once in,
there's only one way out. Are you with us?'

Hoche stood and thought. He thought of Braubach, and
Braubach's manner, and Braubach's trick. He thought of the
works of Chaos hidden downstairs, and he thought of what
other evils might be covered by a veneer of dusty scholarship. He thought of heresies and things unspoken.

He thought of blood dripping from a regimental banner,
and of the feel of a tentacle tightening around his neck. He
thought of Hunni's eyes and lips, and then he thought about
far-away Marie, and he thought about Marie for a while.
Then he thought about the Empire, and he thought of the
Emperor. He thought about the camaraderie of the army
camp and his men, and the spirit, zeal and energy that came
with battle. He remembered Schulze, and how Schulze had
died, and he thought he had decided.

But there was something else, dark in his mind, half-
forgotten memories or half-remembered dreams. They
disturbed him. They were not dreams a soldier should have.
He had changed in these last weeks, and he didn't think it
was for better. If he went back to the army with what had
happened and what he had learned, would he be a good soldier?

He didn't think he could be.

He swallowed hard. 'I am with you,' he said.

'Good. Excellent,' said Zerstückein. 'In that case you'll be
glad to hear we have a mission for you. Nothing too strenuous – a continuation of your training, except you'll be
learning how to take what you've learned here and use it in
the field.'

Zerstückein glanced at Braubach, who still sat silent. The
old man gave a shrug and continued: 'We're putting you on
the trail of a deserter. A renegade, one of our officers who's
failed to report in. His tracks are probably cold but your mission is to learn whatever you can about what happened to
him. You'll leave tomorrow morning. Report back here
within two months. If you find evidence of his death, bring

it with you. If you find a warm trail, send word back and keep following it. Understood?'

Hoche nodded.

'Good. Captain Braubach will brief you further on the man you're looking for: appearance, mannerisms and so forth.' The major-general paused. 'Lieutenant Andreas Reisefertig,' he said thoughtfully. 'An officer with a good deal of promise, we thought. You never can tell.'

Reisefertig. Hoche felt tension crawling up his spine. The major-general was sending him to track down his teacher's former protégé. Something didn't add up. Was this Braubach's idea? Surely they didn't expect him to find Reisefertig, he thought, and then he realised that was the one piece of information they had not given him.

'Sir,' he said, 'what is my course of action if I find Lieutenant Reisefertig alive?'

Braubach sat forward abruptly, his face moving into the light. His expression was cold and dry.

'Kill him,' he said.

There was a dead silence in the room. Hoche's eyes flicked to the general's face, looking for a signal, some sign that this was an order, but saw nothing there. He looked back to his teacher. The air was full of tension.

'Kill him,' repeated Braubach. 'You will do that?'

'I will,' Hoche said, knowing he would.

'Swear it,' Braubach said, staring at him.

'In Sigmar's name,' Hoche said slowly, 'I swear.'

Chapter Five
IN AT THE DEEP END

A YEAR AGO, Hoche reflected, he would have had no idea that Marienburg was a city at war. There was no sign of conflict in the city's streets, taverns and coffee-houses, only the normal rivalry of merchant families and trading clans, dock guilds, and the criminal gangs that populate every major port, and they kept their fights to themselves. The great seaport at the mouth of the Reik seemed to be what it always had been: the busiest melting-pot of races and trades in the world, where money ruled and a man's word carried no more weight than the gold in his purse.

But Marienburg had a second, lesser-known trade: in knowledge. The Unseen Library, an archive of scholarship so secretive that most researchers had never heard of it or believed it a fable, had been a cynosure for those desperate enough to seek it out and pay its entry price. A year ago there had been a disaster and the library had flooded, its collection destroyed. Only the scrolls, books and manuscripts that had been outside its catacombs when the waters flowed in had survived, though beggars scavenged scraps of parchment and vellum from the river's foreshore over the months that followed, selling them to eager collectors.

Now the religious and academic groups that had centred on the Library were warring for control of the remaining books and the allegiance of their members. For a struggle fought by academics, priests and half-blind scholars, it was surprisingly fanatical and bloody. And somewhere in the midst of the mess lay Andreas Reisefertig, or the clues that would lead to him.

Hoche stood at the prow of the river-barge as it swept downstream at full sail. They were approaching the spiralling stone columns of the Hoogbrug Bridge, its great span high enough to allow the masts of the tallest ships to pass underneath.

On the right bank was the Paleisbuurt, where the city's governors and rulers had their opulent dwellings; on the left lay the Suiddock district, the city's main docks, where the real government went on, the buying and selling of goods from all over the world. People said that anything that could be given a price could be bought in Marienburg, and on the city's great scales, a man's life was among the cheaper items.

It had taken him three weeks to reach Marienburg, on horseback as far as the border between the Empire and the Wasteland, and then taking passage on one of the riverboats that sailed the Reik between the trading town of Leydenhoven and the sea, its holds filled with grain from the summer's harvests upstream.

It was not safe to ride all the way to Marienburg without an escort, since the marshy outreaches of the Wasteland were populated by bandits, mutants, and, some said, weird creatures of legend.

Three weeks. If it took him as long to get back to Altdorf, that left only two weeks for his investigations. He would have to move fast.

The barge docked, the stevedores moved in to unload the cargo, and street urchins swarmed around the gangplank to offer the passengers cheap trinkets, grubby sweetmeats and guidance through the city's maze of streets, bridges and islands. Hoche shouldered his bags, selected the least dirty of the pack, gave him half a penny and told him to lead the way to Duck Street.

Duck Street was at the west end of the Suiddock, away from the commercial part of the borough. A canal ran along one side of the street, filled with thick brown water. On the other side, the plasterwork of the high-gabled houses was decorated in many colours, though several were looking the worse for weather and time.

Hoche found the only door without a symbol on it and knocked. After a while it opened a crack and an eye of some age and indistinguishable sex peered through at about waist height. No voice spoke. Hoche cleared his throat.

'I'm sorry to trouble you. I'm looking for my son,' he said.

'Ah,' said the voice. 'I believe he is in the eighth house, perhaps? Ha ha! Come in, come in.' A chain rattled and the door swung open. In the dimness of the dusty hall beyond stood a figure just too tall to be a halfling but of much the same build, wearing a long red robe fastened at the neck with an ornate clasp. His features were drooped and reddened, and he had a bald patch on the top of his head, amidst grey hair, making him look monk-like. A pair of lenses in silver frames were clipped to his nose, magnifying his eyes so they looked huge and distorted. Like an insect, Hoche thought.

'Lieutenant Hoche, I assume?' the figure said.

'Erasmus Pronk,' Hoche said, stepping inside. 'It is good to meet you.'

'A pleasure, a pleasure,' the shorter man said, ushering him into a large room filled with well-stuffed furnishings. 'Your timing is good. I have some tea infusing, and some excellent cakes left over from the Mittherbst feast last week, which should tide us over until supper.'

'I regret that I cannot stay,' Hoche said, aware how stiff his language was. 'I came to pay my respects and to see if there was any news from Altdorf. But I must get to my inn and prepare. I begin my investigations this evening.'

'Oh well.' The diminutive Pronk seemed disappointed. He lowered himself onto a darkwood chaise longue. 'That's so like you younger agents; an investigation stews for a year, and once it's finally assigned you won't waste a single second in the execution of your duties. You'll learn. I don't suppose a bottle of Majjeran wine, aged twelve years, would tempt you to stay? No? Ah,' and he looked sad, 'then I'll have to drink it on my own.'

'News from Altdorf,' Hoche reminded.

'Yes, yes,' Pronk said, waving a hand airily. 'Altdorf told me you know Gunter Schmölling.' There was a note of expectation, even hope in his voice. Hoche sensed it and it made him uncomfortable. There was something about this whole encounter that put him on edge; he couldn't explain it but he felt nervous and jumpy.

'I didn't know him, exactly,' he said, 'but we spoke a few times. We both served under Duke Heller this summer. He was the general's aide-de-camp, calling himself Johannes Bohr. I commanded a platoon of pikemen. He recruited me. In a roundabout way.'

Erasmus was smiling now, appearing genuinely happy. He swung himself to his feet and came over to sit beside his visitor.

Hoche realised belatedly that he should not have given away such information, even to another Untersuchung agent: Schmölling was in an undercover role and information about him was privileged, need-to-know. He hoped that word of his slip wouldn't get back to Altdorf. He wondered if he could trust Pronk.

'How was he?' asked the old man. 'How was he looking? Well?'

'Very well,' Hoche said, thinking of Bohr's fox-like eyes and duplicitous dialogue. 'The general trusted him and gave him great responsibility.' He was surprised to find how fresh his sense of injury at having been deprived of the chance to run the investigation was.

'I'm glad,' Erasmus said. 'I'm very glad. He left the city so suddenly, without so much as a word, that I knew it had to be something very important. And of course the code of silence forebade him from writing to let me know. But friends worry about friends, you understand? I was concerned. I had these absurd nightmares–'

'You knew Schmölling well?' asked Hoche.

'Like he was my son, Lieutenant Hoche. Better than a son.' Erasmus clapped Hoche on the knee and left his hand there an instant too long before springing to his feet. 'This news does call for a glass of that Majjera. I insist.'

He produced a glass bottle filled with a dark, syrupy wine that tasted of oak, smoke, and rich, deep fruit. 'You're certain you won't stay for supper? I have a wonderful halfling cook.'

Hoche smiled politely, insincerely. 'I must begin my work. Is there news from Altdorf?'

Pronk shook his head. 'No messages, I'm afraid. The only pigeons I've seen are the ones we'll be having for supper, with raspberry sauce and roast parsnips. You're sure you'd prefer the slop at your inn?'

Hoche smiled again.

Pronk lowered himself back onto the chaise longue. 'Well, if you must... How do you propose to proceed with following Reisefertig's year-cold trail?'

Hoche had expected the question. 'I want to find out which books and documents he was trying to locate. We know what he had been reading in Altdorf, and the topics he had been researching. The failed entrapment operation had used a forged copy of the missing pages of the Lexikon of Eber Keiler as bait, and Reisefertig was involved in creating it. It's possible he was looking for the real pages.'

'Possible. Yes.' Pronk refilled his glass. 'And what do you hope to discover from these musty documents?'

'Clues,' said Hoche. 'Perhaps something in the texts themselves will indicate where he may have gone. Possibly he made notes in the margins; many scholars do. More likely the books' guardians may recall him, and if he said anything. And it's possible that by reading the same books, I may be able to work out his state of mind and divine his intentions that way.'

Pronk made an amused clucking sound. 'Really, my dear lieutenant, I think that's taking optimism a little far. Many men may read the same book but each takes away his own interpretation. Nevertheless I believe your scheme has a chance of success, which is to say slightly more than none.'

Hoche was stung. 'What do you mean?'

'Altdorf expects you to fail, you know, but they want to see *how* you fail. Take back a single trace of Reisefertig and they'll be astonished.'

Hoche was taken aback by the old man's good-natured pessimism. 'I think, sir,' he said slowly, trying to control the anger rising in his throat, 'that you do me a disservice.'

'Possibly. Possibly,' Pronk said. 'On the other hand, if you think I've spent the last year sitting in my house drinking alone and mooning over Schmölling, you'd be wrong. No, I've spent my share of time chasing after the bad lieutenant. Sniffs I have had: three in a year; and solid leads none. I wish you the best of luck, but if you find more than I have, I will kiss you.'

Hoche resolved that if he did find anything, he would not tell Pronk.

'Besides,' the old man continued, 'how were you proposing to discover and infiltrate these secretive, defensive, factionalised cults that now control the few books that are left of the Unseen Library? You'll need to know who to contact and where to find them, and have papers to show you're a man with good reasons to seek these books.'

Hoche tried to avoid smiling. He knew the old man already knew his answer. 'I was planning to ask you for your advice.'

'Aha!' Pronk crowed, reaching for the bottle of Majjera. 'And to do that you have to keep me happy and entertain me with talk of the fashionable people in Altdorf before I'll give you the benefit of my wisdom and experience. You see, you are going to stay to supper, I knew it all along. Come, pass over your glass for a refill and tell me, what news of the Emperor's son?'

Hoche sighed and handed Pronk his glass.

'What is the subject of your studies?' Father Willem asked.

'Dreams,' said Hoche.

They sat on the wooden pews in one of the side-chapels of the Cathedral of Verena, in front of a fresco showing the goddess in her aspect as the protector of justice. Pale light filtered through high windows, throwing slanted shapes against the plaster of the walls and the dark wood of the furnishings. The goddess's symbol, the owl, was everywhere: carved in the woodwork, painted in the fresco, in brass on the small altar, a senate of all-knowing eyes staring at them. Apart from the owls, they were alone.

Hoche had met Father Willem in the public room of the Grape's Progress, a seedy wine-seller in the Tempelwijk district close to Marienburg's university. Pronk had set up the meeting for him. The priest had bustled in after the morning service at the cathedral nearby, had downed two glasses of Bretonnian brandy, out-haggled a beggar for a few water-logged scraps of vellum the man had found on the Reik's foreshore, had a furious argument with a gaunt scholar who had been beaten in the haggling, clapped an arm round Hoche's shoulders, declared that any friend of Erasmus Pronk's was a friend of his, and bought him a large brandy. It was very bad brandy. Then he had suggested that they adjourn to his 'office', which had turned out to be this chapel.

'Dreams,' said Father Willem thoughtfully. He had a weaselly face on a portly body and an accent that betrayed his birthplace in the Empire. Hoche guessed he was in his late thirties. He was, so Pronk had said, the top information-broker in Marienburg. He didn't keep libraries of musty books and decaying scrolls, but he knew who did. Now the Unseen Library was no more, that knowledge made him an important man. And a rich one.

Father Willem leaned back against the smooth wood of the pew. 'So which books of dreams do you believe are here but not in the libraries of Altdorf or Nuln?' he asked.

'I am looking for–' Hoche paused. It didn't seem right to name the blasphemous book in a holy place like this, even if it might lead him to Reisefertig's trail. He licked his lips. 'I am told there is much I could learn from the last volume of the New Apocrypha.'

The priest steepled his fingers and brought them close to his face, hiding his expression. 'We in Marienburg may have more liberal views about such things than your colleagues in the Empire,' he said, 'but possession of those books is still a capital offence here. I believe I can help you, but it will require a fee to cover my personal danger. The guardians of the book may require concessions of their own.' He stopped, observing Hoche's face.

'I believe you may be after more,' he said. 'There is something you want but have not mentioned.'

Hoche felt a rising fear. Pronk had warned him that the priest was a shrewd judge of character, but this insight felt so piercing it was as if the man had read his mind. Was that possible? Or... No. He remembered what Braubach had said. Today he was not a spy, nor a soldier playing at being a spy. He was a student, needing forbidden texts to further his research. That was all. There was no secret for Willem to discover. He banished other thoughts from his mind.

'You are right,' he said. 'There is more. But I am afraid to ask.'

Father Willem smiled indulgently. 'What is it?'

'The lost pages of Eber Keiler's Lexikon.'

The priest laughed, the sound reverberating off the high hard walls of the chapel. 'Ah, ah,' he said. 'No, I will not help you there. I won't say that such a thing does not exist, even within a half-mile of these stones, but to ask for it is like marching to the Imperial Palace in Altdorf and asking to hold the Hammer of Sigmar. To see those pages you would have to study here for many years, gaining knowledge and trust, and probably lose your tongue into the bargain.'

'Lose my...?' Hoche was taken aback. Father Willem grinned.

'You didn't know?' he asked. 'The inner circle of the Unseen Library, the Readers, they took a vow of silence. To encourage them to keep it, their tongues were cut out. Although the Library is no more, the Readers are still with us, guarding the texts they saved from the flood. They're still cutting out the tongues of their new initiates, and some are said to have found new, even darker ways to protect their secrets. So be on your guard.

'Don't look so disinterested,' he added. 'Whose libraries did you think you'd be visiting for your studies?'

TWO DAYS AND forty golden guilders later, they came to his inn-room before dawn: four men in dark-grey robes. They said nothing as they frisked him, removing his knife, and escorted him downstairs and into the stable-yard's chill morning air. Hoche let them blindfold him.

They led him through the quiet streets. He tried to make a mental map of the route, the turns and distances, how far they'd walked, but by his estimate they re-crossed their path twice and should have been a hundred yards into the river. Finally there was the sound of a door closing, a change in the echoes as he was led down a corridor and some steps. Then the man leading him stopped, he felt himself being spun round, and the blindfold was removed. Not a word was spoken.

The library was the size of the back room at the Tilted Windmill, with no windows and only one door. Every wall was covered with shelves, and every shelf was filled with books. Tall church-like candles stood in the corners, their flames thin and motionless in the still air. It smelled of age, dust, old leather, tallow and ink. In the centre of the room was a plain wood table and a chair. On the table was a small book.

One of the grey-robed priests stood by the door, his scalp bald and flaking, his long beard flecked with white. His eyes were trained on Hoche, following everything he did. Hoche forced a smile and nodded a bow of thanks to the man, who did not respond. Under the thin cord that served the man as a belt, a knife of strange design was tucked. It was clear that he was not a trusted guest.

The book drew his gaze and beckoned to him. He sat down and looked hard at it. The New Apocrypha, volume thirteen: a collection of lost learning and false scholarship. Braubach had told him about it. The book was an inch thick, bound in a whitish leather, stained and warped from old water damage. The damage seemed to have loosened the binding as well; one page halfway through stuck out a little further than its fellows. A modern book as these things went; new enough to be printed, not a hand-made copy.

He did not want to open it. The thing repulsed him. The thirteen volumes of the New Apocrypha, though not one of the great works of Chaos, were banned across the Empire:

possession of a copy or knowledge of the information
within were capital offences. Logically he knew that Jakob
Bäcker was right: it was just a book and could not change
him. But Chaos did not follow the laws of logic, and neither
did his emotions.

He thought: I have to do this. In this room I am not Karl
Hoche, soldier, agent, faithful son of a priest, loyal to my god
and my emperor; here I must be Karl Hoche, scholar, seeker
of knowledge. The information I need may be in that book.
There is nothing to fear here.

He reached out and opened the cover, and he was right: it
was just a book.

Hoche turned the pages slowly, noting the subjects of the
essays within: one on the distillation of hallucinatory
liquors; another on how to draw magical energy from the
corpses of wizards; a third on ritual techniques of thought to
cleanse the mind and control dreams; a fourth on the his-
torical links between labyrinths and sites associated with
Chaos. Here and there were woodcuts of an intricate and disturbing nature. Hoche was careful not to look at them too
closely. There was no sign of marks in the text or observa-
tions scrawled in the margins.

He reached the loose page and realised it was not a page
at all. Someone had left a piece of parchment in the book as
a place-marker. He turned it over, seeing if the previous
reader had noted anything of interest on the other side, and
stopped, frozen. There was a symbol on it, drawn neatly in
thin black ink. Hoche knew it.

A circle. A single line led from its centre down to its lower
edge, with four short flecks flicked out from its right side.
Hoche had seen similar diagrams chalked on stonework or
scraped on paving-stones. It was an Untersuchung symbol,
used to show the location of hidden items to agents who
might need them. Braubach had taught it to him.

The circle meant a hidden cache. The line indicated its
direction, the flecks its distance. The line stayed within the
circle, symbolising information, not equipment. The marks
were on the right of the line; that meant there was danger or
risk involved. To an outsider it would have looked like a
scribble or a random arrangement of lines, possibly an

alchemical symbol. To Hoche, it was proof he was right. Four feet away, in the direction of the line, another Untersuchung agent had stashed something of value.

Had it been Reisefertig? It was impossible to say. It could have been Gunter Schmölling as he left the city, or any other Untersuchung agent who had passed through in the last year. It could even have been Pronk.

He looked up. The silent scholar at the door was staring at him, unmoving. Did he suspect anything? Did the mysterious librarians know this parchment was concealed in the book? If so, did they have any clue to its meaning? Was this all a test, to see if he was really the scholar he claimed to be? The air was still; the candle-flames did not flicker. Hoche put a hand to the back of his neck and twisted his head from side to side as if loosening stiff muscles, glancing back behind him. The bookcase was at least five feet from the table, maybe even six. The line pointed to a space in mid-air.

Obviously the book has been moved, Hoche thought, it hasn't lain on this table for a year. But where had it been when the unknown agent put the note in it? No, he would have known it would be moved. But where to?

Its place on the shelf, of course.

Hoche leaned over the book again and read on, not focusing on the words at all. Curiosity was burning too hot in his mind. After twenty pages he looked up and let his eyes roam the room, the rows of bookshelves, the regiments of spines and bindings.

It wasn't hard to spot, and under his breath Hoche thanked the orderly minds of all librarians. On the far side of the room, on a shelf four feet above the floor, bright among the reds, browns and blacks of the other books, stood twelve white spines and a dark space where the thirteenth would fit. Below them, at the bottom of every section, wooden panels ran between the lowest shelf and the floor. Hoche hoped the one under the Apocryphas was loose. But with his ever-vigilant guard, how could he find out?

Time to be an Untersuchung agent again.

He pretended to read on for another few pages, then raised his head and caught the eye of the priest. It wasn't hard; the man's stare never left him.

'Excuse me,' said Hoche.

The man raised a bony finger to his lips. There was a thin sound of escaping breath, a 'Shhh' from a mouth that did not have a tongue. So he was among members of the Ancient Illuminated Readers. Hoche stared back. There was something about his appearance that was wrong, uncomfortable, but he couldn't work out what it was.

'I need to make water,' he whispered, and stood up. It wasn't a great excuse, but it would do. The priest nodded and took the blindfold from his pocket, gesturing Hoche over. Hoche gauged the distance between them and took three short steps towards the man. Hand on shoulder, leg out, push the right way – and the priest was falling to the ground face first, Hoche twisted behind him to land on his back, driving the air from his lungs as they hit the bare wood floor.

He didn't have much time. He quickly gagged the man with the blindfold and tied his hands with his cloth belt, then moved to examine the panel he had noted earlier. It was loose but he couldn't prise it free with his fingers.

The Reader's knife had fallen to the floor, and Hoche picked it up. The handle felt strangely shaped, but there was no time to worry about that. He slid it into the gap at the edge of the panel, prising it apart. The loose wood front came free, revealing a space beyond and a piece of parchment in it, a page torn from a large book, folded into quarters. Hoche reached for it. It was dusty.

Time was running out. He should be running now, but he needed to know what the paper said: it might indicate something else in this room. He unfolded it and held it up to the light from the nearest candle. There were words scrawled in one of the margins, as if written in a hurry: 'The one you seek, I left in the care of Saint Olovald. Beware: you are among worshippers of Tzeentch.'

'The one you seek' had to be Andreas Reisefertig, but who was Saint Olovald? And Tzeentch worshippers? It seemed unlikely, but Father Willem had warned him that some of the librarians had turned to darker ways. Here was proof.

He caught the stare of the man struggling on the floor against his bonds, and gazed at him in horror and hatred.

His soldier-self wanted to kill him, his Untersuching training urged him to question him – hard with no tongue but there were ways. Then he heard a creak from outside and knew his time was up. He had to get out now, before the other Readers returned.

He crossed to the door and twisted its handle. It would not move; it must be locked. He probed the keyhole with the dagger but something was blocking the blade. The noises outside were getting closer.

He put his shoulder to the door, ramming it, but with no effect. He grabbed the chair and battered it against the door's panels. On the second blow one of them cracked, and he hit there again and again until it shattered, then he dropped the chair and pulled the pieces away. There was brickwork on the other side.

It was a false door.

From behind him came the sound of a sword being drawn, and he snatched up the dagger and turned. A bookcase had swung back to reveal a passage. The other three Readers stood at its mouth, two with crossbows and one with a sword. The one in the middle moved the end of his bow. Hoche weighed the dagger in his hands, sensing it wasn't balanced for throwing, but he was out of options.

He shrugged as if surrendering and began to raise his hands, then hurled the knife at the three people in the doorway and sprang as they flung themselves out of the way, ramming one with his shoulder. For a second he thought he was through, then a crossbow caught him across the back of the head and he staggered, tripped over another Reader's leg and fell. The men collapsed in a heap. He felt his wrists grabbed and bound, and a blindfold was looped over his eyes. He was dragged to his feet. The point of a dagger dug into his neck and he was pushed forward.

'This is a mistake,' he said. 'I'm not who you think I am.' Panicked thoughts cleared for a second. 'I am your brother in Tzeentch, come from Altdorf to make contact. I bring news.'

Predictably there was no answer.

Had the other Untersuchung agent, the one who left the message, been through this too? How far were they going to go? He was fairly sure he could withstand a beating, but would they torture him? Were they going to cut his tongue out?

He threw himself forward, trying to break away, feeling the dagger-tip rip against the left side of his neck. For an instant he was free of their hands, then his face slammed into a wall and, stunned, he slumped against it. What happened? Then he remembered the morning's entry, and a right turn in the corridor before the room. His neck hurt. Something trickled down his skin. He was bleeding.

He was pulled upright. Someone pushed him from behind and he stumbled forward a few paces, his shoulder hitting a wall. Somewhere a door opened and he felt a breeze. The smell of filthy canals was strong.

Something looped around Hoche's ankles and was drawn tight, and a moment later someone shoved him hard in the small of the back.

He lost his balance and fell. And with the disorientation and the panic, suddenly he had an overwhelming sense of déjà vu. He had been here before.

Then he hit the water. He flailed, and kicked, and sank as the cold canal closed around him. Something heavy tied to his legs was dragging him down. He struggled against the ropes binding his wrists and ankles but the water had swollen the cord and any slackness was gone.

His lungs burned. His heart roared. He thrashed against the bonds that held him, the weight that pulled him deeper, struggling to hold onto life, consciousness, who he was.

The water swallowed him and crushed him. He was drowning in darkness.

He had felt this death before.

His lungs burst, and he breathed in the black water.

He sank.

Chapter Six
OLD FRIENDS

HE DREAMED HE was buried deep under the ground, in darkness and solitude. Something had been planted inside him, some dark and vile seed, and it was growing within his body, drawing its strength from his flesh and weakening him. The awful way it grew, spreading its thin tendrils through his veins and muscles, growing out of him like mistletoe or some strange rot, was a slow and gradual thing, but he dreamed this dream a long time.

'YOU'RE NOT DEAD.'

Consciousness floated and sparkled above him, like sunlight seen through riverwater. He swam towards it.

'Lie still. Don't move. You're very weak.'

His eyes were still blinded. No, the room was dark. He was lying in a soft bed, the mattress distorted by the weight of someone sitting beside him. He felt very tired. His thoughts were shadows and mist.

'You've been very ill, at Morr's door, but the physician says you are getting well now. Don't try to move. Can you hear me now? Can you speak?'

Hoche flexed his stiff lips, croaked, 'Yes.'

'Good. Know that you are safe, and sleep.' The weight lifted from the mattress and moved away. A door closed. Hoche wanted to ask him so much, to learn what had happened to him, but he was too tired. Sleep fell over him like a soft veil.

'How long have I been like this?' he asked a while later.

'Six days,' Erasmus Pronk said. The little man rose to his feet and walked to the window, pulling open the heavy curtains to let daylight flood in. Outside the sky was overcast, heavy with potential rain. In the small room on the top floor of Pronk's house on Duck Street, the atmosphere was no less pregnant.

'Six days,' Pronk repeated. 'You were unconscious for the first day, then the fever took hold. You nearly died. Hardly surprising, with so much Doodkanaal water inside you. That place is a disgrace, little better than a sewer.'

'I thought I was dead.' Hoche paused, reaching for a tumbler of water on the table beside his bed. His arm was weak and his hand shook, rippling the water as he sipped it. His thirst was terrible. 'How did you save me?'

'Dear boy.' Pronk looked mock-shocked. 'You don't think we'd let someone out on their first training mission without some kind of back up? It was important that you thought you were working alone, but we were following every step of the way. They threw you into the canal, and we pulled you out.'

Hoche felt a sense of bitter despair. He had failed embarrassingly badly. He would have died if not for the little man whose help he had disdained. And all this would be in Pronk's report to Altdorf. Like many times before, he asked himself what he was doing in this job and this role, and he yearned to be a soldier again.

Pronk must have seen his expression, because he laughed out loud. 'Don't count yourself a failure, Karl. You got into one of the Ancient Order's libraries, they think you're dead – which is always a useful thing for a secret agent – and I don't believe they broke your cover, or they'd have treated you a good deal worse. Not so bad for your first time out.

No permanent injuries either – that cut on your neck has festered a little, but keep that poultice on it and it'll be fine in a week. Did you find anything in the library?'

'Tzeentch worshippers.' Hoche slowly hauled himself up to a sitting position. 'Who is Saint Olovald?'

'Saint Olovald? One of the saints of Manaan, the city's patron-god, but not a major one.' Pronk walked to the window. 'There's a church to him not far from here, but it's quite run-down. Look, you can see it.' He pointed to a spire a few hundred yards away.

'I believe Reisefertig may be associated with it,' Hoche said. 'I found a note, hidden by an Untersuchung agent. It said someone had been left there.'

Pronk scratched his chin, his fingernails rasping against the coarse grey of his stubble. 'Well, at least that implies he's not dead – it's not used for burials. Do you know who left the note, or how long ago?' He sat back down on the bed.

Hoche shook his head, feeling the bandage around his neck shift with the movement. 'No. I didn't recognise the writing.'

'There haven't been any other agents in town for four months at least,' Pronk said, 'and if something has been at Saint Olovald's that long, it'll wait another day till you're fit to be up and about.' Hoche was about to protest that it was too important, but Pronk stilled him with a raised hand. 'No, no. This is your mission, I wouldn't dream of taking it away from you.'

Perhaps he's right, Hoche thought. At least this is a chance for me to do something on my first assignment more impressive than almost drowning.

PRONK HAD HIRED a carriage to take them to Saint Olovald's. Hoche had thought it unnecessary, but it wasn't until he had sat at the bottom of the house's stairs and panted to get his breath back that he realised how weak his forced rest had made him. The vehicle's iron-rimmed wheels clattered and rang over the cobbles of the narrow streets, scattering pedestrians. The area they were entering, on the largest of the Suiddock's islands, was run-down and shabby.

'An ants' nest of scum and villains,' Pronk said. 'And more inside the church. I've made enquiries. Drunks, derelicts, people with nowhere else to go. Still, it's had a few miracles ascribed to it, and they say its priestess is a good woman. Maybe she can help.'

The carriage stopped outside the church and Pronk helped Hoche down. It was a strange, squat and solid building, built of white stone discoloured by moss, lichen and dirt. Hoche guessed it was at least a thousand years old, built centuries before Marienburg and the Wasteland had split from the Empire to form a separate country. Unlike its city, the church had not prospered since: its stonework was worn and in need of repointing and paint. Seagulls perched on the roof.

'Not a prepossessing place,' Pronk said.

Hoche smiled. 'An Untersuchung agent should never judge by appearances.'

Together they passed through the worn arch of the porch, through the battered wooden doors and into the body of the church. Even before his eyes could adjust to the dim light, he smelled the decay and destitution of the place. Then, as the darkness cleared, he saw it was as Pronk had said. The pews were occupied with the poor and the desperate: filthy people in filthy rags, cripples, idiots, the hopeless and the mad.

A woman moved away from a slumped figure on one of the pews and came toward them. She was in her late twenties, Hoche guessed, with light-brown hair, long and tied back, a hard face and plain bluish-grey robes that had seen better days. Her hands were clasped in front of her and she had a half-formed smile on her lips.

'Good morning, gentlemen. Welcome to the temple of Saint Olovald. Are you here to pray?'

Hoche looked at Pronk, waiting for him to reply. He was used to the chain of command and the short man was his superior in the Untersuchung. Instead, Pronk deferred to him with a smile: 'I am merely an observer,' he said, then turned to walk slowly down the aisle towards the altar, stopping to peer at the faces of the people gathered in the pews.

Hoche swallowed to clear his throat. 'Sister, I am looking for a man who may have passed through your church in the last year. Possibly he came to you injured and needing healing. My information is not complete.'

Her half-formed smile neither grew nor faded. 'I hope you seek this man for good ends, and do not wish him ill.'

Hoche smiled back. 'He is a friend and former student of my master. We are worried for his safety.'

'In that case I will be pleased to help.' Her expression didn't change. Did she know he was lying? Her smile seemed to mock his deception. 'What is your friend's name? What does he look like?'

'He is–' Hoche stopped. Reisefertig would have been unlikely to use his real name, and although Braubach had described him – tall, dark, late twenties – he would have almost certainly changed his appearance too. That was basic Untersuchung training. For the first time Hoche understood how difficult tracking a renegade secret agent was going to be. 'He may have been much changed,' he finished lamely.

The priestess began to reply, but a cry from deep in the church stopped her as they both turned to look. The cry came again, louder, a howl of shock and sorrow. Hoche ran to it, the weak muscles of his legs protesting. Behind him, the priestess's sandals clattered on the tiled floor.

It was Pronk. He was kneeling on the floor before a bearded man in filthy rags stained by soup, vomit and spittle, cradling the other's head on his shoulder, his hands wrapped in the man's grease-matted hair. He was sobbing helplessly, words spilling from his mouth in incoherent syllables as he rocked back and forth.

'Who is that man?' Hoche asked the priestess. She shook her head.

'We don't know. We call him the Useful Idiot,' she said. 'His mind has gone.'

'How long has he been here?'

'A year, perhaps a little longer. Is he the one you're after?'

Hoche said nothing.

The other people in the temple were moving away from them, disturbed by Pronk's sobbing. The beggar's blank eyes stared ahead as his body rocked in time with Pronk's movements. He was grinning a huge brown-toothed smile as if he was enjoying the experience, or possibly just the unaccustomed attention. Hoche realised how much the man stank of his own filth. His face was unfamiliar.

Pronk's words were becoming clearer. 'Gunter,' he cried, 'Gunter, Gunter, Gunter,' over and over. His face was red with the effort of weeping and his body shook.

The idiot's mouth lolled open in a big dog-like smile, making strange guttural sounds with his throat as he lifted his head to gaze at the ceiling. Hoche could see deep inside his mouth, down to the strange twisted lump of scar at the back where his tongue had once been rooted.

THERE WAS LITTLE else to do. The priestess had checked the temple's records and confirmed that the Useful Idiot had been living on its charity for a few weeks over a year. Hoche left the two of them, Pronk and the husk that had once been Gunter Schmölling, at Pronk's town-house. Pronk had tried to help him analyse the situation, to work out what might have led to the crippling and abandonment of an Untersuchung agent, but the little old man had been too distraught to focus his thoughts.

Besides, there were too many unknown factors to be able to work out exactly what had happened. The only thing Hoche could be certain of was that Reisefertig – if it had been him – would have left Marienburg after abandoning Schmölling at the temple, and therefore he could return to Altdorf. The long journey back would give him the chance to think through all the possibilities, and sort the information he had into a picture of Reisefertig's movements and motivations. He would report back to his superiors, and then he'd insist on taking his overdue leave. Now, more than ever, he wanted to go home, to be himself for a few days. And he wanted to see Marie. Would one of her letters be waiting for him at the barracks? She couldn't write so what she dictated to one of the junior Grünburg priests was necessarily circumspect, but each letter still made his heart surge with emotion.

The Reik barge docked at Leydenhoven and Hoche disembarked, pushing his way through the busy streets to the watch-station where he picked up his horse from the stable-boy, tipping the man a few pennies. He rode south east, passing a steady flow of carts on their way into town, laden with wares to sell to the river-traders. It's all about currents and flows, eddies and tides, he thought. The Reik flows to the sea, the traders follow their own streams, letting money lead them wherever they will find the best market for their cargo, and the gold they receive flows backwards against the current, passing from hand to hand, flashing gold and silver like a bright stream in sunlight. One could not predict the path of a twig on the current, but the direction of the river was as old and as changeless as time.

Fate, too, was an unpredictable current, throwing men from bank to bank along the course of life's stream, now drifting slowly through a slow pool where big fish moved below the surface, unseen and unsuspected; now tossed in rapids; now beached, waiting for the next flood to move them on.

What strange tides had carried Gunter Schmölling to Saint Olovald's temple, mind-raped and tongueless? Pronk had said that the brothers of the Ancient Order would have done worse to an agent of the Untersuchung than merely killing him, had they found one trying to infiltrate their library. Yet there was no evidence that Schmölling had done that; he could not have left the clues in the New Apocrypha, since the note clearly referred to him. Had Reisefertig written it? And if he had, was he the person who had ruined Schmölling's mind and body before dumping him at the temple, or had he recognised the destroyed agent and taken pity on him? Or was there another Untersuchung agent at work within Marienburg, unknown to Pronk, following another agenda?

For that matter, how far could he trust what Pronk had told him?

And while he was thinking about it, who was the man who had signed Schmölling's name to the letter that had started him on this journey, an age and an era ago, and thereby convinced Braubach to save his life? If Johannes Bohr was not really Gunter Schmölling, as he had claimed, then who was he and what part did he play?

It was no good. He needed more information before he could reach any kind of answer, and that meant Altdorf, the barracks, dusty papers, and probably a long night drinking with Braubach, Bruno and Hunni. Hoche shook his head. Under the poultice on his neck the knife-cut twisted, sending harsh pain through his mind. It must be inflamed, he thought. I should take Pronk's advice and find someone to heal it.

THE SACRED GROUND of Blessed Shallya monastery lay two miles outside the market-town of Scheinfeld, a relic of the days of plague. Hoche had seen many like it and knew their story; the horses that pulled the carts filled with the infected becoming so familiar with the route that they no longer needed drivers to guide them, but could plod to and fro on their own. The healers of the monastery could do nothing to halt the illness and often became infected themselves. But that was all history. There hadn't been a serious outbreak of plague for at least eight years.

It was nearing dusk as Hoche took the track from the Carroburg road towards the monastery's low buildings, their uneven roofs casting long shadows in the dying sunlight, the graveyard obvious and sombre outside the walls. The track was muddy with late autumn rains, and on the overhanging trees the last few leaves were brown and crumpled. The long dark months were not far off.

As he drew near he could tell the monastery was well fortified: its high outer walls protected by a steep-sided double ditch, able to see off a raid by orcs, beastmen or outlaws. The sense of security gave Hoche solace: even here, close to a large market-town and a week's ride from Altdorf, it was not safe to travel after nightfall.

The clatter of the heavy iron ring on the main gate was answered by an initiate in the order's traditional white robes. She showed Hoche to a small room with a simple bed in the west block of the building, told him a bell would sound for the evening service in the temple and again for the start of supper in the great-hall, and left before Hoche could ask to see a healer. A few minutes later the bell called him to worship and he walked across the open yard to the small temple where the order had gathered.

He should have felt glad to be back in a country that followed gods that he recognised, not the foreign Manaan and

Hændryk of Marienburg, but for some reason he didn't. Perhaps it was the unfamiliarity of the Shallyan rituals, but he had hoped to feel calmed and spiritually refreshed. Instead it made him disquieted and uneasy. The temple was simple, with whitewash and wood carvings, and the chanted hymns and blessings of the service were pleasing to his ear, but something here felt wrong.

At the evening meal in the monastery's great hall, Hoche found himself seated next to the temple mother, an elderly woman in a white headscarf who spoke with long pauses between her sentences. Hoche never learned her name, as everyone addressed her as 'Mother'. They spent the meal exchanging the latest news: Hoche bringing the word from Marienburg, the priestess from Altdorf.

'How is the capital?' Hoche asked and then, thinking of Pronk, 'What news of the Emperor's son?'

The thick lines around the old priestess's eyes crinkled in thought. 'No news of the Emperor,' she said, 'but I hear Chaos has been at work in the city.' She paused. 'They say a great cult of worshippers of the vile gods has been unearthed within the army.'

'Oh?' Hoche said, trying not to look as interested as he was. 'Which regiment?'

The priestess shook her head. 'I know little of armies. But it was close to the Emperor, I do know that.' Pause. 'They say the bodies of the heretics were burning for three days and three nights.'

Hoche finished his bowl of vegetables quietly, thinking. It sounded as though the Untersuchung had moved against the Knights Panther. The news should have cheered him, but it did the opposite. Something in the place's atmosphere was still unsettling him. The palms of his hands were slick with sweat.

As the meal ended and the priestess stood to leave, Hoche touched her arm. 'Mother, I have a wound on my neck,' he said, 'and it is not healing. Would it be possible...?'

She smiled. 'Of course. I will send someone to your room, to clean and bless it for you.' She gestured to a tall young man a few places down the table. 'Brother Tobias is a gifted healer. I will ask him.'

The way back to Hoche's room led across the square between the buildings. Above, the stars glittered down from a clear sky and a full moon glistened with cold light so sharp it cast shadows across the ground. He shivered. It was chill, and there could be a frost on the ground in the morning, the first of the season. But more than that, it reminded him of another well-lit night, when he and Schulze had gone walking by moonlight. It felt like it had been years ago.

He gazed into the heavens, wondering where he would be if fate's guide had led him down a different course. Promoted? With Marie? Gutted by an orc raider? He'd heard Duke Heller's army had met an orc army three weeks after he had left, and had not fared well. Perhaps their morale was low, he thought. But with winter coming on the army would have returned home; no army campaigned after the Mittherbst festival, with the weather to add to their list of adversaries.

It was peaceful, and he stood a while, trying to understand what it was about the place that made him feel so ill at ease. There was no rational reason, like the cultist's knife in Marienburg; this was simply a feeling that had lodged deep in his gut and would not be shifted. I'm safe here, he told himself. Be sensible: there is no need for concern. He breathed deeply, tasting the freshness of the night air, stretching the muscles in his arms. Then the wound in his neck started to hurt again, and he walked on.

Brother Tobias was waiting in his room, a shallow bowl of water and a bag of herbs, preparations and bandages at his feet. He stood awkwardly as Hoche came in. 'The temple mother asked me to attend to you,' he said. His voice was young and nervous.

'Thank you,' Hoche said, sitting down on the bed. 'I was wounded in the neck some days ago. It does not seem to be healing, and it gives me pain.' He indicated the ragged poultice. Tobias peeled it away and made a small noise of concern.

'Is it bad?' Hoche asked.

'I can see no sign of rot, but the wound is inflamed and filled with pus. The skin around it is strangely puffed up. I've not seen one quite like it.' Tobias moved to his equipment.

'I'll wash it and apply a fresh poultice with a blessing.' He hummed for a moment, sorting through wilted herbs and jars. 'What kind of weapon did this?'

'A dagger,' Hoche said.

Tobias stood up, holding a dampened cloth. 'Just a dagger? It must have been sharp. Was the blade serrated? I see marks of that.' He touched the cloth to the wound and a dart of unexpected pain made Hoche flinch. He forced himself to think himself away while the young monk cleaned the filth from his injury.

He hadn't seen the knife that cut him, but he had seen the one on the belt of the greybeard who had watched him in the library, and all the scholars – the cultists – had worn similar weapons. What had it looked like? He remembered its strangely curved handle, almost serpentine in its irregularity, and there had been a black stone high up on the handle, like an eye. Now that he thought about it, the shape of the weapon reminded him of something. Something from one of Jakob Bäcker's lessons.

Tobias finished cleaning the wound. He reached into his bag and brought out a flask of water. 'From the holy spring at Vorsfelde,' he said, dabbing a fresh bandage, 'and I've added burned seaweed to purify the wound.' He began to chant in a low voice, giving it Shallya's blessing to heal and restore the flesh.

Hoche, distracted, nodded. In his mind he was back in the long room of the Untersuchung barracks, watching Bäcker leaf through his books. His memory shifted and he knew what the shape was: the symbol of Tzeentch, the Changer of the Ways, one of the unholy quartet of the Chaos Gods. The dagger was longer and thinner than the vile lord's sigil, but was unquestionably the same shape. Further proof that the librarians had been cultists. He had been lucky to escape with drowning. Torture and sacrifice was not an unusual fate for those caught infiltrating or stealing from such groups.

'I'll put a blessing on the wound now,' Tobias said, holding the bandage he had prepared. 'This may sting a little.' He placed the cloth on Hoche's neck.

The explosion of pain was instant and all-consuming. A blazing lance ran through his body, filling his mind with unspeakable agony, as if someone had poured burning oil into his blood and acid on his thoughts.

He was on his feet, screaming and roaring. With one arm he backhanded Tobias and the young man flew across the chamber, crashing into the stone wall and dropping, stunned. Hoche staggered around the room, clawing at the bandage and ripping it off his flesh, but the ruinous pain did not ebb. He grabbed the bowl of water, pouring it on his neck, scrubbing at the wound with his hand, trying to remove whatever the monk had placed there.

He realised he was still shouting in pain, and forced himself to stop. His heart was racing and he was panting as if he had sprinted a mile. Brother Tobias lay slumped on the floor, not moving. A small pool of blood was forming around him. How had that happened, Hoche wondered? I only meant to push him away. Maybe he fell badly. He began to move towards the fallen figure, but then he heard voices. People were moving in the corridor outside.

Hoche grabbed for his sword with one hand, and snatched up his pack in the other. Something was wrong here, something rotten and decaying. He had sensed it when he entered the monastery, but now he knew for sure. The dark powers were at work in this holy place. Their fingers were everywhere he looked, now that he could recognise the signs. He didn't want to show it, but he was scared.

There were too many people here for him to take on alone. He had to get out, get back to Altdorf to let the others know. The wound in his neck throbbed and ached as if it was alive.

He yanked the door open and stood, sword raised against the group of unarmed Shallyans who were gathered outside. 'Get back!' he demanded. 'Get out of my way!'

They moved, but not fast enough. Hoche grabbed a youth little more than a boy, pulling him close like a living shield, and put the sword to his throat. 'Nobody move!' he demanded. 'Get my horse prepared and brought to the door. No trickery, no weapons, no spells. If I see a glint of steel or hear one word of a chant, the boy dies.'

He hoped it worked. It felt like he'd taken them by surprise, that they weren't ready to find a warrior in their midst. Maybe they'd hoped Brother Tobias would have finished him off.

They shrunk back against the wall. Someone at the back began a prayer to Shallya, but was silenced by the others. A novice scrambled down the corridor and out of the door at the end, presumably towards the stables – or possibly to raise the alarm. Hoche began edging down the corridor, his back to the wall, scanning for any sign of movement or hostility. There was none. The boy at his side whimpered.

The door at the end opened and the temple mother stood framed against the night. 'What is going on?' she demanded. 'What has happened?'

'There is corruption here,' Hoche said. 'I felt the signs as I entered. Now your brother has tried to harm or kill me as he tended my wound.' He paused, summoning part of the old Karl Hoche, the part of him he thought had been left on the battlefield, remembering his tone of command. 'Get me my horse!'

People scattered to do his bidding.

THERE WERE NO swordsmen waiting for him outside, no archers at high windows, but he kept close to the walls just the same, holding the boy as a shield in case of sudden attack. His horse was at the front gate, saddled and ready. A few Shallyans remained in the courtyard and others gathered in doorways, watching, muttering in low voices.

He let the boy go, swung into the saddle and rode away as fast as the rough track would let him. It was not far to Scheinfeld, and he would find an inn there, where he would wash and bandage his wound himself. With one hand he reached up to feel it. The flesh was raw and soft, and it ached with a dull throb.

The monastery of Shallya receded into the distance, but his sense of unease did not leave him.

Chapter Seven
THE HERETIC

RAIN WAS SPATTERING against the hard city stones as Hoche rode back through the north gate into Altdorf a week later. It was a cold miserable rain that permeated the thick wool of his riding cloak, dampening his clothes and his spirits. The gate guards were subdued, huddled under their wet-weather cloaks like fattened geese waiting for the Mondstille feast. The whole city seemed muted. The streets were emptier than usual, and there were fewer traders in the marketplaces, and fewer barges at anchor in the river. At least the place didn't stink as badly in this weather.

He heard the temple bells striking to call worshippers for the afternoon service, first the booming call of the Cathedral of Sigmar, and the answering chimes of the other temples ringing out across the city. His friends would be finishing work soon and heading to the Tilted Windmill to start the evening's drinking. Although he was supposed to return to the barracks and begin his debrief at once – and, he reminded himself, there was urgent news to be passed on – the official stuff could wait until morning. He had been on the road a long time, and he was powerfully hungry.

And, he thought, it would be good to see them all again, Hunni, Bruno, Anders, Jakob and even Braubach, with his cynicism, his moods and the strange tangents his thoughts took. He wanted to hear the news, to know how the raids on the Knights Panther had gone, and who was in favour and who was out, before he became caught up in the official rote of meetings and paperwork. He tugged the reins, steering his horse away from the barracks and towards the inn.

He left the horse in the tavern's small stable and pushed open the side door, expecting a crowded room, loud conversation, the smell of fresh-poured beer and hot meat. Instead, in the quiet room a few strangers looked up from their platters, meeting his gaze with interest or suspicion. He did not recognise any of the drinkers, but Ralf the landlord was standing behind the counter with a jug of black beer, watching the tankards. Hoche gestured across the floor to catch his eye. Ralf looked up. He seemed surprised to see him.

'Anyone in the back room, Ralf?' Hoche asked. The fat man shook his head. Hoche grinned back; it was odd that none of the others was there yet, but perhaps they were in a meeting, or the rain had delayed them. Still, he could use the waiting time. 'Bring me a trencher of beef and a pint of black,' he instructed, and pushed open the door to the inner sanctum where Untersuchung members habitually drank and talked.

The room was silent, the long table and benches clean and bare. Hoche sat down at the end nearest the doorway, ready to surprise his friends when they arrived, and waited for his food and beer to arrive. He stared idly at the unpolished surface of the table, and the pattern of scratches and marks that time had left there. Previous occupants had carved sets of initials he didn't recognise, the outlines of the letters filled in with years of grime. Someone had scratched a round marker-symbol there, like the one he had found in Marienburg. Its cuts were fresh, not aged at all. It pointed to the centre of the table.

Hoche stared at it, his attention caught. The mark had to be a joke. Someone had been sitting there, perhaps, and someone else had drunkenly scratched it to point at them. He stood and leaned over the table, checking the indicated spot to see if anything else had been carved at that point, but there was nothing. Nothing but a joke.

And then again...

He knelt and ducked his head under the edge of the table. There was something there, a rectangular shape wrapped in cloth, held to the underside of the wood boards with tacks. He reached out for it, and it came away from its fixings without too much difficulty. What in Sigmar's name was it? What was it doing here?

He placed the bundle on the table and unwrapped it: a small book, untitled, bound in cheap leather. He opened the front cover. There, on the verso, was the owner's name. 'Gottfried Braubach, his journal.'

A sound came from the doorway. Hoche turned, expecting his colleagues or Ralf with his food, but the latch did not lift and the door did not open. Instead there was the rasping clunk of a key turning in an unoiled lock.

Hoche was about to shout out in protest, and then he stopped himself. That wasn't an accident, he thought. They have locked the door deliberately. They're not going to let me out, and shouting will let them know I've learned I'm a prisoner.

Wondering about reasons can wait. First I need to get out of here.

He glanced up at the room's high windows, but they were both barred, as they had always been. There was no other doorway. Think, think, he told himself. This is a room used by a group of somewhat paranoid occult investigators, with a lot of enemies. They wouldn't come here unless they felt safe, and they wouldn't feel safe unless there was another way out. That's the way the Untersuchung think. They may not have told me about it, but it has to exist. Somewhere.

Mentally he mapped the room, working out what was beyond each of its walls. The east wall, with its windows, faced the street. The west, with its large fireplace, probably shared its chimney with the kitchen. South was the door to the main room, so north had to be the stables. All the walls were brick, and not much chance of secret doors in any of them. He bent to peer up the flue of the fireplace, but the chimney was too narrow for a child, let alone him. He kicked the back of the grate but it didn't move: no false back there.

He looked up. No hatches in the ceiling. Then he stopped and mentally kicked himself. Tavern, he thought. Beer-cellars.

The trapdoor was under the table, which he had to shift by lifting it from one end of its solid wood bulk so it didn't scrape across the floor as he moved it. The hatch led to darkness, the room's light illuminating a patch of brick floor about eight feet below. Hoche thought for a moment about how he was going to close the trap to conceal his exit, but realised that if the table had been moved they'd work it out soon enough. He grabbed Braubach's journal from the bench, wrapping the cloth around it, and lowered himself through the hole in the floor.

It was an eight-foot drop onto a rough, dark surface. He landed in a crouch and paused for a second, letting his eyes adjust. The cellar room was abandoned, with only broken barrels and an empty wine-rack. At one end thin light filtered down from cracks around a heavy shutter: the old street entrance, Hoche guessed, and too obvious for what he needed. Then, as his vision cleared, he saw a passageway in the east wall. It was only two feet high and about the same across, but that was enough to crawl through. He dropped to his knees and crept into the darkness.

The tunnel sloped down at a shallow angle for about fifteen feet and emerged into a wider, vaulted one with a stream of water running down its centre. It smelled of rot and decay but it didn't stink. A disused sewer, Hoche thought, or a storm-drain. He stayed close to its wall, following it by touch, glancing up at occasional shafts of light from broken brickwork above. There were no sounds of pursuit.

What just happened, he asked himself? Nobody's in the Windmill. I show up, and Ralf locks me in like a prisoner. Was it the Knights Panther? Are they still on my trail? He shook his head: it was possible but it seemed unlikely, particularly if they'd been raided. Perhaps it was a matter of revenge?

But Braubach had hidden his journal under a table in the tavern. He'd left a sign so any Untersuchung agent could take it, but nobody had. Why would he do that? Hoche stopped for a moment, the water of the storm-drain running over his shoes, soaking his feet. That question was at the heart of it, he felt. Why had Braubach tried to pass his journal to some-one else – and why had nobody else taken it?

There were two possible reasons. Either all the other agents knew it was there, or there were no agents left to find it.

Hoche knew he desperately needed answers. The obvious place to look for them would be the Reiksguard barracks, but he knew that if his sudden suspicion that the Untersuchung was in trouble was right, then going there would put him in mortal danger.

He sloshed on through the darkness.

BEING SWORN SERVANTS of Sigmar, most witch hunters never let alcohol pass their lips. For the few in Altdorf who did, the place they gathered was the Fist and Glove, an ancient drinking-house in the back-streets behind the Cathedral of Sigmar, not far from the Street of a Hundred Taverns. Centuries of repression, the disdain of priests and the occasional suspicious house-fire had not been able to remove it from its location, nor the patrons from its bar.

Inside its cracked oak door, the low ceiling and the lack of windows added to the inn's atmosphere of cramped gloom. The only light came from candles fixed to the wooden pillars that dotted its floor, marking off the booths with their hard wooden benches, worn smooth by generations of clenched witch hunter buttocks. It smelled of tobacco, wood smoke, incense, stale beer and stale sweat. Its patrons preferred the company of their own thoughts and the counsel of their beer. The atmosphere was sombre and heavy. It was as if centuries of earnest discussion over points of religious doctrine and agonising over matters of conscience had soaked into the walls, the woodwork, the beer and even the air itself, darkening them, weighing them down.

Occasionally, however, the spirit might be lightened if a visitor was present: a delegation from another city, perhaps, or pilgrims laughing, joking and telling stories, or a devout trader fresh from saying prayers in the Cathedral of Sigmar since Altdorf, unlike Marienburg, did not have a god of trade. This evening was one of those: a merchant from Carroburg had come in, one-eyed, his left arm bandaged, black curly hair visible under one of the flat velvet hats in the Tilean style. He said his name was Hans Frei and he wanted to speak to a witch hunter, to tell them about a Shallyan monastery he had visited. An astute observer might have noticed the stained bandage around his neck, and the fact that his sword was of a military, not civilian design. But when a stranger is so convivial, has such an interesting tale and is so free with the drinks, who has time to notice details?

'It was a godless place,' Herr Frei said, and shivered, and supped his beer.

'You didn't see any solid evidence of Chaos-worship? Symbols, tattoos, unholy rites? Sacrificed babies?' asked a witch hunter, one of the three who had been listening to the story. His name was Theo Kratz, he was Altdorf born, four years in the service of the Order, and had burnt thirty-four witches. Everyone knew he would go a long way.

'I saw nothing like that,' said Herr Frei. 'But my senses were telling me that something was wrong. There was none of the tranquillity I expect from a shrine of the Mother of Peace. My father was a priest, and I am told I am sensitive to such things. And as I said, there's the matter of their strange healing practices.'

'Very strange,' agreed Erwin Rhinehart, who had drunk more of Herr Frei's beer than the others. 'I will instruct our brothers in Carroburg to make investigations. Be assured the matter will be examined.' He drained his tankard and put it down rim-first on the table, with a sound like a cracked bell.

'Thank you, gentlemen. In Sigmar's name,' said Herr Frei. 'But tell me, what news of Altdorf? I heard of a discovery of a great cult of Chaos-followers. Was that your work?'

'Aye,' said Anders Holger, the third of the listeners, and the only one wearing their distinctive dark clothes and high-collared shirt. His accent was from the western Empire, and he had taken a particular interest in the earlier talk of Carroburg. 'It was our business, and bad business it was. The work of the Foul Lords, so close to the Emperor's court. But we rooted them out, and their smoke has risen to the sky.'

'Close to the Emperor?' Herr Frei looked concerned. 'I heard tell it was one of the great regiments. Is that right? Members of the Knights Panther?'

'The Panthers?' Theo grinned in amusement. 'No, your tale-teller has his facts twisted. It was the Reiksguard.'

'The Reiksguard? The Emperor's bodyguard?' asked Herr Frei. There was a strange note in his voice.

'No. Well, not that way,' said Erwin. 'A secret division of the Reiksguard. You wouldn't know the name. They were a subtle crew.'

'Too subtle for their own good. Or ours,' Anders said. 'It's public knowledge now. The Untersuchung, they were named, and charged with protecting the Emperor from the schemes of Chaos. The Lord Protector received word they were harbouring heretics and dealing with the dark forces they had sworn to revile. They thought they were safe, see, because they had special protection for their work. But Lord Gamow obtained a dispensation from the Grand Theogonist himself to search their barracks.'

'And what a haul we found!' crowed Erwin.

'You were there?' Herr Frei asked. If the room had not been so dark, his skin might have looked pale, like ashes. Then he gestured across the room to the pot-boy to bring more beer and for a few seconds everyone's attention was drawn to the other side of the room, away from him. By the time they looked back he had recomposed himself.

'I was there.' Theo watched as his tankard was refilled, paused to drink, and wiped his mouth on his sleeve. 'Heretical documents, foul forbidden books, parts of mutants, two wizards with expired licences – such a gathering of idolators, false priests and dark things I have never seen. We burnt every one of them, and used their vile books to stoke the blaze higher still. The bone-fires burned for three days, and their hot fat ran down the gutters like rainwater. It was a sight to behold.'

'Sigmar's work,' said Anders.

'Sigmar's work,' echoed Erwin.

'All of them, you said,' Herr Frei asked. 'How many were they?'

'Fifty-seven,' Theo said. 'In Altdorf, that is, and another fourteen in Talabheim. Some escaped us but we have their names and there are warrants out for their arrest, with a bounty of a hundred crowns on the head of each man. They had agents in every city in the Empire, but we will have them all by Mondstille. Their souls will answer to Morr's justice, and they'll learn what good their vile masters are to them then.'

'Sigmar's work,' said Herr Frei thoughtfully. He looked up from the pint-pot he had been staring into, and narrowed his eyes across the half-empty tavern, to where a female figure sat alone at a corner table, in the robes of a priestess. Erwin followed his gaze, then looked back to smirk at the other two witch hunters. Herr Frei caught their smiles and broke his stare.

'You know her?' he asked.

'She's one of us,' Erwin said.

'A witch hunter?' Frei asked.

'Yon's Sister Karin Schiffer, assistant to Lord Gamow,' Anders said. 'A pain, she is. You'd think she followed one of the cold gods of Kislev, for the frozen water that flows in her veins. Not one to talk to us. Keeps her own company. But drinks, she does, and a good deal of late.'

'She's an uncommon handsome woman,' said Frei. 'I feel that I've seen her before.'

''Tis possible,' Theo said. 'She has been in the order only a year or so. But Lord Gamow has taken a powerful liking to her. If you know what I mean.'

'I follow your sense,' Frei said, looking across the room at her. As he did she raised her gaze, scanning the room, and met his stare. Their eyes locked in mutual recognition. Then she dropped her head again, looking back to her clasped hands, hiding her face behind the dark waterfall of her hair.

Herr Frei stiffened, and his right hand dropped from the handle of his tankard to rest by his side. A suspicious man, or one more alert and less drunk than his companions, might have wondered if he was about to draw his sword. But Sister Karin did not move from her table, and he relaxed.

Nevertheless, a minute or so later he made his excuses, paid the pot-boy for the night's beer, and left the tavern. The path to the street took him past the table where the priestess sat alone. He did not look down, and she did not look up until the door had thudded shut after him.

HOCHE WAITED UNTIL he was streets away from the Fist and Glove before ducking into an alley to remove his hat, eye-patch and the sling around his left arm. Perhaps the disguise had been too much, but he had wanted to distract attention from the bandage around his neck. And yet, despite it all, Sister Karin had recognised him. He would have to leave the city that evening. Where he'd go, he wasn't sure. Home to Grünburg, perhaps, but even that wouldn't be safe for long.

The news was still sinking in. The new Hoche, the trained agent, was performing almost by rote, information-gathering, asking the right questions, thinking about plans of action, plotting survival. Underneath, at a more human level, he was numb.

He hadn't believed it until he had heard it from the witch hunters' mouths, but it was true. His colleagues were dead, burned. All of them. Braubach, Hunni, Anders, Bruno, Jakob and all the rest. For a moment he pictured them screaming in flames, bound to stakes, their clothes and hair on fire, blazing. He closed his eyes hard, pressing his fingers against them, to banish the image.

All dead. The Untersuchung all dead, denounced as heretics and daemon-worshippers, followers of Chaos. The organisation that had ended his career as a soldier to recruit him was now itself ended, and with it his new life. This morning he had been an agent of the Empire returning home with important news. Now he was a wanted criminal, a consort of Chaos, an enemy of the state.

Was it true about the Untersuchung? He'd seen the damned books with his own eyes, and heard the oaths and the heresies. But had his fellows been followers of Chaos, or had they just strayed too close to the line that separated black from white, so lost in that twilight region that they didn't realise they had gone too far? He couldn't believe it. He hadn't liked them all, but he had trusted them. Nothing they had done had given him cause to doubt their integrity.

If so, if they were innocent, then who had ordered the raid? The Knights Panther, still fighting to save their reputation? Possibly, but it must have been someone who knew that enough evidence lay there to convict the whole order, to damn them by association. The raid had come from the witch hunters, directed by Lord Gamow. Hoche resolved to learn more about the man.

Gamow was Lord Protector, second-in-command of the Order of Witch Hunters. His ruthlessness and zeal had taken him to the top of his Order, and he was renowned for his ability to seek out groups of Chaos worshippers. Some of those arrests, Hoche had learned from Braubach during his training, had been based on tip-offs from the Untersuchung. Others had been groups of frightened innocents, tortured until they would admit to anything if it ended their suffering. Braubach had disliked the man. In the last few months that dislike had increased and become tinged with fear.

After Hoche had clambered from the storm-drain through an access-tunnel in the slums and bought some clothes from a grubby pawnshop by the docks – too risky to return to the Tilted Windmill for his saddlebags – he had sat by candlelight in the Cathedral of Sigmar and studied Braubach's journal.

His mentor's crabbed script and frequent crossings-out did not lend themselves to fast reading, and Hoche had only studied the last few entries in detail. They had not been illuminating: the normal minutiae of Untersuchung bureaucracy and life. Only the final entry, written in a scratched, swift hand different from Braubach's normal elegant script, gave any hint of what had happened.

'They came for us this morning. No subtlety, battering at the barracks door with staves, which gave us a few moments to hide the most precious items in the prepared places. Many were arrested in their homes before dawn, and the hunters have taken the chance to settle many old scores. I escaped over the ladder and am leaving this for whoever has the wits to find it, for what good it may do you. I suggest you flee to our

*allies in Kislev. Or, if you are brave, stay low in the city to
learn what scheme was behind this. Learn why the witch
hunters moved against us now, who gave the order and what
his motives were, and avenge us. Sigmar be with you. Pray for
our souls.'*

That was the end.

Hoche stopped, considering his options. This late at night
the bridges and the city gates would be closed. He could not
venture north of the Reik, and to leave Altdorf now would
mean passing through the needle's eye, the narrow doorway
set into the walls beside the great gates, passing under the
eyes of watchful guards. Better to spend the night here and
depart at dawn as the gates were opened, in the crush of people entering and leaving.

He wasn't sure where he should go: somewhere he could
lie low and be unobserved until the news of the
Untersuchung's burning had died away. Altdorf would be
too hot for a former agent for a while. Possibly literally.

There was still the question of how to spend the night. The
safe-houses in the city would all have been purged. The
bounty on the heads of all Untersuchung agents meant the
inns would be scrutinising everyone who came in, and trying to find a room this late at night would rouse suspicions.
Besides, he knew he would not sleep a wink. Maybe he
should find a tavern down by the docks, drink and silently
mourn his comrades until dawn.

No. No more drinking. He needed his wits about him.

He thought back to Braubach's journal, and its mention of
escaping from the barracks 'over the ladder'. That implied
there was another way of getting into the Untersuchung's
headquarters. If he could get in, and if the searchers and
scavengers of the witch hunters had not found all of the hidden documents Braubach had mentioned, he might be able
to learn something about what had happened, or glean
some information he could use.

It would be dangerous, even foolhardy to try to break into
the barracks. On the other hand it was one place they almost
certainly wouldn't think to look for him, and if he was
forced to become a fugitive with a price on his head then he

wanted to know why. And, he reasoned, breaking into the Reiksguard barracks at night couldn't be that hard. He'd already done it once.

THERE WAS ONLY one moon, and not much of it: the crescent of Mannslieb glowed from behind drifting clouds, edging each one with faint silver. By its faint light the brick bulk of the Reiksguard headquarters was a black mass, its rear wall shadowed and textureless. No lanterns or torches lit the narrow street, no candles glowed in windows or firelight from behind shutters in the wood-framed buildings that stood opposite the back of the barracks, their gabled roofs jutting out, overhanging the street and blocking out the few stars that had fought their way through the clouds. It suited Hoche fine.

He stood at the base of the barracks wall, trying to work out what Braubach had meant by 'the ladder'. The wall was blank and featureless, without so much as a window or gutter to help him up. Three storeys above the roof was pitched steeply, tiled with slates, black and sheer. There were no handholds or footholds anywhere, apart from rainspouts on the roof corners, carved like the heads of horses with laughing mouths. There was no sign of a ladder here, and it would have had to be over thirty feet high to reach the barracks roof.

It occurred to him that the route Braubach had mentioned had been designed for escape. It might not be possible to get in that way. Altdorf's cat-burglars were notorious for their expertise in climbing, and only a fool would give them a way to break into a building, even one as unfriendly to thieves as a barracks. Perhaps Braubach had used a rope secured to a window-bar on the top floor to escape. Perhaps he was being a fool.

What would Braubach have done? Laughed at him, along with the horse-head gargoyles? Or told him to think harder, walking away, waiting until he'd found the answer on his own? Hoche could almost feel his tutor's presence, a shadow against the bricks, like a ghost.

He stared at the wall. It reminded him of something: a summer evening in the Windmill, with Braubach and some of the others swapping riddles. 'Faced with a wall,' Braubach had said, 'an elf will try to go over it, a dwarf under it, and men of the Empire through it. A halfling will look for the door. I once told that to a scholar from Cathay, and he said that in his country a wise man would turn his back and imagine there is no wall. And who's to say that won't work as well as the others?' He'd laughed. Nobody else had.

Hoche stared at the barracks. What if there is no wall, he thought? Or rather: don't think about the wall. It's part of the problem, but it's not part of the solution. If the wall is unclimbable, ignore it. The answer lies elsewhere.

He turned and studied the houses on the other side of the street. With their overhanging upper floors they were worse than vertical, almost impossible to climb without a rope. He took a step or two closer. The white plaster fronts were smooth, the windows high and shuttered. But in a slight gap, a corner where one building stood a foot further back than its neighbour, he saw it.

An iron lightning-rod, about as thick as his thumb, reached up the side of the houses and along the chimney-stack, jutting into the night sky like a taunt to the thunder-god. Hoche walked over to it and leaned close until the shadows melted and he could see there was an inch of room between it and the building: enough for his fingers. He reached out and tugged it: sometimes these things were fixed so they would pull loose in the hands of a burglar. This one was sound.

This wasn't going to be easy. The temptation to give up was strong. It would be simple to walk away, leave the city, get away from the forces who were chasing him, to live with not knowing what had happened. But he had never been one to take the easy way out.

Muttering a short invocation to Sigmar he reached up, took a firm grip around the iron rod, and let his hands carry his weight. Then he bent at the hips, walking his feet up the side of the wall in careful inches, letting the mass of his body push them against the side of the building. Walk up two foot-lengths, then move his hands up the same distance. That was the tricky moment as his fingers scrabbled for a new grip against the pitted metal, his knuckles barking on the dirty plaster of the wall. The first ten feet were the hardest, but after that he began to develop a rhythm and a momentum. Nevertheless it was slow going.

After six or seven minutes he lifted himself over the edge of the low parapet and lay in deep shadow, out of breath, in the deep gutter on the other side. From here he could see over the city, the occasional glare of lanterns marking the cobweb plan of the narrow streets. Opposite, the roof of the barracks lay no more than fifteen feet away, its sharp slope ending in a narrow ledge. The curious geometry of the pigeon-coop stood in its middle, outlined in shadow against the dark sky. Thirty feet below, the street lay as empty as before.

Fifteen feet was too far to jump. There was no space to take a run-up.

Hoche stood to get a clearer view of the surroundings. Perhaps a hidden wire would pull some kind of bridge across. Or maybe, he wondered briefly, the bridge was only accessible from the other side: an exit, not an entrance. After all, why would the Untersuchung have made an entrance to their headquarters that any roof-walker could find? That would have been careless.

His foot struck something long and solid, lying concealed in the darkness of the gutter. Hoche bent to pick it up, and found how careless his late employers had been. It was a fifteen-foot ladder.

THE PIGEON-COOP was empty, its hatch swinging, a few feathers patterning the floor. The birds hadn't been killed, they had been taken. Braubach had told him that it wasn't possible to interrogate a messenger-pigeon. Hoche wondered if the witch hunters knew that.

The passageway below was dark and still, its doors opening into empty and strangely tidy rooms on either side. Hoche had expected strewn papers, bloodstains, broken furniture and signs of carnage, but there was none of it. The place didn't feel as if something terrible had happened there, it was more as if the occupants had moved out or were elsewhere, like an empty schoolroom on a feast-day.

He reached the stairs and began to descend towards the main room below, then stopped. The door at the bottom was closed. Why that door, but none of the others? He moved to the side of the stairway and stepped slowly down, transferring his weight carefully from foot to foot, leaning on the banister to put as little strain as possible on the stairs, in case they should creak and give him away. If there was anyone to hear it.

The windowless landing at the bottom of the stairwell was almost completely dark, but a thin sliver of light crept under the bottom of the door, giving away its position. Hoche stopped, mentally picturing the long room, working out the position of the moon. It wasn't possible; the first night he'd seen the place the moon had been half-full but none of its illumination had filtered through the slit windows. The light was coming from inside the room. Someone was in there.

Hoche found he was gripping the stair-rail with all his strength, and forced himself to be calm. He hadn't expected this, but of course a site used by a Chaos cult would have a night-watchman. They could have no idea he was here. It was probably some greybeard, asleep by now. The door was well oiled and, Hoche remembered, did not creak on its hinges. He could push it open a crack, to see if it was safe to enter.

He took two cautious steps towards the door, reaching for its handle, then stopped. it would be safer to have his sword drawn. He reached for it, pulling it free of its belt-loop. The tip caught in the unaccustomed folds of his merchant's cloak, wrenching out of his grasp and springing away. He grabbed for it with his left hand but missed. The sword fell with a metallic clatter, spinning away across the wood floor. Hoche dived after it.

In the other room, someone pushed a chair back. A voice said, 'Sigmar! What was that?' Another said, 'Quiet!' Hoche froze, listening. Two of them. They sounded young.

Footsteps moved towards the door. No time to find his sword; it was gone in the darkness. He drew his belt-knife and stood to one side of the door, his back against the wall. His heart was pounding.

Someone on the other side pulled the door open and a rhombus of low light blocked out across the floor. The first voice said, 'It's either one of those rats, or another fool for the fires.'

Hoche held his breath, watching as the first man stepped into the landing. He carried a longsword in one hand and the lantern raised in the other. He wore the dark tunic of a witch hunter.

'Come to Sigmar, you Chaos-scum,' he said.

Hoche stepped up behind him and stabbed him in the side of the neck, left-handed. The blade sunk deep, cutting blood-channels and opening the man's windpipe. He gave a throttled cry and his body thrashed. Hoche twisted the knife with his left hand and reached for his victim's sword with his right, snatching its hilt as the witch hunter's grasp loosened and he sank to the ground. The lantern fell with a crash and went out.

'Sigmar!' said the second voice.

Hoche took a quick step back, turned to his left and swung the sword through the sudden darkness at the point where the voice had come from. It struck something with a metallic clang – another sword, a lucky parry. Then he realised there was another light in the long room and it was moving, throwing shadows of other figures against the walls.

'Bring lights!' one shouted. Someone else: 'Raise the cry! Bolt the doors!'

He had surprise, subtlety, experience and a borrowed longsword on his side. They had at least three men awake, hundreds more asleep and, if the lucky parry was anything to go by, Sigmar's blessing on theirs. Hoche knew when he was outclassed.

He ran for the stairs, taking the familiar risers two at a time, and sprinted to the message-room and its steps up to the pigeon-coop. In seconds he was back on the roof, skidding down the steep tiles to the spot on the parapet where he had left the ladder propped between the buildings.

It was gone.

Hoche looked wildly to either side, down into the darkened street, then across to the opposite roof. There, wreathed in shadow, a figure stood in a dark priest's cloak. Her hood was pulled back and the starlight gleamed idly on her mass of dark hair, contrasting with her complexion and her eyes like firelight glinting on coal.

'Don't do anything you might regret,' said Sister Karin Schiffer, and smiled.

Hoche stood dumbfounded, completely lost. He felt a part of his senses fall away, tumbling down into the city, and for an instant he was tempted to jump after it. Instead he said, 'You followed me.'

'It was easy,' she said. 'My tutor was the finest of his kind.'

They stared at each other across a gap too wide to cross. It occurred to Hoche that if he hadn't left his knife in a man's neck downstairs, he could have thrown it at her.

Heavy feet rang on the steps of the pigeon-coop, and two witch hunters, swords drawn, emerged onto the roof. They spotted Hoche and moved defensively, blocking his possible escapes along the long gutters. One, with long tousled hair, had an expression that jerked Hoche back to the Old Bridge and the faces of three Knights Panther. This was a man who wanted revenge, and wanted it now.

'Stop!' Sister Karin shouted. 'We need him alive and unharmed!' The witch hunters glanced up at her voice. A third man appeared at the pigeon-coop. Hoche looked at them, then across at the priestess on the far roof, and down into the street thirty feet below. There was only one way he could avoid capture, he knew, but he did not feel like joining his colleagues in the afterlife yet.

He raised his hands, letting his sword hang loosely from his grip, and dropped it. It struck the parapet at an odd angle and fell clattering down the side of the building into the street. Sister Karin was watching him. For a second, as in the tavern, their gazes locked and held. For a second time she was the one who broke away from the stare.

'Bring him to the inner temple,' she said. 'He has questions to answer.'

Chapter Eight
A REASONABLE MAN

THEY HAD SEARCHED him and tied his hands. Two more witch hunters had arrived and together they walked, Sister Karin taking the lead, through the streets to a small Sigmarite temple close to the south wall, through a side-entrance and down a set of stone stairs into the earth, curving anti-clockwise in a lazy spiral lit by oil-lamps that flickered and smoked. They had gone down a long way. The air had become cold and damp.

The chamber at the bottom gave into a series of dark corridors. The witch hunters had taken torches and led him down one of them. It was lined with wooden doors, each offset so that no two faced each other.

As the torches moved down the passage, casting brief light through the small window with vertical bars set in each door, Hoche heard voices shout, guttural and inarticulate. Some of them were speaking his language, others in tongues he did not recognise, a couple in shouts and howls that seemed barely human. Filthy hands grasped at the bars, ragged fingernails reaching out imploringly towards the guards. They dodged them with an ease that spoke of much practice. As the light moved away, the cries died back to silence.

Hoche felt completely passive, drained of all resistance. It was as if he was watching himself be marched down this corridor, observing what was happening but not taking any part in it. So much had happened. He felt very tired.

A door hung open, the space inside pitch black. The witch hunters stopped outside it. One untied his hands. Hoche looked up and down the dark corridor, stretching away into night in both directions. A few cells away someone shouted a few words. Something made a wet noise. He noticed Sister Karin was not with the group any more.

'Your chamber awaits,' one of the witch hunters said, his voice laden with sarcasm. 'Breakfast will be served in your room. If you're lucky.' Hoche looked at them, expression and mind empty of emotion. Then he stepped into the darkness, and heard the hard wood door swing closed behind him. Heavy bolts slid into place.

'A hundred and fifty-four,' someone said.

'Enjoy your stay,' said the sarcastic one. Their footsteps moved away, the light fading as they went, the cries of other prisoners following them away down the corridor. In less than a minute all was silence and darkness.

Hoche moved carefully to one wall of his cell and felt his way around it, foot by foot, working out the dimensions and contents of the room. It was about eight feet square. There was a wooden bed, cunningly assembled without nails or pegs, with a thin straw mattress on it. An iron ring, set into the wall. A pile of rags that might have once been a blanket. A grating in one corner of the room, stinking of human filth. Nothing else. A patch of wall above the bed was curiously uneven, as if someone had scratched some words or message there, but in the total darkness his fingers could not begin to decipher it. He lay on the bed, closed his eyes and tried to sleep.

'Hey!'

He opened his eyes to the enveloping darkness. He didn't move.

'Hey, new man!'

The voice came from outside, from one of the other cells. It was low and rough, with a faint Altdorf accent. He ignored it. He wanted to sleep.

'New man, what news? What news?'

The voice was insistent, and Hoche could tell it was not going to shut up. He stood and walked slowly to the door, one arm outstretched so he did not walk into it. The wood was rough and cold under his fingers.

'News of what?' he said.

'Any news! Tell us of the outside. What season is it?'

'Almost winter. The month is Kaldezeit.'

'What news of the Empire?'

'It stands. Karl Franz reigns still. There was war with the orcs in the south this summer.'

'And you, new man? What news of you?'

Hoche considered. He knew nothing about the voice; it could be a prisoner desperate for information, or a witch hunter informant. He wondered how much it was safe to say. 'My order was arrested and burnt. I was out of the city, and captured on my return.'

'Are you clean?' the voice rasped.

It seemed a strange question. 'As clean as any man,' Hoche said.

Silence from the other cell.

'And what of you?' Hoche asked. 'What brought you here? How long have you been in this sunless pit?'

More silence. 'Are you clean?' he asked.

The silence stretched until Hoche turned away. He felt his path back across his cell, lay down on his bed and tried to sleep again.

A COMMOTION AWAKENED him. Light shone in from the corridor outside. Blinking, he went to the cell door to see what was happening.

The cells' builders had done their job well: it was impossible for him to see further than a few feet in either direction, but from the sound of the activity there was a struggle going on. Shadows leaped and there were shouts of activity, the smack of thrusts and parries, and snarls of pain. Hoche listened intently; he'd heard enough brawls to know what was happening. Three people with swords, he guessed, trying to subdue an unarmed man. There was a smack and a crunch, and he revised his opinion: now two men with swords against a strong unarmed man.

The swordsmen won. The sounds of fighting died, there was a rattle of chains and a few seconds later two figures walked past his cell, pulling a bowed figure after them. Its wrists were shackled behind its back, its ankles hobbled and its head hidden by a rough hood. Behind it a third witch hunter moved slowly, holding a torch in one hand and his bloody forehead in another. The light dimmed as they walked away.

The noise had come from the direction of the voice that had called to him. Was that his mysterious questioner, he wondered? The cells around were silent, probably out of fear that the escorts could come for them. Hoche felt tense. The cell had seemed bad enough, but now he suspected there were worse things to come.

WHY HAD HE killed the witch hunter, he asked himself? Logically he should have hidden or run, to get out of the building as soon as he knew it wasn't empty. Instead, almost without thinking, he had stabbed the man in the throat. It had been unnecessary and dangerous.

No, it had been fear and hate, he told himself. He had been far more tired and scared than he had dared to admit to himself. His experiences in Marienburg had unsettled him more than he wanted to acknowledge, disturbing his image of himself as a man who could cope with anything. Even before that, since he came to Altdorf, he had been shocked out of his sense of self and forced to acknowledge how little of the world and its workings he understood. His self-assured soldier personality was no more than a memory now. Those had been simpler times. He wondered if he could ever go back to them.

The long journey from Marienburg had exhausted him. He had been on edge, and the events of the day had thrown him even further off-balance, with no chance to rest and calm his nerves. Then the conversation with the witch hunters in the inn, their smugness and nonchalant arrogance at the deaths of his comrades, had fired him with a hatred and anger that he could not show at the time. Because of that, because of all those things, he had glimpsed a man in a witch hunter's uniform and had killed him in a single blow. And it had felt good. Better than good: it had felt purifying.

The unhealed wound on his neck throbbed under its filthy bandage. He turned over and tried to go back to sleep.

SOMETHING CHANGED. OUTSIDE, someone with a torch was moving down the corridor. Hoche felt himself drawn to it, like a moth. Anything to relieve his senses from the awful, unending night.

He could not see anything except the wall opposite his cell, but he could hear other inmates calling out, howling and yelling. The sounds echoed, distorting off the stone walls until they sounded like the gibbering of beasts.

The light grew brighter. He strained to see down the corridor. A bald man in rough clothes was pushing a hand-cart, with pieces of black bread, chunks of meat and apples. A ewer of water hung from it, and a strange two-handled cup. Hoche was suddenly aware how thirsty he was. He watched as the man stopped at the cell before his, thrusting bread and fruit through the bars, and holding up the cup so the inmate could drink from it.

The man wheeled the cart towards Hoche's cell and past it. Hoche watched in disbelief.

'Hey!' he shouted. 'What about me?'

The man stopped and turned to look at him. His face was ravaged with scars, his eyes dark pits in the flickering light. 'Nothing for you,' he said.

'Please! Some water! Please!' Hoche shouted, but the man was already pushing his cart away and out of view. He did not look back. Hoche stood at the door, his hands through the bars, watching the light recede and fade to nothing, as if it had never been there.

SOME WHILE LATER, he realised the hooded prisoner had not come back. It was hard to gauge time down here, but he guessed it must have been at least a day, maybe two. Maybe he had been asleep when the witch hunters had returned the man. Maybe he'd been freed, or moved to a different cell. Or escaped. Hoche knew the prisoner could have found other less optimistic fates but he didn't want to think about them.

HE WOKE WITH a start from a dream of night and fire and fighting. The details were not clear, but images of twisted people and the faces of friends flitted in his mind before they faded. Since what happened in Marienburg, he thought, I have not dreamed of drowning. Now I only dream of fire and blood.

In the darkness he whispered prayers to Sigmar for strength, to Verena for justice, to Shallya for mercy and to Morr for the souls of his comrades. As far as he could tell, nobody was listening.

'WE'RE REASONABLE PEOPLE, Lieutenant Hoche. Give us what we want and we can make things easy for you.'

They had come for him at last, chaining his wrists and leading him through a maze of passages and the shouts of other inmates to this large, high-vaulted room. The light from the oil-lamps hurt his eyes. On the table in front of him was a goblet of wine, but his hands were tied behind the back of the chair he sat in. A platter of fruit lay out of reach: apples, plums, even an orange.

On the other side of the long table sat two people. One was Sister Karin, the other a tall, elegant man in his early thirties. His hair had the same dark lustre as the priestess's but his eyes and lips could not have been more different: the former a piercing ice-blue, the latter a thin, terse line. His complexion was white-pale; there was no blood in his face. He wore the tunic of a senior witch hunter. The order's badge of office, a gold warhammer, hung around his neck. They looked healthy, serious, concerned and powerful. They looked like reasonable people.

'What do you want?' he said. His voice rasped dryly in his throat. For a moment he was aware how he must look to the witch hunters: his filthy merchant-robes, still spoiled with white plaster and blood, now with a layer of grime from his cell; his hair matted, his face unshaved, his skin slack from lack of food and water. He wanted so much to be anywhere except here. Anywhere except back in his cell.

'Information,' said the man, and clasped his hands in front of him. His voice was filled with the rich, stretched vowels of a noble upbringing, and his fingers were long and elegant, almost elf-like. If he ever got his hands dirty, he only did it metaphorically, Hoche thought. 'We want to know about three things. Firstly, the Untersuchung. Secondly, your recent mission. Thirdly, the matter of a sect of Chaos-followers among the Knights Panther, the details of which' – he glanced at Sister Karin – 'remain unclear to us.'

'What do I get in return?' Hoche asked. He knew he was in no position to make bargains, but he felt he had to try, if only to show some bravado in the face of these smooth, superior, supercilious beings.

The man smiled. 'That depends what you want.'

'I want my life back,' Hoche said with feeling.

'Your life as a soldier? I see no reason why not. If we receive your co-operation, we can return you to your command under Duke Heller, and no questions asked.' The man smiled. 'Don't look startled. The point is, Lieutenant Hoche, that you were only with the Untersuchung for a short time. A matter of weeks. Not long enough for them to get their claws into you, we believe. If we are satisfied that you are clean of the taint of Chaos, then of course we will arrange for you to be returned to your former life.' He smiled with seeming sincerity. 'I am Lord Gamow and my word carries much weight. If I ask for it, it will be done. The death of a witch hunter notwithstanding.'

Lord Gamow. So this was the man who had ordered the death of the Untersuchung. Hoche could see why Braubach had disliked and distrusted him: even from these few minutes he could tell the man was the polar opposite of the Untersuchung captain, whose sardonic and cynical exterior had concealed a core of humanity. The offer Gamow was making seemed generous, but something dark and sinister lay below its surface and Hoche felt wary of accepting it. What kind of a man would write off the murder of one of his men in exchange for some information? Nevertheless, he was out of options.

'I will give you what I can,' he said.

Gamow smiled. 'Very well. Let us start with your recent mission. What was it?'

Hoche stared at the goblet on the table, saying nothing. He felt incredibly thirsty. 'Let me drink,' he said. 'I have had no water since I came here. I must drink.'

'No water? None at all?' Gamow said. He sounded shocked. Sister Karin walked round the table and lifted the goblet to his lips. It was good wine and strong, but Hoche would have drunk it if it had been horse-piss. He did not stop until the goblet was empty, feeling the cool liquid sluice through his dry mouth like a summer storm, and when he breathed in the air smelled clear and fresh.

A full goblet on a tired empty stomach, a part of his mind noted, you should watch your words now. He ignored it.

'Your mission,' prompted Gamow.

'I went to Marienburg on the trail of a deserter who fled the Untersuchung a year ago. I was not expected to find him.'

'His name?'

'Andreas Reisefertig.'

Gamow nodded, as if Hoche had confirmed something he already knew. 'Start at the beginning. What were your orders, and when did you leave Altdorf?'

He told them everything. He told them about the slaughtered soldiers and the bloodied battle-standard, about the meeting with Duke Heller and his discussion with Bohr, his journey, his meeting with the Knights Panther, and the rest of that night. He told them about Jakob Bäcker, Hunni, Bruno, Anders, Major-General Zerstückein and Gottfried Braubach. He told them about his training, about the books in the shelves, and about the two cultists killed in the warehouse. He told them about Braubach's demand that he swear he would kill Andreas Reisefertig.

He told them about Marienburg, about Father Willem and the cultists, the library and the message. He told them about Gunter Schmölling and the damage to his body and mind. He told them about the knife shaped like the symbol of Tzeentch, and the incident in the temple of Shallya.

Through it all Gamow watched him, nodding in acknowledgement and agreement. Sister Karin refilled Hoche's goblet twice, lifting it to Hoche's lips herself.

Finally it had all been said. He sat back, exhausted and light-headed. He must have been talking for hours. His throat was raw. His buttocks ached from the hard chair seat.

'Thank you, lieutenant,' Gamow said slowly. 'You have an astonishing memory for detail. This fills in much that we suspected but could not prove. It has been a useful morning.'

Morning? To Hoche it felt like the middle of the night. He paused, looking at the platter of fruit. 'I am starved,' he said. 'Please, an apple.'

'Of course. Let us call in the guard to unfasten your wrists so you can eat it yourself. Sister, would you oblige?' Sister Karin rose and went out of the room. Hoche realised she had not said a word throughout the entire session.

'One other thing,' Gamow said smoothly. 'The name of your Untersuchung contact in Marienburg – what was it?'

Had he not named Erasmus Pronk yet? He must have gabbled past that part. How stupid of him. Of course Gamow would want to know it. He opened his mouth to reply, and then he halted. It would be easy to tell everything he knew about the strange man, but was it right? Pronk had saved his life. Was Gamow testing him? Did he already know? Pronk was a deep-cover agent, the people it would have been hardest for the witch hunters to find. And he was in Marienburg, outside the Empire and their jurisdiction.

'We used cover-names,' he said cautiously.

'What was his address? What did he look like?' Gamow demanded.

Hoche stopped. Nothing would be simpler than saying 'Pronk'. One word, a funny little name for a funny little man, and he would get to taste that apple, that beautiful green *Oma Schmidt* like the ones in the orchards around Grünburg, and feel its crisp flesh and its juices in his mouth. He knew how his teeth would pierce its skin, and how it would crunch as he bit into it. He could remember nothing in life he had wanted more.

Pronk had saved that life. He had showed Hoche kindness, and now his own life was ruined because of what had happened to Schmölling. He was a strange man, Hoche thought, but strangeness is not inimical to goodness. Deep down, beneath the tiredness, the hunger and the fumes of wine, he knew that naming Pronk would be wrong; it would be a betrayal. Not just of friendship, nor of the Untersuchung, but of who he was.

Could he do this? He had changed so much. Surely one more shift in his personality wouldn't matter. He stared at the apple. He was so hungry. It would be so easy.

Such a little thing. One word. One word and he was a free man. The wine encouraged him, making it all seem simple. Say it. Say 'Pronk'. Don't think about it. Just say it.

But he was not a man who gave his friends to his enemies, and he could not become that. It was a matter of honour, of sense of self. Surely Lord Gamow would understand that. He was, as he had said himself, a reasonable man.

Hoche licked his dry lips. 'I cannot,' he said. 'I owe him my life.'

There was a pause, an uncomfortable silence.

'It is a matter of honour,' he added.

'A soldier's honour,' said Gamow, rising to his feet. He crossed his hands behind him and walked around the table to where Hoche sat. 'I thank Sigmar for it, because without it our armies would fail, our troops would falter and run before our enemies, the Empire descend into civil war. It is a soldier's honour that holds it all together. However,' he moved behind Hoche's chair, 'the good soldiers are the ones who understand there is a point when honour is not enough.'

Hoche plunged forward towards the table, the chair yanked from under him. He yelled, twisting in his seat to stop his head ramming into the hard edge of the wood. He was partly successful. His face did not smash down on the sharp surface, but the edge caught the side of his skull. There was a crunch, then a jarring shock as the chair hit the floor, crushing his right arm beneath it.

He lay dazed, his vision and sense of balance shaken by the blow to his head. He was sideways, his hands still bound behind the chair, his head partly under the table. It was confusing. What had happened? How had he fallen?

Above him Gamow's face appeared, looking down at him, it seemed, from a great height.

'Loyalty!' Gamow said and kicked him in the stomach, hard. He gagged, vomiting wine, and tried to double up, raising his knees to protect his groin and gut. The heavy chair held him down.

'Loyalty is more important than honour!' Gamow said and kicked him in the stomach again. 'Loyalty is what keeps this empire together! Loyalty to your emperor!'

Hoche twisted and yelled. Gamow kicked him in the gut.

'Loyalty to your country!'

Kick to the ribs.

'Loyalty to your race!'

Kick to the neck.

'Loyalty to your blood!'

Kick to the head.

'Loyalty—'

Kick.

'to—'

Kick.

'your—'

Kick.

'god!'

There was a rap at the door. Gamow stopped, panting, his face sheet-white with anger and adrenaline. 'Think about what I've said,' he said. 'We will continue this discussion later.' Then, to the door, 'Enter!'

Hoche lay on the floor, aching and bleeding, his head too filled with pain to think. From where he lay he could see the bottom of the door as it opened and a pair of high black leather boots with silver buckles and a slimmer pair of boots under a dark robe enter.

'Take this man back to his cell,' Gamow ordered. 'Give him water now, but keep him off solid food.'

'A doctor?' asked Sister Karin's voice.

Gamow spat on the floor. 'Get him out of my sight.'

THEY DRAGGED HOCHE down the corridors, to the shouts and screeches of the other prisoners, pushed him into his cell and bolted the door after him.

He crawled to the bed and huddled there. His head roared with pain. His chest and belly ached so hard he could hardly breathe. His mouth was filled with the taste of blood. He would be pissing blood for a week, if he had anything in his bladder to piss with. Why hadn't he given them Pronk's name? He would still be in the room if he had, drinking wine and eating fruit and talking like civilised people. Like reasonable people.

He tried to laugh, but it hurt to even think of it. Reasonable people. Reasonable people negotiate, they don't pull the chairs from under their prisoners and kick them almost to unconsciousness. Hoche had the measure of Gamow now, and he agreed with Braubach's opinion of the man.

He moved, trying to find a position that didn't mean lying on his wounds. There was a hard lump under the ragged blanket. It hadn't been there before.

With careful, slow movements he sat up and pulled it out. It was a rectangle of wood, about six inches by ten. One side of it was covered in a waxy substance. Marks were scratched in it.

Slowly he let his fingertips trace the marks. Words in block capitals, inscribed into the wax with some sharp point. He felt it out, spelling it letter by letter:

DO NOT GIVE ME UP. KEEP HOPE AND FAITH. I WILL HELP YOU.

What was that, he wondered. Another way to break his spirit by promising false optimism? Or a real message from a sympathiser among the guards? Either way, it did him no good. With the nail of his index finger he gouged 'NEXT TIME LEAVE FOOD' across the inscription, threw the plaque to the floor, and turned back to his pain.

It was only there, curled up in the darkness like a foetus in the womb, more alone than he had ever been, he realised he could have answered Gamow's question with a false name.

WHEN HE WOKE he was stiff all over. His fresh bruises throbbed. He felt his face, mapping the cuts and splits, and then unwrapped the bandage from around his neck and gingerly touched the wound there. It was still puffed up but he felt no pain from it so the infection and inflammation must have gone away. It felt moist, so it must still be healing. He retied the bandage. One less wound to worry about.

* * *

HE LET HIS thoughts carry him away to Grünburg, to the streets and alleys where he had played as a child, the faces he had known and might never see again. The last time he had written to Marie was weeks ago, before he'd left Marienburg. She would be worried. He had never mentioned the Untersuchung to her. Dear, sweet, simple Marie. She would have no idea why the letters had stopped, no way of linking that to the news of a cult of Chaos worshippers caught and burnt in Altdorf. Or maybe witch hunters had already been to Grünburg, looking for him, spreading word of his disgrace. In that case she would think him already dead, burnt with the others. Nobody knew he was still alive. Here, trapped in this dark place, it was as if he had been buried.

His chances of leaving here alive were null, he understood. For all his sweet words and wine, Lord Gamow lived up to the implacable reputation of the Order of Witch Hunters as it had been in the days after the fall of Mordheim, centuries ago, when the order had run out of control, a law unto itself. In Gamow's eyes he was tainted by Chaos and nothing could remove that taint. There were only two ways he would leave here: on the way to a place of execution, or already dead.

Months ago Braubach had told him he was a dead man. He had not believed it then, but he believed it now. He resolved that if they were going to take his life, they would not take his honour with it. He would not give them the information they needed to find Pronk. They could kill him in the attempt, but as he was going to die here anyway, it did not matter. If his death was to be unnoticed by the world, it was still better to die with a shred of honour than with none.

SOMETHING IN THE distance was making wet sounds, like slobbering, like the mastication of fat jowls. He wondered what it was. Perhaps some faint sound amplified by the strange architecture of this deep, dank place – perhaps even a natural sound like water trickling from the ceiling, dripping in odd patterns.

Or maybe it was something more sinister. He had seen pigs slaughtered and butchered, and there was a quality to the sound of the way that guts and innards would pour from an inexpertly slit stomach, to slop to the ground in a wet heap.

Maybe some poor soul had given up or snapped, found something sharp and used it to eviscerate himself. Or…

He turned away and tried to think his way back to Grünburg.

IT WAS PARTICULARLY cold. He had wrapped himself in the blanket and huddled in a corner as he waited for his cup of water. He heard the cries and pleading before he heard the boots: four heavy sets marching down the corridor, the dim aura of torchlight proceeding them. Not the food-wagon, he thought. And they're not bringing another unfortunate with them. They must be coming for me again.

He was wrong. The four guards moved past his cell. Despite himself, he moved to the door to see if he could see anything. His mind was numb from lack of stimulation, and even shadows were better than the eternal night of imprisonment. He was desperate for someone to talk to, but every time he had shouted to the voice who had called him on his first night, there had been no answer.

He couldn't see them, but he could guess from the length and direction of their shadows that they had put their torches into wall-sconces by a cell-door some twenty feet away and stood in a group, discussing something in low voices. The words were unclear but their tone was worried. He heard the sound of a crossbow being drawn and nocked, chains, and a rusted bolt being drawn.

Something rumbled, so low he couldn't tell if he was hearing it or feeling it. Despite the cold, Hoche felt his hackles begin to rise. Then the note changed and he recognised the sound. It was a growl. What in Sigmar's name was growling down here?

There was a crash; something heavy throwing itself against a door. Someone was muttering a prayer.

The crash came again. The third time he heard a spang as something metal broke and ricocheted across the corridor, and an instant later the crash of the door rebounding on its hinges. Then many things at once: someone shouting, 'Now!'; a cry of 'Sigmar!', a crossbow firing, a roaring snarl. Thuds, slaps and crunches. The shadows on the wall outside danced and flew in confusion. There was a flash of light, hurting his eyes, and an instant later a sharp explosion of flame flashed down the corridor. A fire-ball spell: Hoche recognised it from his lessons with Hunni von Sisenuf. So the chanting hadn't been a prayer, he thought, and: witch hunters aren't supposed to use magic.

Something snarled again. Someone shrieked, yelling and pleading, and there was a sound like a young tree-branch being twisted and splintered. Hoche recognised that too, he'd heard arms and legs breaking often enough. Someone else was shouting orders above the screaming. Nobody seemed to be paying attention.

Then the shadows shifted and darkened as something moved to blot out the light and Hoche involuntarily shrunk away from the door. Whatever had been in the other cell was running down the corridor, away from its attackers, towards him. Its footsteps were fast but heavy. It was clearly injured, but none of the witch hunters were following it.

Hoche only caught a glimpse of it in the faint light, but a glimpse was enough. A huge, misshapen body, massive legs, a beast-like head atop hunched shoulders, a broad mouth with too many teeth. Slit eyes. Muscles. And, thinking about it later, he remembered something about the way the skin had glistened in the torchlight that suggested scales.

It ran away. One of the witch hunters shouted something after it, perhaps a warning. For a few seconds there was only the sound of its fading footsteps, and groans from the men who had tried to subdue it. Then there was a different roar, a fusillade of muskets and flintlocks, their thunderclaps reverberating and echoing down the stone walls. It sounded like enough firepower to tear a man to pieces. It sounded as if it had.

AFTER THEY HAD carried the dead witch hunter away and a carpenter had fixed the door back on its hinges and hammered new bolts into its timbers, and all was quiet and dark once more, Hoche heard the voice again. It was calling from down the corridor, close to where the fight had been. He couldn't make out what it was saying, but he got up from his bed and moved to the door.

'What in Sigmar's name was that?' he said.

'It ate the food,' said the voice, hoarse and low. 'It ate the meat. There are things in the bread. Drink the water but do not eat the food.'

'Answer me! Was it human, or some beast?'

'I told you, new man, the food makes us unclean.'

'What do you mean, unclean?'

'You said you were clean, new man. If you wish to stay so, do not eat the food.'

'How can I live without eating?' Hoche asked. The voice did not reply and the corridors were silent. He held the cold bars for a moment longer and then returned to bed, wondering how it could be, after he had been down here for so long, he was still the 'new man'.

THE NEXT TIME the guard with the food came by, he held the cup of water while Hoche greedily swallowed his few mouthfuls, then pushed a lump of hard bread through the dull iron bars. 'Knock yourself out,' he said.

Hoche sat on his bed and held it in his hands. He held it to his nose, recognising the sharp smell of yeast and rye, feeling the coarseness of the cheaply milled flour that had been used to make it, finding whole grains in there. He had been without food for what felt like weeks. He had feel himself thinning, his muscles wasting, his thoughts becoming dull and tired from lack of nutrition. How could he not eat it? He was a dead man already. If the bread hastened his death or moved it further away, it did not matter either way.

He bit into it, gnawing hungrily at its dense texture, savouring the acrid flavour on his long-neglected taste-buds. He deliberately ate slowly so his empty stomach did not revolt at the sudden invasion. He thought about keeping some for later, but by the time he reached a decision he had already finished the last crumbs.

He lay back on his bed and thought about what a pure pleasure the act of eating was, how simple, how satisfying. Then he slept, and when he woke up he was somewhere else.

* * *

'SO GOOD TO see you again, Lieutenant Hoche,' said Lord Gamow, looking down at him. 'I apologise for the restraints, but we had a little trouble recently, so we take more precautions now.'

He was staring at the ceiling, strapped to some kind of table. His arms and legs were tied, and a belt held his head down against the cool wood. The room, what he could see of it, was walled with bare stone, not plaster. Racks of tools hung from iron hooks: saws, pliers, hammers, awls. More hooks in the ceiling held pulleys, half-inch ropes over them. There was a smell of burning coal and hot metal, and under it sweat and roasted meat. The dull taint of stale blood hung in the air. In one corner was a door, heavy and oak, probably locked.

'Very good. Your Untersuchung training is still in place, I see,' Gamow said. 'I imagine that even at this moment you are compiling a list of items that could be used as weapons, possible escape routes, all that. Best of luck.' He walked to the far end of the table, where Hoche could not see him. 'Once you've realised how futile that is, I hope you remember our last conversation. Honour and loyalty are all very well for soldiers and citizens, but neither are much use for a man in your position.'

He reappeared on the other side of the table. 'I imagine that you've been doing some thinking,' he said. 'You'll have reached one of three conclusions. Number one: you will give me the information I ask for, without any trouble, in exchange for your freedom – which is still a possibility. Number two: you will give me information but it will be incorrect, either because you do not know the truth or because you wish to hide it from me. The former is foolish, the latter unadulteratedly so. Sister Karin has been schooled in the art of detecting lies from a man's voice, his expression, the tension in his muscles and the beating of his heart. She will be watching you. Or thirdly, you may have chosen not to co-operate and to say nothing at all. That is not stupid, that is simply wrong. You will tell us. You may not think so, but you will.'

Gamow vanished from view. Hoche said nothing. He knew that if he began to talk, even to voice his refusal to answer, it would be one step towards breaking. If you start to communicate with your torturer, it makes it easier for them to crack you, Braubach had said. He lay back. So Sister Karin was here, though he couldn't see her. He knew she could do what Lord Gamow described: he had been taught some of the same skills by the Untersuchung, and Hunni von Sisenuf had been a master of them.

He could see no reason to change his mind from the course he had decided. The talk of freedom was only a tempting lie. It and Gamow's smooth words were nothing more than a veneer over the rough truth: that he was bound to a table in a torture chamber, with two ruthless people prepared to get the secrets out of his head if they had to bore holes in his skull to do it.

On the other side of the room was a hiss and rattle as someone poked a brazier of hot coals. He could smell the strange hard tang of metal brought to red heat. In his future he could imagine only pain. Well. There were worse things, he told himself.

Gamow loomed into sight above him, wearing a white apron. In one hand he held something like sheep-shears, half way between scissors and pliers, long and wicked. 'Many of my colleagues believe that to be effective, pain has to be seen. The inflictee must witness his own defilement,' he said. 'I cleave to the other view. I believe the true horror of torture lies in the unseen and unexpected. You know that whatever happens will be painful, but you cannot anticipate the nature and scope of the pain, its texture or duration. In its unknowing state, the mind amplifies the pain, and as the Reman scholar Lipocratus informs us, it is the pain itself, not its expectation, observation or dread, that leads the inflictee to give up his secrets. That is why I am going to start on your feet.'

He moved out of Hoche's field of vision. Hoche tried to pull his head up, to see what Gamow was doing. but the leather strap restrained him. There was a sound of blades sliding against each other, and something sharp and cold pricked the sole of his left foot. From somewhere to the south came Gamow's voice. 'You would save us both a great deal of trouble if you talked now,' it said. 'I'm a very busy man.'

Hoche tightened his lips.

'Very well then,' Gamow said. Hoche braced himself, tensing his muscles where the sharp point was still touching him. With awful suddenness something dug deep into the sole of his other foot, above the heel, and so far it felt like it would come out the top. The pain hit him so hard it drove the air from his lungs before he could scream, and his whole body contorted, twisting against the tight straps, desperate to break away and curl up. Through the agony he could feel the instrument moving, turning inside his flesh. It hurt worse than anything he had ever experienced, and it went on and on.

He had no idea how long it lasted, but eventually the anguish began to ebb. Out of sight, Gamow chuckled. 'I think you begin to see the truth in the words of Lipocratus,' he said. 'Is there anything you want to tell me? Other than the fact I'm a foul whore-son pig-sticker or any of the other usual insults?'

Hoche opened his eyes and breathed deeply. To resist torture, focus on the furthest thing you can see, Braubach had instructed him – years ago, it felt like – and think of the furthest thing you can imagine. Don't think about what's happening. Lose yourself and you lose the pain.

It had sounded convincing at the time. Hoche stared at the ceiling and tried to think of Grünburg. Then something sliced through a layer of skin and flesh, peeling it away, setting his nerves on fire, and he screamed.

The next few minutes were unbearable. After that it got worse.

AFTER AN ETERNITY of agonies it was over. There was no sound in the room except for Hoche's ragged breathing and the slow drip of viscous fluids falling to the floor. Gamow's face, out of focus, blurred into view above Hoche's tear-filled eyes. His face and hair were blood-spattered and he was smiling.

'Well,' he said, 'I think we've got the measure of each other now.' He raised an elegant goblet to his thin lips and sipped from it. 'Your resilience is strong for a man in your condition. Do you have anything to say to me?'

Hoche licked his dry lips with a dry tongue. The pain was less than it had been, but it still made it hard to find enough clear space in his head to form coherent thoughts. He said nothing.

Gamow looked thoughtful. 'Nothing? Not a word?' he asked. 'You know, I wonder why you're working so hard to protect a minor, almost inconsequential member of your organisation when there are so many larger fish we could be chasing. Think of this' – he waved his hand vaguely in the direction of Hoche's feet – 'as an exploratory mission, a scouting trip to see how much pain you can bear, how much further we're going to have to go in future sessions. You'll notice that while I was slicing you apart, I wasn't demanding the name of your Marienburg contact.'

He bent closer to Hoche's face. 'Do you know why?' he said, with breath that smelled of rich dark wines.

Hoche said nothing.

'Because he's dead.'

It had to be a bluff. Hoche lay still, his sweat-covered clothes suddenly chill on his body, staring up, trying not to listen. Gamow straightened and took another sip from the goblet.

'Erasmus Pronk is dead,' he said, stretching the syllables of the name. 'Your colleagues gave us his identity before we'd even dragged them out of the barracks. We sent agents to Marienburg the same day. You probably passed them on the road. Ironic the way these things happen, isn't it?

Hoche closed his eyes. Tears, born of pain, fatigue and wild sorrow, trickled either side of his face, past his temples and were lost in his hair.

He wanted to grieve for Pronk, but he knew that to survive this and outwit Gamow he had to keep his mind as clear as possible. There would time for mourning later. He hoped.

'So,' said Gamow from somewhere on the other side of the room, 'that pain-befuddled head of yours is probably trying to work out whether this is some intricate game of bluff and double-bluff. How much do I already know? Was I certain that Pronk was the man or had I just heard the name? Has something in your reaction told me if I was right or wrong?

And above all, why would I have caused you so much pain if I already knew the answer?

'They are all good questions, and I think that as an intelligent man you understand that if I was to answer them it would spoil the fun for both of us. But I'll give you a moment to consider them, as well as two new questions that along with your calves will comprise the next act of this entertainment.'

His voice was now coming from Hoche's side. Hoche kept his eyes closed, his breathing shallow, trying to think his way back to the escape of Grünburg. It seemed too far away, hidden behind mists of deception and hills of pain.

'The questions are these,' said Gamow. 'Firstly, we know that the Untersuchung placed a deep-cover agent within the Order of Witch Hunters here in Altdorf. Who is that agent?'

Hoche did not move. The question meant nothing to him. Even if it had he would not have answered.

'Secondly, where is Andreas Reisefertig?'

Hoche said nothing.

'Would you like some water before we restart?'

Hoche said nothing.

Gamow sighed. 'You're going to be a tough nut to crack, aren't you?'

Hoche said nothing. Abruptly he felt fingers pulling his eyelids apart, forcing him to look upwards. Gamow's face leered down at him from inches away.

'You will crack,' he said. 'I will get answers, if I have to flay every inch of skin from your body, reduce your muscles to shreds, and hollow the marrow from your living bones to do it. And I will do those things. I have done them before, many times. I will get my answers.'

Gamow stood up, picked up a knife from the table and began to cut away the stained and soiled merchant's clothes that Hoche still wore, piece by piece, dropping the scraps to the floor. 'You may ask yourself how it is that a man of the cloth like myself can do such vile things. There are many reasons. Because I know that what I do is in the service of Sigmar. Because giving pain to the enemies of the Empire gives me pleasure. And if I am honest, because I enjoy it. I enjoy the control. I enjoy the mastery. I enjoy the practical application of the science of pain. And I enjoy seeing the blood. In particular, I will enjoy seeing your blood.' He licked his lips.

Hoche said nothing. Gamow cut away the last of his shirt, leaving him bare-chested and goose-fleshed in the cold air of the torture room. He began to slice at the bandage around Hoche's neck.

'You still think you can hold out,' he said. 'You think you're in control of your body and your mind. But you're wrong.'

The bandage came away in his hands and he stared down. As far as Hoche could tell, he was looking at the scarred-over wound on his neck. His face showed an expression of surprise, giving way to pleasure.

'Oh yes, you're wrong,' he said quietly. 'Lieutenant Hoche, you are full of little surprises.' He reached out a finger and caressed the scar. Hoche could feel the gentle stroke of his fingertip as it ran over its odd contours. 'The next few weeks will be interesting for both of us,' Gamow said, 'but for now, this discussion is over.' He took a couple of steps down the table and rammed something hard into the ruined flesh of Hoche's right foot. Every nerve screamed in sudden agony and Hoche blacked out.

HE CAME ROUND in pain. He was lying in darkness once more. The air was cold on his bare skin. His feet were unbearable.

Gingerly he felt his surroundings, both relieved and despairing that his hands recognised the familiar outlines of his cell. On the bed was a pile of clothes, cheaply made but thick, and next to them a wooden platter with some bread, a slice of some unidentifiable meat and an apple on it.

Slowly he sat up and began to pull on the clothes, moving gently so not to jar or sway his feet lest the pain increase. Someone had bandaged them, and his neck too, but he was too afraid to feel below his knees to see what awful damage had been done there, or find how much of him was missing. Dressing took a long time. Then he lay down and ate the food. The bread had a strange gritty texture and the meat was chewy and bland, but it felt like a banquet. Then, as he pushed away the wooden platter, he realised it was coated with wax. There were more words scratched on it.

So they had brought food after all.

He traced the words with his fingers. THERE IS HOPE. RESIST THE QUESTIONS AND YOU WILL BE HELPED.

More useless platitudes. He dropped it to the floor, tried to find a position where his feet hurt the least, and began to think.

So the Untersuchung had placed an agent in the witch hunters, and somehow he had escaped the purges. That might explain who had been leaving the messages for him. One of the guards, perhaps.

And for some reason the witch hunters wanted to know about Andreas Reisefertig. No matter how he worried at it, Hoche could not untangle that one. Why were they interested in a renegade Untersuchung agent who had disappeared eighteen months ago? Certainly he was a heretic by association, and the evidence from Marienburg suggested he was involved in something, but it didn't seem important enough for torture. He had already told them all he knew of Reisefertig; there was nothing more to say.

It had to be another of Gamow's mind-games. The witch hunter would refuse to believe that he knew nothing else, so that he would be more likely to tell anything he knew about the deep-cover agent, to appease his torturer and make the pain stop.

He didn't know if that was right, but it fitted what he knew of Gamow and his deceitful ways.

And Pronk was dead.

Hoche lay in the silence and recited the traditional blessings for the dead. They were the prayers he had learned in the army, to be said over the bodies of the Empire's soldiers. Pronk had been a civilian and a citizen of the Wasteland, but Hoche was sure the little man wouldn't mind.

EVERY TIME HE heard the yells heralding a visit from guards or the food-cart he lay in dread, waiting for them to carry him back to the torture-room and Gamow, that voice with its cloak of civility hiding the brutality below. But each time the footsteps passed his cell, and after a while he learned to count the passage of days by the rumbling passing of the food-cart, and tried not to number them.

They were feeding him now, lumps of the gritty bread and coarse meat, undercooked. Starvation rations, and yet he did not feel unfit or unhealthy. His feet pained him less every day, though he couldn't walk on them. His beard grew. From time to time the scar on his neck ached or gave him strange pains, and he would press on it through the bandage, and eventually it would cease.

His waking hours were spent in daydreams of Grünburg, the friends of his childhood and the faces of his family. His sleeping dreams were darker and more troubled, fighting endless battles against faceless warriors, the darkness lit by the glare of red flames, and broken by the sound of a strange ululating voice that he knew he had never heard before, and yet which he recognised.

'NEW MAN! NEW man!' came the cry. From where Hoche lay it had a strange echo, as if a man was speaking and his words were copied an instant later by the shrill voice of a child. Was he still the new man? It felt like he had been living in the darkness forever, but nobody else was answering. 'What do you want?' he called back from his bed.

'Are you eating the food, new man?'

'If I did not eat it, I would have starved weeks ago,' Hoche shouted, hearing his voice reverberate down the corridor.

'Then you are a new man in truth.'

'What do you mean?' Hoche shouted. There was no sound for a moment until the voice came again, the strange under-notes of the child's piping adding an eerie counterpoint.

'Have you received a gift from the gods?'

'No gifts, no blessings, no solace,' Hoche called. 'The gods have forgotten us here, buried so far under their temples.'

'Maybe we speak of different gods, new man,' the voice said, and Hoche felt a chill run down his spine. He did not answer.

THE FOOD-CART had come and gone twice more. Hoche lay in half-sleep, remembering his early days in the army, the unaccustomed strain of order, discipline and responsibility, how he had grown used to them, and good at them.

Something pulled him to alertness. There was a movement in his room. Something almost silent, but not so quiet that it did not gently scuff against the grit on the floor and move the still, damp air. Something about the size of a large dog.

'Who's there?' he whispered. 'Who are you?'

He could sense the unseen figure shift its weight. A gentle hand rested on his upper arm. 'The sun is in the tenth house,' said a soft voice. He recognised it.

'Sister Karin,' he said. 'You left the plaques?'

'Yes. Can you walk?' she asked.

'I can crawl.'

'Then crawl. You have to get out of here.'

She helped him to all fours. Even without putting weight on his feet, their pressure on the floor felt like treading on the roasted stones by a blacksmith's forge, but he could do it without crying out, and that was enough. They made slow, silent progress out of the cell and down the dark corridor, Sister Karin leading, he following like a dog on the ground. It took a long time before he saw the first torchlight in the distance and knew he was away from the cells.

'Is it safe to rest a moment?' he asked. Her nod was just visible in the half-light and he slumped against the wall, stretching his legs to take the weight off his agonised feet. He stared down at them, expecting to see the bandages dripping with fresh blood, but the only stains were dark and encrusted. Karin sat beside him.

'Where are we going?' he asked.

'You're escaping. This is your miraculous one-man jail-break. Upstairs are clothes and a purse of gold, and there's a horse tethered outside. Ride south and make your way through the mountains to Tilea. They don't have much truck with Imperial witch hunters down there and you'll be safe. Or head to Kislev, if you prefer.'

Hoche said nothing, trying to understand what was going on. Was this another of Gamow's tricks, to raise his hopes only to dash them later? Beside him, Karin scanned the corridor, checking both ways.

'What is this unholy place?' he asked.

'The witch hunters' prison. They hold heretics here for questioning. Mutants too; Lord Gamow studies them.' She looked around. 'I couldn't risk you in another torture session,' she said. 'I'm sure Braubach taught you well, but I was afraid you'd give me away.'

'Give what away?' Hoche asked.

She stared at him. 'You don't need to lie to me,' she said. 'I know you know. Braubach told you.'

What did he tell me, Hoche thought. Instead he said, 'Is Braubach dead?'

She said nothing, but in the faint torchlight Hoche saw a single tear glisten on her cheek. Suddenly he understood it all, from their first strange conversation in the Tilted Windmill to her reasons for helping him escape now.

Sister Karin was the Untersuchung's agent among the witch hunters. She was the one who Hunni von Sisenuf had told him about, the one Braubach had trained, and who had been his intimate. She believed that Braubach had told Hoche this secret, and she was helping him escape before he could crack under torture and reveal her to Gamow.

'Why did you help them capture me on the roof?' he said. 'You knew it would endanger you.'

'I wasn't thinking,' she said. 'Or I was thinking like a witch hunter. Lieutenant Hoche, the Untersuchung is dead. You have to understand that. Its members are dead, its mission is over, its ideals are dust. Time rolls on and we must find new paths for our lives. Understand the situation and make the best of it. I have. You must too.'

He stared at her, feeling the bravado in her words and the sorrow that lay under them. She had loved Braubach, he understood now, and in the Tilted Windmill had been confused and hurt by his aggression and insolence. But he had been playing the new roles that had been assigned to them: opposites, not lovers. Now she found herself as a witch hunter, Lord Gamow's lover if the men in the Fist and Glove were right, and she was trying to convince herself that she was happy to play the part. Hoche hoped for her sake that she succeeded.

'I'm rested. Let's go,' he said.

THEY REACHED THE stone antechamber at the top of the helix of stairs, with its wooden door that led outside. Karin passed him new clothes, and he sat on a chair to strip off the ragged prison-wear. In the light from the oil-lamps in alcoves on the wall, he was startled to see how thin his arms were, how wasted his muscles, how exposed his ribs. The act of dressing felt strange, like a half-forgotten skill. The hardest part was pulling boots over his bandaged feet.

'A horse is tethered at the gate,' she said. 'There's food and wine in your saddlebags, and a dagger. I couldn't get you a sword.'

'How did you know there would be no guards?' he asked.

She grinned at him. 'It's the night before Mondstille. Half are in the temple for the midnight service, the other half are drunk.'

Mondstille, the great feast-day at the end of the year. So he had been in the prison six, maybe seven weeks. He didn't know if that seemed a long time or not: part of him felt he had been there forever, and yet for another part it felt like a blink, a dream already fading. He pulled on the clothes: thick wool britches, vest, linen shirt, a jerkin with a high collar and a travelling cloak. He fastened it around his shoulders. Karin reached out and tugged it higher.

'Keep your neck hidden, for Sigmar's sake,' she said.

Hoche looked at her, puzzled. 'Thank you,' he said.

'Don't thank me, just go. The sooner you're out of Altdorf, the safer we'll both be.'

He stood on feet that ached like fire, put one hand on the door latch and looked back at her. She smiled, and for an instant he saw a different face, a happiness he hadn't seen for half a year, and he knew where he would ride first.

'Happy Mondstille,' he said and opened the door.

There could have been anything on the other side. He expected men with swords, Lord Gamow laughing, crossbow bolts piercing his body. He didn't care.

The door swung wide, its rectangle framing nothing but the night and the city. A chill breeze blew in, bringing with it the smell of the world. He stepped outside and stood for a moment, marvelling, ignoring the pain from his feet. He breathed deeply. His eyes were running. It's the light, he told himself, and the cold air. From the sky and stars he guessed it was approaching midnight. It was a wonderful clear night, the crispness of frost in the air, clean and cleansing. He felt refreshed, revitalised, returned to life.

A horse was standing at the temple gate, tied to the hitching-post by its reins. He hobbled to the post and unfastened them, then climbed into the saddle – no strength or energy to swing himself up – and gently geed the horse into motion, trotting away down the street. He did not look back.

He did not ride for the south gate. After a few hundred yards he turned left, down a side-street and away from the city walls, making for the great square and the Cathedral of Sigmar.

There were people on the streets in winter clothes, rich with colour, and occasionally a street-trader with a brazier selling hot chestnuts, chunks of sausage or stew served in thick bowls of hard-baked bread. The smell of food made his saliva run, but he knew it was dangerous to stop. Every extra second he spent in the city was an added danger, every person he spoke to an extra witness for the manhunt that would surely follow his escape. Just being here was perilous, he knew, but there was one final thing he had to do before he left Altdorf.

The cathedral was full, the citizens in their finery worshipping, giving praise for the year just past and making their prayers for the one to come. The pews were crowded all the way up to the high altar and there was a throng of late-comers at the back. They did not look round as Hoche, shoulders hunched and head lowered, pushed his limping way through them to the aisle that ran along the west side of the building.

There were no people standing here and his slow path across the pattern of black-and-white tiles was clear, past the tombs of dead emperors and long-forgotten Grand Theogonists, statues of saints, relics and doorways.

The side-chapel of Sigmar the Crusader was a third of the way down and he disappeared into its shadows. It was unlit and unoccupied as he had hoped: nobody prayed for war or gave thanks for past ones at Mondstille. A solitary candle burned low on the altar, casting pale light onto the statue of the god in his armour by the Tilean artist Hawkslay. The deep shadows around its eyes and face made it look corpse-like, a ghost dressed for battle. It reminded Hoche of a figure from his dreams of fire, and he shivered.

He sat in the rearmost pew, resting the searing pain in his feet and surprised to find himself out of breath after so little exercise. Then he dropped to his knees and reached in the darkness below the seat, feeling across the dusty floor. It was still there: the cloth-wrapped journal he had hidden in this spot before he was arrested. He pulled it out slowly and looked down. The dried leaf he had tucked into the fold of cloth was still there: nobody had tampered with it.

He lifted the book. It was heavy in his hands, his last connection to the Untersuchung and the way of seeing the world that Braubach had taught him. He was tempted to leave it here, to abandon that part of himself as Sister Karin had suggested, but there were answers he had to find, truths he had to know. The book was his only hope of learning them. He tucked it inside his new jerkin, smoothing the fabric so the lump did not show.

Then he hobbled to the small altar, took a new candle and lit it, and prayed for the Fifth Reikland Pikemen, for the Untersuchung, and for the souls of Rudolf Schulze and Gottfried Braubach. He was about to ask for the god's blessings for himself, but held back. It would be wrong to pray for himself here. He was no longer a soldier, he was a fugitive. He would find a better place and a better time to make his peace with Sigmar.

Outside in the cathedral the service was over and people were milling out into the streets, talking and laughing, calling out Mondstille blessings, heading home to jugs of mulled wine, pies and cakes, sweetmeats and the company of friends and family. Hoche felt alone among this bubbling torrent of humanity, isolated and cut off from it. He did not know them and they could not know him. He needed time to rest, to think, to regain his sense of being human. Grünburg was the place for that, and Mondstille week the time. If he rode hard he could be there in under four days.

He made his slow, painful way out, remounted his horse and rode to the south gate, passing though the needle's eye and returning the guards' Mondstille greetings with a raised hand. The Nuln road stretched away into the distance, lit silver by moonlight on the frost. A new year lay ahead. He did not know what it would bring, but for the first time in months he was eager to find out.

Chapter Nine
LEAVING IT BEHIND

HE RODE LONG into the night. The moon was bright enough to illuminate the countryside for miles around: fields divided into strips and ploughed, the bare earth black in the moonlight, pastures and commons dotted with sleeping sheep, rabbits that scattered away at the disturbance, villages lying silent and ghostly, bathed in pale shadows. Once a deer looked up from the road ahead and leaped away.

Above him the sky was full of stars and constellations: the scorpion, the serpent, the gibbet and the axe, brilliant in the darkness. He hoped to see a ring around the moon or another sign of good luck, but there was nothing like that this night. Sigmar's birth, so the priests said, had been heralded by a twin-tailed comet blazing in the heavens. Hoche had never even seen a shooting star.

He stayed on the main road, eager to put miles between himself and Altdorf. Later, he decided, he would take one of the tracks through the Reikwald forest, to avoid pursuit. It would be safe enough. After all it was Mondstille, and even bandits had families, homes and a need to celebrate the passing of the year.

The air was cold in his lungs, his face numb from the wind and the night, the horse warm and vital as it cantered under him. He wrapped his cloak around him and grinned into its woollen folds. The world outside the prison felt so vivid. It filled him with the strength of its sensations and the energy of freedom. He wanted to stand in the saddle and shout. He could sense every muscle in his body wanting to be used and stretched, tested and exercised, and he laughed out loud: let the witch hunters come. He could dodge their bolts, parry their spells, duel armies and leave them broken and beaten.

He felt as if he could run alongside his horse for miles, leap trees, chase the deer and outpace it, catch it up and lift it over his head, tear its neck open and let its blood pour over him, bathing in its heat, letting it splash into his upturned mouth and drinking it down as the beast thrashed its life out.

He stopped abruptly, his horse standing in the road. Where in hell had that thought come from?

THE MOON SET and an hour later the sun rose, staining the eastern clouds with pink. He stopped by a stream and splashed freezing water on his face, gasping, then scrubbed fiercely at his skin with his cloak. After two months underground he would be filthy and he did not want people to remember him. He rummaged in the saddlebags, finding bread, boiled eggs and cheese, and ate while the horse grazed on frost-rimed grass.

He knew his horse was tired, and so was he. His muscles had atrophied while he was in prison and it would take work to rebuild his strength, no matter how energised he felt from his escape. But every mile he put between him and Altdorf widened the circle that pursuers would have to search. He kept riding.

Not long past noon, past the village of Rechtlich and with the foothills of the Hagercrybs rising above the forest to the south, he turned a bend in the road and saw a coaching inn. There was still plenty of daylight but he had to rest a few hours. If the moon was as bright tonight, he could travel on later.

No groom ran from the stables, the windows were shuttered and the door closed, but smoke rose from the chimneys and he was hopeful. He tethered his horse, and walked to the door on legs that felt like aspic. I am Leo Deistadt, a traveller, he thought, carrying urgent news to Grünburg. No, Kemperbad. He rattled the heavy iron ring fixed to the door.

There were faint sounds from the other side, bolts were drawn back and the door swung inwards. Even before he could see the fire and feel the heat of the room spill out, he could smell the meat. Then a great round figure stepped out to block the doorway, carrying a curved knife.

'Come in, traveller, come in! Mondstille greetings to you!' it boomed. 'No greater blessing than a stranger to share the Mondstille feast, and we're sitting down to carve this very moment. This year my wife has stuffed the goose with chestnuts and cherries, and you won't believe its succulence. Welcome! Welcome! Sit! Sit! Sit!'

Hoche let himself be pulled into the inn and sat at the table. A glass of hot sweet wine was pressed into one hand, a cloth napkin into the other. The fire was at his back, drawing the cold from his bones. The landlord who had greeted him was introducing himself as Stefan Kanonbach, his wife Olga, their children – one daughter was comfortably fat, the image of her mother with her face creased by smiles, the other lovely with sly dark eyes, and the son was sent to deal with the horse – and the only other traveller in the inn, a brandy-merchant from Kemperbad, who rose from his seat brandishing two bottles of his stock to toast the feast-day and the meal. Hoche didn't pay much attention. He couldn't take his eyes off the food.

There were roasted potatoes browned to perfection, chipped swedes, a dish filled half with rich purple sauerkraut and half with steamed cabbage, a great tureen of thick dark gravy, sauces of wild berries, a long loaf of nut-bread made with rosemary and raisins, two roasted pheasants and a great goose resplendent on a silver platter, basted in butter and its own fat, its skin as crisp as an autumn leaf, layered with bacon and surrounded by tender dumplings.

At the centre of the table, with the dishes of vegetables and poultry clustered around it as if in supplication, stood an oval dish-cover of silver, rounded and swollen like a pregnant belly, covering a white china plate more than two feet long, hinting of wonders. From beneath it the smell of rich roasted flesh rose above the rest of the food, crowning it gloriously, filling Hoche's whole body with a fierce, wonderful hunger. It was as if the heat of this room and the warmth of the Kanonbachs' hospitality had thawed him out, letting all the pain, fear and horror of his recent experiences melt away. He felt fully, truly human again.

Stefan appeared before him, his red face jovial with cheer, wine and years of happy life. 'Herr Deistadt? Would you do us the honour of carving the meats?' he asked, proffering the knife handle-first, the sharpening-steel in his other hand. Hoche tested the sharpness of the knife against his thumb and gave it a couple of strokes along the steel. Everyone gathered round the table and bowed their heads as the brandy-seller recited a prayer to Rhya the mother-goddess over the food, then chairs were pulled out, napkins flapped open, and the chatter of anticipation filled the room.

Stefan leaned over the long table and grasped the handle of the silver dish-cover. 'The centrepiece!' he proclaimed. 'What our Bretonnian cousins would call the piece of resistance!' He whipped the cover away with a flourish and a grin.

There lay fat sausages, black and white puddings, thick slabs of salt beef, mutton, pork, ham and venison. A heap of kidneys, liver and sweetbreads dewed with drips of white fat. Meatballs in jelly. Tripe in breadcrumbs. Oxtail. And at the centre of the dish, nestled like obscene lovers, sat two fat organs, their surfaces thickly veined, their orifices stitched closed with black thread. It took Hoche a moment to recognise them.

'That one is a bull's heart, stuffed with mushrooms, onions and bacon and seasoned with thyme, roasted whole,' Stefan was saying, 'and the other, on the right, is a stag's heart pickled in sweet cider vinegar with rosemary and pearl onions, preserved this six-month.'

All Hoche could see was two other hearts lying on a blood-soaked cloth on a makeshift stone altar, given faint texture by summer moonlight. For a second his senses were filled with that night, the smell of human blood congealing. The horror of the moment poured back, the feeling of the world he knew dropping away from beneath his feet and letting him fall. He was, he realised, still falling. With a clatter he put the carving irons on his plate and stood up.

'I'm sorry,' he said. 'I can't do... I–' He stopped. Leo Deistadt, he remembered. 'I was riding all night and I'm near dead from lack of sleep. I have to rest an hour. Eat without me, please.'

'Are you all right, Herr Deistadt?' the landlord asked.

'Nothing an hour's rest won't cure, I assure you,' he said. 'I can only afford a cheap room, a simple bed...'

'Nonsense! Nonsense! It is Mondstille and the hospitality of the house is yours,' Stefan declared. 'You'll take the finest room we have, and may your dreams be as sweet as the food you'll be missing.'

It was a fine room. The bed was a four-poster with two mattresses, the sheets recently laundered. There was a carpet on the floor, an ewer of fresh water on the mantel, and thick brocaded curtains over the windows. Most luxurious of all was a looking-glass almost a foot in diameter on the dressing-table.

He lay on the soft bed and could not sleep. The sight of the two hearts had disturbed him and cast doubts into his mind. The plan that had seemed so simple last night now looked like the scheme of a fool. What kind of refuge was Grünburg? It would be the first place the witch hunters would look for him. He had even dreamed of going back into the army. Maybe he could change his name and identity, become a new soldier. The great Thomas Recht, hero of the Arabyan campaigns, was said to have done that...

It was no good: his mind was too busy to sleep. He sat up and went over to the mirror, peering at himself, shocked by the length of his beard. It did not suit him. He dug out the dagger Sister Karin had given him and tested its sharpness. Not ideal, he reckoned, but he had shaved with worse. He poured water from the ewer into the bowl on the table, sat in front of the mirror, wetted his face and began to shave.

It took almost half an hour of concentration, during which he cut himself twice and did not think of hearts, cultists or dark cells once. When he was done he sighed and looked down at his feet. He didn't want to know how bad the damage was, but he knew he must. Under his boots, the bandages were dark and stiff with dried blood. He emptied and refilled the bowl, then dipped his left foot in, let it soak, and began unwrapping the wet cloths. They came away in strips, exposing pale skin beneath.

There was no blood, no open wounds. All his toes were there, their nails gleaming like wet pearls. He could see cuts and scars, but nothing worse. Gingerly he lifted his leg, twisting the foot to study its sole. No gaping holes. How could that be? He remembered the agony, the searing pain, the strange grating as a blade had been dragged across a bone. He was sure his feet had been turned to bloody lumps by Gamow's tortures. Either the witch hunter was a very skilled inflictor of pain, or something curious was afoot.

The other was the same, its flesh tender, the nerves still raw, but it was whole. Hoche ran his fingers over it, wondering if his mind could have tricked him, if perhaps he had been given some pain-amplifying drug. No matter now. They were healed and he could walk on them if he had to.

He scratched at his newly bare chin and brushed his shirt collar. He had never seen the scar on his neck, the one that had interested Lord Gamow so much. Moving back to the mirror, he pulled the shirt down. The mark was towards the base of his neck, an inch above his left shoulder. It was an odd shape, strangely swollen, as if something was trapped under the skin.

It looked somewhat like a mouth, he thought. Yes, the edge of the scar was a little like a lip. It was still new, it would go down in time. He reached up to touch it.

It moved.

The lips parted.

He stared at his reflection, terrified, unable to move. In the gap between the lips, he could see the gleam of teeth.

It was a mouth.

He fought down a scream, but could not tear his eyes away from the looking-glass. It seemed to be shaking. No, he was shaking, his whole body juddering with tension and fear. In a second Hoche was on his feet, staggering away from the table and the glass, bumping into the bed.

It was in him. The stuff of Chaos was in him. The dark gods had placed their mark on his body and it was changing under their power.

He was damned.

So many thoughts crowded into his horrified mind, demanding attention and priority, that he couldn't make sense of them. He was a mutant. He was cursed. He was an exile, no longer human. He could not go home. No regiment would ever take him. He could never show himself to Marie, never. He was not fit to be among people, lest he infect them too.

Braubach had told him about the marks of Chaos. Even the smallest mutation will grow and spread, he had said.

Had it been the Marienburg cultist's blade that had infected him? The tentacle of the mutant who had strangled him? The work of Gamow – the voice from the other cell had warned him not to eat the food. But what if the fault was his? 'Something is rotten within,' Braubach had told him. He had consorted with heretics and blasphemers, and they had made him doubt his faith in Sigmar. He had touched damned books, had read their words. The sin of Chaos was in his soul.

The Shallyan monastery. That must be it. The healer had touched his wound and it had burnt. No, the wound had been touched with holy water and a blessing from an honest priest. It was he, not the monastery, that had been unclean. And dear god, he had sent the witch hunters there.

He was defiled. He was a mutant.

He had to flee. He could not bear to stay in this place, these people, making merry with their Mondstille feast. They would be waiting for Leo Deistadt to return, but he knew he could not keep up that deception any more, nor any other. The truth was too horrible for any mask to hide it.

He glanced out of the window. It faced the road in front of the inn, a drop of around twelve feet. He could not get out that way. Ramming his feet roughly back into his boots, he left the room, crossed the corridor and pushed open the opposite door. That room had a window with a view over the courtyard and stables. He threw it open, crouched on the sill and slipped out, hanging from the window-ledge before dropping to the hard ground. He landed awkwardly, pain shot through both feet and his ankle and he staggered sideways, knocking a bucket at the foot of the wall. It clattered over.

His horse was stabled, its saddle and tack hung beside its booth. Hoche was strapping it back on when he heard a noise behind him. It was Stefan.

'Herr Deistadt, what is it?' he asked.

Hoche tried not to meet his eyes. 'I have to go,' he said. 'I cannot stay.' I dare not risk tainting you, he thought. If the witch hunters find that a mutant had stayed here and eaten at your table, they will burn it to the ground and you with it.

'But why?'

'I can't explain.' He dug in his pocket for the purse that Sister Karin had given him. He thrust it into Stefan's hands. 'Take this as payment. For all your trouble.'

Stefan looked startled. 'Herr Deistadt, are you well?'

Hoche stared at him. How must he look, he wondered: wild-eyed, tousle-haired, his face cut and his hands stained with blood from the bandages. He realised his shirt collar was hanging open, and turned away to hide his neck.

'No,' he said. 'I'm not well. I'm very unwell. Keep the money. I don't need it where I'm going.' Where was he going? Away, far away from everyone. More than that he did not know.

Stefan had loosened the neck of the leather pouch and was staring at the coins in his palm. 'I – this is too much,' he said. 'I will keep them here for you, in case you change your mind.'

Hoche let out a sound that was half laughter and half sob. 'Stefan,' he said, 'you are a good man, and there is a shortage of those in this world.' He reached forward to clasp the landlord's hands, but recoiled. He must not touch him. He was unclean. Instead he swung himself into the horse's saddle, tugging on the reins to turn it towards the road. His eyes met Stefan's. There was nothing but confusion in the man's face.

'I'm sorry,' Hoche said. He didn't know what he was sorry for, but he couldn't think of anything else to say. He geed the horse and cantered towards the gate and the road.

'Sigmar go with you!' the landlord called after him. 'Blessings of the season! May the new year bring more joys than the old!'

Fat chance of that, Hoche thought. Too late for that. Too late for anything. Too late for him.

He rode away, leaving the inn and humanity behind him.

HE WAS TERRIFIED. Of discovery and arrest; of the thought that he might have infected the people at the inn by his presence; most of all by what he had become. His image of himself had been shattered. The Karl Hoche he thought he was, the identity that lay at the core of his soul, was destroyed.

He rode with no thought to direction or destination. At every branch in the road he took whichever fork looked wilder, more desolate, until there was no more road and the last track ran out, and then he rode on through the forest. He ate rotten apples he found fallen beneath a wild tree, their mushy flesh made crunchy by crystals of frost. When night fell he huddled beneath the thick branches of a fir tree. At dawn he rode on into the depths of the Reikwald forest, the horse's hoofs crunching through drifts of dry leaves between bare trees.

He drank from puddles, ate moss and fungi, acorns and rose-hips, watercress grubbed from the banks of sluggish streams and the few sweet chestnuts that the forest's squirrels and wild boars had left uneaten. Once he found a hazel tree with nuts still on its branches and ate them, cracking their shells between his teeth. When a thought about his past or his future emerged he pushed it away, keeping in mind only the journey through the forest, the search for food, and survival. By day he rode with fear and despair at his back, by night he dreamed of fire and damned figures writhing and twisting in its heat, transforming into vile things, and he would wake cold and scared, and ride on.

After four days he reached the Reik.

He heard it before he saw it, a low rushing sound like wind through wheat fields. He did not see the river until he was almost at the edge of the forest. The trees had been cut back a few yards to form a footpath and beyond it lay the water, wide and flat, grey-brown, cold and desolate, flowing endlessly away to the north. On the other bank, the forest continued. The sun was low on the horizon, wintery reds and yellows above the skeletal trees.

Hoche scrambled down to the edge of the muddy water and cupped his hands to drink. He stood and looked around. The river was wide here, so he must be downstream of the point where the Reik and the Teufel joined in the shadow of Castle Reikguard.

Grünburg lay upstream, perhaps only forty miles, but the mass of water flowing endlessly away blocked him from it, taking his desire to go home and dragging it downstream. He would never hear his mother's voice again, never see his father preaching from the pulpit of the temple, never kiss Marie, never gaze into her eyes and feel her trust and love. Never marry her. Never raise children. Never be happy. Die alone.

With that, all the emotions he had been forcing to the depths of his mind as he navigated the forest came pouring out. Everything he had thought he knew about himself, everything he thought he could rely on in this world, had been torn away from him. He felt like a sleepwalker who finds himself on a narrow window ledge, clad in a night-shirt, as a winter storm whips him with hail. He felt he was going mad with despair, uncertainty and impotent rage at the world that had brought him to this state.

The river rushed past, untouched by his agony. It would be easy to surrender to their implacable flow, to swim out to the middle of the current and stop, letting the cold waters carry him away, filling his lungs and mind with their dull emptiness. The Reik would tumble his pale corpse downstream, gnawed by fishes, under the stone bridges of Altdorf, and on through the Empire, past Marienburg and out into the Sea of Claws, lost and gone.

No. That was a coward's way out. He was afraid, but he was not a coward.

He felt a desperate need to talk to someone about what was happening to him, but all his friends were either in

Grünburg, or in the army, or burnt at the stake. He could not visit those who were alive without endangering them and himself; and he could not know what the dead were thinking.

Or could he?

He walked to his horse and unbuckled the saddlebags, drawing out the cloth-wrapped bundle he had recovered from the Cathedral of Sigmar. Braubach was dead, but perhaps the words in his journal would still bring peace and reassurance, or at least advice.

He opened it, turning the pages until he reached the first entries after he had arrived in Altdorf. Braubach's writing was sharp and unsmudged.

> *'Altdorf, 30th Vorgeheim*
> *I do not trust Lieutenant Hoche, and I do not think he will do well.'*

Everything was against him. He drew back his arm to hurl the book into the middle of the river, but stopped. This was all the advice he would get, and too many of the Untersuchung's books had been burnt already. He reopened the book and read on.

> *'I do not trust Lieutenant Hoche, and I do not think he will do well. His strengths are his ambition, his military mind and his willingness to receive advice. These are also his weaknesses. He is too ready to take things at face value, and lacks guile and suspicion. Something in his manner reminds me of Andreas Reisefertig, and that worries me.*
>
> *Yet he has the seeds of a good agent within him. Give him space and the time to reflect and consider his new position, and I believe he will come to terms with his new role.'*

He closed the journal. It might not be the finest advice, but he had no other ideas. Solitude, a time to come to terms with what had happened to him, far from the distractions of humanity – it seemed to fit.

He clicked his tongue and the horse lifted its head from cropping the grass and ambled over. It didn't seem worried by his change. He had heard animals were more sensitive to such things than men, but it didn't seem true. Maybe, he wondered, that was because it was a witch hunter's horse, accustomed to such vileness. Maybe it was just stupid. Maybe he thought about these things too much.

He climbed into the saddle and rode downstream.

IN LATE AFTERNOON he came to a cluster of houses, where foresters and woodsmen sold timber and skins to river-traders. A wide flat-bottomed punt was moored at the dock, and he was able to find the boatman and persuade him to ferry rider and horse across the river for sixpence. He knew he had no money or kit to barter for the ride, so as the punt's bow touched the far bank he threw himself onto his horse and galloped away down the towpath to the sound of the ferryman's fading curses. He hated himself for doing it, but he had no choice.

After a mile or so he dismounted and looked around. The river marked the western edge of the Great Forest, stretching untroubled by towns or roads to the Barren Hills in the east. It was a darker place than the Reikwald forest, the trees older, taller and less tamed. Folklore filled it with marauding orcs and goblins, beastmen, even lost elven settlements. Few ventured here. It was a perfect place for a man to lose himself.

Judging from prints in the path's soft black mud, this side of the river had more foot-traffic. That was good. He needed a few supplies before setting off into the forest's depths: an axe, a tinderbox, some twine to make snares. He should have stolen them from the trading village but it was too late for that now. But the number of fresh tracks showed he would find other settlements on this side of the river before long.

The sun was low over the trees. It would be dusk soon. He rode north beside the river.

After a mile he saw a hut. Even in the fading light it looked dilapidated and no smoke rose from its chimney. As he drew closer he saw something lying outside it, a figure in dark clothes face-down in the mud and unmoving. It looked like the aftermath of a raid or a robbery, or perhaps the hut's inhabitant had collapsed and died outside from his dwelling.

He felt he had to investigate, to see if the body was still alive, or at least if it had any items or clothes he could use. Besides, the hut would be a good place to spend the night. He dismounted, lashed the horse's reins around a tree, and walked towards the body in the mud.

There was no sign of movement or breath. There was no sound apart from the flowing of the river. The world around was silent as he approached the corpse. It was wearing a loose shirt, tattered trousers and no shoes. He could not see any wounds. He studied it for a moment, then kicked it in the ribs.

It flinched. 'Bastard!' it said.

Hoche's hand went instinctively for his sword, taking a bewildered second to remember he did not have one. He grabbed at the other hip where his knife was sheathed, but the body was already scrabbling across the ground to get away.

Drifts of dead leaves in the undergrowth exploded as figures reared up, charging towards him with swords and cudgels. They were vilely shaped: one huge like a bear, one with weirdly stretched arms and no head on its shoulders, one with horns. He didn't have time to take in the others before they were all around him.

He was completely outnumbered. Even back when he was in the Reiklanders he could not fight more than two people at once, and that had been when he was fit and fed. He was far from that now.

He backed towards his horse, making feints with his dagger that kept them away. How many were there? He had been too startled to count as they appeared, but now there were four – no, five.

His horse whinnied and he jerked sideways. A club whirled past his head. He twisted, thrusting with his knife at something at the edge of his vision. The figure dodged but the blade slashed it open and it shrieked in pain, leaping away. Hoche tried to regain his defensive stance, but something exploded against the side of his head.

Stunned, he tried to turn. Behind him was a man with bizarre lumps on his skin, swinging a heavy club. He dodged clumsily. The first blow must have barely hit him; if he had taken the full impact he'd be flat in the mud.

One of the creatures thrust with a sword. He parried it with the dagger but his angle was wrong. The knife was knocked from his hand and spun away. His knees felt weak.

His pain-dulled mind realised these creatures were all mutants. By luck he had chanced upon his own kind. Maybe they could help him, tell him how to live in his new body. He had to make them understand he wasn't their enemy.

'Wait,' he said, holding up his hands. 'Stop. I'm–'

The largest, a head taller and a foot wider than any of the others, stepped towards him.

'–one of you,' he said. A fist the size of oblivion crashed into his face. He felt his nose disintegrate in a gout of warm blood.

He staggered backwards, to be caught from behind. He tried to speak, but before he could he was pushed forwards. The huge figure in front of him, more like a bear than a man, smiled with foul teeth and smashed him in the face again.

Then they were all on him, punching and gouging, kicking, scratching, pulling at his clothes.

It seemed to last a very long time.

Finally there were no more blows. He was lying on the ground, his face covered in flowing blood, his body afire with pain. They stripped his cloak, jerkin and shirt, and his boots too, holding him down as he struggled. Now they stood round as one, a pale-haired youth, knelt over him. The boy had three arms, and in his right hand Hoche recognised his own dagger.

'I'll do the bastard,' the boy said.

'Leave him, he's no use,' the wart-skinned man answered. 'All skin and bone, no flesh. We've got his horse, that's meat for a fortnight. Come on.' The boy looked back at Hoche for a second, hatred in his eyes, and jerked the dagger at him. He flinched. The boy grinned, spat, and jumped to his feet. The pack moved off, leading his horse away, disappearing into the darkness of the forest.

Hoche rolled over and climbed to all fours, then to his feet. 'Come back,' he cried through the blood in his mouth, staggering after them into the twilight. 'I must – I have to…' He didn't know what he had to do.

One of them was coming back, stepping through the trees. It was the pale youth, and he was carrying a sword. Hoche felt weak and uncoordinated, but adrenaline and aggression were surging through his body, letting him ignore his pain. He saw a broken tree-branch on the ground and picked it up, swinging it, striding unevenly towards the boy.

'Come on,' he bawled. 'Come back, I'm ready for you this time. You want a fight, I'll show you...'

The youth crossed the distance between them in a skipping run. As he came in Hoche swung at him with the branch, but he dodged past it and drove his fist into Hoche's stomach. Hoche doubled and collapsed into the dark mud again. The youth looked down at his contorted body, face oddly tranquil in the fading daylight, and then kicked him three times in the back. 'Bastard,' he said, turned and walked into the forest.

Hoche lay in the mud, bleeding, feeling sore and void. He stared through the crossed branches of the trees into the black-blue early evening sky. The first stars were visible through streaks of cloud. It was cold and the air was still.

He thought about moving, but he didn't. He couldn't see the point.

Chapter Ten
LETTING GO

HE LAY STILL for a long time. His attackers had left no sign they had been there, apart from him and his injuries. From where he was, lying on his back half out of a shallow puddle among the trees, he could still hear the river. The sound of its waters was low, like wind in leaves. Somewhere in the forest a wood-pigeon called and another answered. The mud around him was cold against his bare skin, but at the same time it felt somehow comforting. It was difficult to breathe through his ruined nose.

He had been a long time falling. The sight of the two hearts at the centre of the Mondstille feast had reminded him of how long it had been, and how far he had descended from the real world into hell. Since he had walked across the moors with Schulze almost exactly a six-month ago, there had not been one moment where he had felt stable or settled, confident in his own abilities, comfortable with his situation. Or happy.

Slowly, one thing after another, all he had wanted from his life had been cut off. The paths to all the futures he had imagined for himself had been blocked. He had been taken from the army and the job he loved. He had been forced to lie, to cheat and to kill in cold blood. His colleagues in the Untersuchung had been killed. He had been made a criminal and a heretic, without ever committing the crimes that had been laid against him. And finally, just as he felt he was free, he had been stripped of his humanity and his soul.

He would never see his home, his family, his friends. He could never speak to his beloved Marie again. He could never hold another human being for fear of tainting them with the curse he carried. He had been forced away from everything he had ever desired. And now he lay wounded in the wilderness, brought so low that even filthy mutants found him so vile that they wouldn't kill him and eat him.

Everything went back to that first moment, that first contact with the two hearts of Chaos under a summer night sky. It seemed such a small thing, so long ago. It was almost funny. If he wasn't in such pain, he might have laughed.

The last traces of daylight ebbed from the sky and the universe of stars revealed themselves in their icy patterns against the darkness. A cold breeze caressed his skin and stirred the dry winter leaves, blowing them against the side of his body. His face was still bleeding. He could feel the blood running from his nostrils, over his stubbled cheeks, and dripping to the ground.

Why had this happened to him? Why had the gods singled him out for this fate? Why had Sigmar, his lord and patron, abandoned him to the powers of Chaos, robbing him of his life? For the first time since the inn, the anger that had burned under his confusion found a focus and he remembered Braubach's words as the two of them had stood before the great cathedral, looking up into a drizzling sky.

'Times will come,' his teacher had said, 'and you'll be confronted with things that rip away all the nice words you've ever learned about the gods. That's when you'll find if Sigmar really is your strength.' There had been more, and at the time he had thought it heresy. Now he wasn't so sure.

Braubach had claimed Sigmar wasn't a strong or wise god. He didn't know about that. But he knew that for the first time in his life he desperately needed the strength of spirit and certainty of purpose that his god had promised, that would show him why he should get up from this place and carry on. He reached out for it, to the place within his heart where he had always thought it would be when he needed it, and there was nothing there. His faith had deserted him.

He felt abandoned, empty and desolate. He had no determination, no strength of will any more. What had happened? In the Reiklanders he had been a leader, one who was liked and respected. Now he couldn't even command his own body. But before, he had always had a reason to carry on. He had been part of a larger whole, the intricate machine of the army, following its orders and purposes. Here, now, he was more alone than he had ever been. There was nobody he could turn to for help. Not even his god. Not even himself.

The moon had risen and was making slow progress across the heavens. The stars were disappearing as clouds dragged themselves across the sky from the north, thick, bulbous and potent. If the sky was covered then there was less chance of a frost. His nose seemed to have stopped bleeding for the moment. His feet and legs were numb with cold. The shape of a large bird, a night hunter of some kind, moved silently across the trees. In the undergrowth nearby something small scurried away.

When had he lost his confidence, his sense of direction? Had it been in prison, in the endless dark, or before then? Was it when he had let himself be caught and tricked by the cultists in Marienburg? When Hunni had told him that his dramatic, dangerous entry into the Untersuchung had all been arranged to force him into joining? Or had it been a combination of all of them, wearing away at him with uncertainties, changing the rules of the game while he was still trying to work out the previous set?

He was a different man now from the soldier who had ridden out from the Grey Hills six months ago, and not just physically. With each new twist his world had changed and he had been forced to change to keep up with it, to find a new way of coping. From soldier to recruit, from recruit to undercover agent, to heretic, prisoner and fugitive. And now one more: mutant.

He remembered something that Braubach had said early in his training. They had been walking down the Street of Tailors, buying the new clothes Hoche would need as an Untersuchung agent. It was mid-afternoon, a bright late-summer day. Braubach had a good eye for workmanship. No bright colours, no distinctive details unless they could be removed quickly. Nothing that would restrict movement or that might catch your sword as you drew it. They had been talking about disguises.

'You still think like a soldier. We have to teach you how to think like someone else,' Braubach had said. And: 'I'm asking you to put on a mental disguise, a mask over your own thoughts.'

He remembered it. At the time it had sounded like a part of the training. But, he thought, it may have been a lesson I learned too well. I was struggling to survive those weeks, the intense work, the strangeness of it all. Yet I couldn't show my true feelings: the confusion and uncertainty. So I pretended. The Karl Hoche they saw was always confident, alert, ready to learn, eager to do well and gain promotion. And all the time the real Karl Hoche was torn with doubts about the Untersuchung and what he was doing there.

I never stopped thinking like a soldier. Instead, without realising I was doing it, I hid the soldier behind the mask of a new Karl Hoche, tailored for the Untersuchung. When I went to Marienburg, and when I returned to Altdorf, each time I created a new mask to fit the needs of the situation. I masked my own thoughts so well with the roles I was forced to play that not even I realised I was doing it.

'You must learn to play a new role so deeply that it becomes your life,' Braubach had told him, and he had done that without realising it. And each change of circumstance, each new role that he had been thrown into had tapped his real self, draining away the drive and determination of the old Karl Hoche, depriving it of the things that would sustain it.

Now, finally, there were no more masks. He could not disguise the mark of Chaos that he carried, create a personality to hide it, or pretend it did not exist. For the first time in six months he was naked, stripped bare, without anything to hide behind.

He looked at himself, and saw how diminished and raw he was, how wounded, how scared. How helpless. How useless. How little of him was left. The year had exhausted him, left him directionless, empty, hollow and void. The codes and values that he had used to define his old self had been proved false and broken, the structure that held his former life together loosened until it fell apart. Was there anything of Karl Hoche worth saving?

He stared at himself and could find nothing.

Perhaps it would be better if he died here.

He heard the raps of raindrops striking earth and leaves, then the rattle of rain though the bare branches above him. Hard drops splashed against his chest and face. He closed his eyes and let the cold water drench him, washing away some of the blood and some of the pain, numbing his flesh. There was a deep tiredness in his body: he had not eaten or slept properly in days and now he was suffering the consequences. Somehow it didn't matter. He opened his mouth, savouring the moisture on his tongue and lips. He could feel his eye-hollows filling with water.

On the side of his neck the new mouth moved. He sensed it opening its lips, then closing its teeth with a slight snap. A part of him, the Karl Hoche part, filled with dread and hatred, but somehow that didn't matter either.

He lay motionless as the rain pelted him, plastering wet leaves against his body, and contemplated the futility of his existence. He could not think of anything he had ever wanted that had not been cruelly ripped away: his life as a soldier, his friends, his family, all his dreams for the future, and his sense of who he was. He was no longer the man he had thought he was. He was not a man at all.

Karl Hoche did not have to die. Karl Hoche was already dead.

A voice in his mind was telling him that this was ridiculous. It was the voice he had listened to for as long as he could remember, the voice he identified as himself. It sounded scared. How could Karl Hoche be dead, it was saying, if he was Karl Hoche?

That was true enough. But Karl Hoche's hopes and dreams were gone, all the truths that made up his view of the world had been shattered and turned upside down, his knowledge and experience had been proved useless. It was Hoche who had ended up in this place. Yet the last six months had not only ripped him apart, it had taught him new truths, shown him new enemies, and made him understand a new way of seeing the world – a world so alien to the old Hoche that he had fractured trying to understand it.

Karl Hoche might try to deny what had happened to him, and prefer a quick death to life without hopes or dreams. The man on the ground could not do that. He had seen things he could not ignore, and had heard questions that demanded answers.

Slowly, dispassionately, he looked into his own thoughts. He had been Karl Hoche from his first memory, but now he understood that what he thought of as Hoche, as himself, was only another mask. Something – someone – lay beneath it, some aspect of himself he did not know, but that knew him.

He tried to concentrate, to understand what part of himself was separate from the part that was Karl Hoche. It was useless. Too much of his mind was still occupied by Hoche, and Hoche was terrified – by what was happening to him, by the unknown, by these thoughts. Terrified by the possibility that without the mask, what defined his humanity, controlled his emotions and gave his life shape and purpose, he might become the thing he feared most. It might not just be his body. He might be a creature of Chaos in mind and spirit too.

He had a choice. Either he could remain as Hoche, and die here, wretched and alone. Or he could lift the mask and see what emerged, for good or ill.

He did not know what to do.

He had no strength to decide. He was too wrecked in body and soul. His injuries, his hunger, the strain of the last few months had left him too weak to make the choice. If he could not choose then Karl Hoche won and he died here, and crows would pick his bones.

But that was not a decision, that was surrender, an acknowledgement that he was powerless and useless, and he knew that was not true. A spark of something still burned within him. He needed to find another source of strength. He was prepared to die here, but if he did then it must because it was the right path for him to follow.

The rain had stopped. He barely noticed. His flesh was numb with cold and exposure, his breathing shallow. The cold mud leeched the warmth from his body. He had no strength to move, even if he had wanted to.

He had no strength. Braubach had talked about strength. 'You'll find if Sigmar is your strength,' he'd said.

This wasn't about his faith in Sigmar, nor about the stories of the god he had learned at his father's knee and recited in the temple every Festag. It was about the true aspect of the god himself.

Sigmar, the warlord-king who had single-handedly defeated a war-party of goblins before his sixteenth birthday, who had united the tribes, built an empire and driven back the greenskin hordes. He had not lain back to die quietly, surrounded by grieving relatives. In his fiftieth year he had taken the great hammer Ghal-maraz and gone to Black Fire Pass, striding away into battle, history, legend and god-hood. Wherever it was he had faced death, he might have been alone but he had been on his feet and fighting.

A warrior never gives up. A true servant of Sigmar never surrenders.

'In the stretch,' Braubach had said, 'he and your sword are the only true allies you have.' And he had no sword any more.

'Sigmar give me strength,' he whispered. His lips were cracked and split, caked in dried blood and scabs. It hurt to move them.

He opened his eyes. Rainwater had pooled in their hollows and he stared at the night sky through a film of blurred water that made the stars and constellations dance.

Everything was silent and still for a timeless moment, and then a streak of light blazed across the black sky. A shooting star, the first he had ever seen. He tried to turn his head to follow its course. The movement rippled the water over his eyes, and for an instant before the star winked out it seemed to split into two.

A two-tailed star in the heavens. The symbol of Sigmar's birth. No sign could be clearer.

He lay back. Calmly, without any fuss, he let the personality that had been Karl Hoche drop away to one side, falling like his sword from the Untersuchung roof, tumbling end over end into dark shadows. Maybe one day he would be able to put that mask on again, to become his old self, think the comfortable old thoughts, perhaps even achieve some of the long-cherished dreams. Maybe one day.

First he had answers to find, a new purpose to fulfil. It was not about revenge, for himself or for his comrades burnt in Altdorf. Nor was it about completing his old life before he put it away. It was more simple. He no longer saw the world as Karl Hoche, with Hoche's preconceptions and prejudices. His new sense of self, still raw and painful, gave him a new sense of perspective.

Everything he did from this point on, he understood, was not beholden to any code of morals or ethics, any sense of duty, or honour, or loyalty. Sigmar had brought him to this place and given him the sign, but it was not Sigmar who would have to stand up and walk away, forging a new path through life. His sense of who he was had to come from within, and his sense of loyalty and honour must do the same. If you cannot be true to yourself, you cannot be true at all.

He knew that the taint of Chaos in his flesh would kill him in the end, and he knew he could not fight that. He could still strike at its root, at the works of Chaos in the world, its followers and its schemes, and if he died in the struggle then that would save him from the agony of a longer, more painful death. But to fight Chaos he would have to understand it, to learn to recognise its workings and its methods. The Untersuchung had started him on the path, but he still had a long way to go.

First he had to learn how to survive. He would have to learn how mutants lived.

Dawn tinted the edge of the sky to the east. The long night was closing. He moved slowly, lifting himself up out of the mud, feeling the pain of every bruise and cut, brushing dirt and leaves from his body. He staggered out of the forest to the edge of the river, splashing the dark water over his face. It was cold and stung, but it refreshed him. He cupped his hands and drank it in slow mouthfuls, letting the overflow wash over his chest.

Then he walked to the dilapidated hut he had seen the evening before and pulled open its rotted door. There was nothing inside except a battered chair, a mildewed straw mattress on a broken bed and a pile of dried leaves in a corner that had blown in through the splintered shutters. He pulled the door closed behind him, judged which corner was the least draughty and dragged the mattress over to it. He piled the leaves in a heap on its rotten canvas, curled up in them and fell into a deep and dreamless sleep.

HE WOKE IN the late afternoon. He rose slowly, examining his body, surprised at how fast his wounds were healing. He felt ravenously hungry, desperate for something to eat, but he had no way of finding food, catching a fish or trapping game. There was only one source of food nearby.

He left the hut and walked into the forest, following the trail the mutants had left.

Chapter Eleven
ONE OF US

THE MUTANTS HAD not gone far, and there were not many of them. His mind, clear of the blurred thoughts and interference brought by emotions and self-pity, knew these things. They had been practiced and coordinated, so they had used this location to ambush people before. They had said the horse would feed them for a fortnight, so there were unlikely to be others back at their camp. And horses were valuable: most thieves would steal one to sell or ride, not eat it. So they were a small, lone group with no use for transport or money.

Which was the leader? He thought over his fleeting glimpses of their faces, bodies and attitudes, and the snatches of their speech. Not the bear-like one: he was muscle, nothing more. Nor the youth, he had the sullen aggression of adolescence and the demeanour of one who had suffered too much strong discipline. Probably at the hands of the one who had ordered the boy off, the one with the warts for skin.

Their trail was easy to find and easier to follow. five humanoids and a horse left a lot of tracks, and they had made no effort to hide theirs. It was about an hour, something over a mile uphill through tangled undergrowth and brambles, before he heard voices and smelled wood smoke. He crouched down, moving slowly and silently, his bare feet touching the ground gently before each step.

Their camp was a crude thing, a circle of low huts made from piled and woven branches, the walls daubed with mud and clay to keep the wind and rain out, the roofs crudely thatched from reeds and bracken. A stream ran along one side of the settlement, widening to a pool roughly dammed with stones. At the centre of the circle was a large rock with a flat surface. A fire burned beside it and the gang was gathered around the flames, roasting lumps of meat on sticks.

He counted five of them. The warty one had ram's horns and wore his jerkin, and the one with no head had his cloak thrown over his shoulders. That one had eyes where his nipples should have been, long arms, and his bare chest was split by a wide lipless mouth that moved strangely as it chewed. The great ursine one was there, and the woman, and another he'd not noticed before, with small wings like an owl's and a face that seemed to change as he watched it. There was no sign of his horse, apart from the lumps on the sticks.

From the darkness he observed them for half an hour, gauging the dynamics of the group, working out who deferred to who, and thinking of a plan. Then he stood and walked into the camp, splashing through the stream's freezing water, making no attempt to hide his approach. They stood up to watch him. He knew he must be a gruesome sight with his smashed nose, his face bruised and cut, his body bloody and mudded.

The headless mutant stood up, his thin arms hanging down almost to his knees. 'He's still alive,' he said in a voice like claws scratching.

'Tougher than he looks,' said the woman. She had huge eyes, a mass of thick blonde hair and breasts as big as her head.

'Too tough to make good eating,' said the wart-faced one, not moving from where he sat.

The headless mutant stepped forward, waving the stick it had been using to cook meat as if it was a rapier, its gash of a mouth smiling to reveal a nest of thin pointed teeth. 'What are you here for? Another beating?' it demanded.

He stood his ground. 'I am here by the will of the gods and I want my rain-cloak back,' he said.

There was laughter. 'You do, do you?' The headless figure stepped forward. 'Then you'll have to fight me for it.' It pulled the cloak higher so the collar sat tightly over its shoulders, and it made come-on gestures at him with its long hands. He raised his eyebrows and held his ground, his arms loose by his side. He hoped he was ready for this. He hoped he had the strength in his body to pull it off. He knew he had the strength of mind.

'Get him, Walther,' called the woman. 'Whip him back into the night.'

The mutant Walther danced in, holding the stick in its right hand like a sword, making thrusts and sweeps with it. It was too light to be any use as a weapon, with no heft or point. He made a show of dodging it, but he knew it was a distraction. Even with its long arms, the mutant was holding back too far. The real attack was coming from somewhere else. That meant it was two against one, and he was too weak to try anything flashy or strenuous. Time to test the value of tactics.

He turned to face the fire and lifted his head to expose his neck, letting his second mouth catch the light. 'I'm one of you!' he declared. 'I bear the mark of Chaos!'

He'd been hoping for more of a reaction, but Walther stopped waving the stick for a second and that was long enough. He darted for it, grabbing its end and yanking it to the right, against the thumb to break the startled mutant's grip. The stick flew loose. He whipped it around, twisting his body, spinning to see what was behind him.

He had been right: the lanky youth with three arms had been coming from out of the darkness, carrying a knife in his right hand. The end of the stick caught the boy across the knuckles, knocking the weapon flying, its blade catching the light from the flames. It was his knife, the one the boy had taken from him.

He dropped the stick and dived for it, scooping it up as he landed and rolling over on the soft ground so he ended up on his backside at the edge of the stream, facing towards the two mutants, his back to the forest and the night.

He gestured in the air with the knife, and the boy stepped back a couple of steps. The group around the fire were jeering at them. 'Come on, Walther,' called one, 'or he'll have that cloak off you as easy as he took your stick.' The headless figure shook its shoulders in annoyance, picked up a thick branch, swung it like a club and stalked forward.

'What are you going to do with your little pigsticker, you dirt?' it asked, the mouth in its breast grinning wide, showing rows of yellowed teeth as it approached. Its club was drawn back to swing.

He smiled for the first time in days, balanced the knife in his hand and threw it. It spun across the gap and buried itself blade-first in the mutant's mouth, the hilt sticking out between its suddenly closed teeth. Walther's weird eyes bugged wide as thick blood oozed between its lips. Its club dropped from its hands and it crumpled to the ground, kneeling, clutching at its mouth.

Behind it the other mutants watched, silent. They couldn't see their comrade's Chaos-twisted face, but they knew something had happened, and the man they had been jeering a moment ago had proved he was more than a joke.

He stood and walked to where Walther knelt, blood pouring down its chest, trying desperately to stem the flow with its hands. 'Don't bleed on my cloak, dead flesh,' he said and kicked the hilt of the knife with his bare foot, forcing it further into the creature, through the spot where a man's heart would be. There was a final gout of blood and it collapsed backwards, limp, dead.

He turned to where the blond youth stood, fixed to the spot, and gestured at him with a clenched fist. 'You want the same? I'll leave you dead beside him.' The youth stared for a second, then broke and fled into the darkness beyond the firelight.

He went to the corpse and pulled his knife from its strange teeth. One had broken off in the polished wooden hilt, a jagged souvenir. He stuck the blade in the waistband of his trousers, then stripped his cloak off the heavy body and pulled it on. It felt warm and familiar, comfortable. As he fastened it, he glanced up to watch the rest of the group. They were standing, weapons drawn, in wary poses. Good.

'What do you want?' the wart-skinned one said gruffly, trying to sound fierce, failing.

He pointed at the corpse lying at his feet. 'His hut.'

THE BED WAS squalid and too short, but it was a bed. He lay on it, picking at a piece of horseflesh stuck in his teeth, and thanked his strange luck that his smashed nose was blocked with clotted blood and he couldn't smell the hut's foulness. He was very tired but he dared not sleep: the pack would be certain to try to kill him while he rested.

It had been a reasonable beginning. The others had sat, sullen and silent round the fire, as he had cut a lump off the carcass of his horse, roasted strips of it in the flames, and retired to eat it in his new hut. Now he could hear them talking outside in low voices. Let them talk. He could guess what they were discussing.

Who would be first to try their luck? Bastard-boy was an obvious choice, looking to restore his damaged pride, but there was something in the youth's demeanour that made him unlikely to be tonight's visitor. It wouldn't be the leader, and the bear-man was too large. That left two. Perhaps they'd try to fire the hut and kill him as he ran out. That was what he'd do. But he suspected a band like this would be looking for something with a little more bravado.

He remembered an old trick. Standing, he stripped off his cloak and trousers and bundled them up, making a man-sized lump under the blanket on the bed. Then he moved to the corner of the hut closest to the thick cloth draped over the doorway, and waited, naked and cold.

It took less than an hour. Soft footsteps came from outside and the door-cloth was pulled slowly aside, letting light from the fire spill across the earth floor. He held his breath. A figure crept in with careful steps – the one with wings, he guessed. It was holding a woodsman's axe. It made its stealthy way to the side of the bed and raised the weapon.

He stepped behind it, grabbed the axe-handle with both hands and pulled it from the assassin's grip. As the figure turned he swung the flat of the blade at its head. The contact was messy but solid, sending the mutant flying sideways across the small room to hit the wall.

'Go! Next time I see you, I'll have your head!' he yelled. The stunned assassin staggered to its feet and ran. He waited a second and followed it outside, stark naked, hefting the axe in both hands. The night wind was bitterly cold on his bare skin. He didn't care.

The strange winged figure scrambled across the open ground, crossed the stream and disappeared into the night. The other mutants were nowhere to be seen, but the flaps of their doors twitched and he knew they were watching and listening.

He strode to the fire, its flames low, and turned to face the silent huts. 'I hear everything,' he declared to the camp, 'and I do not sleep.' Lies, but lies they would believe, he hoped. He threw the axe onto the embers, stirring sparks into the air, and the flare of heat was warm on his skin.

He went back into his hut and slept, and his sleep was not disturbed by anything more than dreams of fire and blood.

HE WOKE BEFORE dawn and rose at once, crossing the camp in the half-light of sunrise, washing himself in the pool of the stream. The cold water carried away the last of the filth and the blood. Gingerly his fingers felt out the new shape of his nose: flatter, lopsided, curved downward now. A mark of his new self.

Many of his smaller cuts were already scabbed over and disappearing. It had only been a day and a half. Perhaps that was another effect of the mutation, the influence of Chaos making him heal faster. He thought back to the prison, and feet that should have been ruined and useless. He had not felt a twinge of pain from them in the last two days. Unless it had been something in the prison food, he could not think what else might have had such an effect on him. Perhaps mutation might have some beneficial side-effects.

Would he continue to change? What would be next? Would it ever stop?

He walked back to the embers of the fire, using a stick to stir them up and threw a handful of kindling on the glowing remnants. A sound came from behind him and he turned to see the wart-skinned mutant, the one he had marked as the leader, emerge from another of the huts. He looked wary, arms folded in an unconvincing show of confidence.

The warty mouth moved unpleasantly. 'Morning.'

He didn't look away from the fire. 'Morning.'

The leader shifted his weight. 'Going to stay long?'

He's frightened of me, he thought, and of the fact I could become the leader of this motley band in an instant. For now I need them more than they need me, so I have to convince him I'm not a threat. Tough, but not threatening.

He looked up and touched the mouth on his neck. It twitched under his fingers. 'I need to learn what this means,' he said. 'I need to understand why I have it, and how I live with it. Have I been cursed? Have the gods of Chaos marked me as one of theirs?' He paused. That much was true enough. 'Can you tell me?'

There was a long pause as the mutant considered his answer. Finally: 'What's your name?'

It was a good question. Since he had spent the night in the mud, he had not needed a tag for his new identity. He had snuffed out the soul of Karl Hoche within him, but did that mean he could never use any part of his history again? The old name felt comfortable. He remembered what Braubach had taught him about identities and disguises. He was no longer Karl Hoche, but he could use that as a mask. He would have to be careful not to slip into old familiar ways, but it would do for now.

'Karl,' he said.

'I'm Max,' the mutant said. 'The one you want to speak with about Chaos is Nils, but you scared him off last night. And, –' he raised his hands defensively '– I had nothing to do with that. It was purely him. They're a difficult lot to control, this lot, you've got to know how much rope you can give them, and they still sometimes pull it out of your hands.'

Karl watched the muscles of the man's face tighten, heard his voice a fraction too controlled, watched how he stopped describing his words with his hands, and knew it was a lie. Max might not have ordered the failed assassination, but he had been involved.

'Did Nils come back last night?' he asked. Max chuckled.

'After you told him you'd have his head? He won't be back till he knows it's safe. Maybe today, maybe tomorrow.' He paused. 'Breakfast?'

The other members of the group emerged one by one from their huts and while more strips of horsemeat roasted over the fire, he was introduced to them. The huge man, his nose and mouth elongated into a snout and his face and hands matted with fur, was Rolf. The three-armed youth was Hermann, the son of Luise, the only woman in the group, a bizarre hyper-feminised figure with exaggerated breasts and hips, a small mouth with fat lips in a perpetual pout, and blue eyes three inches across, under thick blonde hair that did not move. Karl noted there was no mention of Hermann's father. Nils, the absent one, was the group's priest and spiritual leader. Max made it clear he was in charge, giving orders and bossing the others around.

'How did you all meet?' Karl asked, chewing a strip of flesh.

'Followed the smoke,' said Luise. 'I fled my town when I realised something was... that I was changing. We'd had witch hunters through that spring so I knew what they did to mutants. I begged my way downriver for a few weeks, then headed into the woods. I was almost starving when I saw smoke. And it was Max's fire.'

Max nodded. 'There's a lot of wild folk in the forest,' he said. 'Some of them far gone too, mad or worse. Beastmen also, vicious sods. Many keep away from each other, and everyone stays clear of the beastmen. But the smoke's like a beacon. Worth the risk. It pulls in all sorts.'

'Elves?' Karl asked. Max shrugged. 'Folk say they're around. But I've never seen one.' He stood up and stretched, his lumpy skin creaking. 'Come on. If you're staying there's work to be done.'

'Work?'

'Gathering firewood and cutting trees. We're clearing a bit of land. I want to plant some wheat or vegetables come spring. No need to look for food today – we've meat to last us for a few days.'

'What about digging a grave for–' Karl tried to remember the name. 'For Walther?'

Max looked surprised. 'It's waste not, starve not out here. He's part of the meat.'

Karl decided to prepare his own food.

HE WATCHED HOW the mutants lived. It was a poor sort of life. Most days revolved around searching for the things that would keep them alive: food and firewood. Max boasted of how good things were, how bad it had been when they were on their own, and making grandiose plans of growing crops and raising livestock – rabbits, chickens, maybe even goats – but the days were hard and the living was poor.

Karl pushed himself into the work. His body was thin and his muscles atrophied from the time in prison, and the relentless physical effort gave him release. All day he would cut trees or dig up the stumps from the ground Max wanted to clear, then eat in front of the fire and ask questions, return to his hut exhausted, sleep, wake up stiff and aching, wash himself in the stream, and start again. It gave him a fierce appetite but he was careful to eat only the horsemeat. Eating human or mutant flesh was a taboo he wouldn't break.

Nils sneaked back into the camp early on the third morning, and when Max introduced him to Karl he pretended they hadn't met. Karl shook his hand, squeezing it until he felt the bones twisting, and smiled conspiratorially. Nils looked down, unable to meet his eyes. The man's face changed constantly, bones and muscles shifting under the skin, his eyes changing shape and colour. At one moment he might resemble a youthful aristocrat with a hawked nose and arrogant mouth, the next a haggard Tilean, a vellum-faced scholar or even an elf.

Most of them were first-generation mutants, the change having come upon them spontaneously. The exceptions were Hermann, who glowered at Karl every time he saw him with the sulky rebelliousness of a lonely adolescent, and Rolf who could not speak but used a language of gestures that Max interpreted for the others. Max claimed Rolf was the offspring of a woman who had been raped by a bear, and from whose womb he had exploded. Karl suspected he was making it up.

When anyone asked about him he was non-committal, eluding the details of his history. He didn't think they would take kindly to a former Chaos-hunter.

The fifth afternoon broke into hard hail, fusillades of ice firing from the sky and forcing them into the huts for shelter. Karl followed Max and Nils into the leader's hut. The conversation was stilted and awkward, Nils looking anywhere except at Karl. Max did not try to make things easier between them. In fact, Karl thought, it felt like the opposite.

QUESTIONS CAME TO him that evening and blocked him from sleeping. What was he doing here? He had hoped to learn the ways of mutants and the nature of Chaos at first hand, and yet this impoverished crew seemed to have nothing to teach him. But that did not mean he had nothing to learn. There were ways of thinking and behaving he had never known before, but which his new self would need in the future. He had to learn how to be manipulative, deceptive, destructive, and ruthless.

He lay still on his bed and listened to the night. He could hear voices. No, a single voice. It was Max, his tones guarded, with long pauses between his sentences. Karl slipped from the bed, crept to the doorway and peered out. Two figures were silhouetted against the glow of the fire, and from its size the second had to be Rolf. He was moving his hands in agitation, using the secret language only he and Max understood. Karl watched and listened.

'No,' said Max. 'No, I agree with you, there's something not normal about our new friend. He took Walther down like he was a trained killer, he beat Nils. I mean, he survived that beating we gave him on the riverbank. By rights he should be dead three times over.'

Rolf gestured, making shapes with his huge hands.

Max sniffed. 'No, you're right, he doesn't like you. He told me during the hailstorm. He's afraid you'll become a monster and go berserk. Says he used to know a witch hunter who told him that happens sometimes, in cases like yours. But I said–'

The bear-like man threw back his head, his hands carving frantic gestures in the air. Max was silent, waiting for him to finish. 'No, no,' he said. 'I'm not saying you're right, but I'm not saying you're wrong. I've had the same thoughts myself. We need to watch him carefully, you and me.'

More gestures.

'No, we need all the live bodies we can get to make it through till spring. We're a man down already, and it's only midwinter. What if beastmen attack? Or wolves? But if you see any funny business, anything that gets your hackles up, tell me and we'll do him.'

Rolf pointed to the huts and made a low growl. Max put his hand on the beastman's arm. 'No need to tell the others,' he said. 'They're women and children, likely to panic or make him suspicious. You and me, we'll have to do it alone. Till the spring brings some fresh recruits, anyway. I'll make sure he doesn't tell anyone else about what that witch hunter said. It's all nonsense anyway. Witch hunters don't know anything.'

The figures sat silent and unmoving for a while, then Max stood up. 'Don't let me down. You know you're the only one I can trust.' He slapped Rolf on the back and walked back to his hut.

Karl returned to bed. He had known the others would be suspicious of him, but he hadn't reckoned on Max using it to help keep them on his side. He would have to move more slowly from now. The thought came that he could leave, but he still had too much to learn from these unhappy beings: about life as a mutant, about the nature of mutation, about treachery and subterfuge and manipulation.

He remembered his first night in the camp, and his declaration that he did not sleep and heard everything. Max and Rolf had picked an obvious spot for their late-night discussion. Had he been meant to overhear it? Was it a warning, or were they testing him? Max wasn't a fool, and did little by accident. Was he not meant to hear their talk, meant to hear, or meant to hear but disbelieve? Truth, bluff or double-bluff?

A man could go mad trying to unravel such things. He turned over and went to sleep.

* * *

THE NEXT DAY was fairer, and Nils left the camp early to check the snares in the woods, set to catch unwary rabbits and the occasional fox. Karl waited a minute and set off after him, following his trail through the dead bracken and leaves until they were out of earshot from the camp. He waited until Nils was crouched by an oak-tree, busy extracting a thrashing rabbit from one of the devices of twine and wood that had caught its leg, and crept up behind him.

'I want to talk to you,' he said.

Nils turned, startled, and dropped the rabbit. It fled for a patch of brambles, dragging the remains of the snare from its foot. He backed away from Karl. His face looked as if it had been scarred by fire, the skin tight and red.

'Please don't kill me,' he said.

'I'm not here to kill you,' Karl said. 'I bear you no malice. I want to talk.'

Nils's eyes were questioning for a moment. 'It was Max's plan,' he said. 'He said he was too heavy-footed to carry it off, and gave me the axe. I'm sorry.'

Karl nodded. 'It's okay. I'd have done the same thing,' he lied. 'I wanted to ask you about Chaos.'

'What about it?'

'Tell me about mutations.'

'Mutations,' said Nils. He put down the broken snare and lifted his eyes to the sky. 'Mutanto mutantis, the alteration of the flesh, the gift of the Lord Seench, the changer of the days, the ineffable, unknowable lord of the Chaos lords, upon those he has marked for his schemes for generations, yes, generations upon generations sometimes, the mutation of one to be passed down the bloodline till the mad god's scheme bloom out to fruition...'

It was gibberish. It might fool these people but it exasperated Karl. He stopped Nils with a wave of his hand.

'I heal faster than I used to. Is that an effect of the mutation?'

Nils nodded sagely. 'A blessing from Lord Seench, that is. Rolf's the same. He broke his arm once, and it was fixed in a week.'

'Does everyone pray to this... Lord Seench?'

Nils nodded.

'When they pray for his blessings, are they asking for more changes, or less?'

Nils looked at him strangely. It was clear he didn't get into many theological discussions. 'The true believers ask for Seench to work his mysteries through them. More gifts for some, stability for others. The chosen of Seench are ever-changing.'

Karl said nothing. The strange-faced mutant studied him for a moment, then walked to the low-hanging branch of a nearby oak. A few acorns still hung in clusters on its twigs, and he reached up to pull them down. Karl expected him to eat them but instead he put them in the pockets of the jerkin. Nils turned and smiled sheepishly.

'If you roast them in a fire,' he said, 'and grind them like flour, and boil them in hot water, it tastes like coffee.'

'How much like coffee?' Karl asked.

'Not much,' Nils admitted, 'but more like coffee than dandelion tea tastes like tea.'

He sat down against the trunk of the tree and sighed. 'It's not much fun, this life. But it's better than the alternative.'

Karl said, 'I'm still trying to get the measure of some people. Does Hermann ever say anything except "bastard"?'

'Not much.' Nils smiled with the plump face of a matron. 'But he's still young.'

'Old enough to know better.'

'He's six, Karl. Luise was pregnant with him when she arrived.'

'Six?' It was impossible to believe.

'Yes. He had hair on his balls by the time he was four. You can forgive him a lot if you remember that. Luise tries to be a good mother, but it's hard for her.' Nils paused. 'I like Luise, a lot.'

Karl nodded. He'd noticed it. But Luise flirted with every-one except Max, and that indicated a different relationship between those two. 'I'm not sure about Max,' he said.

'What do you mean?'

'His plans. He's been in the forest longer than anyone, and what has he achieved? You still have no regular supply of food. How many years is it going to take to clear that field? And you're setting snares for rabbits, but not for waterfowl down by the river, or leaving lines or nets for fish. That's not sense.'

'Max is a good man,' Nils said. 'He's a good leader. He does his best. He plans the ambushes and keeps the others under control.'

'Under control?' Karl remembered the conversation he had overhead.

'Yes.' Nils paused, hesistant. 'When I found the village, I told them I was a priest of Lord Seench. The others were frightened of my powers. They were plotting to kill me or drive me back into the forest. Max let me know, and he talked them into letting me stay. I wouldn't be here if it wasn't for him.'

And Rolf was afraid he might turn into a monster. 'I see,' Karl said. He saw a skilled manipulator, controlling a group by making them fear each other, pretending he was their only ally against the rest. He wished Nils luck with the rest of the snares, walked back to the camp and chopped wood all day, thinking.

ON THE TENTH morning Max came to him. 'Meat's low. You're going hunting with Rolf. See if you can bring back a deer or a wild boar. Rabbits if there's nothing else.'

'I thought you ambushed people on the river-path?'

'In summer, but there's not enough traffic this season. We got lucky with you, saw you crossing on the bargeman's boat. Ran ahead and set up a welcoming committee.'

'What weapons do we hunt with?' Karl asked.

Max rubbed his nose, dislodging one of its warty growths of flesh. He put it in his mouth and chewed. 'There's a sling or a spear. Or your knife.'

Karl thought of Schulze, walking in summer moonlight and talking about poaching. 'I'd prefer a bow.'

'I'll hie down the armoury and get one. Would m'lord like a suit of armour and a warhorse while I'm about it?' Max gave him a look of contempt that faded into thoughtfulness. 'Though if you know about bows, you could make one. There's a yew-tree not far off, and you could take some sinews from your horse's legs. That'd be right useful.'

Karl took the spear, left the hut and followed Rolf into the woods.

The going was not hard, but Rolf walked fast and surprisingly quietly, and it was hard for Karl to keep up. Several times Rolf would stop, look back over his shoulder and raise a hairy finger to his lips and Karl, admonished, would try to move more carefully through the maze of branches and brambles, until he found he was dropping behind again.

Here and there he saw deer-tracks in the black earth, and their teeth-marks in the soft bark of the birch-trees, but the animals had gone and their trail could have been hours or days old. At least, he thought, there's no sign of the forest's other inhabitants.

They visited thickets of birch, pools in the stream and other places animals might gather, but they found nothing except old tracks and spoor. There was a light wind that made the air cold and the walking hard.

Around noon they paused, and sat on a fallen tree to eat the dried meat they'd brought with them. Karl studied Rolf, and Rolf studied the forest, sniffing the air and not looking at Karl at all. How scared of me is he? Karl thought. How much has Max made him fear me and what I'm supposed to know about mutations? Because this would be an easy place for me to have an accident.

'Rolf,' he said, 'I'd like to learn how you talk with your hands.'

The great hairy head turned slowly to study him. If there was an expression on Rolf's face it was impossible to read it. 'It would be easier if someone apart from Max could understand you,' Karl added.

Rolf shook his head slowly and took another bite of horse-meat.

'You're happy that Max is the only one who knows what you're saying?' he said. Rolf nodded.

'So it's a private language between the two of you.'

A nod.

'You don't want anyone else to understand you?'

Another nod, slow and deliberate.

'Did Max told you that you'd be in danger if the others knew what you were saying?'

Rolf nodded. He trusts Max implicitly, Karl thought, and in all things. I wonder how deep that trust runs, and how fragile it might be, and where a man could strike to break it.

He was about to ask more, but Rolf raised a hand and pointed. Through the trees Karl could see a deer, a good-sized doe three or four seasons old. It was cropping bark from a tree some sixty yards away.

Rolf slid down from the tree-trunk, crouched low and began to move towards it. How could someone so large be so quiet? Karl let him get five or ten yards ahead and then followed, watching his feet to make sure every step was silent.

The breeze shifted, and a second later the deer raised her head, looked at them, and with a flick of her white tail was gone into the depths of the forest. Rolf gave chase, sprinting between the trees, his feet pounding the earth. Karl, taken by surprise, watched for an astonished second. He tried to follow, but his boots were still on Max's legs and the cloths he had wrapped around his feet for protection did not make running easy.

The doe leaped round bramble-patches, darting to avoid webs of interwoven branches or piles of fallen leaves. Rolf ignored them, his bulk and speed crashing a new trail through the undergrowth. If it hurt him he did not show it. The deer changed direction to avoid another fallen trunk; Rolf had anticipated the movement and was already moving to cut it off. It jinked, twisting between the trees. He followed. It slowed for an instant and he leaped, knocking it down.

Karl stopped and watched. The deer was struggling to get up but Rolf reached out, grabbed one of its legs and pulled its flailing form towards him. His other hand wrapped around its thick neck and squeezed. The deer's legs thrashed the ground. Karl could see it tossing its head, trying to move away from the crushing pressure on its windpipe, but Rolf held it firm. Slowly it ceased to move.

Karl approached, holding his spear and feeling redundant. The deer's tongue was extruded between its slack lips and its eyes were glazed. He stared, still not quite believing what he'd seen. A man had run down and strangled a deer.

Rolf looked up and smiled. His teeth were long, and this smile showed all of them. Karl tried to smile back.

'Tell me,' he said, 'wouldn't it have been easier to break its neck?'

Rolf made a circle round the deer's neck with his two hands. Huge though they were, the neck was thicker: too large and flexible for the bear-like giant to snap its spine. But he had completely crushed the deer's windpipe with one hand. The imprint of his fingers were still visible there. Karl looked at it and shivered, hoping he never felt Rolf's hand around his own.

Chapter Twelve
PRACTICE

THE DAYS PASSED until he lost track of them. He cut more wood, felling trees, splitting them into logs and carrying them to the rock in the centre of the camp. His muscles grew, and his appetite with it. For a week it snowed and they huddled in Luise's hut like rabbits in a burrow, conserving warmth. They caught no meat that week, the snares useless in the snow, and the stocks of food began to dwindle. When the snow cleared Luise showed him how to grub up the roots of plants below the frozen earth, and for some days they ate the few they could find. Then Rolf killed another deer and there was meat for several more days.

The worst of the winter passed and the trees began to produce signs of hard buds. The forest was quiet, the inhabitants out of sight. Food was scarce and the hunting trips more frequent. Rabbits and roots were the usual fare. Some days they had nothing. Karl began to yearn for the taste of horsemeat.

All the time he watched the others, judging how they interacted, thinking about how he could disrupt the network of control and lies that let Max keep his leadership of the group. It was clear that none of the others wanted to lead, but it was also clear that Max had arranged things so that the subject was never discussed. Each mutant thought Max was his ally against the rest, who hated their particular aberration and wanted to see them ousted or killed. The only exception was Luise, and Karl had noticed that though she and Max never slept in the same hut, they were often absent from the camp at the same time. He knew Hermann knew that too, because he saw the boy watching the two of them.

Spring was coming. It was time for a change.

THE DATE MEANT nothing in the forest; only the sky, the temperature and the slow growth of the new buds on the forest branches were important. This day was grey. In the morning the snares had been empty, and their bellies too. It was a hunting day.

Karl and Nils went north, Rolf and Hermann south. Max and Luise stayed behind, 'in case someone passes on the river path', they said. Karl doubted it. There had been a late frost in the night and the ground was chill under his feet. Nils was wearing extra clothes, including a jerkin that Karl recognised. It had been his once.

The forest was empty and still. In the upper branches sparrows and starlings twittered and squawked, but at ground level there was nothing. They walked in silence, Karl content to let Nils take the lead. Once Nils gestured to him to stop, hefted his sling and crept forward to peer round a bramble patch, but on the other side was only a rabbit-warren, with no sign of life. Nils muttered something about ferrets and they walked on.

It was past noon when they stopped at the edge of a stream, near a tall elm tree that spread great ridged arms to the sky. The water was cold and clear, filling their stomachs in the absence of food. They sat to rest for a few minutes: Nils with his back to the elm, Karl on a fallen branch a few feet away. The clouds were heavy with unfallen snow, and the light in the air was muted. It was a depressed day.

Karl toyed with his spear, spinning its shaft in his hands, looking at its two pointed and fire-hardened ends. 'Where did you learn about Chaos?' he asked.

Nils looked at him sharply, his face with the features of a young girl, though drawn with hunger. 'I stood at the right hand of the great priest of darkness in the city of Nuln,' he said, 'head of the covenant of pain, the congregation of Lord Seench the changer of the days, but I was driven away when my visions threatened his status, forced by his followers into the forest...'

'What I'm asking myself,' Karl said, 'is how you picked up the few bits of information you do know, when you've never been near a dark rite in your life. For a start it's Tzeentch, not "Seench", and he's the changer of ways, not days. You repeat the one name you know, but you make up the rest as you speak.'

Nils didn't move for several seconds. Then he said, 'Am I so obvious?'

'Who are you really?' Karl asked. 'What did you do? You know enough to have tricked Max, and he's no fool. But you were never a priest of Chaos.'

Nils paused. 'I did work at the temple in Nuln,' he said, and paused again. 'The temple of Morr,' he added, dug an acorn from his pocket and chewed on it. 'I was a gravedigger. One of the priests was teaching me to read. He said I had potential and I might find a place inside the temple, in the brotherhood. Then my wings started sprouting, and I fled.'

'How long ago was that?'

'Seven summers. Seven years in this forest. It's not been easy,' Nils said. His face slowly became lined and worn, growing dewlapped, pock-marked and sad. He fished another acorn from his pocket and offered it to Karl. 'You won't tell Max, will you?'

Karl took the acorn and ignored the question. He said, 'This is what interests me. None of us had any contact with Chaos before we started to change.' Except me, he thought, and I'm not telling you that. 'If we had been Chaos worshippers, we'd have seen the mutation as a gift from our gods, not a reason to flee. Yet here, instead of cursing Chaos and turning to Sigmar and Morr, you and the others follow this debased form of Tzeentch-worship, a god you know almost nothing about. Is there something endemic in mutation, that it turns the bearer towards the Chaos gods? Or is it in the nature of Man, that we feel the need to grovel towards whatever power seems to control our lives? Because if it's the former–'

A thudding crash came as something ploughed through the undergrowth, heavy footfalls shaking the earth, breath snorting like thunderclaps. Karl was on his feet in a second, spear raised. Nils scrambled up as a huge black boar bolted through the bushes. It looked as large as a horse, with yellow tusks six inches long. Its breath was plumes of steam in the cold air.

Karl held his ground, one end of the spear planted in the earth, braced against a tree root. He didn't move. Nils did, diving round the trunk of the elm, trying to keep it between the boar and himself, shouting words in panic. The beast changed its course. It struck him on the back of the leg, its tusk tearing his flesh, its momentum pushing him down and crushing him. There was the snap of bones. Nils, on the ground, screamed.

'Hoi! Hoi!' Karl yelled.

The boar stopped, turning to the noise. Karl stamped his feet, moving from side to side, distracting it. The beast stood for a moment, tossing its head, its wet button eyes glinting. Its black fur gleamed dully. Three hundred pounds, Karl guessed, and all of it muscle, fury and near-blind aggression.

It snorted and charged. Karl bent low, bracing the spear's point level with its neck. The tactic had worked before, with the wolves in the Grey Mountains and with the assassin in Altdorf. He hoped three times was the charm.

The animal flung itself forward, directly at Karl. He faced it, his legs tense, his heart thudding, until the last possible moment, then he stepped left to let the beast's rush carry it onto the spear, as he reached to his waistband for his knife. The boar reacted to his movement faster than he imagined, swerving to follow him. The spear pierced it above the leg, and the thin wood bent and splintered. The boar's great angular head lunged sideways and one tusk ripped through Karl's thigh with searing pain.

He felt himself falling, and twisted forward towards the mass of black hair. Moving away would be death; if he was on the ground the boar would gore him. There was only one safe place to be.

He landed across the boar's back, forcing it down. The beast squealed and tried to move away but its wounded leg and the remains of the spear would not let it. In a moment Karl had his arms around its neck, hanging on, slashing desperately at its throat with his knife. Hot blood gushed over his hands.

The boar bucked, bellowing in agony and rage, throwing itself across the clearing. Karl felt his new muscles strain and tear, and dug the knife in as hard as he could. Then as the monster rolled over to crush him, he let go and dived away, grabbing for the other end of the broken spear on the ground.

The beast heaved, blood gouting from its neck and pooling on the forest floor. It clambered to its feet as Karl did the same, and stared across the short distance that separated them. Its dark eyes were full of bloodlust and hatred. Karl stared back, implacable, his half-spear held ready for a final charge. Neither moved.

The huge animal exhaled with a fierce heave, sank to its knees, and died.

Karl stood, not breaking his stare. For a second he could hear nothing but the sound of its blood as the thick liquid ran down the hilt of his knife protruding from the boar's neck, and streamed to the earth. There was a lot of blood. The beast's bristled flanks were covered in it, and more coated the ground. Red and hot, it steamed in the winter air. Its blood was drying on his hands and forearms like a second skin.

It called to him.

Karl

Blood was what he needed.

Karl

He raised a hand to his mouth, to lick.

'Karl!'

Nils lay at the foot of the elm, one leg twisted wrongly, as if it had a second knee. 'I can't get up!'

Karl shut his eyes and shook his head hard, to clear it. Was this bloodlust or something worse? He'd never felt a thing like it before – no, he had, riding on the road from Altdorf. The thought made him feel sick. Something was terribly wrong. He had to concentrate. He had business to finish.

He walked over to Nils, limping from the wound in his thigh, and knelt to touch the bent leg, making the mutant grunt in pain. The flesh was torn open and the bone was shattered. 'Is it bad?' he asked.

'It's a clean break,' Karl said.

'That's good. We can use your spear as a splint to get us back to the village. Tear strips from your cloak, bandage it, tie the splint on.'

'My cloak?' Karl said. He stood up slowly, inspecting his own wound. It was long but not deep; enough to slow him down but not stop him.

'I don't understand why it didn't attack you first,' Nils said.

Karl indicated the body. 'You moved. Beasts like this see movement better than they see shapes. You see, Nils, this is what I was talking about. You did something you thought was sensible, but it wasn't. You shouted something as you ran, too. You made yourself the victim.'

'That was stupid of me.' Nils tried to shift, and winced.

'It's not your fault.'

'What do you mean?'

Karl looked down at the mutant, helpless on the ground before him. 'Do you remember what you shouted?'

'It... no.' Nil's features were agitated, unable to settle on one face or expression.

'It was "Seench", Nils. You shouted the name of a god you don't know, that you admit you don't understand. By sense, you should have no faith in this god, and yet in your distress you called his name.' Karl stepped away, limping around the clearing, testing his leg. He bent over the still carcass of the black boar and pulled his knife from its throat, wiping it clean on his trousers. 'You answered my question.'

'What question?' Nils looked agitated.

Karl didn't look at him. 'Whether the worship of Chaos among mutants is a conscious reaction against old gods who have abandoned us, or whether it lies deeper. Does the fact that we bear the mark of Chaos make us things of Chaos? You, Nils, you were closer to the old gods than any of us. But in your panic you didn't call for Morr or Sigmar. You called for Tzeentch, the god who made you this thing of corruption.'

From behind him he could hear Nils shift position, probably towards a weapon of some kind. 'So what?' the mutant asked. 'What does that have to do with getting back to the camp with a ton of pork and a man with a broken leg?'

'It's about what you believe,' Karl said. 'I believe that the works of Chaos are intolerable and must be destroyed. And though I believe you do not understand it, and you think yourself a good man who has been used cruelly by fate, you are in your heart a thing of Chaos.'

'But you can't exorcise the Chaos out of me,' Nils protested. Karl stood and turned, tucking the knife into his trousers. He picked up the broken spear, adjusting his grip on the wood, and advanced across the clearing. Nils saw his expression and tried to scrabble away, around the trunk of the elm.

'Seench! Seench!' he whimpered. 'Why like this? Why didn't you let the boar kill me?'

'I wanted you to know why you're going to die,' Karl said, 'It's not personal. All things of Chaos must be destroyed, it's as simple as that.'

Nils kicked out with his good leg. Karl dodged it and put one foot on the mutant's broken limb, pressing down. Nils screamed in pain, flailing his arms, tears streaking his bizarre face.

'For pity's sake,' he pleaded.

'I pity you, but that will not save you,' Karl said. He took aim with the spear, careful to avoid the jerkin.

'But you're marked by Chaos too!' Nils squealed.

'My time will come,' Karl said, and thrust downwards.

HE STAGGERED INTO the circle of huts at a limping run, his trousers torn and bloody. 'Nils is hurt!' he shouted. 'He's been gored by a boar!'

The curtain of Max's door flapped open and Max lurched out, pulling on a jacket. 'Seench!' he said. 'Badly?'

Karl nodded. 'It smashed his leg and ripped him open on the ground,' he said. 'But he was still alive when I started back.'

'Where?'

Karl pointed. 'About three miles, by the big elm by the stream.' Max nodded. Behind him Luise emerged from his hut. Her hair was perfectly in place, but her hair was always perfectly in place.

'Nils?' she said. Karl nodded. 'He looked pretty bad,' he said.

Max pursed his lips. 'What happened to the boar?'

'I cut its throat.'

'You got it?'

'Yes.'

'Well then,' Max said, 'we should wait till Rolf gets back, so he can carry it. Nils is either dead already, or he'll survive.'

Karl nodded, his face deliberately grim. 'If he's dead,' he said, 'his jerkin's mine.'

THAT NIGHT HE lay on the hard bed and stared up at the holes in the thatch. Nils didn't answer my question, he thought, I did. Chaos is in me deeper than I had thought. It has my body, and now it is starting to grip my mind with these thoughts of wild death. That's why I dream of blood and fire.

I must resist it as long as I can, and I must know when I can hold it back no longer. I must be strong in body, mind and soul, but I cannot be strong forever. Chaos has twisted me, and I must learn to twist the power it has given me for my own ends. We have to play the hand of cards that fate deals us in this life. Only a coward throws in his hand before the game is won or lost, though if you find yourself playing with cheats, only a fool continues without cheating against them.

But how does a man cheat Chaos? It was like cheating a mountain, setting one's shoulder against a river, stabbing the sun in the back. It was a thing that gods and the heroes of legend might have done, but he was just a man. Less than a man.

No. That was his old voice, like an echo from the past. If he learned to use what Chaos had given him he could be at least equal to other men, or even more. He healed faster than he had as a man. He felt his senses were more alert, more acute. Other changes might follow. For now, it was enough that he knew the path he had to follow.

He drifted into sleep.

Hours later he suddenly woke. There had been a voice. Something had said a word or a sentence. It had sounded like the speaker was in his hut. Without moving his head, his eyes searched the shadows for an intruder. Nothing.

Perhaps someone was outside the door, trying to attract his attention. He had told them he didn't sleep, and it was possible they still believed it. Maybe it had been an owl. Or a dream. He didn't think he'd been dreaming.

'Is anyone there?' he whispered.

'Sssainie-unn thare? Unn-thare?' said the voice in his ear.

Not his ear. His neck.

He could feel the lips of his second mouth move as they tried to enunciate the syllables. Like a baby, he thought wildly, and reached up to clasp a hand over it, to silence its babbling. He felt hot breath, and then the wet sensuousness of the tip of a tongue licking the palm of his hand. There was no sense of taste from it and, more horrifying, no sense of control. He could not make this tongue move, and he could not stop it.

The mouth was possessed. It could breathe and speak.

He kept his hand over it, stifling its words. He could feel it moving under his palm. Then it bit him, hard.

He gasped in pain, threw off the blanket and tore a long strip of cloth from it, winding it around his neck several times and tucking it around itself to muffle any more sound or movement. Then he slumped back onto the bed. His mind was whirling so fast his thoughts were dizzying.

AT FIRST LIGHT he ran to the stream. Leaning over the calm edge of the pool he pulled the lips of his second mouth apart and stared at the reflection. The angle was bad but he could see it had sharp pointed teeth, like a fox's. He stared at it for a long time, until he became aware of someone coming up behind him. It was Max.

'I heard you talking in your sleep last night,' Max said.

'I don't sleep,' said Karl. Max gave a sarcastic smile and walked off to the fire-pit.

* * *

THE SPRING SUNLIGHT was too bright, sparkling off the surface of the Reik, hurting Karl's eyes and distracting his focus. He tried to concentrate his mind, but Rolf's great arm wrapped around his neck did not make it easy. He tightened his own grip on Max, pressing the knife against the coarse skin of the man's throat. The mutant leader inhaled sharply and pressed his head back against Karl's face. How could a man who washed himself in the stream every day smell so rank?

Across the patch of muddy ground stood Luise and Hermann. She was holding the reins of a horse, whose rider sprawled in a bloody heap a few feet away. Hermann was holding his broken arm and whimpering.

It had all gone terribly wrong.

Spring had come but the warmer weather had not brought more food and there had been long weeks of hunger in the camp. In desperation Max had decided to go back to the river path in the hope of ambushing a traveller. After three days of lying in wait they had got lucky: a uniformed man on a horse, riding south. Karl, hidden in the undergrowth, recognised him as an Imperial messenger, carrying letters from the court or the generals in Altdorf to the outlying regions of the Empire.

The man had not dismounted, but had ridden cautiously around where Hermann lay face-down and corpse-like in the mud, looking at the body. The horse had stepped on Hermann's arm and it had broken with a crunch. The youth had screamed. The ambushers had rushed from their hides, the horse had reared and unseated its rider, and Karl had sensed his opportunity, and lunged for Max.

It had gone wrong.

Really, his hand had been forced. The mood of the camp had been different since Nils's death. Partly it was the void created by the absence of a member of a small community, but there had been no one to lead the mutants' prayers to 'Seench', nobody to make up consoling gibberish about the Lords of Chaos to explain bad luck or dreams. The life of the group had lost a dimension.

He knew the others suspected him of killing Nils. He was still the new arrival, the unknown quantity, and Max would not have missed a chance to divide the mutants further, separating Karl from the others by making him a threat. But in the last few days things had come to a head. The lack of food endangered Max's position as leader, and there was only one person who had the strength of character to take over: Karl. Even though he didn't want that, Max still saw him as a problem.

Two days ago he had heard Max talking to Rolf. I'm sure Karl killed Nils, he'd said. I'm sure he wants us all dead, he'd said. If you find yourself alone with him, kill him, he'd said. After all, he'd added as an afterthought, we need the meat.

Now Karl stood sandwiched between Rolf, who had him in a stranglehold, and Max, who was at his mercy. It was a stalemate, and all three men knew it. If Karl felt Rolf's arm tightening then he would slash Max's throat in an instant. If he moved, either to kill Max or to get away, then Rolf would break his neck.

The three of them could stand there forever, in balance, except that Karl could feel warm blood running down his leg. He hoped it was from the stab-wound he'd put in Max's back. He hoped it meant Max was bleeding to death; but then if Max died Rolf would kill him too. It looked like the only one whose life was assured was Rolf.

Luise and Hermann kept their distance. The sun bathed them all in golden light.

It was all over bar the talking, he thought.

Max started. 'Have you gone mad?' he asked. 'What the hell was that for?'

'Yeah, you bastard, what was that for?' Hermann echoed. Rolf grunted. Karl thought fast, knowing that his chance of dividing the others, using Max's own tactic against him, was weakening every second. If he hesitated too long they would regroup against him.

'I saw you going for Rolf, you bastard,' he said.

'What?' said Max.

Karl paused, working out his words. Give them some truth, tell them their suspicions were right, then build the lie on that, he told himself. He swallowed and took a breath. 'I know you all think I killed Nils,' he said. 'Well, I did.'

Rolf's arm jerked tighter round his neck. Luise gasped. Karl knew he had to continue or he was dead. 'I did it on Max's orders,' he said, 'just like Max ordered Nils to kill me the first night I was here.'

'What the hell are you talking about?' Max demanded. Karl dug the point of the knife into his skin and he shut up. Rolf's arm relaxed slightly, enough for him to breath. The big man wanted to hear what he had to say. That was something.

'He knew Nils had been having visions from Tze... from Seench, predicting doom for the camp if he remained in charge,' he said. 'He was scared Nils would tell the rest of you. Nils told me, but I trusted Max more than I trusted Nils. And look at the result.'

Max struggled. 'This is nonsense. It's a trick! Not a word is true!' he shouted. Karl kept him in a tight grip. Behind him he could feel Rolf shifting.

'Max told me not to tell anyone, so I didn't. I didn't know then how he likes to set us against each other, to keep himself on top of the heap,' Karl said. 'Then two days ago he gave me another order. He told me to kill Rolf.'

Rolf growled and his arm round Karl's neck tightened. Karl had no idea if the huge man was believing him or preparing to kill him.

'He was afraid Rolf would become a monster and kill us all,' he said, and then in a flash of inspiration: 'And he said we needed the meat.' Max's line to Rolf.

There was hubbub. 'The meat?' Luise demanded. Rolf was growling. Max was shouting, 'I didn't, I did not!' but nobody was listening. Hermann watched with narrowed eyes. Karl waited. The person whose reaction he wanted to see was the one person he couldn't. The thoughts would be working their way through Rolf's mind, linking to his conversation with Max. Would the two ideas knit together, the fact and the lie? Would Rolf think what Karl wanted him to think: that Max had set the two of them against each other, not caring who killed who?

Karl waited a second, and another, and delivered his last shot. 'Because he's not going to eat his woman, is he?' he said. 'Or his son?'

Hermann's eyes snapped open wide and he took a step forward. Right reaction, wrong person, Karl thought, and then he felt Rolf's arm pull away from his neck. The huge man roared with anger and his hand with its huge meaty fingers reached around Karl to grab Max by the hair and lift him into the air. Karl released his grip on Max's neck and ducked away.

'I didn't! I swear I didn't! By Seench! I swear!' Max was shouting, scrabbling at the air, grabbing at Rolf's hand as his feet swung. Rolf's face, now that Karl could see it, was set firm with fury. He had been right: they all knew Max's manipulative ways. They had been ready to believe anything that affirmed their suspicions, and his lies had played to their fears.

Hermann was running forward, shouting something incoherent, his broken arm hanging loose, his other two waving wildly.

Almost in slow motion, Rolf reached up with his left hand, gripped Max's shoulder and twisted.

Many years before Karl had heard the two-inch mooring-rope of a hundred-foot Reik river-barge snap as the boat was torn from its dock in a storm. Max's neck breaking sounded like that.

Luise screamed. Rolf dropped the body and it crumpled on the ground, limp and thin. The man-bear stood straight, looking down at his work. Hermann collided with him. 'Uff,' Rolf said and pushed the youth away. It was only then that Karl saw the knife in the boy's middle hand. It was red with blood.

Rolf saw it too, now. Hermann thrust again, but Rolf swatted him out of the way before the knife touched him, the strength of the flat of his hand throwing the youth away. He fell and lay still. Luise ran to him.

Rolf looked down at the wound in his stomach, the blood emerging in lazy pulses, running over his hairy skin and falling to the ground. He looked across at Karl, and there was pain and puzzlement on his strange, stretched face. He growled, low and rumbling. Karl looked back, fighting to keep his expression blank. He said nothing.

Rolf started to gesture at him, his hands spelling out the incomprehensible words of his manual language. Then he looked at Karl, his eyes pleading.

'I don't understand you,' Karl said. 'None of us can.'

Rolf's gaze dropped to the body of Max, twisted and still in the mud. Tears welled in his eyes. He dropped to his knees beside the corpse of the only man who could have translated his grief, closed his eyes, threw back his head and howled his rage, pain and sorrow at the sky.

Karl stood beside him, lifted his dagger and drove it down into Rolf's right eye, putting all his strength behind it. He felt it pierce tissue and punch through bone, and he forced it down, deep into the bear-man's brain, up to the hilt. Then he twisted it.

Rolf still howled as his body fell forward but the sound was dying, fading to a sigh, an exhalation, a last breath. The ground shook slightly as the huge body hit it, the mass of muscle trembling, then lying still. Karl studied it for a moment. Hermann's dropped dagger was lying close by, and he picked it up.

No point in trying to retrieve his own; it was stuck against the bone and pinned under hundreds of pounds of dead mutant.

Luise crouched beside the unmoving body of Hermann. Her huge eyes were wet with tears, the moisture running down her face as she looked up at Karl.

'He's not dead,' she said.

Karl said nothing.

'Help me,' she said.

'That seems unlikely,' he said.

The words seemed to have no effect for a few seconds, then she brushed her hair out of her eyes. It was the only time he had seen it out of place. 'Are you going to kill us all?' she said.

'Yes,' said Karl.

'Why?' Her tears were drying, her bizarre, exaggerated beauty flowing back across her face like thick oil poured on water.

'Call it my mission,' he said.

'But we helped you,' she said. 'We gave you shelter, food...'

'You left me to die, in this spot,' he said, 'and by doing it you saved me from myself. Do not think I am not grateful. I will repay you by doing everything I can to destroy the forces that made you what you are.'

She stared at him uncomprehendingly for a long moment and then turned back to Hermann, laying a hand on his forehead. 'Max wasn't his father,' she said. 'I don't know why you said that.'

'He wanted a father,' he said, 'and he wanted it to be Max. He could count: he was six, you'd been here six years. He thought you were keeping the truth from him for some reason. I just told him what he wanted to hear.'

'How did you know all that?' she asked.

Karl stared at her, his face hard. How could any mother know her child so little? 'Our worst insults are the ones we fear the most,' he said. 'There was a reason he called everyone a bastard.'

KILLING LUISE AND Hermann was not pleasant, and he did not enjoy it. Once they were dead he checked the messenger and found his neck broken by his fall. His horse had wandered a few hundred yards down the path and was cropping grass. He found it, led it back and tethered it to a tree. It found more grass and cropped on, unconcerned by the presence of so much death.

He opened its saddlebags, drew out the letters the messenger had been carrying, and broke their seals. As he finished reading each one, he crumpled it and tossed it into the river, letting the current bear its news downstream, back to the capital. Most of them were pointless and a few were tedious: matters of church intrigue or court orders. A couple were in code. A couple were personal, not to say intimate. He read them all. He had forgotten the pleasure the written word could bring.

Of the stack, only one caught his interest. The Second Nuln Lancers were instructed to ride north with all speed, in defence of the Empire against an army of Chaos forces said to be travelling south. They were to travel to the Eiskalt valley, thirty miles south of Wolfenburg, and rendezvous with the main force of the army led by Duke Heller.

Karl smiled, folded the letter and tucked it in the pocket of his jerkin.

He stripped his clothes from the corpses – his shirt from Hermann, his boots from Max – and put them on. Apart from the knife, which he left lodged in Rolf's eye, he had recovered almost everything he had taken from Altdorf. It seemed like a lifetime ago. In a way, it was. The time he had spent here had taught him much. There were still things he needed to finish, loose ends to tie up, but now he had everything he needed to do that.

Everything? He thought for a moment in the afternoon sunlight, then strode back into the forest, walking the trail he had grown to know, back to the empty camp, the smouldering embers of the untended fire, the pathetic scrap of land that Max had seen as the future of the community.

Karl did not stop to contemplate it, or recall memories of the last few months. He walked to Luise's hut and ducked inside, emerging a moment later with the saddlebags he had brought from Altdorf. He unbuckled the fastener and drew out Braubach's journal from the dark leather where it had sat untouched since the mutants had taken it from him. He held its familiar weight in his hand and felt calm for the first time in many days. Then he walked back to the river, untied the horse and mounted it, turned up the collar of his cloak to hide the mark of Chaos on his neck, and rode away towards the north and Wolfenburg. Duke Heller's army was there, and answers.

Chapter Thirteen
BLOODY THINGS

KARL REINED IN his horse and stared out across the flood-plain. Below him, in the distance, the silver-grey trail of the Eiskalt river snaked across the landscape, bounded by hills in the distance on either side. Over millennia the spring floods had washed down the contours of the land, depositing silt from the Middle Mountains to the river Talabec, creating a valley floor of dark, rich soil that stretched from the foothills around the city of Wolfenberg thirty miles north all the way to Talabheim more than a hundred miles south. In the last few days of his ride he had passed prosperous villages fortified behind stockades, their fields green with the shoots of young wheat, barley, rye and oats. There would be a good harvest this year.

But not around here. This was where the civilisation of the Empire met the wilderness of the Forest of Shadows. The floor and sides of the valley were thickly forested by a green blanket of oaks, beech, ash and firs, still in their spring leaves. The wide band of the Eiskalt cut through it like a highway, dotted with sandbanks and islands. There was little traffic on the river; the places it connected had nothing to say to each other.

At the edge of the forest the terrain broke for a hill that rose above the valley floor, its steeply contoured sides abrupt and alien. Between it and the river the hand of a celestial architect had drawn a great square on the landscape, imposing geometrical rigidity and rules onto the world. Karl could make out the ramparts, rows of tents, the stockade, even the figures of the soldiers moving between them. Around three thousand men, he estimated: a thousand more than they'd had in the Grey Mountains. A formidable force, and more to come. They had cut a new road across the plain and carts and cattle progressed along it in trains. It took a lot of food to sustain an army that large.

Karl nodded to himself. The camp was in a good position, easily defensible, protected on two sides by the hill and the river and far enough from the forest to make ambushes and surprise assaults difficult. The officers had made their quarters on the hill itself, for greater protection and to let them plan the defence and set pieces of any battles that might come. That would be where he would find Duke Heller.

He focused his gaze on the hill. There were buildings there, more substantial than a summer encampment would erect. Old stone walls stood white and solid between the tents, and the banner of the army flew proud and high from a crenellated tower at one end. It looked like a ruined fortification, a large one, but he could not remember ever having heard about such a thing up here. But then he was from the Reikland, the south. Ostland was a foreign country to him. Things were different here.

He spurred his horse and started down the side of the valley, descending to meet the road below.

THE GATES TO the camp were almost identical to the ones he had passed through nine months ago, probably built by the same tools, wielded by the same carpenters, following the same plans. As before, two Reiklander pikemen were standing on guard, their white and red uniforms emblazoned with a campaign medal from last summer's wars against the orcs. He didn't recognise them.

He rode up and they crossed their pikes in front of him. 'State your business,' one said.

He should have anticipated that, but he had been thinking what he would say to Duke Heller. Of course they would stop a man in civilian clothes, on a strange horse. 'I am Lieutenant Karl Hoche, formerly of the Fifth Reiklanders,' he said. 'I need to see the duke.'

'Papers,' the guard said.

'I have none,' said Karl.

'Can't let you in without papers.'

'He doesn't need papers, you oafs,' said a familiar voice behind them. 'Haven't you heard about Lieutenant Hoche, who saved the battle of Wissendorf?'

'Sergeant Braun!' said Karl.

'Well met, sir,' Braun said, walking over. 'And a surprise it is too. We heard you'd got caught up in the affairs of the city and wouldn't be back. Are you rejoining us?'

'That depends on the duke,' Karl said, and paused. He didn't know what to say: of all the conversations he had rehearsed on the long ride from the Reikland, first along the Reik and then up through Talabecland, Hochland and Ostland, this had not been among them. How could he talk to old friends and comrades when the man they had known was so greatly changed? He had nothing to say to them.

'I heard you were in the wars,' he added finally.

'You too, sir, by the looks of your face,' Braun said.

Karl started, his hand rising involuntarily to his collar. Then he caught himself and deliberately continued the movement, lifting his fingers to his nose. 'This? Not a war. Hardly more than a skirmish.'

'Jealous husband? Angry father?' Braun said, laughing.

'Six mutants in the forest,' Karl said, and Braun stopped.

'Six?' he said. 'Blimey. How many were you?'

'Alone.'

'What happened?'

'I killed them all.'

Braun's mouth hung open. 'That must have been some fight,' he said.

'It was,' said Karl, 'though it took longer than you'd think.'

His cover story was simple: riding back to the regiment he had been attacked on the road and badly wounded. He had

sought sanctuary in a village temple where a priest of
Shallya had brought him back to health. It had taken
months. Once healed, he had learned where the army was
and had returned. It was a simple story but hard to disprove.
He told it to Braun, practising the details as the two of them
walked through the camp towards the hill and the duke's
tent. The sergeant led Karl's horse and Karl walked beside
him, glad to stretch his legs after the long morning in the
saddle.

'It'll be good to have you back, sir,' Braun said. 'The lieutenant who they brought in to replace you is, if you don't
mind my language, a bit of a nob. Lieutenant Knopf. Not a
pikeman at all. Doesn't understand the tactics and can't be
made to learn them. Be nice to have a Reiklander in charge
again. The men still talk about you. They would do anything
for you if you gave the word.'

Karl shook his head. 'I don't know if Duke Heller will give
me my command back,' he said, 'or even if he has a job for
me. There's been to be some bad blood around after what
happened with the Knights Panther.'

Braun looked across at him. 'I'd been wondering,' he said.
'What did happen with that?'

Karl stopped so abruptly that the horse, walking behind
him, bumped his back with its nose. 'What do you mean?'
he said. 'Wasn't there an investigation?'

'Oh yes,' said Braun. 'It lasted two days and decided that
some cook had picked a wrong mushroom for the Panthers'
stew or they'd eaten some mildewed grain and all gone mad
or something. That was the last of it. They didn't even send
out a patrol to find them.'

'That was all?' Karl was horrified. 'But I took the news to
Altdorf about what Schulze and I found in the wood...
Nobody came? No witch hunters, no Imperial agents?
Priests of Sigmar? Nobody at all?' He could tell from Braun's
expression that his fears were correct. There had been a
cover-up. Perhaps the council of the Knights Panther had
managed to hide the truth and protect their reputation after
all, he thought. Perhaps Braubach had even been in on the
scheme, keeping him from the witch hunters so they could
not investigate properly.

No. He was overreacting. He needed to find how the land lay before he could start guessing where his enemies were hidden.

'I'M SURPRISED TO see you again, lieutenant,' Duke Heller said. 'Pleasantly so, but still surprised. I had feared that the delights of Altdorf had robbed the army of a good man.'

The duke's tent was the largest in a semicircle beside the main part of the ruined fort, a maze of foundations and crumbled walls. From the style, Karl guessed it had been built around three or four hundred years ago and by human hands: a dwarf-built fort of the same age would still be standing strong. He and the duke sat outside the tent on camp stools, next to a low table with a flagon of wine on it. Spread out below them, the camp lay quiet in the afternoon sun.

'Why is the army here?' Karl asked.

Duke Heller drank wine and sniffed. 'An oracle in Altdorf reckons there's a Chaos force coming in from the north-east. We're here to meet them,' he said.

'So you're waiting for them to come to you?'

'Essentially yes. We've got scouts out in the field, looking for their outrunners, and the men train, build fortifications and get accustomed to the terrain every day. But it's a waiting game, and a damned tedious one.'

'What type of Chaos force?' Karl asked.

'Not specified. You know oracles. Can't ask them if they want a drink without getting three stanzas of metaphysics. Bloody things.'

Karl sipped his wine. 'What happened with that business last summer?' he asked, choosing his words carefully. 'I handed in my reports in Altdorf and that was the last I heard of it.'

The duke drummed his fingers on his empty goblet in a basic staccato rhythm and paused. 'Well,' he said at last, 'it seemed our suspicion was right: some drug had been slipped into their food. Not an accident, but we hushed that up, though we got the villain responsible. Not the dread hand of Chaos, more the dread hand of Tilean agents. I know,' – he held up a hand to silence Karl's unspoken question – 'that you were sure it was your Chaos God theory. No evidence for it, I'm afraid. When in doubt apply Occam's Broadsword: the simplest explanation is usually the one that's right. And with respect you're a low-ranking layman in these things, whereas Johannes Bohr has had some training.'

The Chaos worshippers burnt all the evidence, Karl thought, and a good man along with it, and they did cover it up. I begin to smell the reason why Bohr was so eager to pack me off to Altdorf with news that would get me killed, and handle the investigation himself. The answers I seek are here but they are patches on a cloak, hiding something larger beneath.

'Is there a place for me here?' he asked.

Duke Heller leaned forward and clapped him on the shoulder. 'For a man with your experience? We couldn't do this without you, Karl.' He stroked his moustache. 'Of course we can't give you your old command, that's with a new fellow, Lieutenant Knopf – a good man but hasn't been properly blooded yet – but there's a company of mercenaries and sellswords, fifty or sixty of 'em, locals and itinerants mostly, who have been scouting for us. They're an absolute shambles and they need to be shown some discipline. Job's yours. Knock them into shape. Now if you'll excuse me...'

The duke stood up, and Karl jumped to his feet and saluted. The gesture felt strange: on one level it was a reflex, automatic and reassuring, but on another it belonged to the life he had deliberately cut off months ago. He felt like an interloper, here under false pretences, his movements false and his every word a lie. I am not the Karl Hoche these men know, he reminded himself, but for now I must put on his mask and pretend to be him. These familiar ways must not become too comfortable. I must not forget what I have been through and what I have become.

He touched the high collar on his jerkin. Little danger of him forgetting that.

THE SELLSWORDS' ROWS of tents were in the far corner of the camp, between the stable and the latrines. It showed the low regard the regular soldiers held for the mercenaries. Karl walked down, examining the empty tents, the unwashed cooking pots, the clothes and equipment left strewn on the damp earth. He wasn't impressed. This was a force without discipline or the right attitude. Men who didn't take care of their living quarters wouldn't look after their comrades in the field. He wondered how they'd do in battle, and suspected it wouldn't be good. He'd seen sellswords break and run too often.

A whistling was coming from one of the tents. Karl rounded its end and saw a short man with dark, close-cropped hair sitting on a camp-stool, a bandaged leg set out straight. He was polishing a sword but looked up as Karl approached.

'Nobody here,' he said, his northern accent strong. 'They're off scouting. Be back before dusk.'

'What happened to your leg? Karl asked.

'Nasty cut. Sword-practice. Can't put any weight on it.'

'How long have you been invalided out?'

'Two weeks,' the man said, 'and I think the surgeon might give me another week if I slip him a shilling.'

'Who's your senior officer?' Karl asked.

'Ralf Langstock,' he said and there was contempt in his tone, 'but he's dead. So we don't have one.'

'You do now,' said Karl. 'And you stand up and salute when an officer approaches, you address him as "sir" and you call him by his proper rank when talking about him. Is that clear?'

The man grinned. 'Yes, all right,' he said.

'Stand up,' Karl said.

'What, with this leg?'

'Stand and salute.' Karl's voice was iron. The man stumbled to his feet, planting the tip of his sword on the ground to use as a crutch. Karl kicked it away.

'Never abuse your weapon like that,' he said. 'What's your name?'

'Tobias Kurtz.'

'Sir.'

'Tobias Kurtz, sir.' When the salute finally came, it was surprisingly sharp.

'Good,' Karl said. 'Smarten up. You're taking the Emperor's shilling and fighting in his army, you obey his rules and respect his kit. Remember it and tell the others. I'm going to the quartermaster for my uniform and equipment. When I come back I want that tent in the middle pitched properly and empty except for a bed and one storage trunk. Got that?'

As he returned, his arms full of new clothes, he could hear Kurtz complaining as he worked but the tent had been cleared, its poles were straight and its guy-ropes were taut. He walked past Kurtz's salute into its cool interior. Inside, the tent was spotless. Karl changed into his uniform, taking care to button the collar tight and high, not daring to take off the grubby cloth that gagged his mutation. It felt good to have a sword on his hip again.

Kurtz was a classic malingerer, doing as little work as possible, but if given the right challenge he would set to the task with a will. He was probably in on every scam and scheme going on in the camp. Such a man could be a valuable ally, or a brutal enemy, depending on how he was handled. If the sellswords were as bad as Karl had been told, he thought, then he would need all the allies among them that he could make. He was here to find answers, not to spend his time butting his head against a bunch of recalcitrant mercenaries.

'Kurtz, come in here,' he said. The soldier came to the tent entrance and saluted. Karl looked for a trace of irony or insolence in the gesture but couldn't find it.

'I need an orderly,' he said. 'Someone I can trust. Someone who'll give me straight answers and not abuse their position too much.'

'You want me to recommend someone, sir?'

'No, Kurtz, I want you.'

The short man's mouth hung open for a second in surprise, but he shut it swiftly. Karl guessed he'd never been given a position of responsibility in his life. Good. It meant he'd work harder to keep this one.

'You'll have to tell me what to do, sir,' Kurtz said.

'You'll pick it up soon enough. When the others get back, spread the word that this group will sharpen up. I know you're irregulars but that's not an excuse for slackness. Right now, every soldier up the hill thinks you lot are a disgrace and not worth the gold you're paid. That is going to change. Am I clear?'

Kurtz grinned. 'As the air, sir.'

'Good. Make them believe it. And while you're waiting for them to get back, you can start clearing up this section of the camp.'

Kurtz saluted again and turned away. After a step or two he turned back. 'Sir?'

'What is it?'

'Do I get more pay?'

'No, but you get more respect.'

'Yes sir!' Kurtz walked off. His limp had disappeared. Karl watched him begin to pick up the mercenaries' detritus and throw it into the tents, or onto a nearby fire. The man would never be close to what Schulze had been, he thought, but it was a start.

THE SELLSWORDS CAME back before the sun had touched the horizon, a motley crew with a mix of clothes and equipment, unkept, surly and hungry. Karl made them practise drilling and defensive formations for two hours until the gong sounded from the mess tents below the hill and the soldiers formed queues in front of the great iron cooking-pots, carrying their tin bowls and spoons.

There was grumbling among the men, some of it within Karl's earshot. He joined the queue with them, took his food with them and sat with them, talking, learning who was experienced, who was dependable, who was trustworthy and who wasn't.

The food was thick stew and coarse bread. Its taste was familiar but he couldn't place it.

'One thing in the army never changes,' he said, 'the food's always slop.'

'Tastes like prison food,' said Johan, a hulk of a man with a Middenheim accent and bad tattoos. Karl grinned. Under the bandage on his neck, he felt his second mouth move, as if it was chewing.

THAT NIGHT HE lay in his tent and refused to sleep, listening. The men murmured around their fires for an hour after he had retired, speaking of him in low voices. He knew they didn't mix much with the regular soldiers, but in a day or so one of them who did would speak to a Reiklander of their new officer, the disciplinarian with the smashed nose, and would hear about Lieutenant Hoche and his reputation. Until then, let them murmur.

A couple of the men snored. In the stables the horses snorted and coughed. The night breeze carried a stench from the latrines; in the morning he would talk to the camp's engineering officer about digging a water-course through the camp so the river sluiced the filth away. In the forest owls hooted, calling to each other on their dark hunts, and in the distance the low rushing of the Eiskalt suffused the night with cool sound. It seemed to call to him.

Around midnight he heard a clatter and an oath. Tent-fabric rustled. He crept to the mouth of his tent and watched. The moon was slim, giving little light, but it was enough to show two figures emerge from their quarters and steal through the silent ranks of canvas towards the camp gate. He let them get around twenty yards, then threw open the tent-flap and strode out.

'Where in hell do you think you're going?' he said loudly.

One of the men started and dropped the bundle he was carrying. The other stopped and turned, but did not say anything.

'Where are you going?' Karl asked again.

'We're leaving,' the second man said. Karl recognised him: a tall Talabheimer who had sat and glowered throughout supper, not saying a word.

'Why?'

'We don't like you.'

Karl threw his head back and laughed. 'Then go,' he said. 'Go at once. You don't have what it takes to make a soldier. If you want to serve someone you like, get a job with your father or your uncle. Marry some girl who'll get fat, raise children who hate you because all your stories of bravery are lies, and die knowing nothing of honour or glory, or what it takes to be a man.'

The first man stooped to pick up the contents of his bundle. 'Leave it,' Karl said. 'That belongs to the Emperor. You leave this camp with nothing but what you brought to it.

Being a soldier takes more than wearing a sword, swaggering and swearing.

'If you had stayed I would have taught you those things, but you're not willing to learn. The Emperor does not need men like you in his service. You're a coward: you don't fear the enemy but you fear hard work, and that's worse. I won't waste my time on you. Get out.'

There was a long, hard silence. Karl could feel the tension all around. Hidden in their tents, the irregulars were awake and listening. Half of what he had said was for their ears.

He didn't move. After seconds the other two did, turning and walking towards the gate, the Talabheimer leading. Karl watched them go, then picked up their bundles of pilfered equipment and put them inside his tent. The tension was still in the air. He walked slowly between the tents, stepping carefully. Some men were whispering. He guessed two, maybe three more would be gone by morning, but the rest would be one step closer to being real soldiers.

He was awake now, full of energy and would not sleep for another hour. Plus he needed time to think, and walking would help him do that. There was still something missing from his picture of the camp.

He looked up the hill to where the officers' encampment was. Above the tents, the ruin of the ancient castle lurked in shadow, still and ominous. Below it, the camp was laid out by sections and he walked its regular aisles between the rows of canvas, noting where the different banners flew, where each section of the army was. There was something about its layout that made him uncomfortable, though he could not name it. He needed some perspective.

He found the section for the Fifth Reiklanders and felt a wave of nostalgia. How many of the men in these tents had he known, had fought alongside him, had obeyed his orders though their lives depended on them? How many had died at the hands of orcs? A part of him wanted to step back into these ranks, to take up his old life, to be the old Karl Hoche, the man he had been before his world had become a wider and more terrifying place. He fought it down. That would not do.

Ahead, a figure flitted between two tents and into shadow. He didn't turn his head or break his stride but watched carefully from the corner of his eye. His Untersuchung training, he thought. Now he knew there was someone there, it was easy to track them. Was it someone trying to get past him, or someone shadowing him?

He walked on, catching glimpses of movement. The figure was keeping up with him, staying around twenty yards away, moving only when Karl's vision was blocked by at least one tent. He could give chase, he thought, but it would likely be fruitless: his stalker probably knew the camp better than he did and would have a bolt-hole prepared. There was only one thing to do.

The row of tents ended at the mess area, deserted at night, its fires out and the great iron cooking-pots cold and empty on their tripods. There was nobody around to hear or see anything. He walked to the middle of the area, stopped and turned.

'Come here,' he said. For a moment there was no movement, then a man dressed in black appeared between two tents twenty yards away. He walked closer, stopping ten feet away, keeping his distance.

'Lieutenant Hoche,' he said. 'Forgive me for this clumsy surveillance. My skills are a little rusty. I'm sure you remember me: I am Duke Heller's aide-de-camp, Johannes Bohr, though perhaps you know me as Gunter Schmölling.'

'You are Lieutenant Andreas Reisefertig of the Untersuchung,' Karl said, 'and I swore to Gottfried Braubach that I would kill you.'

Reisefertig smiled. 'My goodness,' he said. 'You don't beat around the bush. How is dear Gottfried?'

'Dead,' said Karl, 'as you know. They are all dead. Why did you do what you did to Gunter Schmölling?'

'Firstly,' Reisefertig said, 'why should I give you answers? Secondly, what makes you think I did it? Gunter and I were working together, infiltrating the Illuminated Readers to remove a book we needed. Gunter went too far. I warned him the cult had turned to darker ways but he wouldn't listen. I found him, his tongue and mind gone, and gave him to the care of Saint Olovald and then, knowing my life was at risk, fled.'

'What book?' Karl asked. Reisefertig smiled again.

'That would be telling,' he said. 'But what of you? How did you survive the purge?'

'Firstly,' said Karl, 'why in turn should I give you answers? Secondly, I don't believe you. I think you found the information you required and left Schmölling as your scapegoat. You came to work for Duke Heller for a reason, and I think it's connected to the Knights Panther who fled last summer. That's why you covered up their crime.'

'So you think I'm a Khorne cultist?' Reisefertig asked, moving to sit on a bare wood bench. 'You think I sent you to Altdorf to die?'

'No. I think you sent me to Altdorf to join the Untersuchung, and Braubach thought so too.' Karl carefully did not answer the question about Reisefertig's gods. 'But what he couldn't tell me, and what I cannot work out, is why you did it.'

Reisefertig tapped an idle rhythm on the wood of the bench and paused. 'I refer you to the previous response about giving answers,' he said. 'If we are to share information and work together, then we must be able to trust each other.'

'Can I trust you?' Karl asked. Reisefertig snorted.

'Of course not! You have no idea what I'm doing, and I know nothing of your reasons for returning.' He looked thoughtful. 'I do hope it's nothing as petty as revenge.'

Karl shook his head.

'That's a relief. But all the same, you'll have to take my word for it that we're on the same side, or at least your enemy is my enemy. Some would say that makes us allies.' He paused. 'Your being here is interesting. The duke himself said so earlier. You're a bit of a wild card in this pack, Lieutenant Hoche, and I look forward to seeing how the game plays out.'

Karl's mind hummed with questions, but asking them would not get him any answers, only tell Reisefertig that he did not know them. He was learning how this game was played fast. The balance of power here was bad; the general's aide had the upper hand. There would be a time for a full exchange of information, but this wasn't it. For now it was enough to know that something was going on, something important enough for people to hide information from him and discuss him behind his back.

Reisefertig looked away, then up into the night sky, and finally back at Karl.

'So are you going to carry out your oath to kill me?' he asked.

'Yes,' Karl said. 'But not yet.' He turned and walked away, back to his tent and his men.

Chapter Fourteen
APPETITES

THE NEXT MORNING Karl drilled the mercenaries for an hour before breakfast, then over bread, mutton and cheese he sat with three who seemed to be natural leaders and talked about the lie of the land.

The news was not good. Their previous officer had obviously had little head for command and less for strategy. The sellswords had been scouting the width of the valley, but not in organised sweeps and only rarely moving away from regular tracks and paths. The groups were too large and had no training in scouting. They were not even sure what they were looking for. This had been going on for weeks.

'Nobody asked about this?' Karl protested.

Johan shrugged wide shoulders covered in tattoos. 'It's the army way. You don't question orders and you don't ask for more.'

Karl sent a messenger to the Fifth Reiklanders, asking two soldiers he remembered to come over and instruct his men in tracking and observation. Meanwhile, he asked Kurtz to call over men who knew the local area to help him understand the layout and terrain. Within an hour he had a sketch-map of the land and landmarks around the camp for ten miles in every direction, the most likely locations for enemy camps and approaches, and a system for patrolling and monitoring it all. The details would need refining, but it would do for today.

He sat for a while, staring at the map and thinking. Something worried him. Mentally, he took the plan and overlaid it on his memory of the view from the hilltop. That was it. He let out a puzzled snort. Kurtz, polishing a breast-plate nearby, looked up.

'What is it, sir?'

'Nothing. No, wait. Kurtz, you're from Wolfenburg. Look at this.' The short man peered at the chart as Karl pointed out positions on it. 'We're here, buttressed against the hill on the west side of the river. The oracle has told Duke Heller the Chaos army will come from the north-east,' he indicated, 'which means they're going to have to cross the river at some point between here–' point '–and here–' point. 'That makes them easy pickings for us: we're well defended on all sides.'

Kurtz nodded his understanding.

'What worries me,' Karl said, 'is if the attack doesn't come from the north-east, or if the army has already crossed the river somewhere upstream. They'll come straight down the west side of the valley, into the north edge of the camp, which isn't well protected or defended. If they used the woods for cover, they could get to within a quarter-mile of the camp before we knew they were even there. An army of decent size could take us completely by surprise.'

'That's what happened last time,' said Kurtz.

Karl jerked round to look at him. 'Last time?'

'When the castle was destroyed, back in the first incursion of Chaos. A big Empire army met a force that was supposed to be coming in from Kislev and the east. Maybe it crossed the river upstream, maybe it was coming from the north, but they charged in at dawn and broke the army's back before anyone knew what was going on. My granddad heard about it from his granddad, whose father had met a man who survived it. The fall of Castle Lössnitz.

'I've heard of it,' Karl said, 'but I didn't know this was the place.' He stared up the hill at the sombre ruins, their broken walls offering no protection now. 'From what I remember the Empire was victorious,' he said. Kurtz shook his head.

'A pretty poor sort of victory,' he said. 'Four thousand men were camped here the night before. You know how many were left by sunset? Ninety. Oh, they stopped the invasion and the general walked away so they call it a victory. But they lost the castle and an entire army.' He stopped and looked away, chewing thoughtfully on his thumbnail. 'I don't like to be here,' he said. 'It makes my flesh crawl. Too much death. It's a cursed place. That's why nobody farms this land. Would you eat crops knowing they'd been grown in earth watered with the blood of four thousand men? They say at sunset that day this whole plain was red, and each year on the same day you can see it again. They call it the field of the cloth of blood.'

'The cloth of blood,' Karl said thoughtfully. He remembered the feel of a sodden Imperial banner, coarse and sticky against his fingers, draped over an altar in the ruins of a farmhouse, dark and glistening in summer moonlight. 'So it all comes round again,' he said.

'So they say,' Kurtz said. 'I'll tell you one thing, I wouldn't have camped an army here.'

'Nor would I,' said Karl. He looked up the hill, to Duke Heller's tent, where figures in a group were looking at charts, consulting. He felt someone had given him another part of the answer, but he had no idea what to do with it.

'Come on,' he said. 'The men should be in the field by now. We're going with them.'

Kurtz looked surprised. 'Old Langstock never–'

'Old Langstock isn't leading this company any more. No more shirking, Kurtz. I need you to be a soldier.'

BIG TATTOOED JOHAN, who Karl was surprised to discover was not only a natural leader but also the third son of a Hochland baron, took twenty men and headed north along one agreed route. An Ostlander named Ludolf who had a head full of sense and the tone of command in his voice went east with another twenty. Karl and the rest followed the river.

The Eiskalt was narrower and shallower than the Reik. River traffic on it was rare, and though there was a path along its bank, it was narrow and overgrown. If the Reik was the backbone of the Empire, this was little more than its ankle.

'Or its arsehole,' Kurtz said, and the men laughed. The afternoon sun hung in the sky, they had seen nothing all day and they were bored. By now, Karl suspected, they would normally have found a shady tree and would be sleeping off their midday meal.

'N-no, Wolfenburg's the arsehole,' said young Ewald and there was more laughter.

'It's people from Wolfenburg who are the arseholes!' declared Matthias, who everyone called Dodger, and there was guffawing and shouts of 'Oy, watch it!'

'Enough! Quiet,' Karl said from the rear. 'This is reconnaissance work. Everything within three hundred yards knows we're here now. That's a good way to get ambushed.'

The laughter died away as the troop walked on. Karl had missed many things about army life, but its sense of humour wasn't one of them. He watched the men, noting who was using their new training and who would need a quiet word this evening.

So, he thought, Duke Heller has camped his army on the site of a centuries-old massacre, and made exactly the same defensive mistake. He welcomes me back and gives me command of a minor section of the army, one that he knows will cause me trouble. He talks to his aide-de-camp about me, and the aide comes to watch me by night, possibly for his own motives but possibly for the duke. This is the same duke and aide who covered up the infiltration of an Imperial regiment and the sacrifice of Imperial soldiers by Khorne cultists the previous summer.

Summer. How long ago was that?

'Kurtz,' he said, 'what's the date?'

Kurtz scratched his head. 'Almost the end of Jahrdrung,' he said. 'The... oh, the thirtieth.'

'Th-thirty-first,' said Ewald.

'Mitterfruhl is not past?' Karl asked.

'Still three days hence.'

Mitterfruhl, the spring equinox, the feast-day of Ulric, Taal the wild god, and the half-forgotten deities of the old faith too. Nine months since he had ridden out to Altdorf.

What things had gestated and grown fat in that time, he wondered?

Whatever was going on, Duke Heller was involved in some way. That was bad. He had no idea if the duke knew anything about his past year. Karl had claimed he had delivered his messages, tried to return and been injured, and the duke had not contradicted him. But the Untersuchung had notified the army that they were co-opting Karl. Had that message reached the duke? If not, perhaps Reisefertig had told him after last night's conversation?

If the duke knew, why had he said nothing? If this was all a plot that involved Chaos, why had he welcomed Karl – an agent of the agency that investigated Chaos conspiracies – back into the camp? Perhaps that was why he had given him the sellswords to command; to keep him distracted. Perhaps Heller believed Karl was not acting alone, and could not risk killing him without drawing suspicion. And if there was a scheme, how many of the other officers and other companies of the army were involved?

Too many unknowns. He would have to start filling in the blanks in his understanding, and quickly. Wandering through the wilderness was not the place to do that. He wondered absently if there might be anything in Braubach's journal that would help him. For a moment he missed the older agent's detached cynicism with sorrow so sharp it felt like pain. He thought of the candle he had lit in the cathedral at Mondstille. It was time he lit another, and made his own peace with Sigmar.

'Kurtz, where is the camp shrine?' he asked

'Up in the ruins, sir, in the remains of the castle's chapel. We went there to pray for Old Langstock when he pegged.'

'Oh yes. You never told me how he died.'

Kurtz coughed. 'He – er, tripped and banged his arm on a pike.'

'Clumsy,' Karl said. 'But that wouldn't kill him?'

'Blood-poison from the wound did. The surgeons bled him and bled him, but it didn't do any good. He–'

There was a call from the front of the group, and the two men broke off and hurried to the front. A long, shallow puddle split the path ahead. In the mud around it were deep hoof prints.

'One horse,' said Karl. 'Either heavy or with a heavy rider. Anyone here know horses?'

There was a pause and some murmuring until Otto, a bald man with thick ears, pushed forward. 'My old dad was a blacksmith,' he said.

'What do these tell you?' Karl asked.

Otto leaned to look, and whistled. 'That,' he said, 'is a big horse. I'd say a big carthorse, but look at the length between the marks. Long legs. Clean prints, no dragging, it lifts its feet. It's been trained.' He bent closer. 'It was shod in iron, but not locally. I've not seen a shoe like it. Look at the heads of those nails. They're spiked.'

'Kislevite, maybe? For riding on ice?' Karl asked. Otto shrugged.

'I don't know. Maybe.'

'Some sort of beastman?' someone asked.

'No,' Karl said. 'They don't wear horse-shoes. Let's follow it. Quietly. Julius, Harro, you're on point.'

The prints led down the path for a quarter-mile, and turned towards the river at a small beach of pebbles. 'The rider paused to water his horse,' Otto said.

'The tracks stop. They don't continue,' Karl said. He stared out across the churning river, full and cold with snow-melt from the Middle Mountains. Twenty yards out stood a large island, its bushes and trees thick with green spring leaves, blocking the view of the far shore. The only movement was the wind in the tree-branches and the river-water surging between it and the shore.

For a second he had a sense of déjà vu, of having seen this place before, but it passed. He stood for a moment, contemplating, then turned to his men. 'Good work. I'll report this to the general; he can interpret it. Time we were heading back.'

AT THE EVENING meal, Sergeant Braun came to find him. 'Do you remember Armin, sir?' he said. 'Young lad, joined up after Wissendorf, showed promise?'

Karl nodded. He'd kept an eye on the boy for promotion.

'Well, he took a bad blow to the head in sword-practice today, and he's in the infirmary. It would mean a lot if you could visit him, sir.'

Karl passed his half-finished bowl to the man next to him, and walked up the hill to the white tent where the surgeons and priests of Shallya tended the sick and injured.

It smelled like all such places did: of vomit, rot and not enough incense. The patients lay on low beds, some moaning, some silent and still. Armin was four beds down, his head shaved and capped with bandages. His eyes moved to watch Karl as he approached and sat on the bed, but he showed no recognition and said nothing. His skin was pale.

'Armin, it's Lieutenant Hoche,' Karl said. 'I heard about your injury. I–' He noticed a clean horizontal cut on the man's forearm. It looked recent and deliberate. He beckoned to a priest.

'What's this mark?'

The priest looked down. 'This man has blood-poison. The surgeons have bled him to arrest its spread, and we are praying for him.'

Blood-poison again, Karl thought, and the same treatment that didn't work for Old Langstock. He didn't like the sound of it.

BACK AT HIS tent, Kurtz thrust a bowl of stew into his hand. 'I saved you some, sir. Hope you've still got an appetite.'

'Thanks, Kurtz.' Karl retreated into his tent. He was hungry; hungrier than he'd realised. The stew smelled like yesterday's, meat and vegetables in rich gravy, but today there were dumplings too.

Then his stomach wrenched and he staggered, almost spilling the bowl, gasping in pain. Simultaneously the mouth on his neck yawned open, wide, trying to get free of the bandage wrapped around it.

The pain eased. He sat, put down the bowl and pressed his belly, feeling where it hurt. The mouth was quiet. Then the feeling came again: the mouth stretched and his stomach spasmed with a primeval, bestial hunger, so deep it hurt.

It's taking over my body, he thought in panic. It wants to be fed. Dare I? What will happen if I do?

The pain struck a third time, knocking him to the ground with its intensity. He lay there as it ebbed away, feeling helpless, loathing what was happening to him. Cutting his throat, he reminded himself, was not an option. He had things to finish first. But this was crippling him. For now, though he hated himself for it, he had to give in.

He crawled to the flap of his tent and tied it closed. Then he unwound the bandage from his neck, glad he had no mirror or way of seeing the mark that had damned him. He could feel it grinding its teeth.

He plucked a lump of lukewarm meat from the bowl with his fingers and, hating himself, fearing what might happen, slowly brought it close to his second mouth. The sharp teeth snapped at it and he jerked away in panic, then steadied himself and gingerly touched the meat to his other lips. He felt them part, the tongue wrap itself around the offering and draw it inside. Then he felt it chewing and, after a long, ghastly while, he felt it swallow.

He wanted to vomit. He wanted to cut the thing out of him. He wanted to scream madly into the twilight. Instead he took another piece of meat and fed it to his infection.

It refused the sixth lump he offered it and he slumped onto his bed, his nerves and mind exhausted and terrified by what he had done. He slept and his dreams were filled with terrible visions. Then he woke and could not remember them, only the fear they put in his heart.

It was still evening. Outside the tent, the men were talking about wives and girlfriends, and for a second he thought of Marie and his eyes pricked with tears, until he remembered those feelings would not help him now.

He did not want to sleep again so he roused himself and left the tent, nodding a greeting to the group round the fire. The sun had set, the stars were out and the camp was preparing for sleep. He walked aimlessly past groups of soldiers cleaning their kit, talking, laughing, singing songs of love, beer and death, and he felt apart from them. He had no connection to their lives. Surrounded by these soldiers, men with whom he had once shared a common bond, he flet utterly alone.

His feet carried him unthinkingly to the infirmary but the tent doors were closed. A field surgeon was sitting outside, his bag of surgical instruments and ointments open in front of him, and he was rummaging in the contents. He looked up as Karl approached.

'Can I help?' he asked. 'Do you have a medical problem? A pain, perhaps?'

It would be so easy to surrender and say yes. 'No,' said Karl. 'I want to see a lad from the Fifth Reiklanders, Armin. Head-wound.'

The field surgeon nodded and disappeared into the tent. A lamp flickered within and there were low voices. A minute later the surgeon reappeared.

'I'm sorry,' he said. 'He died a half-hour ago.'

Karl froze. He was no stranger to death, but this had been unexpected, and fast. There was no reason to die from a head-wound like that.

'What happened?' he asked.

The corners of the surgeon's mouth tightened. 'Blood-poison,' he said. 'You know.'

'I know,' Karl said. 'May I see the body?'

The surgeon led him around the tent to a separate area at the back, half morgue and half storage area, and left him there. Armin's corpse lay on the end of a row of wooden pallets, naked apart from a loincloth. Even in the lamplight Karl could see his skin was as pale as candle-tallow. There were two more cuts on his arm. What had Kurtz said about Langstock? 'They bled him and bled him.' Blood-poison or not, they had drained the life out of the lad.

He saw a sheet spread out over a pile of equipment and went to take it, to drape over Armin's body. It was the smell that hit him first: heavy, cloying and sickeningly familiar. Under the sheet lay a bucket filled with thick crimson fluid. He knew what it was. But this was a medical tent, and bleeding patients was a normal part of treatment. There was no reason to suspect anything out of the ordinary.

All the same...

He left the tent and walked away, making a five-minute loop through the camp and returning from a different direction. Maybe it was only morbid curiosity that made him want to know how the camp disposed of blood and bodies, but he had learnt to trust his feelings. He hunkered down behind a supply-cart and waited.

A while later, after the camp had gone to sleep and the only activity was the guards patrolling the ramparts in the distance or figures heading to the latrines, the shadow of a man crept down the aisle between the tents. There was even less moon than the previous night and Karl could not see his face, much less recognise it. The figure slipped into the tent and emerged a minute later with a bucket in either hand. From the way he staggered, both were full. He set off down the aisle.

My night to be the follower, Karl thought. This was probably nonsense. The man would pour the buckets into the latrine, or at the worst into the ditch around the camp, or to the pigs. It was done after dark because blood made some soldiers squeamish. But then he remembered the field of the cloth of blood, and shivered.

The man was making steady progress. Karl kept his distance but kept following. With a dreadful inevitability he realised what lay at the end of this aisle of tents. He had come this way last night. It led to the mess-area where he had spoken to Reisefertig.

He hoped that the man would turn aside, but he did not.

He wished the man would not walk up to the great iron cooking-pot, suspended over the embers, but he did.

He closed his eyes and prayed he would not hear, but the sound of thick liquid being poured into echoing iron carried through the night air with horrible clarity, and he knew why his new mouth had craved the stew.

He did not sleep that night. He lay awake, afraid of what his dreams might bring.

Chapter Fifteen
BLESSED FRIENDS

THE MORNING WAS overcast and the men seemed the same. Karl moved among them, joining in conversations, answering questions and trying to build morale, but it was as if a cloud had fallen over this part of the camp. Their spirits were damp and Karl's presence drew glowering looks and silences. This was not going well.

He called the section leaders together, gave them their routes and sent the men out into the valley. Then he sat beside the fire and thought. He was hungry, but he would not touch the breakfast meats.

After half an hour he knew he had to confront Duke Heller. He did not know what was going on, how all the strange pieces fitted together or what bizarre picture they would form when they did, but he was sure that if the duke was not at the centre, then he was at least involved. That left the question of who might be running the plan, whatever it was.

Reisefertig? Reikhart the regimental priest? Someone else, keeping their profile low? Even the mysterious forest-rider from the day before?

Those paths were blocked. He had to follow the one that was open, even if it might lead into a trap. He got to his feet, drank a cup of water, turned the collar of his uniform up, and climbed the hill to talk to the duke.

He heard him before he saw him. At the centre of the half-circle of tents around the duke's, a group of men had formed a second crescent. Two figures danced and darted at its centre, sword-blades glinting, the ring of clashing metal reaching his ears a split second after he saw the strike. The men wore heavy padded tunics and helmets but the swords were full-length battle-weight blades.

A third man entered the fight; tall, light on his feet, favouring an Estalian style of attack. It was two against one, but the one did not give ground. His parries quickened and flowed into ripostes, and his blade whirled with feints and thrusts as he held off both men, forcing them to change their guards and sidestep unanticipated swings. It was a virtuoso display.

One of the attackers was struck a ringing blow across the helmet and fell back, but his place was immediately taken by a man with a shortsword and a shield. The defender changed his stance, moving to circle his fresh assailant, trying to keep him between himself and the other swordsman, probing for gaps in his defence, adapting his style in a second depending on which man he faced. The three stalked each other.

In an instant it was over. The second swordsman charged past his ally in an all-out assault. The lone defender parried and sidestepped simultaneously so his riposte came from the flank, sweeping under his guard to strike at his legs. The swordsman dodged back to avoid it, into the shield-wielder's guard. He stumbled. The clangs of the defender's sword ringing off his assailants' helmets echoed out over the camp.

Karl walked up as the victor stripped off his own helmet and handed it to a squire, revealing a face cragged with experience and sporting a brush of a moustache. It was the duke. 'Good,' he said to the crowd. 'You're getting better. After breakfast, three on one.' He turned towards his tent and the crescent of men parted to let him through.

'May I speak with you, sir?' Karl asked. The duke turned to look at him. 'Good morning, Lieutenant Hoche,' he said. 'I

was wondering when you'd make another trek up the hill.
We can talk now if you don't mind watching me eat.'

Inside, the tent's fittings were as luxurious as they had
been in the south the summer before. Andreas Reisefertig
rose from his desk as the two men entered, but the duke
waved him down. 'The lieutenant is breakfasting with me,
Johannes. You remember Lieutenant Hoche, don't you?' Not
waiting for an answer, he passed through into the inner
room. Karl caught a scowl from Reisefertig, and followed.

The duke was loading a plate with meats from dishes on a
sideboard. 'So, lieutenant,' he said without turning round,
'you've been sniffing around.'

Karl's guard was up as fast as the duke's outside. That was
a statement meant to confuse him, draw him out and make
him confess what he knew. But he had to keep the upper
hand in this conversation.

'Yes,' he said, 'and something smells.'

The duke walked to the table and put his plate down, then
looked at Karl before sitting. 'Not going to eat?' he asked.
There was a smile on his lips. The fingers of his left hand
tapped out a short staccato rhythm against the rim of his
plate.

Karl said, 'When you chose to camp here in the shadow of
the ruins of Castle Lössnitz, did you know it was the field of
the cloth of blood?'

'Sit,' Duke Heller said, pointing at the chair at the other
end of the table. Karl sat. The duke forked a kidney, put it in
his mouth and chewed. 'Of course I did,' he said through the
meat. 'I'd be a damned fool if I didn't. Most of my officers
think I'm intent on expunging the shame of that battle, but
they're fools if they believe that. Tell me why.'

'Because you've not defended the flank that made the
camp vulnerable two centuries ago,' Karl said.

'Exactly,' said the duke. 'You're a good soldier, Karl. Sadly
you're a bloody awful negotiator, or you wouldn't be here.
Let me save us some time so we can get this finished before
the poached eggs go cold. You're going to tell me you've seen
things that make you suspicious. I shall nod sagely. You will
ask why there was no proper investigation of the Knights
Panther last summer. I say because there was no need. You

present more evidence and reveal you suspect me as a worshipper of Khorne or at least sympathetic to those who are, and you threaten me with investigation. I look shocked, and tell you that in my desk I have a warrant for your arrest on grounds of heresy, murder of a witch hunter and escape from Imperial prison, so you'd be on thin ice there. You are silent. I ask for your motives. You decline to answer, but ask me why I didn't arrest you. I say I wanted to let you show your hand in your own time. You ask what hand. I say that I never believed for a second your story about being attacked by mutants and recuperating in the forest, because I know you joined the Untersuchung, a heretical organisation covering for a Chaos cult, and spent months working with them. You say that proves nothing and possibly you protest your innocence. Again I nod sagely, before telling you that I'd like to believe you, but I don't.

'When you returned, Karl, I thought you'd worked out our scheme, helped by your Untersuchung masters, and you'd come to be a part of it. But we've watched you these few days, my colleagues and I, and I'm not so sure. It's possible you're part of the great work, on our side. But I think you've been looking a little too hard for that. I think the shocked expression on your face is in earnest, and that you're horrified that one of the Emperor's most respected generals – though I flatter myself – could be in league with dark powers.'

The duke speared another kidney on the tip of his knife and waved it to emphasise his words. 'So that's the way the discussion would have gone,' he said. 'Don't worry. Nobody can hear – nobody who isn't already one of us. All secrets are safe between friends, and Karl, it comes down to that: are you our friend? Either you show me proof that you're a follower of the true gods, or I shout for the guards and you'll be arrested, tried and burnt before noon. Your word against mine, and I run this bloody army. Go ahead.' He bit down on the kidney.

Karl fought to find a clear thought amidst the hubbub in his mind. The upper hand was completely forgotten. Duke Heller, a great man, a hero of the Empire, had admitted he was a follower of the Chaos powers. Thought he was a follower of the same warped gods. Was inviting him to join with them – or die.

He was supposed to prove he was a cultist? His spirit rebelled against that; death would be a more honourable course. But honour was something that had belonged to the old Hoche. It had no place in his new life.

How could he prove he was a cultist? He thought back to his Altdorf training. Cults used signals to reveal themselves to other members: gestures, movements, tics, styles of clothing, secret hand-shakes, phrases, tattoos, anything that a layman would miss but another member of the cult would recognise. What had he missed – not just now but when he first entered the camp? What had the duke done earlier in their meeting, that he had dismissed as a habit or a nervous tic?

A tune echoed in his mind, a short rhythm of staccato beats. The duke had rapped it on the rim of his plate minutes ago, and on a goblet two days before. Reisefertig had knocked it on the mess-bench with his knuckles. Then they had paused, and then they had lied to him.

That must be it. If it wasn't, he was finished.

He lowered his fist to the table and beat out the same staccato rhythm.

'Good,' said the duke, 'but your Untersuchung could have taught you that. I need more to know you're a friend.'

'I am a blessed friend,' Karl said, and he turned down the collar of his uniform to reveal the mouth, his mark of damnation.

Duke Heller stared for a long moment. Then he rose to his feet, walked round the table to the sideboard and lifted the cover off a dish. Steam rose. 'Still warm,' he said. 'Excellent. Nothing worse than a cold poached egg. Eat up. Then we're going for a ride.' He caught Karl's expression and grinned under his moustache. 'Don't worry, it's clean food,' he said. 'Inedible muck, but clean.'

AFTER BREAKFAST THEY took two horses and rode out of the camp across the plain. Wind rustled the grass and shook the branches of the few trees. To the north the forest spread, dark and ominous, like a carpet before the grey might of the Middle Mountains. Below the ground, the ancient blood of

Empire soldiers fed roots and worms. Duke Heller reined in his horse and began to talk.

It was a long talk and it rambled, and Karl didn't know how much of it to believe. As far as he could tell the duke trusted him, but he didn't know if he could trust the duke. The man was filled with enthusiasm but there seemed to be gaps in his understanding of the scheme. Or, Karl thought, there were things he wasn't saying.

It boiled down to this: the stories about the field of the cloth of blood were true. Two hundred years ago there had been a great massacre. The duke wanted to recreate it, but not to slaughter another army. This was not a sacrifice to Khorne, it was to be the creation of a great army of Khorne that would sweep down and destroy the Empire's heart.

The door that led to it all was the location. As Karl had realised, the camp was vulnerable to a sneak attack from the north, and that was where the attack would come from. Repeating a great act reinforced it, gave it potency and allowed the power of the first act to be tapped and used for new ends. Not magic, just ritual, acceptable in the eyes of Khorne.

The lock was a feast day, the equinox, two days away. It was a holy day and a time of power, of balance between light and darkness, each holding the world in equal sway. A push could swing it either way.

The key was the blood. Blood in the land and blood in the food, one giving the camp's site dark power, the other priming the men, like a goose being fattened, not knowing that Mondstille is coming. When the time was right and the correct rites were performed, the power of Chaos would flood through the army, their bodies fed on the blood of their comrades, and change them.

'Change them? You mean twist their minds to follow Khorne?' Karl asked.

The duke smiled. 'Not just that. We will have them body, mind and soul.'

'Who turns the key?' Karl asked.

'Old friends,' said the duke.

'Old friends?' Karl said. 'From where?'

The duke looked at him, smiling under his moustache. 'From last summer,' he said.

Suddenly it all fitted together. All of it. 'Sir Valentin and the Knights Panther,' Karl said.

The duke shook his head. 'Knights Panther no longer,' he said. 'You think you had a hard winter? They've been up in the Chaos Wastes at the top of the world, fighting to survive and to learn. They have gone through the great change to become knights of Khorne, true servants of the Blood God. They're out in the forest, waiting, and we shall all join them soon.' He chuckled in his throat. 'It's been a long time since I had a promotion.'

'Where are they now?'

The duke shook his head. 'Enough. They'll be missing us back at the camp. I need to out-fence a few more of them or they'll think I'm losing my edge.'

They rode back in silence, Karl trying to understand what he had learned. His thoughts shot off at tangents. The plan sounded insane: only a madman would try it, and only a madman would dream it could work. Back in Altdorf, Jakob Bäcker had said Khorne worshippers did not use rituals. But the symbols from last summer had come from a sect that had left written records. Bäcker would have known more, and could have told him if the plan might work. He felt a sudden tremendous fondness for the baby-fat man and his obsessive knowledge of the ways of Chaos. That learning and the rest of the Untersuchung's wisdom had risen to the sky as ash or run down the gutters of Altdorf as molten fat.

Not all of it. There was still Braubach's journal. He vowed to spend the afternoon combing it for anything that might explain what was going on, help him stop it, or simply to make him feel more in control of the situation. He felt out of his depth, bewildered, with nobody to turn to. Even a strong swimmer can drown if stranded in midstream.

He went back to his tent and the place under his mattress where he had left the journal, and it was not there. He shouted for Kurtz, but Kurtz had seen nothing and nobody all day. He searched the tent, checking the mattress three times. The journal was gone.

He stalked round the tent swearing under his breath. He had deliberately delayed reading Braubach's thoughts, partly for fear of learning something he didn't want to know about himself, and now he had lost the chance. Who had taken it?

He could think of only one person: Reisefertig, who had manipulated him once before, and who now seemed to be pushing him into a confrontation. Very well, he would talk to Reisefertig, but at least this time he knew who was playing games with who.

THE OPEN SPACE at the top of the hill was unoccupied and empty. Inside the duke's tent Reisefertig sat at the desk in the outer chamber, reading papers in the daylight that filtered through the canvas. He looked up as Karl entered.

'Lieutenant Hoche,' he said. 'What a pleasant surprise.'

'You have taken something not yours, and I need it,' Karl said. Reisefertig smiled wryly.

'The same applies to you, lieutenant. You have acquired information that I need. Perhaps we can effect a trade.'

So that was it. Reisefertig wanted to know what the duke had told him.

Karl couldn't believe he knew anything that the oily aide-de-camp had not already learned but he had sensed a shred of jealousy that morning, when the duke took him in to breakfast. Well, the trade could be useful to them both.

'Are we safe to talk?' he asked.

'Oh yes,' said Reisefertig. 'The duke is touring the camp and will be gone an hour at least. Though perhaps we should move outside to be sure we are not overheard.'

They stood overlooking the camp. Grey clouds rolled across the sky as Karl told Reisefertig the scheme that the duke had unfolded to him. A line of blue began to appear in the south.

Reisefertig was silent a while. 'Heller hadn't trusted me with half of that,' he said. 'How did you wheedle it out of him? What do you have that I don't?'

'You don't want what I have,' Karl said.

'It is an extraordinary plot,' Reisefertig said. 'Not a regular piece of Khornate scheming. Almost as if–'

'It had come from a book or copied from history?' Karl said, remembering what Bäcker had said about the cult's rituals from the summer before. Reisefertig shook his head.

'No. This is too exact, too planned for this particular situation. Old Heller didn't come up with that on his own. I'm not even sure he understands it. He's too literal, too straight-ahead. He likes to make it seem he is at the head of things, and perhaps he believes he is, but someone else is running this scheme.'

'Do you know who?'

'No,' said Reisefertig. 'But of course I could be lying to you. You can't trust me. I could even be the person behind it all. This could be a test.'

Karl smiled humourlessly. 'I hadn't ruled that out,' he said. 'But will the plan work? Positioning a camp to be attacked by Chaos forces is one thing, but having thousands of Imperial soldiers taken over by the will of the Blood God is a different kettle of—'

'You state the obvious,' Reisefertig said. 'It could work. It doesn't fit the rigid structures of magic theory, but it's not implausible. It'll be interesting to see.'

'To see? You want it to go ahead?' Karl was aghast. 'You are part of it!'

Reisefertig shook his head. 'I'm here in... ah, an observational role.'

Karl eyed him through narrowed lids. 'I don't believe you. I don't understand your purpose for being here, but I don't believe you'd sit in the background and let this happen or fail. A horror like this forces all men to take sides.'

'You'd think so, wouldn't you?' The aide shrugged. 'Whether it works or not, you have to admit it's an extraordinarily bold scheme.'

'Feeding blood to his own troops,' said Karl. 'It's monstrous. Bestial.'

'Those are the ways of Chaos,' Reisefertig said. 'Still it could have been worse.'

'How?'

'It could have been Khornish pasti– hold on, what's that?'

In the valley below, a long column of men had appeared on the road from the south, marching in military ranks.

Supply wagons and baggage carts followed them. Banners flew over their heads. Both Karl and Reisefertig shaded their eyes and stared at the tiny figures in the distance.

'Greatswords from Altdorf,' Reisefertig said. 'Two companies of them, unless I miss my guess. Another five hundred skulls for Khorne's skull throne.'

'They're not alone,' Karl said. At the back of the column he could see another banner, this one not a battlefield pennant. It bore the crest of a golden warhammer, the symbol of the Order of Witch Hunters. He watched as it drew closer, and could not work out if it presaged good or ill.

'Should we go and see what this means?' he said, but found he was addressing the air. Reisefertig was nowhere to be seen. The man had gone without fulfilling his side of the bargain, the return of the journal.

He shrugged and walked down the hill and through the camp as the first of the soldiers arrived at the main gate, a sea of blue, white and red uniforms, their mounted officers directing them to the site where they would pitch their tents and mingle with the rest of the army. He waited by the gate, watching as the men streamed through the narrow opening, followed by their baggage train.

The witch hunters were at the rear of the column: four men on horseback in sombre robes, riding at each corner of a large carriage. Its windows were curtained and he could not see its occupants, but baggage was piled high on its roof and rear stand. It was the last vehicle to enter the camp. The earth around the gate had been churned to rutted mud by the wheels of the laden carts that had gone before, and it lurched between the gateposts, dropped into a fresh furrow, and stuck there.

Karl heard a voice shout, 'Watch out, you oafs!' from inside the carriage, and he turned his face away before anyone looking out through a crack in a curtain might see him. He recognised the voice. It still haunted his dreams, laughing and taking pleasure in his torment. Lord Thaddeus Gamow, Lord Protector of the Order of Witch Hunters, had come to Castle Lössnitz.

Chapter Sixteen
BETRAYED

KARL WATCHED THE carriage roll into the camp, wondering why Reisefertig had disappeared so suddenly. Did he have a reason to fear Lord Gamow, or was there a more prosaic explanation? Of course: as Duke Heller's aide-de-camp he would have to warn his superior of the new arrival, and prepare him for the meeting and questions that would inevitably follow. Karl smiled.

He had no reason to like the witch hunter in the carriage, but the man's zeal and his ability to sniff out conspiracies was unmatched. His appearance would put the cat among the rats in Duke Heller's tent. That, Karl thought, was a meeting he would give much to witness. Keeping his distance, he followed the carriage through the camp.

It stopped at the base of the hill, and Lord Gamow clambered out of its narrow door and down its steps, looking up at the ruins of the castle above. Then he turned back to the carriage and held out his hand to help someone else climb out. She emerged backwards, her legs and bottom appearing first. It was a shapely bottom, in the robes of a priestess. By the time her long fall of black hair appeared, Karl knew it was Sister Karin. Today was proving to be full of interesting incidents.

They stood and talked a while, then Lord Gamow started up the hill towards Duke Heller's tent, flanked by his entourage of riders. Sister Karin began to follow but he waved her back towards the carriage. She walked back towards it, and Karl started in her direction. As she reached it a soldier stepped in to hold the door for her but Karl caught his eye and signalled him to move away, then strode over, took the door and saluted, making sure his hand hid his face. The priestess did not look at him, but climbed up the steps and into the carriage. Karl rapped the painted panel beside him, and as the carriage began to move he swung himself up the steps and inside, swinging the door closed behind him.

'Forgive my intrusion, sister,' he said, 'but I never thanked you properly for the horse you lent me at Mondstille.'

The interior of the carriage was dark and intimate. For a moment Sister Karin did not reply.

'Lieutenant Hoche,' she said quietly. 'This is unexpected. You are aware there are warrants for your arrest.' She leaned towards him. 'By the grace of Sigmar, what happened to your face?'

'I shaved,' he said. 'Sister, there is much wrong in this camp, and I need to know who I can trust. You helped me three months ago. Do you still have any loyalty to the Untersuchung and its ideals?'

She said, 'That was last year, and much has changed. I told you in Altdorf that we each had to find a new path for our lives. I have found mine, with Lord Gamow. Gottfried Braubach was a good man and you should treasure your memories of him, but live your own life now.' She turned away and stared ahead. The carriage rumbled slowly through the camp.

So, Karl thought, here we have gathered: Braubach's three pupils, all of us working for different sides. An unlikely reunion, and a poor epitaph for a man who deserved better. Then he thought: did Braubach mention Sister Karin in his journal? Is there enough detail for Reisefertig to be able to work out that she used to be part of the Untersuchung too?

He looked Sister Karin in the eye, determined to try once more to persuade her. 'I don't think you understand me,' he said. 'Foul, vile things are happening here. Chaos warriors are gathering in the woods. A bizarre ritual is planned. The men are being fed on human flesh...'

Something in her expression that stopped him, a hint of a smile. 'What?' he said.

'I'm surprised that horrifies you,' she said, 'given your recent past.'

'What do you mean?' He felt outrage. The memory of the winter in the forest, the long days of hunger because he would not eat the fleash of men or mutants, was still sharp. With vile guilt he thought of the night before, feeding lumps of foul meat to his other mouth. But there was no way she could know of that.

'In prison, Karl,' she said. 'The meat you were given. Did you not know, or guess?' Her smile had gone, replaced by pity. 'Thaddeus has been studying the effects of Chaos on the flesh of civilised races. He is writing a treatise on mutation, and working on a greater theory of change and transformation. When a mutant in the prison dies, he gives its flesh to the others. It accelerates their changes and brings on new ones.'

They didn't give me meat until Gamow saw my neck, Karl thought. They gave me meat after that. There was damnation in the meat. Part of what I am is his fault. Oh, Sigmar, Sigmar, Sigmar. I will kill him. I do not care if he can put an end to this Chaos plot, he will die for what he did to me.

The carriage stopped and the coachman shouted something that Karl didn't catch. Sister Karin leaned forward and placed a hand on his knee. 'I know what's going on in this camp,' she said. 'You have a part to play in what is to come, Karl, though it may not be the part you expect. Remember, when the time comes: heart is better than head. Now help me down from the carriage.'

The reunion was over. Karl opened the door, stepped out and held her hand as she descended. She walked away from him without a second look.

They had stopped by the space where the Altdorfers were pitching their tents, the rows of canvas hard up against the north rampart of the camp. Karl watched her walk through the sheets, ropes and baggage, towards where a larger tent was being erected. He turned and stared out at the edge of the forest a few hundred yards away. Deep in the trees lurked a force of unspeakable evil, but he had no idea where, or how to stop it. And the same was true of the evil within the camp.

Sister Karin had given him no clues, only raised new questions. He needed to talk to Reisefertig again. The man owed him answers, and he had to get Braubach's journal back. He began to make his way back up the hill.

OUTSIDE THE GENERAL's tent, officers in the uniforms of Talabheim and Hochland were talking to their newly arrived fellows from Altdorf, sharing news, gossip, stories of past campaigns and fallen comrades. Karl pushed through them, trying to give the impression of a man in a hurry, possibly with important news. They parted for him and moved back after he passed as if he had not been there.

Reisefertig's desk was empty, his chair cold. Karl tried the drawers to see if he had been careless enough to leave the journal there, but found nothing except parchment, quills and reports from the quartermaster. Most likely it was in the man's quarters, wherever they were.

Voices drifted faintly from the inner chamber and he felt his hatred rise as he recognised them: the duke's rumbling tones, heavy with consonants, and Gamow's higher replies, more nasal and vowel-filled. He could not make out what they were saying and moved closer to the heavy brocade curtain that separated the two chambers, to hear more clearly.

So they were in a private meeting already. That did not bode well, Karl thought, particularly for him. If the duke mentioned that he was here, Gamow would demand that he be arrested and burnt.

Could Gamow be a part of the scheme? Impossible. Karl had experienced his religious zeal at first hand. But it did not alter the danger to him. If Gamow was untainted by Chaos he would see Karl as a mutant and cultist; if he was within the conspiracy then he would know Karl was not. Whatever happened, he would have to keep a low profile.

'...with the cavalry,' the duke was saying. 'And the usual trouble with deserters. Plus there are superstitions about this place, so local mercenaries have been hard to come by, and the ones we've been able to recruit have mostly been a shifty lot.'

Don't mention me, Karl prayed. Don't say my name, don't even refer to the mercenaries again.

'But we're up to the strength we need?' Gamow asked.

'Close to it. I still...' The duke's voice was obscured for a few seconds. '...any day soon. There will be more than enough come Mitterfruhl.'

There was a break in the conversation, and the faint clinks of crockery and cutlery. 'Is a site prepared?' Gamow asked.

The duke's reply was muffled. Kidneys, thought Karl. 'We have a place,' he said, 'though it waits for your approval. The chapel in the castle ruins. The old altar is...'

The next few words were unclear. A breeze blew through the tent, making the heavy curtain move. Karl stepped back in case a shadow gave him away. What if someone catches me listening, he thought. But he could not leave now. He had to hear more, to see if Gamow was part of Duke Heller's plot. Something was planned, but it could have been as simple as a rite to bless the troops, or an investigation, or a trial. Though why the second-highest witch hunter in the Empire would travel hundreds of miles for that, he did not know.

When he stepped back to listen, the conversation had moved on. '...showing the necessary dedication to the plan?'

Gamow's response was hard. 'Do not question my commitment. I am prepared to die for this, you know that.'

'Of course.' There was an uncomfortable silence.

'...things in Altdorf?' the duke asked. 'The Emperor's son, how is his health?'

'Fine, so I hear. Though the rumours are not true: he's not... let's say he doesn't sympathise with our position.'

The duke laughed and paused. 'Speaking of sympathisers, Thaddeus, I have not congratulated you on closing the Untersuchung. I had not suspected they might be followers of another dark lord. What were they? Tzeentch worshippers, I'll be bound.'

A frisson ran up Karl's spine and he bent closer to be sure he caught every word of Gamow's answer. The noble priest's voice was clipped and dry.

'Augustus,' he said, 'Things are not as the reports claimed. The Untersuching was not a cult front. One or two of them had been beguiled by dark forces, certainly, and that gave us the excuse to move against them. But they had begun to get an inkling of our great work, and were asking questions better left unsaid. So we got rid of them.'

'They weren't cultists?' Duke Heller asked.

'Not at all.'

Karl's mind filled with wild hatred. Up to now he had believed the accusation laid against his old order because in the depths of his heart he had believed it could be true. To hear the man who had put his old comrades and friends to death admit that it was done as a piece of politics, to remove an inconvenient barrier to his own plans...

He felt himself shaking with sorrow and fury. A wild part of his mind wanted to draw his sword and rush in, revenging himself on the two men who had conspired to destroy his life. A calmer voice told him this was not the time. Duke Heller would cut him down like a sapling. Even if he succeeded, the plan would be seen through by the other unknown cultists of Khorne in the camp.

He moved away from the curtain; he had heard enough. And there was another danger now. Duke Heller had previously thought the Untersuchung really were Chaos cultists. Now he knew that they were innocents, he would be sure to look again at whether Karl really was in sympathy with his plans. And if there was one thing Duke Heller did not tolerate in his officers, it was the slightest hint of betrayal. Karl's life was in further danger.

He walked out of the tent. The sun was low in the sky and the officers had moved away to find beer or food.

He could not move against the duke or Lord Gamow; even if he succeeded in killing them their places would be taken before Mitterfruhl. He thought about rallying the officers, telling the troops the truth of what was going on, but he had no proof and would be dismissed as a madman – worse, a mutant, a thing of Chaos. He could flee and let fate take its course, but with what he had learned today, he could not do that.

That left only one option: the band of Chaos warriors, knights of Khorne, somewhere in the forest. Thirty of the most fearsome fighters in the world, with inhuman strength, cursed weapons, their bodies twisted and reshaped by the anvil of Chaos into forms built for war, bloodshed and death. He didn't even know where they were. But they were the hand that would turn the key, the duke had said, and if they could be broken then the door could not be opened.

How could he do that?

WHEN HE RETURNED to the camp the mercenaries were back. They had nothing to report. Normally Karl would have given them drill-practice until the gong sounded over the camp for the evening meal and retired to his tent to plan, but not this evening. He had too much on his mind to think clearly.

'Kurtz,' he said, 'call the men.' And when they were gathered, disgruntled at having their recreations and conversations disturbed, he told them what he wanted to know.

'Most of you grew up within fifty miles of here,' he said, 'and that makes you unique in this army. Somewhere in the forest, within a few hours' ride, a band of thirty warriors has hidden itself so well that three thousand men cannot locate them. We need to find them.

'Think of everything you've ever heard about this valley, from the day your grandmother told you the first tale about the field of the cloth of blood, to this afternoon as you walked through the forest. Every thicket. Every ruined keep, house or hut. Every dell, cave, island, cliff, every legend and rumour, anything at all.'

There was a deep silence.

'Think about it tonight,' Karl said. 'I'm not expecting the answer right now. But there's a purse of twenty gold crowns to the man who gives me the right answer.'

The men shuffled, murmuring among themselves. Then young Ewald spoke up from the back.

'Wh-what about that island?' he said.

'What island?' Karl asked.

'Y-y-yesterday,' he said. 'The island b-by the tracks we found y-yesterday.'

'Don't be a bloody fool,' Karl said. 'It's twenty yards out in the river.'

The lad tried hard to speak, made nervous by the attention on him. 'M-m-m-my brother's a b-b-boatman,' he said. 'I've travelled with him. He w-won't take the west channel round that island. It's t-t-too shallow, even for a river-barge.' He swallowed and sat down, red with embarrassment.

Karl stared at him. An unladen river-barge this far up the river wouldn't draw more than three or four feet. A man could walk to the island if he didn't mind getting wet.

'We've got them,' he said. 'By Sigmar, we've got them.'

He was about to say more but the low thudding of the meal-gong reverberated out across the camp and the sense of tension broke, the men moving, talking, gathering their bowls and spoons.

'Stop!' Karl shouted. 'Don't eat the food!' Calm down, he told himself, or the men will think you're mad. 'There's no time,' he said. 'Eat what rations you have here, gather your kit, get your armour on and douse the fires. Prepare for a night assault. I'll be back shortly.'

He set off up the hill.

AMONG THE QUEUE at the huge iron cauldrons he found men of the Fifth Reiklanders who he recognised and who recognised him. He greeted them, asked after their wives and girlfriends, gave sympathies for the death of Armin, and asked where he could find Sergeant Braun. They pointed him out, sitting on the benches with the enlisted men.

Karl walked over to them. The men around Braun looked up from their meal, and Karl restrained his urge to tell them what they were eating. It would not achieve anything, and he needed them on his side.

'Sergeant,' he said. 'Can I have a moment? In private?' Braun nodded, and together they walked away from the ranks of men who chatted and laughed as they ate their dead comrades.

Karl turned to face him. 'A few days ago you told me the men would still do anything for me,' he said. 'Is that true, or were you being polite?'

'It's true, sir,' said Braun. Karl did not hear the words but he watched the man's face and listened for the stresses in his voice, and knew he did not lie.

'I have a mission for tonight,' he said. 'We've located a small force of the enemy – not the main army, just thirty outriders. They're on an island in the river, but it's fordable. There's going to be a night assault, but I'm afraid the sell-swords aren't up to it – they have no training in night-fighting. I need men from the Fifth to show them how it's done.'

'How many men do you need?' Braun asked.

'As many as you can persuade to come. This isn't an order. I'm asking for volunteers.'

Braun looked contemplative. 'Night-fighting in the forest isn't work for pikes,' he said, 'but we've got plenty who are handy enough with swords. I'll get you your men, don't you worry, sir.'

Karl placed a heartfelt hand on his shoulder. 'Thank you, Braun. I'm truly grateful. We'll see you and the men outside the main gate in half an hour. If anyone asks, you're helping to train the mercenaries in night-attacks.'

'Glad to be of service, sir. Be good to fight beside you again.' Braun smiled. 'It'll mean interrupting the men's supper, though.'

'I'm sorry,' said Karl, not feeling sorry. 'Tell them hunger sharpens the senses and quickens up the blood. And tell them that there's glory to be had tonight, and legends to be made.'

'Is that true, sir?' Braun sounded incredulous.

'I'm afraid it may be,' said Karl.

THE TWO FORCES met outside the main gate as the last of the sun was sinking below the rim of the valley, staining the clouds with vivid streaks of scarlet and gold. There were around a hundred men assembled, the two forces eyeing each other, and not mixing.

Sergeant Braun had brought four horses for the officers to ride out and the wounded to ride back. Karl mounted and

gave the order to form a column, Reiklanders at the front
and mercenaries to the rear. He was concerned that there
would be trouble but his fears were allayed: both sets of men
obeyed his command. He spoke a few words to them,
repeating what he had already said: a small force of outriders camped on an island; a surprise night attack; glory to be
had.

'Johan, you know the territory, you lead. I want dead
silence in the forest. When we reach the island the two tallest
men – Julius and you, there – ford the river, find the shal-
lowest track. Take ropes, tie them to trees on the far bank.
The rest of you follow, using the ropes as guides. Reiklanders
first, fifteen at a time. Absolute silence. No talking, not even
a whisper. Don't lift your feet or splash, and don't get out
onto the island: stay in the river, the water will mask your
footfalls. Wait for my command, then sack the place. Kill
everything. We'll be back in time for breakfast. Questions?'

'Sir?' asked a voice. Karl looked around and saw bald
Johan. 'Why tonight?'

'Because we don't know when they're going to change
their location, so we have to act fast.' He couldn't tell them
the truth: that tomorrow he would be arrested by Gamow or
Heller, and by Mitterfruhl night it would be all too late.

'When do I get my gold purse?' Ewald wanted to know, to
a gale of laugher.

'When we get back,' Karl said. He was about to give the
order to move off when Kurtz spoke up.

'I've brought flasks of lamp oil,' he said. 'Rub it on your kit.
It'll stop leather squeaking and metal chinking. Your blade
won't get stuck in its scabbard and won't rust from the wet
neither.' He passed them out. Karl took one, grateful for his
orderly's forethought. Lamp oil was an old poacher's trick,
he remembered.. Perhaps Kurtz and Schulze had more in
common than he'd first thought.

They set off towards the forest at a steady march, Karl at
the rear. Once a few soldiers had been relieved of equipment
that creaked, clanked, grated or squeaked, the unit moved
with a satisfying lack of noise, though the difference in discipline and professionalism between the two sets of men
was obvious and, to Karl, worrying. The three days he had

spent with the sellswords had sharpened their teamwork and attitude but they were still essentially untrained, handy with a weapon but with no battlefield experience. What right did he have bringing such a raw band to ambush a force of Chaos warriors? If this attack went wrong, the blame would be his alone.

As the head of the column entered the treeline, Karl turned to look back at the camp. The last rays of the sun reflected off the coloured clouds, tinting them, and for a moment the valley floor and the trees, the river, the tents of the army and the walls of the castle were all bathed in red. Under his uniform his second mouth writhed, and for a second he felt a spasm of last night's inhuman hunger. He fought it away.

HIS EYES ADAPTED quickly to the darkness of the forest and he was able to see the track that Johan had chosen. His horse seemed to have no problem picking its way through the gloom and shadow of the fading daylight, and he let it have its head, following the column of men. It gave him a chance to think about the day.

He still couldn't fathom Reisefertig. The man had said he was here as an observer, but he had been involved in the cover-up last summer, and had sent Karl to Altdorf, out of the way. It was impossible to tell whether Reisefertig was telling the truth, lying or concealing how much he knew; and there was much he was concealing. Neither he nor his words could be trusted: he regarded Karl as an information source, not an ally. It was a shame. In quieter times, Karl felt the two men could have been friends.

Who was Reisefertig? Braubach's journal might have revealed something, but it was gone now. Braubach had trained him and they had worked together for eight years. Then, after the failed raid, Reisefertig had left without a word and gone to Marienburg, where he had infiltrated a library controlled by Chaos cultists, and his actions had left an Untersuchung agent mindless and mute. From there he had gone to work for Duke Heller, where Karl had met him the previous summer. Whether there had ever been a real Johannes Bohr, he did not know.

Back in the torture-chamber under the temple in Altdorf, Lord Gamow had mentioned Reisefertig, asking where he was. Why would he do that? Why would he even know who Reisefertig was, or care? He'd put the question immediately after asking about the Untersuchung's deep agent in the witch hunters. Was there a connection?

Karl chuckled to himself. He had not told Karin that he could not have betrayed her cover in prison because he did not know it. Evidently Braubach had trusted her with more information than he had given to Karl. But then Braubach had not trusted him. 'I do not trust Lieutenant Hoche, and I do not think he will do well,' he had written in his journal. Now Karl was the only one of Braubach's three apprentices who was still doing the work of the Untersuchung – or something like it.

At the front of the company Johan held up his hand: a quarter-mile to go. This was where they had found the track the day before. Karl and the others dismounted and wrapped cloths around their horses' hoofs to muffle their sound. The dark sky cast everything in blacks and blues; neither moon was in the sky tonight but the band of stars across the heavens gave a cold, faint light. The troops moved on, the river beside them but running the other way, a wide band of shining grey pouring back towards the camp.

What had Karin meant in the carriage when she said Karl had a place in the scheme? Over the last two days, he had watched the pieces of the plan fit together, but had not felt there was a place for him. Now she said there was. Did she mean a place could be found for him, or was there a more sinister meaning to her words? Had the smooth coming-together of the threads of the conspiracy included him, possibly from the moment he had disturbed the doings of the Knights Panther at high summer? And would he ever be able to find the answers?

They reached the island. Karl tethered his horse downstream as the troops spread out along the bank. There was no sign of movement from the island, and no firelight broke its dark outline. That could be a good sign, or might mean that their quarry had already gone.

He watched as Sergeant Braun gestured silent orders to the men. Julius the mercenary and the tall Reiklander slipped into the chilly water carrying coils of thin rope and waded out into the stream, their steps careful. The water was lapping around their waists, but came no higher. It was slow going.

The two reached the far bank and tied their ropes on the trees that overhung the river. They signalled, and the first of the Reiklanders began to follow them, fording the stream, swords held high above the current, and taking up their places in the shallows on the other side as they waited for their comrades. A steady flow of men made their way out. This was the trickiest part of the operation, moving all the men into position without alerting the enemy. Compared to this, the killing should be easy. Karl watched from the undergrowth.

The last of the Reiklanders started across, the strong current cresting against their chests in waves. Their comrades were arrayed along the far bank, the water there up to their knees and thighs. Half the men were across now and the first of the mercenaries was in the water, one hand on the rope, the other holding their weapon. Others moved to follow him, the two slow lines of men in constant motion against the surface of the river.

In midstream one man missed his footing and slipped, losing his grip on the rope. He disappeared under the water, but didn't flail or splash. In a second he had surfaced and the man next to him had grabbed his forearm, giving him the stability he needed to find his feet. He stood up, wiped the water from his eyes, found the rope again and waded on. All without a single shout or splash, and he hadn't even dropped his sword. Hoche's heart swelled. His soldiers. They were everything he could have hoped.

Suddenly there was a cry close to him, an alarm call, like the screech of a great black bird. It shattered the night, echoed from the far bank and rolled across the forest. The soldiers were frozen, the few men left on the shore startled and confused. Karl stared across the river. What had happened? Should he give the command to attack? Were they safe? Was it too late?

'What the hell was that?' he heard Sergeant Braun say.

The trees on the island were black against the dark sky. A shape moved against them, a hulking silhouette darker than the shadows. Another emerged further down. Great armoured men on great black horses, with swords and axes the size of doom.

They hear everything, Karl thought in terror, and they do not sleep.

'Attack!' he shouted but his command was lost in the roaring cry from the island as the horsemen charged forward. A horde of dark riders poured from the treeline, charging into the river and the lines of soldiers with great splashes, swinging their huge weapons.

The soldiers scrambled away but the water slowed their panicked legs. They staggered, tripped and fell as they were cut in half, decapitated, or crushed and drowned by the cruel hoofs of the horses.

A few men tried to charge forward, to meet the enemy, yelling battlecries. They were cut down before their feet touched dry land.

The horses crashed on across the river. The ropes were severed and men clinging to them were swept away. On the riverbank, the men who had not crossed fell back, drawing their weapons. The first of the huge riders reached them, cutting down two with a single stroke.

They were magnificent, these knights of Khorne. As a salmon leaps or an eagle dives, so they killed. It was their purpose, the climax of their existence, and they did it spectacularly well. Karl felt himself awed by their skill even as his horrified eyes watched them massacre his troops, leaving blood and bodies to ebb downstream, staining the river red.

He bolted for his horse and leaped into its saddle, severed its reins with a stroke of his sword, and galloped away, his mind full of madness and confusion, the hordes of Chaos in pursuit. At least here he had the advantage: his horse was smaller, nimbler and had travelled this path already once tonight. He had to get back, to rouse the camp. The riders were coming.

He wanted to go back to the river and see if any of the men had survived, like a leader should, but he knew that was death. They were all dead. Braun, Kurtz, Josef, Dodger, Ewald and Julius, all the men who had trusted him. All of them.

And he was responsible. It was his fault they had been cut down. Not because his plan had been bad, or his leadership poor. The weird cry that had raised the alarm and roused the forces of Chaos had come from him. He had felt the mouth on his neck open, draw breath and scream.

He had killed them all.

Chapter Seventeen
TRANSFORMATIONS

'TO ARMS!' HE shouted as he galloped through the gate past the sleepy sentries. 'The enemy is coming! To arms! To arms!'

The alarm was like a stone dropped in thick oil: it disappeared and for a moment seemed to have no effect, and then the waves began spread through the tents, growing outwards as the word was passed on. Lights appeared as men emerged and thrust torches into the embers of their fires or stoked braziers to new life. Cries came back: 'What?', 'Where?', 'Who's coming? What enemy?'

'Defend the north wall!' Karl shouted but his voice was lost in the hubbub. Lights spread up the hill as people carried the word to Duke Heller and his officers. The soldiers closest to him were standing in confusion. 'Put on your armour!' he screamed at them. 'They're coming from the north!' There was no reaction. He wheeled his horse, riding further into the camp towards the mess area, shouting as he went. Milling bodies blocked his path. One man blundered into his way wearing a night-shirt and carrying a mace. 'Give me that!' Karl shouted and snatched it from his hands.

The mess area was as empty as it had been the last two times he had visited it at night. There was no sign of the gong used to signal meals, but the huge cooking-pots hung cold and empty from their tripods. He jumped off his horse, ran to the nearest and swung the mace against it. The shock jarred his hands but sent a booming clang across the camp. He hit it again and again until the clangs merged into a single continuous note of warning. Soldiers began to move towards him, looking for orders or clarification.

Karl could see torches moving in the tents on the hill, and figures milling in their light. I've sprung your trap early, he thought, and your plan is useless. Mitterfruhl is two nights away and Gamow's ceremony is not ready. Men will die but the forces of Chaos will be destroyed.

A rider was galloping down from the ruins, the hoof beats of the horse audible above the confused noise of the camp. It turned and headed for Karl, and he recognised the man on its back. It was Duke Heller. Karl dropped the mace as the general rode up to him.

'Good evening, sir,' he said and drew his sword.

'You bloody fool,' the duke said. 'You bloody, bloody fool.' Then he raised his voice. 'Soldiers! Arrest this man! He is a servant of Chaos and a mutant!' Karl lunged for him but his horse stepped nimbly away. Someone grabbed Karl from behind, pinning his arms behind him. His sword was knocked away. Rope was lashed round his wrists.

'What should we do with him?'

'Kill him,' the duke said. 'No. Take him to Lord Gamow, in the old chapel in the ruins.' Then to Karl, 'This doesn't change anything. Two days is nothing. We have been ready for weeks.'

Karl did not look at him. He was staring down at the camp, and the edge of the circle of illumination created by the mass of torches and fires within it, pushing back the night beyond the ramparts and ditches of the wall. The air was warm, thick and still, heavy in his lungs. He heard hoof beats from the north.

The Chaos knights galloped out of the night, charging for the north wall. The lead rider hit the line of stakes and it did not slow him. His horse leaped the ditch and slammed into the wooden wall with a crash that shook the earth. The wall gave way, timbers falling. The huge horse stumbled but did not fall, and galloped on into the camp. Its rider swung his massive sword one-handed and one of the Altdorf greatswords fell. A brazier toppled over onto a tent. Flames leaped and dry canvas blazed.

Another knight hit the wall, punching through it. Soldiers scattered in panic.

'Doesn't change a thing,' Duke Heller repeated and spurred his horse, heading off into the camp.

One of the soldiers kicked Karl in the back and he staggered forward. 'Come on, you bastard,' Four men grouped round him, leading him up the hill. Around them soldiers ran in disorder, half armoured, trying to find officers or anyone who would tell them what to do. The air was full of shouts and cries.

From the bottom of the hill came the bellowed war-cries of the knights, screams, and the crackle of flames. It was chaos.

'Look over there,' said one of his guards and Karl turned to see men in the field below trying to form up a wall of pikes, blocking one of the aisles between the tents in both directions. As he watched the tent next to them was knocked aside by a charging horse that ploughed into the middle of their ranks, its rider swinging his axe through the few men who did not flee.

Something was happening to the soldiers below. Their bodies were wrong. He squinted, trying to focus on them, but the air seemed thick and blurred.

'Keep walking,' muttered one of the three escorts. Three? A second later there were two, and one had bloody hands and a knife. The two faced each other. 'Run if you know what's good for you,' one growled. The other ran.

'You said you were here as an observer,' Karl said as Reisefertig used his knife to slice the ropes from his wrists.

'I said we shared an enemy,' the man said. 'Why in hell didn't you tell me you were going to start things tonight?'

'You disappeared when the witch hunters arrived,' Karl said. 'There was no more time. Lord Gamow would have recognised me.'

Reisefertig grimaced. 'Me too. I – look out!'

With hoof beats that shook the earth, a dark rider charged at them. He whirled a huge axe above his head. Splintered stakes and the remains of pikes hung from the horse's armoured body, dripping with blood. It did not notice them. Reisefertig dived to the left, yelling. Karl snatched up a longsword from one of the corpses. If he tried to flee, the great horse would ride him down. He faced it and stood his ground. The horse thundered in. The axe swept down.

He judged its curve and sidestepped, ducking. The blade whistled inches from his head as he turned to slash at the back of the horse's galloping foreleg. His sword bit through muscle and ligaments. The horse flew past, the hoof landed for another pace and buckled. Karl heard the bone break. It started to fall to the left, its momentum carrying it forward, its head dropping even as its back legs pushed it onwards. The rider threw himself to the right.

The horse hit the ground and a gout of blood erupted from its mouth and nose. One of the stakes embedded in its flesh had been pushed deep by the impact, puncturing heart or lungs. It was finished.

From the other side of the horse rose a mountain of red and black armour, ribbed, curled and spiked, brandishing the axe. Its helmet was dented, and it ripped it away to reveal a twisted, skull-like face, a mouth distorted into a horrific grimace, red eyes with pinprick pupils. Karl recognised him.

'I have followed your tracks a long way, Sir Valentin,' he said. Sir Valentin, the Champion of Chaos, the leader of the men who had once been Knights Panther. He showed no recognition of his name.

Reisefertig charged in from the Chaos warrior's flank, swinging his sword down. Valentin reached up one mailed fist with incredible speed and snatched the weapon out of the air by its blade, pulling it out of Reisefertig's grasp. He smashed the hilt across his assailant's face and, as the dark-haired man staggered back, twisted the weapon round and thrust a foot of the sword through Reisefertig's chest.

'A skull for the skull throne,' he said in a voice like iron grating on rock and turned to Karl. Behind him, Reisefertig's knees gave way and he fell to the ground.

Valentin bent to retrieve his axe. Part of its blade had broken off. He straightened up, a foot taller than Karl, clad from head to foot in Chaos-blessed plate armour. His ghastly mouth smiled and he hefted the axe.

Karl swallowed and prepared to die.

Then he felt his neck twist under his metal collar, and a second later his other mouth gave voice to the same unearthly sound that it had used to warn the Chaos warriors of the ambush. Valentin stood transfixed for a second, then moved his head to study Karl with unseeing eyes.

What fresh hell is this? Karl thought. Am I becoming one of them? Do they recognise me as one of their own?

Valentin turned and strode away across the camp. A man ran out of the darkness at him, yelling, sword raised, and he decapitated him without breaking stride.

Karl went to Reisefertig. The man was curled on the ground, six inches of sword emerging from his back. His face was distorted from pain, but there was no blood in his mouth.

'It's in my lung,' he said, his voice husky and weak, 'but he missed my heart.'

'Don't move,' Karl said.

'I can't.'

'You can do one thing,' Karl said. 'Tell me why Lord Gamow would recognise you.'

Reisefertig tried to suppress a cough. 'I was a witch hunter once.'

'You were?'

'I was. Lord Gamow sent me to infiltrate the Untersuchung.'

There was a scream and something rushed out of the darkness towards them: half a soldier, his flesh melted and twisting into new forms as he ran. In his left hand was a sword. In a movement Karl was on his feet. He knocked the clumsy attack aside and thrust through the decaying man's heart. Blood arced wide, splashing him, but the man didn't fall. He turned and tried to bring his sword to bear. Karl thrust again; the man offered no defence, but he would not die. He swung. Karl parried and swung his sword with both hands, slashing through the man's neck. His head lolled as blood gouted and he fell backwards, snarling and dying.

'It's begun,' Reisefertig said. 'Nice work.'

'What was that?' Karl asked, but he already knew. The soldiers were being warped into new forms by the force of Chaos. Body, mind and soul, the duke had said. At least he had saved his men from this unholy fate.

He stared at the corpse. The skin was flowing off its bones like liquid. What about me, he thought? I ate the food too. Does my damnation make me immune, or more likely to succumb?

He could feel the atmosphere of the camp thickening, heavy with the smell of blood and the sense of death. It was powerful. He could feel its tug on him.

'How do I end this?' he asked.

Reisefertig coughed again. 'Only you can answer that, Karl. But remember that Chaos rules the emotions, not the intellect. Let your head rule your heart.'

'My heart?' Karl said. 'Andreas, what are the two hearts? What do they mean?'

Reisefertig shook his head weakly. 'Two hearts? I don't understand. Lovers, perhaps?'

Lovers. That fitted. 'I have to stop Lord Gamow,' Karl said.

'Give him my regards,' said Reisefertig.

'I will come back for you,' Karl said. He turned to look down into the camp below. It was a scene from hell. Half the tents were ablaze, shedding flickering yellow light over the corpses that strewed the ground. Some of the Chaos knights had fallen, others had lost their horses. Shrieking men twisted and deformed, their limbs reshaping in the vile atmosphere, becoming living weapons, servants of Khorne, to rejoin the battle on the other side. Soldiers clustered in groups as the great figures of the Chaos knights swept past them. The earth was dark with blood and the air was full of screaming. In the distance, the river's water was red in the firelight.

Unholy things were walking the cloth of blood.

He made his way towards the ruins, stepping over the burning remains of tents and the bodies of dying men. The ground under his feet was soft with blood. Behind him, he could hear battle-cries, the clash of weapons and the sound of great death.

THE CASTLE STOOD like a ghost against the night, its walls reflecting the light from the flames below, imperial and oblivious. The ruins of the keep stood cracked and crooked and at the other end, by the rubble of what had been the curtain wall, a lone watch-tower still held together, gazing out over the devastation below. It had seen it all before, and it did not care.

Within the ruins, torchlight danced and flared. Voices chanted, insistent low rhythms filling the night. This, he could sense, was the heart of everything that was happening here; without this ceremony, the carnage in the camp would be nothing but bloodshed. Yet there were no guards, nobody watching or protecting the ritual that was going on within. Karl found that strange.

He climbed over fallen limestone blocks, encrusted with lichen, unmoved for centuries, and made his way through the network of fallen walls and overgrown rooms to the heart of the place.

Two walls of the chapel still stood. Poles had been stuck into the ground and torches strapped to them. The altar, a raw stone block the size of a butcher's counter, stood draped in a dark red cloth. Karl knew what it was. He did not have to look up to the watchtower to know the Imperial standard was missing from its pole.

On the altar, a knife and a bowl gleamed silver. Around it, four witch hunters, their eyes covered by hoods, droned the low notes of the chant. Two figures knelt before the altar, their heads uncovered, praying soundlessly: Lord Gamow in his Imperial uniform, and Sister Karin in the formal robes of a priestess of Sigmar. It was as if they had been waiting for something, or someone.

Karl looked at them, considering and planning. He was too far to charge across the uneven ground and catch them off their guard, before they could draw swords. He had no throwing knife to end this quickly. And he wanted to hear what Lord Gamow had to say.

He walked forward, his sword held loosely at his side. Lord Gamow looked up and rose to his feet. 'At last,' he said. 'The mutant. The final card in the spread.'

Karl stared. 'The two of hearts,' he said.

'No, you vile fool. The two hearts are much more important than you. The two hearts must be pure.' Gamow pursed his lips in a sneer. 'You don't understand, do you? For all your sniffing and searching, for fooling Duke Heller into telling you our plan, you still have no idea why you're here. If this is the best the Untersuchung could manage, little wonder it was so easy to have you all burned.'

He's trying to goad me, Karl thought, and it's working. He felt his anger rising. 'Let us end this,' he said, raising his sword. Lord Gamow laughed. Under the rising sound, the witch hunters' chant droned on.

'Yes,' he said, 'let us finish this. I started this by making you the filthy thing you are, so it's justice that I should finish it too.' He drew his sword.

Why is he doing this, Karl asked himself? Why challenge me when he has a ritual to complete? But it was not the time to think about reasons. This was a time for vengeance: for his fallen friends, for his soldiers, and for himself. This was a time for blood.

Under his collar, his second mouth began to make a sound, a low moaning drone that merged with the witch hunters' chant. So he was part of the ritual now. Well, so be it. Gamow must die. He lunged forward, and their blades met with a crash that shot sparks flying. Gamow smiled, his mouth wide and white. Behind him Sister Karin had risen to her feet and was watching the fight, her hands clasped hard in front of her.

'Avenge the Untersuchung, Karl!' she shouted.

Karl easily parried Gamow's thrust, turning it back into a low cut the other only just avoided. Avenge the Untersuchung? Hours ago she had told him to forget the Untersuchung and find a new path.

But what else had she said? Heart is better than head. And that he had a place in the scheme. Was this his place? Fighting Gamow? Was he meant to fight this duel and lose, and become a sacrifice to Khorne? That made no sense.

Too much thinking; not enough blood. He wanted to kill Gamow; that was all that mattered. He wanted to slice through the man's flesh, watch him fall to the ground, cut off his head, rip out his heart and squeeze the blood from it. Then he would do the same to the woman. Their deaths were all that mattered.

Gamow came at him with a flurry of blows and he knocked each one away, blocking Gamow's advance and advantage. He thrust forward. Gamow's parries were slowing.

'Come on, you abomination,' cried Gamow. 'Show me you mean to finish this!' Karl's rage surged forward, and as it did the chanting from his second mouth grew louder. The swords rang against each other as the two duellists moved across the chapel. Nobody else moved. Nobody tried to stop the fight. The chant continued.

Heart better than head, Karin had said. Two hearts better than one. The two hearts must be pure. Reisefertig had said two hearts meant lovers. So Gamow and Karin were the lovers, that was clear. But what did the two hearts signify?

Gamow was tiring now, his blows slow and his parries weak. Karl roared his hatred and moved in to kill. Gamow dropped to his knees, offering no defence. Karl swung his blade at the man's unprotected neck, the instinctive move of a killer faced with a helpless victim. All the emotion of the last year was in that blow, all the sorrow, all the vile thoughts and self-loathing, all the desire for vengeance concentrated into pure animal rage and directed at one point of soft flesh. The killing blow.

No!

His blade stopped an inch from Gamow's neck, frozen by the power of his new will. The muscles in his arm shook with the effort of restraining the sword-stroke. He was meant to kill Gamow, here, like this. His place in the ceremony was to sacrifice the priest, the leader of the ritual. That was what they had meant, and that was why they had goaded him, making his bile rise. That was why his mouth had responded. The man of learning had to be destroyed by the thing of Chaos, raw emotion, and bloodlust.

Him.

Karl Hoche. The old Hoche. The Hoche of grief and revenge, of emotions and frailty. The man.

He had played the role of Hoche too well in the camp, The mask fitted too well and felt too comfortable. He had become his old self again, with his old doubts and fears, commanding men, thinking like a soldier. That was what had brought him here. No, they had brought him here. This had been planned. He didn't know for how long, but this was what Karin had meant. This was his place in their scheme.

Karin and Gamow intended to die here, to be the sacrifices for their own plan, to create the army of Khorne. They needed him to kill them in bloodlust and fury. And he wanted to, more than anything he had wanted before: to sate his boiling rage and kill Gamow, and then to kill Karin too, Gamow's lover and the second heart.

It must not happen.

He fought down his emotions and lowered his blade.

'What are you doing?' demanded Karin.

'Defeating you,' he said. 'Without this, you do not have an army. Your warriors are tearing each other to shreds. I will not be your tool to bring about the final change. I am not the man you think I am.'

He turned away. Behind him, Gamow rose to his feet. 'You are not a man at all,' he said and charged.

Karl spun and parried, expertly. They traded blows, neither breaking the other's defence. It was not easy. Gamow was a better swordsman than he had pretended.

Karl tried to remain detached, not to think about what the man he was fighting had done to him. That version of himself was dead and buried in the Great Forest. There was no place for vengeance or fury in his new life. He could lose this fight in two ways: by dying, and by losing his control. But he did not know how he could win it.

'Let your head rule your heart,' Reisefertig had said.

Reisefertig.

Karl locked eyes with Gamow across their clashing swords. 'Andreas Reisefertig sends his regards,' he said.

Gamow's eyes blazed. 'Reisefertig! You know him?'

'He is here. He helped me,' Karl said.

'That traitor!' Gamow exclaimed and Karl knew he had him. Anger was a weapon that could be turned both ways. Now he was in control, and Gamow was out for vengeance. His sword deflected Gamow's frenzied attacks, as he let the man wear himself down. Around them, Sister Karin and the witch hunters watched them, unmoving. The low chanting continued.

He still needed strength to win. Unbidden, Braubach's words came back to him, from a rainy afternoon an age ago. 'Not a strong god, and not a wise god,' he had said. 'But in the stretch, he and your sword are the only true allies you have.'

Gamow swung, a hard blow a fraction of an inch too high and a fraction of a second too slow. Karl's blade slipped under it, through the armour under the priest's robes and into his heart. Gamow froze, eyes wide, his sword falling. Karl watched as the witch hunter slumped to his knees, sliding down the blade to collapse on the ground. His body cried out with the urge to rip Gamow apart and wallow in his hot blood. He resisted.

'Die in the name of Sigmar,' he said, and as he did he felt an inner calm spread through him. His desire for revenge, the fury of the man he had once been, slipped away and was gone. But as it fled he grasped one last shred of it and held it back. He still had a use for that.

Slowly, with awful deliberateness, he turned his face to the other figures. Karin looked shocked. The witch hunters had stopped chanting.

'It is over,' he said.

Sister Karin ran at him, a knife in her hand, a clumsy charge. It would be easy to let her run onto his sword and die beside her lover because he sensed that was what she wanted. Instead he sidestepped, swiping her arm with his blade, knocking the knife into the night.

'Kill me!' she screamed.

'No!' he said. 'Is this all you learned from the Untersuchung and the witch hunters? Was this your new path, to die to raise an army of Khorne?'

'You don't understand!' she howled, falling to her knees.

'I understand,' he said. 'I know the ways of Chaos better than you ever can.'

He left her there, by Gamow's body. The witch hunters had gone, the ritual was broken, and he had other things to finish.

BEYOND THE RUINS, the officers' tents blazed. In the semicircle of flames two figures stood and fought, hewing at each other. One danced and spun in silver armour, twisting away from blows and darting in with feints and clever attacks, the other stood like a mountain of red and black, his broken axe thrashing like a tree in a storm. Duke Heller and Sir Valentin were fighting to the death.

Karl marvelled. This was swordsmanship in its purest and most elemental form. There was no overlap between the way they fought and yet they were evenly matched, completely absorbed in the fight. Every thrust, dodge and parry was perfectly judged and perfectly met. It was beautiful and terrible to behold. Below them, on the slope of the hill down to the river, the camp burned.

Karl walked closer. They were unaware of him, wrapped completely in their duel. If either of them faltered, even for a second, they would be lost.

The weapons clashed, sending up sparks. He was yards away now and still they had not seen him.

'My lord duke!' Karl shouted. 'Your promotion is refused!'

Heller's head jerked round in horror. His eyes met Karl's, and the Chaos champion's axe passed through his neck like a hand through mist. A fountain of blood shot into the air, glinting with firelight. His body fell, his head a moment later.

Sir Valentin studied the corpse of the man who had wanted to take his place at the head of the Chaos army, and then turned to look at Karl. Karl knew with awful certainty that his mutation would not save him this time. The knight was a giant in armour, tireless and unstoppable, driven by the power of the dark gods. His armour was studded with arrows, broken swords and bits of pikes where others had tried to stop him and failed.

Karl lifted his sword. The two faced each other for a moment, then the giant took two steps in. The great breastplate he wore was decorated with the eight-pointed star of

Chaos. Under it, the joints of his armour moved, sleek and organic. Was a Chaos warrior's armour a part of their body, a new hard skin, like an insect? It moved more smoothly than any metal armour Karl had ever seen. It was as if every joint had been oiled.

Oil, Karl thought, and then the knight was at him, the axe swinging down. He dodged back from its sweep but the Chaos warrior's great forearms twisted the blade's parabola and he had to meet it with his sword to knock it out of the way.

He noticed a wooden shield on the ground and grabbed it, sliding it onto his left arm. Better than nothing, he thought. Then the axe-blade swept in again, and in seconds the shield was nothing. Karl backed away, giving ground, trying to buy time. With his left hand he groped in his belt-pouch to find the flask of lamp-oil that Kurtz had given him earlier, before the night-attack and the massacre.

The axe crashed down and he stepped under it, inside its reach, right up to the great steel bulk of Sir Valentin. With the sword in his right hand he thrust clumsily. The warrior blocked it easily, but while the giant was parrying Karl had pulled the flask of oil from his belt. He swung his arm up, smashing the container against the neck-rim of the champion's dark armour.

The flask shattered. Oil poured over the armour and inside it.

He ducked and dropped. The axe-head thudded into the earth beside him as he rolled away, and the great figure stepped after him. Karl was back on his feet, sprinting away, trying to find a torch on the plateau. He had left his sword behind. It didn't matter.

He could feel the thud of Sir Valentin's footsteps behind him. The champion bellowed, a sound of elemental rage, calling for his blood. There were no torches here, only the blazing remains of the tents all around him. That would be enough.

Karl charged into the roaring flames, closing his eyes, feeling his flesh burn as he pumped his legs in a sprint. The Chaos warrior followed him into the inferno, bellowing above the sound of the blaze. He ran on until he felt cool air on his skin. Then he threw himself down and rolled to extinguish his clothes, and lay still.

Behind him, Sir Valentin exploded out of the fire. He was burning. Flames leaped from every joint of his armour and he was tearing at himself, trying to rip the steel plates off his body. Chunks of flesh came away with them, but the oil had soaked in too far and he was roasting in his metal skin. His head was on fire, his short hair blazing. He bellowed like a dying ox, fell sideways with a ground-shaking crash, and flailed at the flames that enveloped him.

Karl fetched his sword. It was a poor thing now, its blade blunted and dented by impacts with the axe. He threw it away. Duke Heller had a sword he wouldn't be needing, and Karl took that. Valentin's body was burning and his hands were still scrabbling at the flames as Karl approached, though the movements were becoming smaller and slower.

The dying figure sensed his approach and rolled onto its side towards him. Valentin's face was a blackened ruin, bone visible through the burnt flesh and his eyes were gone, but the jaw still moved.

'Blood for the blood god,' it whispered.

'Vengeance for Rudolf Schulze,' said Karl and sliced through its neck. The skull dropped and rolled free, its empty eye-sockets staring up into the black sky. Karl looked at it. With this last exercising of duty, this final ritual, he felt the last shreds of the man he had once been slip away like a snake's old skin. Karl Hoche was gone forever. The process that had started on the banks of the Reik at Mittherbst was complete, and he was something new and powerful.

He left the bodies and strode back into the camp, to speak with Andreas Reisefertig.

Chapter Eighteen
LOOSE ENDS

THE BATTLE WAS all but over. The Chaos knights had been unhorsed and destroyed one by one, but at awful cost to the army. Those soldiers who had felt the warping power of the Khornate ritual had been cut down by their comrades. Men were extinguishing the burning tents, bringing aid to the wounded, dragging away the bodies of the dead. There were a lot of dead.

Reisefertig lay four yards from where Karl had left him. He had pulled himself into the shadow of an overturned wagon and lay there. He had lost a lot of blood, but he was still alive. The sword through his chest moved slightly as he breathed, and his eyes flickered open as Karl approached.

'You came back,' he said.

'I keep my word,' Karl said.

'Is it over?'

'It is.'

Reisefertig lay silent and still for a moment. Then he gestured to the sword projecting from his chest. 'I'm in a bad way,' he said.

Karl shook his head. 'That wound won't kill you.' He leaned back against the side of the wagon. 'Where is Braubach's journal?'

Reisefertig slowly unbuttoned his jerkin and pulled the leather book out from where it lay over his heart. 'Sir Valentin thrust the wrong side, or it might have saved my life.'

Karl took it. 'Now this is over, he said, 'which side were you on?'

Reisefertig smiled. His teeth were red with his own blood. 'You haven't heard of us,' he said.

'Not working for Gamow?'

'Not for years. I was a witch hunter once, and he trained me. Then he sent me into the Untersuchung, to report on their work. Undercover.' He laughed weakly. 'All the training in subterfuge Braubach gave me, and it didn't occur to him that I was using the same techniques against them. I was the reason so many Untersuchung operations failed.'

'Including Braubach's?'

'Yes. When that collapsed I realised the witch hunters had tipped off the cultists, to make the Untersuchung look bad. They were letting Chaos worshippers escape to score political points. That night I knew I had to leave, and left.'

'Where did you go?'

'Marienburg. It was after the Library had flooded, and the sects were fighting for control of what was left. I joined a group of former witch hunters and scholars, disaffected like me. The Cloaked Brothers. Research is what they do, Karl. Discovering the true nature of Chaos so it can be beaten – not the short-term victories of battles and burnt cults, but learning how to force it from the world. They knew Duke Heller was plotting something and sent me to infiltrate. It wasn't till later I found Lord Gamow was involved.'

'You were here to observe? To report back on how the plan went, whether it succeeded or failed.'

'Yes.'

'You would have let thousands die to form a Chaos army?'

'Yes. For the greater good. We needed the information.'

'Then the Cloaked Brothers are insane and you are no better than Lord Gamow.'

Reisefertig said nothing. Karl wanted to think the man agreed with him, but he knew he did not.

'Why did you send me to Altdorf?' Karl said. 'Why did you force me to join the Untersuchung?'

'Because I thought it would do you good.' Coughing jolted Reisefertig's body, and he gripped the sword to stop it shaking in the wound. 'You needed to be set on a new path, Karl. You were destined for more than the army.'

The horrors of the last year flickered past in Karl's mind. If he had known how any of this was going to turn out, would he still have gone out to the wood that hot summer night? Yes, he would. Even the old Hoche was not a man who would have turned away from his fate.

'Yes,' he said. 'Destiny. Was I meant to be a part of this plan? Was my place in tonight's ceremony set last summer? Did you know I would be here?'

'You or someone like you,' Reisefertig said. 'You were meant to be here. But it was not mortal hands that guided you back.' He coughed. 'We're alike, Karl. Even Braubach said so. Go to the Cloaked Brothers. They can use men like you.'

'Everybody wants to use me,' said Karl. 'I've had too much of that. From here I follow my own path.'

'We share a common enemy.'

'Being the enemy of my enemy does not make you an ally. It just means you're another unknown quantity, another unturned card. I need fewer of those.'

Reisefertig smiled ruefully. 'What are you going to do?'

'I will hunt the things of Chaos: its cults, its worshippers, its trappings and its schemes. I will destroy them with no mercy. Including the Cloaked Brothers, if I find them.'

Reisefertig pulled himself up and stared out over the ruins of the army camp. He was silent for a moment. Then: 'At what cost, Karl? How many people will die to sate your revenge?'

'No revenge. This is what I am now. I swore an oath. And I keep my word.'

'Yes,' said Reisefertig. 'You do. And you have sworn to kill me.'

'I had not forgotten.'

'Last time you said, "Not yet".' Reisefertig tried to smile. 'Do I get another stay of execution?'

Karl said nothing for a while, then: 'Very well. But the next time I see you, I will kill you.' He sheathed his sword, took the book in his right hand, and walked away up the hill, towards the castle. He did not look back.

'Do well, Karl,' Reisefertig shouted weakly. 'Be true to yourself. Fight the good fight.' His voice faded in a spasm of coughing.

THE RUINED CHAPEL was quiet and still. One of the torches was still alight, making long shadows. The body of Lord Gamow lay slumped where it had fallen. Karl dragged the blood-soaked cloth from the altar with the silver bowl and the knife, and piled them on top of the corpse, followed by the torches and their wooden poles. Lastly he threw the one remaining lit torch on top of the pyre, and stepped back as it burnt.

He looked at the book he held. It was last remnant of the Untersuchung, and of the thoughts and teachings of Gottfried Braubach. He had tried to pass on his knowledge to three apprentices, and they had all proved false: one had betrayed him; one had turned to Chaos; and one had become a thing of Chaos.

What lay within the book? What ideas and insights, what secrets, what details of schemes unearthed and cults destroyed? How much had Braubach written of his own life, his hopes and dreams, the things that drove him? Did he talk of Sister Karin and Andreas Reisefertig? What else had he written about Lieutenant Hoche? Did he have insights that could help Karl learn more about himself?

So many possibilities. So much that the book could teach him. But he was an apprentice no longer. He had passed the final test. He did not need it any more.

He threw it onto the flames and watched until it had burnt to ash.

ANDREAS REISEFERTIG TRIED to push himself back up against the wagon. He dared not move the sword that bisected him in case the wound started to bleed harder. He could feel blood pooling in his punctured lung and knew he needed help if he was going to survive. But he was confident. Survival, sick leave, possibly a promotion. All things considered, it hadn't gone badly.

'Injured man! A surgeon here! A priest!' he called weakly.

There was no answer. After a minute he called again. A figure stepped out of the night, walking towards him.

'Thank Sigmar,' he breathed.

'Sigmar will not save you,' said Karl, and drew his sword.

Reisefertig looked at him in horror. 'Damn you! Damn you!' he cried.

'We are all damned,' said Karl and pushed the sword through Reisefertig's throat.

HE STOOD LOOKING at the corpse for a moment, then turned away. There was nothing left here for him, and there was much work to do.

He walked into the darkness, his sword drawn and ready.

ABOUT THE AUTHOR

James Wallis started his first magazine at fourteen.
Since then he has been a TV presenter, world-record
holder, games designer, political firebrand,
auctioneer, convention organiser and internet com-
mentator, and has written for publications from the
Sunday Times to the *Fortean Times*. He launched the
magazines *Bizarre* and *Crazynet*, and his books have
been translated into eight languages. His proudest
moment is being called 'sick' by the *News of the
World*. He lives in London, has no cats, hears everything and does not sleep.